THE SECOND NARRATIVE

OF

JOHN TANNER

The Second Narrative

of JOHN TANNER

As Recorded by Constance Mesare

With an Introduction by the Editor
T. Forrest Treadle

A Novel by J. Todd Gillette

College of Mines Press

2025

THE SECOND NARRATIVE OF JOHN TANNER

To Connie

INTRODUCTION

John Tanner's remarkable second narrative, contained within seven 8" by 13" half-leather bound ledgers, came into my hands nineteen years ago. The ledgers, brittle though largely undamaged, together with two books on 18th century English peerage and several grade school primers from the 1820's, were the contents of a zinc box discovered in the crawl space beneath the home of George Zech, in the southwestern Michigan town of Berrien Springs. Zech shared news of his find with a number of friends, including Stuart Bartkowsky—an alumnus of the Michigan College of Mines and apparently a student of this editor's in the early 1980's—who, upon inspecting the first of the ledgers, noted a recognizable bit of longhand, "John Tanner," inscribed along the margin of a page otherwise bristling front and back with faded shorthand. Recalling the tragic, demonized, and ultimately enigmatic figure whose historia vitae I was perhaps justly accused of over-emphasizing in my Michigan History Overview, Bartkowsky hypothesized a connection worthy of investigation and contacted the School of Arts and Humanities on Zech's behalf. The seven ledgers were soon thereafter acquired by The College of Mines and delivered to me, in March 2006, for evaluation.

The shorthand text itself, though undated, spoke to the document's age, authenticity, and importance. The recorder's employment of Pitman shorthand was of particular significance. The Pitman method, introduced by Samuel Pitman in 1837, was considered to be far superior to the Taylor shorthand system which it soon replaced, and the academic as well as government and judicial fields were among the first to adopt the improved Pitman system; it seemed reasonable, then, to assume that the recorder of this narrative, self-described as a young school teacher educated at university, should have been trained in the new method. Were the document not authentic but a later fiction or forgery, it seemed all but certain that either longhand or the Gregg shorthand system, which began replacing the Pitman following its introduction in 1888, would have been employed.

Also supporting the authenticity of this record, subsequent to its conservatorship and transcription (the laborious process of transcribing the Pitman into English text, generously aided by faculty and graduate students of the Eastern Michigan University School of Administrative Assistance, began in 2007), was its felicity to known historical events related to its narrator, as well as to the documented life of its recorder, Constance Mesare.

Although the birth record of Mesare has not been located (she was by her own account within the narrative born of Swiss immigrants in Ontario), records of her employment with the Baptist mission at Sault Ste. Marie from 1844 to 1846 do exist, as do annual records supporting her residency at the Episcopal mission in Sault Ste. Marie, Ontario as a student from 1832 to 1842. Evidences of her later life, including her attendance at the University of Michigan from 1842 to 1843, surfaced here and there, which records were located with the assistance of staff of the Berrien County Historical Association, located in Berrien Springs, Michigan—the town Mesare made her home following her encounter with Tanner in 1846 and preceding her death in 1904. From these records we know that Mesare owned her home (the same simple frame structure much later occupied by Mr. Zech), served as a public school teacher in Berrien Springs until her retirement at the age of seventy-eight in 1900, and that she never married. Beyond that sparse documentary trail, no other recorded, epistolary, or anecdotal information regarding Mesare has to date been uncovered.

The transcription of Mesare's shorthand was followed by two years of editing and formatting by this editor, as well as historical research for purposes of annotative footnotes. The narrative, in the form presented here, was completed in August 2012.

A striking and initially problematic characteristic of the narrative was its readability, notable given Tanner's tentative command of his native English even as late as 1837—as made pathetically evident by his letter of November 10th of that year (possibly taken down by his daughter, Martha, but in any event never mailed) to President Martin Van Buren, which begins

> *I take opportunity this day to reach my words to you with tears calling upon you for help. Because of my long sufferings by the hand of Mr. Henry Schoolcraft. It is 7 years past he lays his hands upon me.*

It is doubtful Tanner's skills increased in later years. Both the vocabulary within the accompanying document, and the semantological and grammatical competency of the text—verging occasionally on eloquence—were major issues casting doubt upon its historical authenticity. Yet, if the document could be otherwise adjudged genuine, it appeared certain, and the more remarkable, that its recorder, Constance Mesare, was editing and shaping the text "on the fly," a feat that, given what must have been on occasion an intimidating endeavor, suggests an extraordinarily facile mind at work.

A second feature of the text attributable to Mesare's effectiveness, and adding significantly to the narrative's significance as historical record, was her inclination to comment on the process at hand—to insert, both contemporaneously and later as longhand insertions—her observations, and even occasional snatches of conversation with Tanner. This portrait of Tanner also benefited from Mesare's reluctance to stop recording her host's words when the monologues were suspended or at an end, and moreover to describe certain gestures and mannerisms.

It can be assumed from the brevity of the nightly output—rarely over 3,000 words—that Tanner was speaking quite slowly, probably pausing to recollect and painstakingly frame his words into English, allowing Mesare the time necessary for her contemporaneous editing, observations, and asides. It is indicated in

Mesare's notes that two hours, from roughly six to eight o'clock, was spent each evening with Tanner throughout the period of the narrative, which began, we have estimated, on or about June 8, 1846.

From the editorial standpoint, it was left to us only to fill in missing language, to insert punctuation and occasional italicization for obviously intended emphasis, to format with respect to paragraph breaks, and to inform the text with appropriate footnotes. Formatting and punctuation were ultimately left to editorial discretion (the shorthand offered extremely limited direction), and, this being the case, a guiding principle was adopted that punctuation and presentation would be used in the service of perceived narrative cadence, situational intensity (e.g., in a dialogue), and other altogether subjective "literary" considerations.

In terms of editorial protocol, Mesare's editorial and conversational insertions have been bracketed. This editor's insertions are enclosed in braces.

John Tanner's life, as characterized by Henry Rowe Schoolcraft, was one of "incongruity and transgression," an existence fated to pivot between two cultures yet belong to neither. He was variously described as fierce, cruel, generous, and wise. Born in 1780 to a clergyman on the frontiers of eastern Kentucky, Tanner was at the age of nine kidnapped from his home by Saginaw Ojibwa Indians. Subsequently sold to and adopted by an Ottawa chieftess, Net-no-kwa, Tanner grew up in the Michigan Territory near L'Arbre Croche. Convinced by the Saginaw that his Kentucky family had been murdered, he gave up for the balance of his youth any intention of reclaiming his white heritage. He as well forgot his surname and any shred he might have retained of his native tongue. He shared with his Indian family the dangers and privations of the woodland life, became an unexcelled hunter, and, through marriage, fatherhood, and tribal intercourse, both in Michigan and in the Red River region of Manitoba, lived in every sense as an Indian, eventually attaining the status a minor chief. But by events detailed in the first narrative (recorded by Dr. Edwin James in

1827-28 and published in 1830 as *A Narrative of the Captivity and Adventures of John Tanner (U.S. Interpreter at the Saut de Ste. Marie) During Thirty Years Residence Among the Indians in the Interior of North America* by C, & G. & H. Carvill (New York and London, later Paris and Leipzig)), and summarized within the accompanying text, Tanner was in middle age expelled from Indian society. By devastatingly painful measures he finally rejoined white civilization; he managed to find his surviving Kentucky family, and thereafter sought to bring himself and his Indian family to terms with white culture. The results were frustration, alienation, poverty, and personal tragedy. Even his famous narrative brought him only grief, as the exploits described therein did not prove credible to a white audience. Tanner did, however, have the good fortune to find employment as a government interpreter for Henry Rowe Schoolcraft, U. S. Indian Agent at Sault Ste. Marie, noted Algonquin languages etymologist, collector of Algonquin lore, geologist, mineralogist, and naturalist. But Tanner was, due to a series of highly charged misunderstandings—these arising from his poor grasp of white customs and poorer comprehension of governmental fiscal matters—soon relieved of that position. This reversal, as well as many to follow, also reflected a notoriously fierce, "Indianized" temperament, characterized by a tendency to threaten the life of anyone and everyone causing him real or imagined harm. With no justification beyond this temperament and charges of unspecified cruelty, his daughter Martha was by a singular legislative act removed from his custody in 1830; his wife was similarly taken from him two years later and granted a divorce. Tanner's resentment, vitriol, and erratic behavior worsened subsequent to these events, allegedly to the point of madness.

When, in July of 1846, James Schoolcraft, brother of Henry Rowe Schoolcraft, was ambushed and murdered by an anonymous assailant, suspicion fell instantly on Tanner, whose house had mysteriously burned to the ground two nights before. Tanner had for years been outspoken in his ill-will both toward Henry Schoolcraft, whom he blamed for the taking of his daughter and wife, and James Schoolcraft, who he claimed had preyed upon him financially. Tanner had even been heard to say that if Henry Schoolcraft, who had by then relocated to Mackinac Island, was beyond the reach of his vengeance, "his brother Jim would do." Seemingly confirming the case against him, Tanner disappeared at the time of James Schoolcraft's shooting, and was never to be seen again. The summer of 1846 was thereafter remembered as "The Tanner Summer," for the citizens of Sault Ste. Marie lived in fear that the "White Indian," the bogey "Old Tanner," lurked somewhere just beyond the edge of the woods, and could strike again at any time.

Schoolcraft, in a journal entry of February 1831, said of Tanner, "This being, in his strange manners and opinions, at least, appears to offer a realization of Shakespeare's idea of Caliban." His written accounts of Tanner's behavior, crimes, and character, nonetheless, stand very much in contrast to the self-characterization Tanner accomplishes within his first narrative and the accompanying text. Tanner does not seem altogether fierce or cruel in either of his autobiographies, but as one functioning within the norms of his Indian upbringing and otherwise behaving as a benign or, at worst, perplexed member of one society or the other. In Tanner, we recognize a complicated, misunderstood, and tragic outsider accused of much and perhaps guilty of much less.

By the same token, Tanner's prejudicial depiction of Schoolcraft here is greatly at odds with what is amply demonstrated by history and the testimonials of contemporaries. Henry Rowe Schoolcraft was in a major sense, together with Lewis Cass and others, a founding father of the State of Michigan. He was as well, unquestionably, the spiritual patriarch of the Michigan College of Mines. One may, I think, read into the text of John Tanner's second narrative a certain element of self-justification and self-serving revisionism. If Tanner was Schoolcraft's Caliban, then, as he himself said, Schoolcraft must be cast as Tanner's Prospero. And, whatever faults can ultimately be laid at the feet of Schoolcraft, like Prospero he retired from the stage a magnificent and munificent character.

T. Forrest Treadle, Professor Emeritus
Michigan College of Mines, Houghton
August, 2025

THE SECOND NARRATIVE

OF

JOHN TANNER

1

[Lightning. Shouts outside, far off.]

Write it that they burn bits of old houses, the scattered bones of lodges, pee-poles.

[He considers, watching my pen.]

Their damp fires are black in my nostrils.

[Thunder. He glances at a rattling window, rearranges himself, winces, raises a hand to make a sideward benedictory gesture, face and eyes following his hand—]

Camps rise across the rapids like a horizon of grassfire. They fill the empty ground from the Superior headlands clear down to the alder swamp a mile south and east of town, where summers the Indians tended their livestock during the annuities; the shoreline swarms with them; the woods are fouled; prices have gone through the roof. No one sleeps. Late, after the songs and fires die, a few tramp down through dew-wet meadows to raid gardens, while others—drunk, belly-sick—creep like moths at lit windows or paw at gates before stumbling, succumbing to little fits of dance, and spilling over like stillborn deer.

In the morning mist they accumulate from cross-legged heaps and with my chair straddling the threshold and my gun resting just out of sight, I mind their passing. Sometimes the road is empty and I'll sneak back to the privy, but often as not I can't pull up my trousers without being frightened halfway to Kingdom Come by some one of them standing outside waiting, or several—some newly arrived, sitting on their packs smoking pipes and chatting with the mindless contentment of voyageurs or priests—until evenings my hands are bloody from throwing them and their bundles into the Ste. Mary's. That's not to say, of course, that it hasn't been worse. Last fall the brush fires drove the township's farmers and Indians into town along with the travelers, and everyone went crazy as bees. In the disorder I was accused of sneaking off with one of the Mission's calves, which was a lie; but Bingham, your Reverend Bingham, had me put away—for the tenth time, by my count—and for the tenth time my house was broken into and sacked. For the tenth time the sheriff blamed the Indians. Of course it will get ten times worse before locks make a bit of difference.

[Takes a deep, convulsive breath.]

Read it back, please.

[I read.]

I did not say those words.

[You cannot very well say such words, I tell him, nor in that order.

He purses his lips.]

Now they've hauled a ship—not a Mackinac boat or a schooner but a ship,[1] a great black lake steamer with mill-wheels gathered upon its rust-bloodied flanks like clenched thighs—up a greased ramp out of the Ste. Mary's onto Portage, where they have it now half-way through town on its way to Superior. A city of men works in its shadow, moving roller-logs and whipping up dust from the backs of oxen and breaking and clearing away countless old cabins and shacks (I lived in one, a long time ago) and cutting centuries-old elms, lightning-white sycamores, pines—ragged, winter-wracked as starving wolves—all along the way—scourging a great,

---

[1] The *Julia Palmer*

sun-scorched, sorrow-littered wake in reverse. If you hold still and shade your eyes it can be observed to shudder now and then, nudge at the clouds. Oshawano, Shegud, a few of the elders, gather near the Mission daily, or when they happen to be in town, to mind its progress. "Aye, gitche-one-gum," they murmur, waving skyward ceremonial pipes, or pretending to offer a pinch of tobacco to the wind (a portage, however monstrous, being recalled as a noble thing); "hoh, gitche-nos!" Only the gulls, aside from a habitual dip as they pass over the decks, seem unimpressed. I go up there myself some nights, late, after the teams are put away and the hubbub dies down, to see how it's coming. It rakes the stars. Men lean over the railings, shout down from decks high as treetops. I reply, show them a finger, toss this and that up at them. They throw shoes, tankards, a tambourine, demand them back. An officer on the ground approaches. I retreat.

[He blinks, pauses to moisten his teeth, swallows; his brow gathers.]

The portents, in any case, are not lost on me.

For their part, the Indians—well, the Indians have all but disappeared. How many are in the mission school now? Did you know your Bingham and I arrived here the same week? How much worse it must be for him, to see the fruits of his labors sent off to the western territories. To be replaced by this. Poor old Bingham. He needs to retire.

I met with your Reverend Bingham just this week. Has he mentioned it? No, I did—I went up to the Mission House the other morning and was admitted into his room, although he declined to come out to greet me, extend his hand, welcome me in as an old friend, once-ally. No, I went in as a supplicant, answering his call to enter, and after he'd finished reading whatever paragraph I'd interrupted and closed his book on a finger and adjusted his neck like an old, harried buzzard, he raised his chin from its nest of beard and acknowledged me. We spoke, and I asked something of him. He refused me.

[Looks me in the eye, unwavering. A wasp works audible swags across the far end of the darkening room. He looks around.]

Still very warm tonight, isn't it?

The travelers are of course miners and speculators. There is copper in the hills west. They come from the east and from Europe. [Waves his hand as if dismissing the subject, sits in silence a time.]

Enough foreground. I thought it might help.

I am nothing now. I am unwell. I was, a long time ago and for many years, an interpreter. I was unfit even then for much else. During my years with the Indians I suffered many wounds and injuries; there were countless afflictions and few remedies, and my constitution was badly compromised. I had been tomahawked [points to a spot at the rear of his head]—and here [then another spot above the left ear]—and shot through the arm and side [brings his left hand to his right arm, which he then raises in order to clasp his ribs], and flung from the topmost limbs of old pines, the backs of horses—whatever fate had handy; I had been frozen to the precipice of death and known the predations of hunger too many times to count, and suffered the effects of every plague inflicted by God and whites upon the Indians. So fierce was my lot that by the age of forty I was unable to so much as lift both arms over my head or bend to touch my feet. My hearing was gone in one ear. I could still hunt, more or less, and in this way had come to terms, like an old cat, with my limitations. But for the white world, be it the world of the sweat-blind plowman or the politician, I was badly equipped. So I became an interpreter.

Kitte-mau-giz-ze.

I am in want.

Not my fault.

Ma-mo-yah-na mis-kwe.

Yet even this I might not have been but for having met, at Lake Winnipeg, an old Indian named Wah-ka-zhe. It was this man, brother of Muk-kud-da-be-na-sa, with whom I had been travelling during the Sioux troubles that year, who took me aside. Wah-ka-zhe in his many years had lived among the whites as I had not—or had not for over twenty years when a child—and had come to work at various trades such as to understand their disciplines and requirements.

"You will live better with the whites," he told me, "but you cannot work as a trader. A trader must be an educated man and you cannot write or work numbers. You are not fit for constant labor for all your injuries, plus you have the indolence of a hunter."

I told him I was not lazy.

"You are for too many years a hunter; you cannot be a farmer."

I did not wish to be a farmer.

"No," he said, "but you must go back among the whites."

Of this, at that time, I was not certain, and said as much.

"Perhaps not," he said; "but you will learn soon enough what you already suspect to be true;" and when I began to speak again he cut the air between us with his hand. "There is but one situation exactly adapted to your habits and qualifications," he said, "that of interpreter." He fixed his mouth and looked at me firmly, so that I could understand he had attended to the matter with much thought.

"Not even between the Ojibwa and Ottawa,"I told him; "I should be equally suited to become a missionary."

"Hoh!" he cried, and in spite of himself laughed—then became suddenly grave, as if realizing I might be serious, and, if so, crazy. I rose and left him thus, for I was less happy for having discussed the idea. My English then was very poor. In truth, I spoke no English whatsoever.

It was Wah-ka-zhe's wish that I guide his band through the winter that was then upon us; so over many fires beside the Be-gwi-o-nush-ko, on the western prairies of the Red River country, a region I knew to be abundant with deer and suitable for our families, we spoke often, and over time his influence upon me grew.

Even to such a degree that sometimes out alone hunting I might find a spot and, forgetting all else, stand with hands clasped behind my back to mind attentively—bent slightly forward and smiling with the bright, vaguely impatient eyes of a Baptist minister—to the weeping trunk of a tree; then, with a nod, turn to a neighboring stump to offer the gift of other-made-known: "Ahneen-a-zhe-ne-kah-so-yun?"[2] To which the stump, through my powers, would reply, "Tree stump." It unsettled my dogs.

My sole, pathetic advantage was my utter aloneness.

I was, during this period, very much alone. The truth that I was neither this nor that, Indian or white, Manito-pagan or Christian, was pressed upon me continually, even by the words and actions of my wife and her family. My entire existence was incongruity and transgression, as Schoolcraft would say; it was so among the Indians as it would be so among the whites—whether I was a blacksmith or a trader or an interpreter—as it would be so later and to this day, regardless of my dreams or prayers or threats of violence, as it would be so in spite of literary accomplishment and fame. But I could know none of this then, and would not have cared, so desperate was I; so I strained with all my being to remember my childhood, to recall the words—as if language itself could transform me back, reconcile all, restore to me my lost family, my former world, end my aloneness. I played games at being civilized. I prattled gibberish, proffering inanities to my wetting dogs; I listened at the windows of trading posts and cabins; I tortured myself. It was hopeless.

[Wind-borne rain rustles along the roof. Desultory conversation of thunder, remote.]

Yet I knew I was not a snatchling infant when Manito-o-geezhik and his son Gish-kaw-ko seized me beneath the walnut tree by my father's home, but had cried out in perfect English (or

---

[2] *What is thy name?*

would have had not my mouth been covered), and I remembered clearly the weathered adz scars and feathers of splintered wood on the logs of my home, and the date I'd carved into one flattened spot with a knife, and recalled as I was dragged off (or up to the instant I fainted, for this was the last I was to remember until laid upon a fallen tree very far from my home) my eyes fastening not on the cabin's windows or doorway, but rather on that receding date; yet could I, as a grown man, speak that date, know those carvings as words or numbers beyond a place in time, or as a place in time beyond a memory of mosquitoes and pride of art? Where had this unused language gone? Of my original tongue, which I somehow recalled as having a quality of lightness and dance, there remained only the shards of names and a few object-nouns useful among the tribes in their intercourse with traders and missionaries: *gun, trap, powder, house, beaver, bear, deer, pelt, peltry, tree, trunk, fire, water, fire-water, God.* Of verbs I recalled not the first, and could not conjugate or structure sentences or think except in the Ottawa-Ojibwa. Such a simple declarative statement as, "I am John Tanner and my father's name was John Tanner and he is dead without seeing his son yet alive," was a world away from my abilities and faculties of recollection (my impression at this time was that my name might have been "Taylor"), yet the desire to speak thus called up painful, urgent memories—about my poor father in particular, of whom I had not spared a thought in a decade—and daily brought me fresh grief. With effort, I recalled my sisters' names, Agatha and Lucy, and those of my brothers, James and Ned; I struggled in vain to remember the name of my youngest brother. My mother's name, though it is true she died when I was but two, was utterly lost.

But I was sure that the words, if only I could recall a sufficient number of them, would release me from my condition, and names and family would be together restored me. I desired to know the universal: not merely the language, but the mind of the white world, as if their magic might be known without thinking, without learning, and thought words would open all to me, would open *me* to me, as in an instant. (This was never to be, or so I am coming now to understand.) I would, more practically, gain a profession. Such was the faith Wah-ka-zhe had given me. But there was no one to help, and ultimately I could remember nothing. At the end of the day, exhausted, sickened by the struggle, I would walk down to the ridge over the river and raise the peeling soles of my hands toward the moonlit streaming landscape of heaven and cry, "Tyau, gitche sunnahgud!"[3] But the trees were blind, the wind impartial; I would not be acknowledged, and the moon would fall.

Yet I could not believe even then, for all my despair, in a world condemned to everlasting futility. I did not often or for long enjoy the comforts of resignation that were second nature to my Indian brethren. I was not one to give up. I had survived and become, against all odds, an unequalled hunter, a leader of families to wintering grounds. A minor chief. I would, if I willed it, become an interpreter.

"That is practical," Wah-ka-zhe said. "You cannot be a trader."

"I will be a trader if I choose," I told him.

"You must find a teacher and endeavor to become an interpreter. Go to a mission."

"My father was a farmer," I said, this to tease him.

"No! You must go to a mission and endeavor to become an interpreter. Of this there can be no question."

I said, "I have committed myself to become an interpreter, Wah-ka-zhe."

"Then you should go with your family to the Place of the Dancing Spirits."[4]

"Is there good hunting at this place?" O-ke-mah-e-nin-ne asked. The sun had set, and O-ke-mah-e-nin-ne, son of Wah-ka-zhe, had brought several pieces of wood, which he laid upon the fire. He

---

[3] *"Oh, how hard is my fate!"*

[4] *Michilimackinac*, as orthographically derived by the French from the Algonquin, later shortened to Mackinac.

sat down with us. His father did not consider the question, but pushed the logs about with a stick and after a moment said, "You are a great hunter, but you will be better off among the whites."

"I should prefer to remain here, father," said O-ke-mah-e-nin-ne.

"Not you, fool."

I had learned the previous year at Pembinah of the war between the United States and Britain, and of the capture by the British of Mackinac, and told Wah-ka-zhe of it. He nodded, remembering. I had grown up in the country around L'Arbre Croche, which was not such a great distance from Mackinac, and had visited the island—or the neighboring Round Island, which provided a good view of the harbor and town yet did not expose me to whites that might seek to take me from my Indian mother, Net-no-kwa—and had considered it myself a good place to go when the time came to leave the Indians. I might have been there at that moment, but for hearing of the war. War had deterred me. This I told him. He looked unhappy.

"They would have need of interpreters there," he said. "It is unlucky."

"Shaw-shaw-wa ne-ba-se,"[5] O-ke-mah-e-nin-ne, who had since our encampment killed seventeen moose but only one bear and but one beaver, said, "what have you brought this day to feed our families?"

I had killed nothing that day, as I had been called upon to help in the cutting and distribution of wood, there being six fires of us together there, but reminded him that I had provided by my hunting not merely one hundred beaver but several moose and seven bears.

"Father," he said, "he is not unlucky. He has in this place translated moose into beaver."

---

[5] *The swallow*, name given Tanner in youth by the Saginaw-Ojibwa, misinterpreted, with Tanner's apparent encouragement, as *The falcon*, or *Grey-hawk*.

It was a better insult than joke, but a good joke for an Ojibwa.

In this phase I thought very often of Mackinac. It is an island of high wooded rocky hills above a shoreline of white scree, with a great white fort atop its anvil-shaped promontory and a village pronouncing like whitecaps along its southern face and many Indian tepees and lodges below town near the water. It was an impractical place for either hunter or farmer—its essential purpose foreign to one of my upbringing, thus attractive—and, being in the Red River country then, with its muddy streams and broken elms and cottonwoods, its colorless plains stretching like worn hides to the horizon, that isle overlooking the great straits of the Ottawa kitche-gawme, Michigan and Huron, stirred in me great longing. In this new phase, whether standing in a snowstorm or in a downpour at the edge of a drumming marsh, my mind's eye beheld only the sun-bleached shores of Mackinac.[6]

[Clap of thunder, nearer.]

I had with me at that time my second wife, Therezia, and our son of four years, James. He had been given an English name, as would his sisters and brother, as it had become my plan to raise my children in white society and for each to attend school. It was for James as well that I had determined to remove to Mackinac and make every exertion to become an interpreter. Yet the war dragged on another year, and the insistent needs of those for whom I had respect or debts of gratitude further waylaid my plans. I travelled with Therezia and James from hunting grounds to wintering grounds, to trading posts and sugar camps, huddling around fires built upon the scatterings of last season's lodges, gaz-

---

[6] The prominent raised beaches of Mackinac Island, a mass of calcareous rock rising from the bed of Lake Huron, and its other glacial and post-glacial features—in particular its peculiar brecciated limestone formations—attracted early geological explorers primarily interested in either the stratigraphy (including the breccias) or Pleistocene history of the region; these explorers included Henry Rowe Schoolcraft, whose reconnaissance in 1820 was chronicled as "Narrative Journals of Travel Through the Northwestern Region of the United States," Albany, 1821.

ing numbly as smoke columns pawed at star-wheeling skies. My feelings of repudiation, otherness, my keen, kithless sense of time and its loss, became unbearable. In the meantime, my Therezia produced two more starvelings. Her family, mind-sick with jealousy of my hunting skills and hatred of my race, sought continually to murder me. I emptied medicine bags praying for guidance. Eventually it would come. Benefactors would come into my life. I would return to my people. I would come to look, stone-tongued, into the tear-filled eyes of my brothers and sisters. And eventually, although it would require many years and the sacrifice of yet another family, I would become what Wah-ka-zhe had determined I should, and would attend to those duties with such diligence and fidelity and sleight of wit that Henry Schoolcraft would mutter to himself, watching as I interpreted—shifting from the very embodiment of nature to one at home with and in service of civilization—pivoting effortlessly between two worlds— "Unheimliche!" Which term Therese Schindler told me was of the highest order of commendation.

What is it?

[There had been, for some minutes, yellow light gilding the outer framing of a river-facing window. Mr. Tanner, having followed my eyes, at this moment turned in his seat with an abruptness that startled me and gained his feet and rose to his full, fearsome height with a violent expression of pain. He went to the window. His jaw dropped and he roared. He clasped at the inseam of his pants before looking suddenly back at me, then threw himself on a slant toward the back door. I was by now on my feet, shaking. I went to the vacated window.

Outside, nearby the riverbank, a canoe was overturned with its bottom facing the house. A fire beyond it threw up amber gems and pulsed orange light through the canoe's ribs and knotted and veined flanks, spidery seams, blue patches of pitch. Half its lanterned length was darkened by the oblique line of a tarp. Mr. Tanner approached, his silhouette bent, hand outstretched, and, crouching, lifted the tarp. I blinked, then found him gone and the tarp settling. The fire went black in a flurry of sparks and the canoe rocked over and bucked upright and the tarp rose like storm-chop. Sickened, I fled the house and ran out into the street, where I tripped and fell headlong into a pocket of sand. I heard shouts by the river, Tanner's, and saw by watery flashes a man running away along the riverbank through the trees. Tanner was throwing stones after him. It was raining then, and a fierce wind had come up. I crawled under the waving, down-spread limb of a hemlock. Tanner, when next I looked, had returned his attention to the canoe. He dragged it out into the river. He pushed it into the current, with the same motion throwing his arms up into the wind. He was still shouting. I believe that his shouting had never ceased.]

{The last bracketed entry is in Constance Mesare's longhand, probably written in her room within the Baptist Mission. There are, on the following two pages of her folio, in Mesare's Pitman shorthand, notes taken at a prayer meeting which occurred, by every indication, the following morning. Interestingly, there is no mention of her encounter, only hours earlier, with Tanner. "How strange and sad it seems," she writes in a singular note of reflection, "that so much of our energy and treasure is expended to bring salvation to the heathens of China and India, great as that cause and acute as those needs might be, when such wretchedness exists here in our own land—indeed, so close at hand."}

2

[A small fire is smoking in a bed of embers over which a kettle is suspended, steaming; the room, again, is stifling. He clears his throat, swallows, rests his eyes on my notebook, folds his arms. I dare to ask him a question.]

That was Trinket last night, youngest son of Shewabeketon,[1] named William by his father. It was his canoe you saw. The Indians gave him the name Trinket. He was weak and shy as a child, of little use to his family, so was cast out and renounced and forced to survive with the tribe's dogs on refuse meats and whatever could be procured without the price of labor or cunning beyond common thievery, and in time distinguished himself as a collector of shiny things, a medal-snatcher. He naturally took after those who treated him with the greatest distain, so to this day affects to be British. Trinket lives alone now. He was drunk last night, and came down from town after getting into a bad fight with another Indian. His face and shirt were covered in blood. I knew it was his canoe by the silver tea service he'd laid out by the fire; I knew of the other Indian by Trinket's nose. He'd been bit. [Holds his nose in his fingertips, each fingernail a tooth.] Indian fights are that way. Don't ask me why. I never suffered or inflicted such injury, although it's true my brother, Wa-me-gon-a-biew,

---

[1] *The jingling metals.*

13

son of Net-no-kwa, had his nose bit clean off. Trinket, the drunken fool, should count himself lucky.

I sent his canoe off down the river. Trinket is not allowed on my property. I committed what I realized, too late, to be an injustice. [Closes his eyes, touches trembling fingers to his cheek.] So I chased it. It was stupid to do so. The current is strong below and carried me against a rock. In truth Trinket had nothing directly to do with this [indicating his bruised, swollen face]; he might have caught me in the eye with an elbow ("Frightfully sorry," I think he whispered), but the rock was always there, so I accept responsibility. The cedar deadfall downstream, that was another matter.

You surprised me tonight. I thought you'd be the sheriff.

Are we ready?

I became desirous to leave the Indians around the time I have described, when wintering with Wah-ka-zhe and his clan. Near before this time I became aware also of my white family. This from a North West Company trader. I had been travelling with a small band in the spring from our sugar camp east of the Red River into the far country west, where we had that winter discovered beaver and Sioux in abundance and suffered terribly. Of our party one had been killed by the Sioux and another captured, yet in our want the beaver had drawn us back to this borderland. On our journey, by a small, deer-hung cabin on a meager, clay-banked tributary reached far up the Assiniboine, we met a trader I remember only as Perry. My companions had been talking of pausing for the night; the sun was setting in thin clouds and the sky was red and the earth before us gone dark and we were tired and hungry and wary. Perry stood from his work skinning out a small doe, wiped his hands on his pants, and took up his gun. He was a big man with a stained white beard. Greeting us in Ojibwa and I him, and seeing I was a white man addressing him in Ojibwa, he took an interest and approached me. He spoke first in English, then French, then Ojibwa. He told me his name and asked mine.

My white name, I told him, was John. John Taylor.

"Taylor," he said. The name encouraged him to speak again in English, but I could not understand, so shrugged and repeated my name as my companions lowered their packs to the ground and seated themselves. They watched us.

"Or something like that," I said in Ojibwa. "Of the *John* I have greater confidence." I did not look the man in the eye. Though I had been in the presence of white men many times before and deferred nothing to them, it suddenly struck me as bad, imbecilic, to lose track of something so basic as one's name. I turned to look upon the horizon, fingered my braids. My name had lived a separate life, I told him. (If he pursued it, I would lay my forgetfulness down to tomahawk blows, or, more generally, trauma visited upon an innocent.) "When a child in Kentucky on the Ohio I was taken by the Saginaw," I said. "They were very cruel."

He studied me a moment, looked down at my companions.

"I was sold to Net-no-kwa, an Ottawa. That is her son," I said, indicating my brother, Wa-me-gon-a-biew, who was sitting pestering another that had opened a bag of pemmican. "I am her son as well."

The trader looked at me. He seemed confused.

"It was what it was," I told him.

Around the mouth his beard drew in; his eyes narrowed. "'John,' you say."

I said again my name and he said it again questioningly, making a sound quite different with it so that it did not rhyme, as I thought it should, with "bone." I said it his way.

"Kentucky?" he said. He pointed a finger at my chest and turned as if to address the others, then grabbed his mouth and looked at me close with one eye. "Where in Kentucky?"

"On the Ohio across from the place the Big Miami enters."

"Then it *is* you," he said, as if not at all to me, still looking closely.

I backed up a step and asked him then what was me.

15

"I have news for you, my Chippewa friend." He showed his teeth.

"Ottawa," I said, and felt my fists gather.

I waited to be told what news, but he turned and said no more, and when I insisted, he merely smiled and opened his palm toward me as if to say all in good time. He moved about quickly, looking over his thick shoulders at us from time to time as he worked the doe, becoming more cheerful; he invited us to spend the night; later he prepared a good meal of venison and poured a little strong rum from a small cask.

There was in the center of his tiny cabin a fire pit and a hole in the roof as in an Indian lodge, and by the fire we sat on packs of peltries and Perry the trader broke the quiet with stories of his encounters with the Sioux, including descriptions of torture I believe were mere tales intended to frighten us. One had a man cut open and his entrails tied to his horse, which was then slapped to gallop away. Another involved marriage to a Sioux princess. The Eternal Crisis of Irresolvability, the Sioux called it. Afterward, my companions were quiet. They laid out mats upon the dirt floor of the cabin and pretended to fall asleep.

He told me then how it was I was known to him. He had waited thus to tell me.

"I," he said, leaning toward me across the smoky fire, "have met thy brother."

"Wa-me-gon-a-biew?"[2] I said, wondering how this was news, as he was among our group here.

"James," he said.

I could not answer.

"At Mackinac," he said, "last summer." His mouth tightened and his eyes smiled.

"Hoh," I said.

---

[2] *He who puts on feathers*

"Have you not a brother so named?"

I nodded, yet unable to speak.

Minutes passed. The man spoke and logs popped and hissed, but I heard nothing. I was stunned. The news, as my heart settled, made me at first happy, then sorrowful. I shook my head, met his eyes. I had thought my family dead, I told him, cruelly murdered by the Saginaw. While still carrying me away through the woods above the Ohio, the Saginaw had produced my brother's hat, split and encrusted with blood, and gave me to understand that my family had been butchered to the last child and negro, leaving me no reason to flee, no course beyond whatever fate the Saginaw would, at their whim, impose upon me. I saw now it was a trick.

The trader nodded. One could see my reaction, my words, had moved him.

This trick of the Saginaw, even beyond my affection for my Ottawa mother, Net-no-kwa, had prevailed against any thoughts of returning to white civilization well into manhood. Yet my brother James, whose hat it was came to me covered in the blood of, probably, a porcupine, had travelled as far as Mackinac in search of me. It seemed impossible. Unimaginable. Yet in my joy I realized that I had in my ignorance abandoned my family to many years of worry and grief, and it was this made me feel sorrowful.

"Stay here with me," the trader Perry said. He sat up and spoke insistently. "I will take you back to the States. There you will be given help to find your family."

I thought on it and told him no. I was very poor, had no peltries of value, and had waiting near the Red River a wife and child.

He squinted, tipped his head to indicate those sleeping, or lying with one eye open, upon the floor. "You can't live forever like this. Listen to me. We'll bring your wife and children. The government and the people of the United States will treat you with kindness. I will myself give you all the aid I can. Stay here, then I will see you back in a month."

But I was not prepared at that time to leave the Indians. I would one day, I told him. I had not yet then determined to become an interpreter, so had no more to say on the subject. I did not tell him that I was afraid and confused. That my mind before such a consequential opportunity, apocalyptic promise, wanted to squeeze into a hollow tree and hide. It would take time, and a season with Wah-ka-zhe, for this to change. I made to appear firm.

He lifted his hat, scratched his head, nodded sadly. "Offer stands," he said.

"My brother you met," I said, "James."

He nodded.

"Taylor?"

"Maybe," he said. He frowned. "Or Tenney, Thompson, Tremain, Trevor, Tanner..."

In the morning, the trader Perry transcribed for me a letter to my Kentucky family, whose name was a T with a line, and gave to us two bark canoes that he would have had need of to transport his peltries—such was his generosity—as well as a keg of rum and other valuable gifts. I thanked him with tears flowing as the others stood about watching or scuffing at the ground with the instep of their moccasins; we then set off. I never saw Perry again, nor heard more of the letter. Yet my world was shifted by my encounter with this man, what balance it had lost forever.

With rum in hand my companions decided to go no farther in the direction of the Sioux then; we travelled instead back toward the Red River, and quickly, yet ever mindful that the Sioux might not be far distant. At the conclusion of our journey, at Pembinah, many such returning Indians were trading their peltries and indulging in the usual drunken frolics, and it was there, at Pembinah, that my brother, Wa-me-gon-a-biew, lost his nose. Old Ta-bush-shish grabbed him by the hair, yanked his head back, and bit it off. Sioux were not required for the infliction of such cruelties. Only rum and a minor misunderstanding.

It happened that Wa-me-gon-a-biew had responded to the cries of a woman who was being beaten and was mistaken for her attacker by the next who entered her lodge, which, as it happened, was the woman's father-in-law, Ta-bush-shish. This man cared little for Wa-me-gon-a-biew to begin with, but felt such remorse over his mistake that he gave Wa-me-gon-a-biew a shirt as compensation for the lost nose. From the cloth of this shirt I fashioned a kerchief for my brother to wear around his face. I mention this only as it occurs to me, Miss Mesare, that Indians wearing such cloths were not uncommon.

But I have wandered off my central concern, which is how I came out of the woods. I will tell you next of Lord Selkirk.

I think the water is ready. Do you take tea?

Of the benefactors that aided my return to the white world none was more important or strange than Selkirk.[3] I became aware of him at the time have just described, 1812 or 1813, when the settlement near the mouth of the Assiniboine was being established. He was a Scot. Though slight of build, he was very strong and vigorous, and never rested long, nor could abide a man to stand more than a second on the same spot, unless to listen to his enthusiasms. I liked his energy, but found his enthusiasms disconcerting and occasionally tiresome—although it is true he helped me a great deal when my personal past and future became such enthusiasms. He died exceedingly young.

If you detect in my speech an accent it is because I learned my first English from Selkirk, who was, as I said, a Scot.

---

[3] Thomas Douglas, 5th Earl of Selkirk, b. June 20, 1771, Kirkcudbrightshire, Scotland; d. April 8, 1820. Selkirk and his partner received a grant of land in the northern Red River region from the Hudson Bay Company, which land, located near present-day Winnipeg and named by Selkirk *Assiniboia*, was to serve as an agricultural colony for the Company. Settlers were recruited from Scotland and Ireland to inhabit Assiniboia. It was there, in 1815, that John Tanner, while employed hunting buffalo to provision the growing community, saw a white woman for the first time since childhood.

[He seems to await a response. I nod and he smiles, apparently having made a joke.]

After the fur war of 1816, both Selkirk and I were compelled to reside the summer of 1817 at Fort Douglas on the Red River. He was there for the hearings, which included inquiries and trials for crimes committed during the dispute between the fur companies,[4] and I had retired there from hunting to avoid being murdered, such was the ill-will against me among the Assiniboines and Ojibwas and half-breeds for my role in the conflict. I had retaken Fort Douglas for the Hudson Bay Company.

[He pauses and I meet his eyes. This I have heard, I lie. He gives a nod, clears his throat.]

Most of the region's Indians were loyal to the North West Company. I was not political. It did not matter. Taking the Fort for Hudson Bay was politically unpopular. So I confined myself to Fort Douglas—it was named by and for Selkirk himself—until things blew over. There Selkirk was acquitted of wrongs by Judge Codman and Hudson Bay was found the offended company and ordered paid a considerable fine by the North West Company. I was relieved at this outcome, as a different one might have resulted in my arrest.

There was present there a Colonel Dickson, who was toward the Sioux sympathetic and who boasted of a minor and ineffectual treaty council between the Sioux and Ojibwa that previous winter. He determined that the Sioux should be made aware of the outcome of the hearings, so sent a man to bring some of them to Fort Douglas. The Sioux came as far as Dickson's own trading house, where, being Sioux, they set upon and killed a quantity of Ojibwa

---

[4] The rivalry between the Hudson Bay Company and the North West Company for dominance in the fur trade had erupted into armed conflict in 1816. During the winter of early 1816, the North West Company had seized control of Fort Douglas as well as a post at the mouth of the Pembina on the Red River. Selkirk was determined to regain the settlements for Hudson Bay and so reassert control over the region's fur trade, and John Tanner would play a pivotal role in that endeavor.

they found there. When this was made known by a party of Ojib-wa arriving at Fort Douglas, Dickson boasted no more of the Sioux and their peaceful intent. But Selkirk took up the remnants of his cause and called the Indians together. He sat in uniform astride his horse, that he might better be seen and heard, whilst a half-breed interpreter stood nearby and shouted his words in Ojibwa. I watched from the porch of the guard house, as it had begun to rain.

"My children," Selkirk said, "the sky which has been long dark and cloudy over your heads is now once more clear and bright. Your great father beyond the waters, who has ever, as you know, nearest his heart the interest of his red children, has sent me to remove the briars out of your path that your feet may no more bleed. We have taken care to remove from you those evil-minded white men who sought, for the sake of their own profit, to make you forget your duty to your great father; they will no more return to trouble you. We have also called to us the Sioux, who, though their skins are red like your own, have long been your enemies. They could not make it today, but have been told they are hence-forth to remain in their own country. This peace now places you in safety. Long before your fathers were born, this war began, and instead of quietly pursuing the game for the support of your women and children, you have been murdering one another. That time has passed away, and you can now hunt where you please. Your young men must observe this peace, and your great father will consider as his enemy anyone who takes up the tomahawk!"

He dismounted, and approaching them extended his hand to each in turn.

The Indians answered with many promises and professions, and that night stole all the horses belonging to Selkirk and his company and disappeared, so that not a single horse remained.

"Wasn't so bloody disposed to leave right now in any case," Selkirk said, standing shirtless in the mud of the empty horse en-closure the following morning. "What the hell."

How much worse it might have been, I could have told him, had the Sioux come all the way.

In the month that followed, Selkirk gave me no peace. He gave no one peace. If he was not ordering men about, he was carrying bark and poles upon roofs or digging new pits for latrines, or splitting wood—shouting and laughing and taunting others to greater effort—or plunging into my lodge to go on in a loud voice about things I could not have comprehended had I understood his English. He brought with him once his interpreter and Codman the judge and a lamp and a half-quart of whisky. It was the middle of the night. Codman had acquitted Selkirk and they were now fast friends. Codman was drunk. I did not want a drink. I had been sleeping. Not only was I still in bed, but I did not take alcohol and was always irritated by its effects on others. I asked them to please leave. Of course they did not.

"This man," Codman said, speaking to Selkirk and seeming very emotional whilst attempting, on his knees in an Indian lodge, to sound judicial, "conducted your party from the Lake of the Woods hither. In the winter season. And performed a very important part in the taking of the Fort."

This was interpreted for me. Selkirk's face in the yellow glow of the swaying lamp was alarming. He was grinning as if about to devour me.

"I took the Fort," I responded. "I captured Harshield myself as well."

The interpreter looked my way as I spoke, then looked again. I don't think he took me seriously.

"At the expense of great labor," Codman went on, "and at the hazard of his very life. And all for the sum, sir, of forty dollars."

I sat forward to ask when that sum might be delivered to me, and asked them again to please leave my lodge; whereupon Selkirk leapt forward and embraced me, which action surprised and distressed me. He seemed very drunk as well.

"The least you ought to do," Codman declared in a louder, yet still formal, voice, "is make his forty dollars eighty, and give him a horse—or an annuity! For life!"

I was at this point incited near to violence, as Selkirk had moved from a brotherly embrace to tickling me. I cried out in Ottawa an oath and the other relented, yet not before calling me "Johnny-Boy" and shouting that he loved me. This last was translated in a sheepish voice by his half-breed interpreter, which started Selkirk laughing hilariously so that he fell off his knees and rolled on the ground. The interpreter fled the lodge.

With his interpreter looking very dark and solemn, Selkirk approached me on the riverbank below the Fort the morning following. The rising sun on the water was very warm and bright, with vapors lifting and white pelicans floating on the current and feeding across near the tree-shadowed cut-bank opposite. The fish here were abundant and could be seen rising. The Assiniboine entered the Red River upstream around a bend to my right; I remembered it had been a gathering place for the Indians for a very long time before the fort appeared. I was thinking of this, and of being at that spot as a boy with Net-no-kwa, when Selkirk approached and apologized for his interference of the night before. Thanking me for my service to Hudson Bay, he told me I would receive an annuity of twenty dollars a year for ten years as reward, this from him personally. When this was interpreted for me, I expressed my gratitude. He wished then to be told more of my part in the retaking of Fort Douglas. This I would gladly do, I said. Selkirk laid himself in the dewy grass and pointed his narrow nose up at the sky. His interpreter did not appear to wish to sit, but did, and I sat facing the interpreter. We glared at each other.

"My wife's family had turned against me," I told him. "This was my second wife, Therezia."

The interpreter translated and, as I had learned to mind the tone of translation, I watched and listened carefully. Inflection was everything in the Ojibwa; I did not know whether this varied much by English rules.

"I had incited the Indians and Therezia's family against me by chiding Ais-kaw-ba-wis, a false prophet then among us, and mocking their gullibility to his artless teachings and tricks."

The interpreter was, I thought, more sympathetic to this message, as he spoke it more quickly, looking not at me but out over the river toward the pelicans.

"Also I had greater success at hunting than they, and at various times their very survival had depended upon me; thus they hated me."

He glanced at me as he translated.

"They terrorized me," I said.

He translated and I did not like his tone, so repeated my words; he said them differently. So this went on.

"It was in the summer of 1816 that, in the company of a trader named Mr. Bruce, I took my family to Rainy Lake in order that I might leave them in the care of the Ojibwa there and alone journey east to the United States. The War of 1812 was over."

The interpreter was now speaking as I spoke, and I hoped listening and keeping up. It was hard to know. Soon he seemed to overtake me, to finish translating my sentences before I'd finished speaking them. Selkirk had closed his eyes.

"Mr. Bruce had given me much information and advice and encouragement, and I might have reached the United States before winter locked in but was then taken in tow by a Captain Tussenon,[5] who was then in charge of a group of Hudson Bay militia at the Rainy Lake post. They had taken the post from the North West Company. But you know this," I said.

I found I was growing tired trying to keep up with the interpreter. I finished my story quickly and without embellishment,

---

[5] Probably Capt. D'Orsonnens of the Hudson Bay Company.

telling him I'd guided Tussenon and his party forty days through the great swamp between Rainy Lake and the Red River, and had designed and led the raid, the silent night raid, on this fort named after thyself, Lord Selkirk. I made a ladder of a pine tree and, emboldened by the fact no had heard me chopping the tree to bits, surmounted the walls of the Fort and crept over the roofs of buildings within and took the Fort by surprise. Not a shot was fired. I had promised Tussenon something and had delivered it. That something being Mr. Harshield in his bedroom.

The interpreter looked at me. I didn't bother to explain. I had finished. The half-breed interpreter looked down at Selkirk and after a moment gently poked his shoulder.

Thereafter, Selkirk button-holed me daily and we talked, with or—as best we could—without his interpreter, about our lives. We always talked whilst walking or climbing ladders to clamber over roofs, and I was continually interrupted by his shouts to others, his pointing out to me this or that, or his sudden and quite violent urges to dive into the river or hug me and thump me upon the back; he was almost always laughing when with me. I put it all down to an inexhaustible spirit and pathological narcissism. I forgave it, as one forgave the A-go-kwa, and sought to learn from him what I could of my native tongue and culture.

Selkirk tried to help me with the English language. We spent an hour or longer each morning together. Never sitting still, but walking or working.

"This," he'd say, holding up an axe.

"Dis," I would mumble.

"This."

"Dis."

"Is an axe." He laughed, pointed to a log perched vertically upon another bigger and raising the axe, said, "And that—"

"A-dat," and I would point, feebly, shyly, as well.

He swung the axe, then picked up the split wood. "Yields the burnable!"

"Yeh-de-bun-a-buh."

He gave to me the axe.

"Dis," I said.

"Axe." He patted me on the shoulder, planted another log, stepped aside. "Axe."

"Axe," I said, holding it up to look at it. I swung the axe and another two pieces flew.

"And those—" he said.

"A-dose." I pointed. "Yeh-de-bun-a-buh?"

"Good!" he'd shout, and, laughing, slap my chest so that I stumbled. Together we produced a great pile of yeh-de-bun-a-buh.

I did not learn a great deal from Selkirk, but it was a start. He too pressed me to leave with him to the United States, but I was yet unprepared. So he took it upon himself to have published in newspapers in every city in the United States my story, and to provide intelligence of my whereabouts and circumstances and thereby locate my family; and he never missed an annual payment of my annuity. He was a kind and true man and I think of him often and was very sorry when told of his death at such a young age. I am twice his age at death now. Such a doubling of waste—

That is enough for tonight. Tomorrow I will find my family for you. May I walk you home?

[Please do not, I say.]

There are travelers about.

[It is still light. I am quite capable of seeing my way home, and in any case I'll be nearby the Agency and the Fort and between those, the ship. There will be just as many soldiers about.

He relents to this reasoning and stands.]

3

I spent the summer there at Fort Douglas, and in the fall Selkirk sent six men to take me to Lake of the Woods, that I might rejoin Therezia and my children. The corn had been gathered, and there was a brief time of quiet accord, although game soon became very scarce. When the snow fell we made to travel into the northern prairie in search of buffalo. I went to Be-gwi-o-nus-ko Lake, where a great many Indians had gathered together, as the word had gone out, and as winter locked in and the snow fell we travelled into the yellow prairie. The northern prairie was harsh country in winter, and only desperation induced us to go there.

We soon began to suffer of hunger. The weather was very severe, and our suffering increased. A young woman was the first to die of hunger. Soon after this, a young man, her brother, was taken with that kind of delirium, or madness, which precedes death in such as die of starvation. In this condition he had left the lodge of his debilitated and desponding parents, and when at a late hour in the evening I returned from my hunt and they could not tell what had become of him, I left the camp (it was the middle of the night) and following his track found him at some distance lying dead, eyes half-closed and teeth bared like an opossum's, in the snow. The winter stars shone in a sky drawn taut by a cold wind, and I lifted a prayer to the Great Spirit. I asked him why in hell he had not had me go with Selkirk.

I myself came close to dying not long after.

Our camp was on the southern edge of a rise of land overlooking a frozen stream and a broad and flat plain. From atop this rise one could see game, or the lack of it, for a great distance. We saw no buffalo. Each day we watched the same distant shrubs, but they did not become buffalo. We cleared snow from the hard clay and pressed an ear, but neither could we hear buffalo. We sniffed the breeze. No buffalo. Where there was fat left on my body I felt a burning, and cramps arrested my walking sometimes and caused me to cry out in the night. More died and were buried in graves covered with stones. No one talked much about it. No one wanted to talk about the hunting of that day or the next. To hunt meant walking terrible distances, and the stubborn pointlessness of each such exertion (you could see every rock for fifty miles) wore on the nerves. But those of us that could went out and drifted silently toward the next rise, eyes cast downward looking for tracks or cow plops or clumps of grass that could throw one headlong upon the miserly earth—from which even the strongest might not summon the will to rise—and from the next hummock scanned a new nothingness, blank-white abyss of hunger and desertion, then dropped our heads and walked on.

One day out alone hunting I scared up a bear from a small draw above the stream. So startled was I that I fell over backward and dropped my gun; the bear bounded off into the blowing snow. I got up and, gathering my gun, gave chase. The wind stiffened and the snow came in waves. He did not reveal himself to me again. I tracked him all that day and night and through the day following, and for a total of three days followed his meanderings about an area I judged to be five miles in breadth. He was himself hunting desperately and without rest for these three days; I don't think he remembered or cared about me by the end. In the end, I sat down exhausted, and, unable to strike a fire or make camp, and knowing I had not the strength to catch the bear or return to camp, resigned myself to die that night. I considered shooting myself rather than freezing to death.

I sat dazed and as one dreaming. The white beaches of Mackinac appeared to me in the snow, and above the horizon the great blue kitche-gawme, and around me the woods and ferns nodding over pebbly streams; and I thought I would be there now, fishing a thousand miles downstream from this agony, but for my stupidity. A thousand miles from the nearest Sioux. But I had refused the trader Perry and I had refused Selkirk. I had been prideful. No. Bashful. Fearful. Stupid beyond belief. It was disgusting. From trepidation I would this night die.

As I sat thinking thus and eyeing my gun in the dying light, there came a voice, and then another. Two men from our band had tracked me as I tracked the bear, and had now found me. When they comprehended my condition, they sat down with me and gave me a little food and some water.

"No bear," one said. He was Pe-to-beeg,[1] a younger cousin of Therezia—possibly also a brother (it was a peculiar, insular tribe).

"I tracked him three days," I said.

He looked at the other, then back at me. "Too bad."

I asked where this meat came from.

"Dead cow," he said.

"Kill?"

"Find. Follow eagles." His breath smelled like the meat, like death.

"It is good," I said.

The young man was studying me intently, or possibly thinking something through. He looked quite like Therezia, very dark with angular eyes and a flat salamander mouth. I remembered he had cried loudly and often during our days of suffering there, and was occasionally beaten for this. It occurred to me now that he might

---

[1] *Dirty pond*

29

be mad, dangerous. Any one of my wife's family was dangerous. They were fanatically insecure.

"Thank you," I said. "I am in debt to you for my life!" I was taken by a tremor as I said these pitiful words, and the effect was both alarming and humiliating. Pe-to-beeg nodded, looked again at the other. It was possible they'd been sent on an errand to kill me. Or by killing me hoped to restore to themselves a measure of honor. In any case, they were of Therezia's clan.

"Did Therezia send you?"

He shook his head.

"Her mother?"

They looked at each other. I bit into the rancid meat, focused my eyes on my shaking hands. When I looked at him again, he was working a knife into a ball of tarry cow-flesh, watching me.

"You are like a brother to me!" I blurted, a little maniacally.

As if in response he handed the knife to the other.

"You too!" I said. "What is thy name?"

The other stuck the knife blade into the ground. It fell over. "Om-waush ke-wa-wa,"[2] he said.

"You too will be greatly honored for rescuing me. You will both henceforth receive the first portions of my kills!"

These words, it seemed, struck a chord with these two; they immediately rose and helped me to my feet. It took us all night to return to camp. In the days that followed, Pe-to-beeg and the other hung about my lodge and with Therezia and my children looked after me—or laid clenched in balls racked with stomach cramps and diarrhea, rolling one then the other out of the lodge to puke up amber-flecked slime. I was sick as well. Therezia glared in disgust; my skeletal dogs whined and chewed sticks by the fire; my children became quiet, their eyes peering out lifelessly from their pile of hides. When I could hunt again, the two young men

---

[2] *Deer lick*

went out with me. It became well-known that they had rescued me, and Pe-to-beeg cried not so often.

~~Finally it happened that the buffalo came and our lives were spared, and I was driven from the Indian world. Not all at once, mind you; but had not the buffalo come I might have remained among my Indian brethren many more years.~~

[On the other hand, you might have died then and there of starvation, I point out.]

Make it as you like.

[I apologize.]

Strike everything after "Pe-to-beeg cried not so often."

[I promise to stop interrupting.]

No, strike it. Read back the part before.

[Which I do.]

Add yellow flecks to the vomit. I believe they had been eating grass.

[Thank you.]

Edit as you go, I always say.

One day soon after, with a soft breeze blowing out of the southwest, we the three of us went across to the same far-off rise of featureless prairie and there, on the other side, found the earth black clear to the horizon with buffalo. Dumbstruck, we were. I sent Om-waush ke-wa-wa back to camp to bring others and instructed him how many should come here, and pointing wildly showed where the others should place themselves. As I waited with Pe-to-beeg, the buffalo continued to move in our direction. We slid on our bellies down the rise as to not be detected. The smell of the herd came to us on the breeze. Their grunts filled the air as with a constant moan. Pe-to-beeg became excited and was very keen to shoot. I deterred him.

"You will kill many buffalo today," I told him, "and we will feast—" (here I became emotional and my voice stopped; I swallowed dryly) "—but you must wait for the others. If the buffalo come over the top we will have to shoot, though there be but the two of us. But when the others come we may kill many before the herd is frightened away."

Pe-to-beeg nodded rapidly. He was sweating, and his eyes were not steady.

"It would be different had we horses," I told him. I asked him was his gun ready. He looked at it as if in surprise, then commenced to load it. He was very clumsy and noisy about it. The others came then, and as they drew near I motioned them get down. They came crouched over but moving very fast; they wanted to see the herd. Three, including Om-waush ke-wa-wa, joined Pe-to-beeg and me; the others were in two groups several hundred paces south and north. Those joining us could not be dissuaded from standing to look, and their example brought Pe-to-beeg to his feet as well; finally, seeing there was no point in putting matters off—they'd scare off the nearby animals whether they shot or not—I got up.

"Watch me," I said, and moved slowly forward until the shoulders of the nearest cows rose over the sky-blue-snowed crest of the hill. They were about fifty paces distant. When one turned to look in my direction and dropped her ears I stood upright and shot her. She fell forward dead. Whereupon to either side of me there came a deafening volley and among the animals a spattering as of hail striking mud, and in the reeling smoke much pitching and bucking and a terrible bawling, though only one other buffalo fell—and this one, a small cow, got up and rocked stiffly away. They all ran away. Some dragging wounded limbs or spilling from gut wounds or flinging blood from their tails and shaking their mangy heads, but these too ran. It was a wretched sight. Pe-to-beeg and the others ceased their yipping and watched in disbelief. They looked at their feckless guns. I held my tongue, went to inspect my cow.

Pe-to-beeg sidled up to me. He was breathing hard. "First portions," he said. I looked and would not have been surprised to find him holding out a platter. He blinked and smiled, but was serious.

I pushed him hard to the ground, then dragged him to his feet and threw him in the direction of the Indians south, who were reloading. "Get them here!" I said. "No one shoots!" He looked back as might a beaten dog, but ran. With this message I sent also Om-waush ke-wa-wa to the north.

Once they had gathered I spoke to them: "I speak to you because I alone among you have hunted the buffalo. I, in the service of Mr. Hainie at Assiniboia, killed over two hundred. This is true. Hear me: With our guns we seek not merely to slay, but to honor our friend the buffalo, and not cause him useless suffering and lingering death. In this way we differentiate ourselves from the white hunter (my example perhaps notwithstanding), who may or may not seek to kill the animal well, but does not, ultimately—because, again, he is a white—give honoring the animal a passing thought. But it goes beyond that. An Indian hunter thinks out a problem in concrete terms, and because he is obliged to deal with particular animals in a particular place—and may die if he fails to kill—gets a truer answer than a white hunter would get. I don't want to be simplistic; of course one can immediately respond that because an Indian limits himself to a particular animal—say, buffalo—or locale—as in the northern prairie on an unnamed muddy creek—he may come up with a *narrow* answer."

They were looking at each other. I could see a more direct approach was needed.

"Aim here," I said, and with my finger jabbed repeatedly into the hair of my cow just behind her shoulder, where, deep within, her heart had minutes before exploded.

"Hoh!" the others exclaimed, and raised their guns to aim at one another.

They killed buffalo that day and in the days that followed, and I was called a leader among them. This caused a disturbance in many minds. Soon I was called arrogant. I was then hated—first by a few braves, then by their wives, then their elderly mothers, and eventually everyone, including Pe-to-beeg and Om-waush ke-wa-wa—for having killed that first cow and, worse, for instructing. I was mocked and provoked. The Hudson Bay business came up again. My in-laws—who, as I have said, were long sick with jealousy of my hunting skills and thought of me only as a white trespassing upon their land and their Therezia—pestered me with coups and half-wit plots, idiotic shrub-shaking ambushes. I had thought we were past all that. It was a sad and frustrating disappointment. When the band withdrew from our camp on the rise in the prairie and scattered themselves in pursuit of the buffalo, I remained behind. Only a few remained with me. Except for these several men and a woman deranged by hunger who would soon die, I was alone. Therezia wanted to go as well, but I would not allow it.

[But you had saved all their lives, I say.]

True. But I had been stupid. Unconscious of my color. Unaware that instruction to the hungry was a gift, but to the once-hungry a tyrannical fraud. Totally stupid.

[How unfair.]

With the men remaining was Waw-bebe-nais-sa. He that hath no ears. This was not his name. It was how I came to think of him. He looked at you from inches away and had the face of a bat. He had ears, but, unlike a bat's, the ears did not invade any impression he made. Waw-bebe-nais-sa remained that he might annoy and torment me. All their grievances, their prejudices, had in his mind boiled and darkened and become poison, so that he hated me and remained. Any other—any sane other—of his youth and strength would have gone to kill buffalo. These Indians had never killed such animals, and there was great excitement and glory in that. He was young and ambitious, yet remained. He gave me to understand by remaining how bad the talk against me had been. I knew them and had sat with them at fires throughout seasons innumerable, and could see how it must have been. How they as they spoke would have leaned in toward the fire so that their faces and gestures would with their words be enflamed, and spoke first quietly and humbly, how those lying about leaning on elbows would take note and, walking their elbows in toward the fire and pulling the bones from their teeth and pushing off the children and dogs that had gathered upon them would also speak and be seen, how the young braves would crowd in and pledge stupid oaths, and how the elders in their shadows would question the talk of the fire-faced, pretending they had no quarrel or particular opinion in the matter. It would have been as this with my situation: there would have been serious talk, truculence, then long and regretful consideration of my value as a hunter-provider— interrupted by an exploding pine log and a frantic brushing-off of embers.

It didn't matter. I was satisfied that one of them, Waw-bebe-nais-sa, one beyond logic and without ears, had remained behind and taken it upon himself to kill me.

He would wander in my direction, pretending to do something. "Nosa," he'd whisper close beside me, seeming to mimic the voice of the deranged woman who had of starvation died in our midst that day, "show us that we might plow as thou the contours." I looked at him. I was not plowing or hoeing (it was February), but hanging beef to dry in a generous sun to make a store for my family. Waw-bebe-nais-sa was immune to the obvious. He put his face in mine, said, "Teach us that our furrows might heed the riparian buffer." He went away, came back, and passing bumped me roughly on the shoulder. I started, looked at him.

"Ha, teacher!" said he.

I told him angrily to leave me be. He turned suddenly and thrust both his hands into my hair, which hung about my shoulders then (as now), and with his fists held me thus; he put his bat face very close to mine.

"This," he hissed, "is the head of thy road. Look down and see the place where the wolves and carrion birds shall pick thy bones." (He forced me to look down, then yanked my head back up so that our noses touched.) "You are a stranger," he said, "and have no right among us, but you set yourself up for the best hunter, and would make us treat you as a great man."

I began to speak, to state in strong yet measured words what I felt needed to be understood, that he judged me without knowing me or my history, why I felt the way I did about the traditions of the Indians and their relationship with nature and kinship to and respect for the dignity of animals, and the imperative for a need-based affinity for those suffering beasts that provided us not merely sustenance but self-definition—even as he proceeded to pound off the bark of a poplar tree with the back of my skull. I thought I heard him shriek like a bobcat, thought I saw flames jump out his eyes; I grabbed his arms, but could not prevail against their iron strength; I tried to get my knee into his groin but missed; he forced a leg between mine and pressed me against the tree, ground his forehead into my temple; he took into his teeth my ear, bit down, lisped: "For my part, I have long been weary of your insolence, and I am determined you shall not live another day!"

"Nor yet a week?" I cried, catching a glimpse of the mountain of meat that had yet to be dried.

He shook his head; I thought my ear would be ripped off; the pain was blinding. "Not another week!" he growled.

"This being what day?" I asked, and I felt his muscles relax, felt his mouth recoil from my ear.

He looked at me, licking his lips. "What?"

I butted him hard in the nose and this made his back straighten and knees buckle, which enabled me to bring a shin forcefully into his groin; he howled and I threw him to the ground and managed to free myself from him, though at the expense of much hair—his hands had not loosed their hold—and in the struggle I found several of the fingers of my right hand caught between his strong teeth; these he bit quite to the bone. I aimed a blow to his eye and his jaws flew open and he sprang to his feet.

There was lying nearby upon the ground my tomahawk, and we both saw it at once; he leapt for it first and taking it up aimed a blow at my head with such force that when I eluded it he was thrown by his exertion to the ground; I seized the tomahawk from his hand and threw it as far as I could. There was also laying there a stout lodge-pole; this I picked up. I demanded he rise and when he did I whacked him upon the head with it. He stood a second stunned, then ducked and fled running. I chased him, swinging the pole with such enraged ferocity that each time I struck him my feet flew from the ground and ran upon the air. He made once the mistake of turning to face me with the intent of grabbing my weapon, whereupon I swung the pole into his forehead and dropped him. I beat him where he lay. Again he rose and tried pitifully to escape, but again I followed, beating him as he cried out and jamming the pole up his backside, and did so as we ran for at least three miles.

[Excuse me, I say; you said three hundred yards in the first narrative.]

Make it three hundred feet, the result was the same.

[Three hundred feet.]

No!

[Well then tell me what you want, I say. He makes an awful howl and strikes the table-top, glares. I apologize. Three miles, I say. He sits, squinting.]

Feet or miles, I never knew it at all. Until now. Then there was you.

[I will write it as you speak it. Or I can leave.]

Don't.

[What.]

Leave.

[Then be civil.]

Three hundred feet is sufficient. Dr. James had a penchant for stretching the truth; if he said yards, I must have first said feet.

[Fine, I say.

37

He sits looking, breathing as if in bad temper, then sighs.]
Epics, though, are of miles made.
[We both reluctantly smile.]

When I returned to my lodge and the task of drying meat, I was
met by the son of Waw-bebe-nais-sa and several other young men
who had heard the cries of the father. "What is it you have in this
place done to my father?" the homely young man, son of Waw-
bebe-nais-sa, asked angrily.

"I have been explaining to him," I said, by which I meant *instructing*, though I was careful not to use that word. Nevertheless
they set upon me. With the aid of Waw-bebe-nais-sa, who had by
now returned, they beat and kicked and strangled me until satisfied I would not get up again. "He is dead," one said. I lay face-
down in the snow, my arms and legs in disarranged attitudes that
must have strengthened this impression. I minded not to defe-
cate, though I felt suddenly an urgent need, for fear they would
bury me on the spot. Finding a reserve of strength, I leapt to my
feet in a bound, and so startled them that they ran, but for the
earless one who was much fatigued. I picked up my lodge pole
and beat him senseless.

So this went for days.

I had reason to fear for the safety of my dogs (Waw-bebe-nais-
sa had thrown a knife into one), my children, and, I supposed, my
wife, so when the Indians moved from the prairie in the direction
of the Lake of the Woods, I stopped and encamped instead at
Rush Lake, where I determined I would spend the remainder of
the winter apart from their annoyances and antagonisms. We had,
by now, a very large supply of food—twenty bags of pemmican—
which needed to be transported.

[I tell him that I have need to leave soon.]

There is not much more to tell. It will not take long if you do
not interrupt.

We established the children at Rush Lake and set about trans-
porting our food, which required several trips. Once, on returning

to camp, we were told by James and his younger sister Martha that their grandmother had visited and left word that I should take Therezia to her, at which place four or so lodges of family and friends had gathered. This I decided, after some thought, to do.

[Excuse me, I say, but I had thought you were to find your family tonight.

He thinks on it.] Wrong family.

[I must go. I'm sorry.]

[Speaking more rapidly:] That night, as I was dreaming, the boy appeared again that had so many times in the past come to warn or comfort me—as before medicine hunts—and came this night down through the fire-hole of my lodge and standing directly before me, real as you are this minute, said, "You must not go." He meant, of course, not go to the encampment of Therezia's mother. "But if you persist, and will disregard my admonition, you shall see what will happen to you there. Look there." And he pointed up where in the sky was flying a small hawk with a banded tail.

[And this hawk you saw the following day as you walked with Therezia to her mother's lodge.]

Correct. It was a warning.

[I tell him I can fill in from the first narrative, which I remind him I am reading, or we can take this up tomorrow, but really I must go now.]

As you like. Fill it in, then. Fill it in how when I went into the lodge of my mother-in-law I sat down between the sisters of Therezia who were married both to the same man—probably also a relative—and was playing with their small children when I heard a loud sound and lost all my senses and awoke surrounded by frightened faces and bathed in a warm liquid that I found was my own blood, and only when hearing the derisive voice of Waw-bebe-nais-sa outside the lodge came to realize I had been toma-hawked by him, which blow would have proved fatal had I not been wearing a very large and thick moose-skin capote upon my head, which I had not removed upon entering the lodge, and that it was this event—you should also fill in—which cemented my conviction to leave for the States, for it was clear to me, as it must be to the reader, that not only my mother-in-law, but my wife had aided Waw-bebe-nais-sa in his plan to murder me; and when I recovered from my wound I did go, and went immediately, with such haste and urgency as you exhibit now—

4

There was much confusion and unhappiness attended my emergence, Miss Mesare, but I will tell only as much of it here as is necessary. The rest is in there in my first narrative. I shouldn't have to go into this at all, but the first narrative is not in wide circulation and is expensive and I would not in any event want to propagate its readership, for it is full of fabulisms.

[Not yours.]

Not mine.

[Fabulations.]

Thank you.

[We should to it, then, I say. I am impatient to meet your family.

He straightens his back and extends his hands—fingers interlaced and palms outward—as if to crack his knuckles; there is a single, loud pop, followed by a cry of pain; he clutches suddenly his hands to his chest, shoots me a fierce look.]

My near-fatal attack at the hands of Waw-bebe-nais-sa, following those of innumerable others, left me few options, and after recovering from my wound and securing and preserving sufficient food to see my family through a year, I left in the spring of 1819 for the States. Members of the North West Company, sympathetic enough to my plight to overlook my past association with the

Hudson Bay Company, took me by canoe from Rainy Lake to Lake Superior, and via Sault de Ste. Marie, or Ste. Mary's, to Mackinac. All this journey not one of these men mentioned a word about the Hudson Bay Company, nor, on reaching Mackinac, was my history in this connection revealed. They were very kind to me.

It had been very warm all the way across Superior, the air hazy and thick with flies and mosquitoes. We kept our canoes several hundred yards out to avoid the worst of the insects, but the nights were terrible. Though we built many fires around us, some of our party would wake in the night screaming, such was their torment. It threatened rain continually, but did not rain. The smell of the pines was carried on the hot and humid breeze, and the shoulders of the trees were blued by the heavy air. At the lower end of Superior the wind rose and came into our faces. I was given a paddle only then, for my strength had not yet fully returned, and the least exertion caused me blinding headaches; we reached the Sault (there was no town then, only a settlement of Ojibwa lodges, a few cabins, and a frame building referred to as the Treaty House, where I met Mr. Ermatinger), and Mr. Ermatinger took me thence to Mackinac, where we arrived two days later, beaching our canoes in the bay below the Fort as the sky behind us over the mainland darkened under piling, towering clouds and went then black as midnight. There were forked spikes of lightning; thunder rumbled. The storm drew overhead and the fort with its white stone walls shone in sunlight that strayed in from the west below the rim of the clouds, and the broad garden below glowed and soldiers stood from their working, faces like candle-flames, to watch as the storm came in. There was shouting. A few carts and carriages passed by on the road going very rapidly. Then a roar could be heard coming over the straits, the mainland disappeared in a whirlwind of water, and everyone was running wildly—including many Indian women and children that popped up from under overturned canoes—for the Indian Agency. The wind brought with it a sound as of a waterfall, and I heard the crashing of canoes behind us. The air filled with sand, leaves. All light, but the faint bleed of yellow that ran upon the grass from the windows of the Agency House, was smothered.

The wide front veranda of the Agency House was crowded with Indians. I saw them in the trembles of lightning—most crouching, arms thrown across their eyes or outstretched, struggling with wind-ripped blankets—as we hurried to a door situated on a near wing; Ermatinger pounded upon it. He pressed his cheek against the wood and shouted. The door was opened to us; there was a heaving of bodies, and the door was shut again. Then it was still. The Indians remained without.

Major Puthuff, who was Indian Agent at this time, stood at a window overlooking the Fort garden. He glanced at us as if we'd been called for, nodding slightly, then returned his attention, eyes blinking with every flicker of lightning, to the window. Another man, his young interpreter, was watching the windows as he lit the candles of a lowered chandelier. The Major suddenly ducked and there came a great crash upon the wall; the building shook. Boards and sticks clattered against the windows. The Major looked around. "Some damned gazebo or other," he said. He talked to the man lighting candles, who then raised the chandelier by a rope and opened a pair of interior doors which slid apart each into the wall; the man, his interpreter, went out of the room. Ermatinger told me the Indians were to be allowed in. I thought this a good thing, for the storm had only gotten worse. Even in the darkness, through the rain-running windows, objects—skiffs, buckboards, shop signs—could be seen sailing through the air, and the Agency House itself was rocking like a ship at anchor in the bay. A door onto the veranda was thrown open. The Indians were greeted by shouts from the Major's interpreter as they pressed in and dispersed quietly about the dim rooms of the residence. A few started up a staircase and were called back down by a woman I took to be Mrs. Puthuff. She came into the room we occupied, which was the Agent's office, took her husband forcefully by the hand, and led him out. The Major came back a minute later. His face was very dark. There was then the loud report, almost directly overhead, of a big tree breaking in the wind. Everyone crouched, eyes on the ceiling. The fireplace at my back squealed. There was a general groan throughout the timbers of the house.

"Storm's about up," Puthuff said, straightening. "Willis, would you please see our guests out?"

But the Indians had more sense than that, and when the interpreter Willis opened the door onto a shriek of wind, they crouched or sat upon the floor. Mrs. Puthuff could be seen carrying a candle amongst them, saying "Shoo!"

The Major called her "Dear" and told her something. She called him a name and told him something back. Her eyes went as my Therezia's would, but when there came a brilliant flash and terrible blast of thunder, she screamed and disappeared. Ermatinger nudged me.

After that, as the storm passed over, Major Puthuff ordered a small keg of whiskey be brought out and he shared it, against the protests of his interpreter, with all present (excepting, of course, the children); in time the windows brightened and the doors were thrown open to let in a cool and fragrant breeze. The Ojibwa and Ottawa and Pottawatomi and Saginaw filed out and stood on the stick-strewn grass in the late afternoon sun watching their children conduct games or chase dogs about, and drank whiskey from cups and spoke with each other about the storm or their year's hunting adventures. They returned the cups and with salutes offered their thanks to the Major, then walked or danced their way back down to the bay. By nightfall they had built many new lodges and the shoreline was rimmed with their campfires and the cool night breeze carried upon it their songs.

[Really, I say.]

What.

[I re-read the last several sentences, which seem to me sanitized, Platonized, something.]

What would you change?

[Really? Nothing. I'm sorry. Go on.]

I had dinner that evening with Major Puthuff and Mr. Ermatinger and the interpreter Willis. We ate in the town at the hotel where Puthuff had determined to spend the night. I think it was called "The Yankee." There I told Puthuff my story. We sat by the fire and a group of young women had taken a table nearby, so it was very hard to hear what the interpreter told me—plus he, Willis, was paying attention to the young women, one of whom he said was to be married in a day or two—but I did learn that Major Puthuff would write a letter for me to take to Governor Cass in Detroit and that the Governor would certainly aid me in reaching my family. Willis told the girls also that Puthuff would supply me with a bark canoe and other provisions for my journey.

We were served beef stew and several glasses of wine and I developed a terrible headache. Major Puthuff arranged for Ermatinger and me to stay at the hotel for the night. Willis knew some of the young women and I think stayed as well.

Some days later, when the lake waters had largely calmed, I thanked Mr. Ermatinger and Major Puthuff for their kindnesses and sailed for Detroit. The canoe given me by the Major was lashed alongside the schooner. It was my first time aboard such a vessel and I spent much time above decks watching the crew work and following the captain about or leaning on the rail watching the coastline of the Canadian side recede to a string of islands that separated from the water as if to float on the horizon as they thinned and in time disappeared. The Michigan coastline was kept closer at hand, as here the lake swells were not bad. Soon the action of the boat caused me to become sleepy; with the captain's seeming permission, I sought a corner of the deck warm in the sun and protected from the wind, and there, resting my head on the bag given me by Puthuff, I slept for a time.

One of the young women from the hotel sailed on the same boat. Early in the day she had been sick; when I awoke I saw her still at the rail with a few others, bent over and her back squeezing violently. She was ill all the first day; but on the second she sat with her head in her hands and was a little better. She spied me and tried to speak with me once. I had again been sleeping in my spot on the deck.

"Hello," she said. She was leaning against the railing with her figure turned as if she'd just noticed me. The coastal hills were moving up and down at the level of her knees, and she wore a white dress to her shoes with the sun behind and her knees uncrossing as she looked back out at the shoreline. She turned again and smiled. Her face was white as a sail and featureless, but for her doubled chin and black-socketed eyes; she held her wild, unbound red hair in her free hand. "I *thought* I recognized you," she said.

I rose to my feet and, holding the wall of the cabin, shook my head and made—I suppose because I was both embarrassed and slightly dazed with sleep and feared also that if I'd attempted to speak she'd have thought me not an Ottawa or a Frenchman or Chinese, but drunk, mad, or an idiot—the Indian gesture, with my finger at my open mouth, that indicates one is of a different dialect. Her eyes started and she turned and left me, walking her hand along the railing, without a word. I went to the railing, relieved myself through its spiles, and sat back down.

We made Detroit late the following morning.

Will you have tea?

I was very fond of Cass.[1] He has gone on to Washington so I probably will not see him again, but when I was young and in

---

[1] Lewis Cass, b. 1782, d. 1866, rose to Brigadier General in the War of 1812, in recognition of which service he was appointed first Governor of the Michigan Territory by President James Madison in 1813, in which capacity he served until 1831. He was a major influence in establishing filial relations between the

great distress he gave me aid many times. He was very kind. I called him Father, out of respect for his position but too because, though several years younger than myself, he was like that also to me. There is a picture of him in the town hall and he has gone fat and jowly, but at this time he was not fat and a very striking man. His eyes were dark and commanding and his brows like the wings of a hawk holding on the wind. You noticed these about him first. His face in youth was narrow, with a very big nose, and his mouth reminded one of an old woman's, though when he spoke you forgot that. He would call me *"John"* comically, so that it sounded again like "bone," and shaking his head would put an arm over my shoulder and say, *"John, John, John."* He was a wise and kind man and I was very fond of him.

I went to his house on arriving in Detroit. It, the Governor's Mansion, was an old French house on a hill overlooking a large farm and beyond that a line of trees and the Detroit River. Across the river were woods and some open fields. There was a soldier or sentry walking back and forth in front of the gate. He stopped me. I could not speak English so as to be at all understood, but seeing a man sitting on the veranda with a straw hat upon his head, which man I thought might be the Governor, I waved my letter from Puthuff toward him. This man then told the soldier to let me pass in.

The Governor's office smelled of tanned hides and had fixed upon the walls the antlers of deer and elk and the swollen black and dusty head of an old bull buffalo. Two or three bear furs were spread upon the floor. To put the Governor at ease I pointed to these and told him, "Good bear, hmm, good buffalo!" and he looked and nodded, sat himself behind a large desk to tell me of

---

federal government and the native Americans of the lakes region, as well an architect of government's policy of acquisition and depopulation of Indian-held lands. He later served as Secretary of Defense and Secretary of State, and was Democratic nominee for the presidency in 1848. He was defeated by Whig candidate Zachary Taylor.

their histories. He motioned me to sit. I did so. When our conversation had nowhere more to go he read the letter. After a moment he looked up at me, now differently.

I pointed to the stove, or to the split wood that filled a great copper bucket alongside it. "A-dose, good yeh-de-bun-a-buh," I said. I think he then asked me how much English I understood. This much, however, I didn't; I told him again my name and, trying unsuccessfully to smile, looked up at the elk antlers on the wall behind him—in my fear and shame I could not bring out the words to compliment them—and grunted. He stood and came around the desk, clasped my hand, and spoke to me in words I knew, without knowing them, were words of pity and charity. He sent a soldier to get his interpreter.

While we waited for the interpreter the Governor had me sit on the veranda with him. We ate cold chicken and he tested my English. He made it like a game, and we both enjoyed it. When finally the interpreter arrived, the Governor was as one thirsty, and commenced to ask many questions; we talked thus for several hours.

Gish-kaw-ko was sent for and joined us. He confirmed for the Governor what I had related of my capture at the hands of the Saginaw. I had met Gish-kaw-ko on the street the day previous.

[That was quite the coincidence, I say.]

Leave it out. I thought not to bring it up and think we might just leave old Gish-kaw-ko out of this. It so strains the credulity, as Schoolcraft would say, as to require a truss. I had not seen this man since my childhood years ago with the Saginaw; in effect I had been Gish-kaw-ko's brother—he and his father, Manito-o-geezhik, had stolen me from my father's house to replace a younger brother that had died—though my treatment by the father was not as a son but as a captive, a slave, and I was only spared certain murder by my sale from him to Net-no-kwa for a keg of rum. It happened that Gish-kaw-ko had been just released from prison in Detroit when I ran into him. He was wandering as was I. We were on the same street. I crossed the street to ask of an Indian directions—any Indian—and was overcome by a feeling of sickness and awe as I comprehended his features. He drew back and flung his arms over his head when I made known my Saginaw name, and he was only able to speak after being assured many times that I intended him no harm. He was a deteriorated old man now.

When he later approached the Governor's mansion in the company of a soldier, Gish-kaw-ko appeared again very afraid. Seeing us on the porch waiting, he spread his arms so to signal the soldier he needed to stop, and, turning, opened his clothing. He lifted his head, Gish-kaw-ko did, and stood thus for five or ten minutes, or until the Governor called out to the soldier either help the poor old man pee or bring him up here. The soldier brought him up. I think Gish-kaw-ko expected to be going back to prison for having taken me so many years ago.

At the close of the day Cass dismissed Gish-kaw-ko and had me go to his interpreter's quarters a mile distant, where I was to reside until preparations could be made for the Council of Ste. Mary's, which was to be held not here at Ste. Mary's but at St. Mary's in Ohio. I would from there go to find my family, below in Kentucky. But the preparations took months, and after two months I could stand to wait no longer. I left with Be-nais-sa, brother of Gish-kaw-ko, and eight other men who were going to the Council; we travelled south by canoe to Lake Erie and up the Maumee and thence up the St. Mary's river as far as the rapids. As we had left without the knowledge of Governor Cass, we were without supplies, and I quickly became deathly weak with hunger and fatigue. We were aided along the way by Indians, one of whom, Ah-koo-nah-goo-zik, had a modest home and was very hospitable and generous and even gave me a horse to take; but the whites gave us no help, though they had large fields of corn and big houses—but refused us and sometimes violently drove us away. In time I reached St. Mary's, and might have recovered my strength, but it was there I was seized with fever and paroxysms and was in such pain and distress I could barely eat. I did not fully regain my health for many months, and by the time I met my relatives I could not walk without aid and was as a skeleton. That was later, after the Council.

Cass arrived at St. Mary's wearing his straw hat and was kept busy with the business of the Council, but at its conclusion called me to dine with him. There were many gentlemen also there that enjoined me to drink wine with them, and Cass put his arm over my shoulder before dinner and did also himself tip a bottle to my glass. Many bottles of wine were consumed with dinner. After dinner a man stood and challenged another to do as he did, and with his arms outspread brought first the finger of one hand to his nose, then the other. Each man there then followed in turn this man's example. I accepted more wine and performed the same maneuver. Afterward, a line was drawn in the dirt with a stick and each walked along the line as upon a roof-ridge, waving arms and some falling over. This line in my moccasins I walked easily. I enjoyed the games—if I thought them more foolish than any invented by tribes familiar to me (though of course I could not speak for the Sioux)—but several days later I was told by an interpreter that the Governor had a curiosity to know whether I had acquired the same fondness the Indians usually have for intoxicating liquors, and whether, when drunk, I would behave as they did. I would have been more displeased by this conspiracy had I behaved badly or become unconscious; but I had proved myself at the games, and had felt better the next day than I had in two weeks, so was only mildly put off by news of this experiment.

[That all inebriates should perform so laudably, I say.]

Soon thereafter I met my relatives.

[Good.]

First my nephew.

[His name is not given in your narrative.]

I don't remember it.

[The wine you remember.]

I've never been good with names.

I traveled south along the Miami with two Miamis from Kentucky who had attended the Council. One had heard of my family. I was soon too ill to sit upon a horse, so a skiff was procured and I was laid in it and taken along the river. When I could no longer travel even in this manner, I was received into the home of a poor white man and stayed with him several weeks. My nephew was located and brought to this house by one of my new companions. He was fair-haired like me, this nephew, but was balding, wore thick spectacles, seemed somewhat lazy or moony, and when he thought he was not being observed was in the habit of sucking his thumb. After all my endeavors and difficulties, it was hard not to feel a measure of disappointment.

I could not converse with my nephew, so our journey down the Miami to Cincinnati was tedious as well as difficult; at Cincinnati we rested a little before proceeding down the Ohio in a skiff to the settlement where my sister's children lived. I stayed a day in one nephew's home (his name, I recall, was John), then was moved (John had small children and feared my fever) to the home of the nephew that had delivered me to him and whose name fails me. He had no children. I was there a month, bedfast and very unhappy (neither my nephew or his wife spent much time at my bedside, or made the first effort to help me with language; I was left to look out a window of the tiny room upon a dreary and unchanging landscape), when a letter arrived for me. It was opened and read to me by my nephew's wife, in a voice as one would speak to an infant. As I could not comprehend a single word of it, I shook my head. She started to read it again, looking at me disapprovingly; when I turned my face away she stopped reading and called for my nephew. He came in and sat down upon the side of the bed and read to me the letter as his wife watched. He smiled, raised his brows; I shook my head. He read it again, looked questioningly back at his wife. He leaned forward to put his mouth in my face and shaped with his thick, unshaven lips several words repeatedly—his breath smelled like socks—then sighed and let the hand holding the letter drop to the bed; he sat hunched thus, staring at the wall above my head, as the thumb of his left hand slipped, as if willed unawares, into his mouth. His wife leapt forward and slapped it out. Her hand was scarcely quicker than mine. There was much shouting that followed, I think some of it directed at me.

A few days later a second letter arrived, and it was opened and dropped upon my bed as if I should clean myself with it. I decided immediately to pretend I could understand it, and took it upon myself, in spite of my poor condition, to prepare at once to leave as if in response to its message. I went back north—upon a horse but otherwise desperately alone—the way I had come. My health was such that I could ride, but I soon became weak with hunger and, as before, received almost no aid from the whites I encountered along the way.

The letters, I was to learn, were from my sisters, telling me that my brother Edward had gone to the Red River country to look for me, and that I should go to their homes, which were together near Port Girardoux. They, my sisters and brother, had been made aware of my fate by, or through the efforts of, Lord Selkirk.

I was two days from Detroit, at the foot of Erie, when a man on horseback passed by me with a Sioux pipe in his hand. So strong was his resemblance to my father, I thought, that I endeavored to stop him and have him take note of me. But he gave me only a hasty look and went on. When I reached Detroit, Governor Cass had me know that my suspicions—that this man was in fact my brother Edward—were well-founded. Similar thoughts on Edward's part were confirmed by people he met along the way, and he returned to Detroit, where we were reunited at the Governor's house only three days following my arrival.

I was dozing in the sun on the Governor's porch when I heard the hooves of a horse on the street, and on opening my eyes recognized my brother, who before I could stand had handed the reins of his horse to the soldier-guard and was bursting through the gate. He shouted my name; I let out a whoop, shouting "Ned!" and we embraced there on the walk before the Governor's house for a very long time. The soldier, who had been made aware of my history and of the possible arrival of my brother, paused beside us, head tilted, eyes filling, before running in to inform Cass, who came out immediately with his interpreter. Edward took the Governor's hand, but continued to hold me with the other. I wept and felt as if floating; I think I'd have fallen to the cobbles had Edward let go his embrace; we started then to verbalize sentiments with the aid of the young interpreter, who was not so moved as Edward or Cass or the soldier or me and so rather dampened, with his business-like translations, the urgent grace of the moment; but we were very happy, and went in and sat in the parlor of the residence and with the aid of the bored interpreter talked for several hours of my father's death eight years before and of the great earthquake and of the morning of my capture by Manito-o-geezhik and Gish-kaw-ko, which Edward remembered clearly (it was Edward found my hat and the spilled walnuts and first deduced I had been taken by the Indians), and of my children in the Red River country and my keen desire to retrieve them. I endeavored to persuade my brother to accompany me there, to my family's lodge at the Lake of the Woods; but to this he would by no means consent, insisting I must go with him to his home near New Madrid, beyond the Mississippi, and we set off together accordingly.

There followed a season of peregrinations whereby I was reunited with my brother James, my sisters, my step-mother, an uncle, and nearly all my living relatives, and at the conclusion of which I returned to Me-naw-she-tau-naung in the Red River country to retrieve my family. One of my children, a child born in my absence, died of measles upon my arrival. We went to the winter hunting grounds and nearly starved. Life became much as before.

In the spring of 1820 I returned with Therezia and my children to the States. We arrived at Mackinac very poor and hungry, and were told by Indians we met there of a woman trader who was very kind and would give us aid. So we erected our lodge in dripping fog in the middle of the night on the front lawn of Therese Schindler's home. She was very surprised to find us so encamped in the morning. Therese was an old widow born of an Ottawa mother and a French-Canadian father, who had succeeded her husband in the fur trading business and lived in a large white house above and east of the town, with a garden sloping toward the bay. She and her daughter Marianne provided for my family; she helped secure for me a position with the American Fur Company that year, and later adopted my infant daughter Lucy.[2] She made a home for Martha Ann and Mary, and showed my children, whose mother Therezia soon ran off to the Red River country only to return and become a fog-eyed Catholic, every kindness.

Much more happened over the next several years, which is all there in my first narrative, but we find ourselves on Mackinac, so I think I'll skip it. Suffice it to say I learned English from my sisters over many months spent in Jackson, which is near Cape Girardoux, and in 1824, having now a working command of English, secured the post of U.S. Government interpreter with Colonel Boyd[3] at Mackinac.

[I tell him the reader will feel a little cheated; I had hoped to become more familiar with his family, in particular his sisters.]

---

[2] Lucy Tanner, b. 1820?, was raised by Therese Schindler and educated on Mackinac at the boarding school for girls, reputed to be the first such boarding school in the Old Northwest, established and taught by Schindler's daughter, Marianne (Fisher). Lucy, who in her later youth also helped teach at the school, died tragically when the lake schooner she was aboard was lost near the mouth of the Grand River on Lake Michigan in 1834.

[3] Col. George Boyd, Jr., b. 1779, d. 1846, served as Indian Agent at Mackinac from 1820 to 1832.

We should move on. Sometimes, as my Wildereen liked to say, you have to do what you have to do.

[We might have dispensed with the thumb-sucker.]

I don't think so.

[Did you want to tell of your shooting?]

No.

5

I had lived then on Mackinac three years when Dr. James[1] arrived in the spring of 1827. He sought me out within two days of his arrival. My situation as Col. Boyd's interpreter would have brought us into contact soon enough, but he went to Therese Schindler's house to find me. We were spading the garden below the house when Dr. James came up. He'd gone off his directions and was in the tall weeds back of the house next door when we saw each other. He waved.

"Mr. Tanner?"[He shouts.] He walked up, brushing at the cockle-burrs spotting his trousers and waist-coat. The five of us— Therese, Marianne, my older two daughters, and I—stood and watched. It was early afternoon and the bay was brilliant and I had a little difficulty making him out, other than he was very thin and walked like a heron on the verge of flight. Over his head in the nodding trees a boat was coming in. He approached directly and I accepted his hand.

---

[1] Dr. Edwin James, b. 1797, Weybridge, Vermont, d. 1861, graduated from Middlebury College and later studied medicine under the tutelage of his brother, Dr. John James. He pursued as well a keen interest in botany and geology, studying with such notables as John Torrey and James Eaton. He was thus uniquely equipped to serve Major Stephen H. Long's expedition to the Rocky Mountains in 1820, as surgeon, botanist, geologist, and reporter. His notes on the expedition were published in 1822. He was, in 1827, assigned the post of surgeon at Fort Mackinac.

"John Tanner. Bless my soul!" he said. "Edwin James!" He was a little breathless, his nose was red and wet. He had thick dark hair, a small tight mouth, and a clubbed chin.

Therese stepped up and introduced herself and the others, and they shook hands in turn.

"Oh, yes, I've heard of you," he said to Therese.

Her kindly old eyes opened a little, but Dr. James said nothing by way of explanation; he returned his attention to me.

"I would very much appreciate an opportunity to speak with you, Mr. Tanner," he said. He jumped a bit and looked down at his trouser leg, which Lucy had just then commenced freeing of cockle-burrs.

"Your child?

I nodded.

"Charming. Thank you, Dear One," he said. If he thought this would stop her, it did not. His face reddened.

"We're at work," I told him.

"I see you are," he said, looking over the turned earth and nodding approvingly. He frowned, grabbed Lucy's hand. "This might not take a minute," he said.

His face did not seem familiar, although he said we had met seven years before at Cape Girardoux. What he said I believed to be true, as I had wintered that year at my sister's home in Jackson, and remembered the arrival in Cape Girardoux of Major Long's party, then just returning from the western mountains, as something of an event. Dr. James, who'd been attached to Long's expedition as surgeon and reporter and, if he spoke the truth, botanist (whatever that was), appeared disappointed that I did not remember him; it did not help when I told of meeting Major Long again in 1823 on Rainy Lake, where I was lodged at a North West Company trading post recovering from my bullet wound.[2] Long

---

[2] Tanner's near-fatal shooting by Ome-zhuh-gwut-oons, agent of his first wife, Mis-kwa-bun-o-kwa, occurred near the mouth of the Sturgeon River in July, 1823. Tanner was at the time engaged in an unsuccessful effort to retrieve to

had been exploring the upper Minnesota Territory, and had taken along not Dr. James, but a Mr. Keating, to report on the journey. I recalled Mr. Keating, I told the Doctor.

"In any case," Dr. James said, tightening his thin lips, "you see, I've done some considerable traveling in the territories and I'm in the course of—"

I interrupted to remind him that we were at work, adding that I could be found any day but Sunday, which day it was, at the Indian Agency.

"I'm a student of the Algonquin languages, you know," he said, apparently not having understood a word I said. "Something of an etymologist. I daresay I am most keenly interested in the possibility of working with you."

"Take a shovel."

"Hah," he said, and smiled. "Yes indeed." He turned and looked out at the bay, then back at me; he made an urgent face. "I am extremely anxious for your conjugation of the Chippewa substantive verb." When he saw I did not understand, he added, "Not just that, of course."

"Here, sir," Martha, standing at his side with a spading fork, said.

He laughed when he saw the fork, but saw that I did not catch the irony and took it in hand. He worked for an hour or so, talking playfully with the girls, stealing glimpses at me and occasionally Marianne, then excused himself.

"You'll stay for dinner," Therese told him.

"I should be honored on another day," he said. "I fear I'm not decent."

"Not decent for a trading house?"

He took her hand, and Therese cocked an eye questioningly at me as he bowed. Then he told me he looked forward to meeting

---

the States his two daughters born of Mis-kwa-bun-o-kwa. Tanner recuperated at the Northwest Company's trading house on Rainy Lake for the balance of that year.

with me at the Agency offices, and we watched him go. He went back through the neighbor's weeds. He was at the Agency first thing the following morning.

I lodged at the Indian Agency. I occupied a room about the size of this [indicating the room around us], in a cedar-barked addition with smoky plaster walls and a hearth of white stone. There were two windows with a view of the street and the bay beyond that and a door between the windows; I was provided a table and two chairs, a washstand, and a bed. A door to the interior of the house was unlocked once a day, the lock-click telling me that dinner had been set on the floor by the threshold. As the room took up the entire addition, it was quiet and gave me a measure of privacy, and it was there—or now and then in Dr. James's lodgings at the Fort Infirmary, if he sent word he was not up to going out— that the first narrative gathered form.

Behind the house rose a steep wooded bluff, and at its base was a patch of grass overhung with pine and birch and protected by the back wall of my addition as well as the east wall of the kitchen; here I maintained the ash frame of a little wigwam. I had built it for my Therezia to stay in during her menstruations, but she was gone now—

{Indecipherable}

So in the warmer months I would throw deer hides over the framework and sleep in it myself.

You see, this was Indian custom.

[Regardless, I say.]

In Therezia's lodge I could hear the wind in the trees and the waves coming into the point, and smelled the lake and pines and the silent hides, and sometimes there were the footsteps and voices coming up from the docks, or down from the fort. Late at night the whippoorwills would start. In winter I moved back inside, and my sleep then was never as good. I awoke with bad headaches.

My days were spent in Colonel Boyd's office, which was the same office once occupied by Major Puthuff, at the other end of the house. His office could be closed off from the residence by a pair of doors that slid back into the wall, and which were to be kept closed throughout the business day. Boyd himself occupied a table at the rear of the room, facing the front outer door. Behind him was a bookcase, and on the wall above a picture of John Quincy Adams, sitting at a table not dissimilar to Boyd's, slouching like Boyd, and perhaps also leaving it to an unseen interpreter to make eye contact with a visitor; and next to it and positioned a little below hung a smaller picture of my friend Lewis Cass, standing erect and reaching into his vest. Two wooden chairs with spindled round backs stood either side of a mantled fireplace, with large windows beside, and there were, as with my room, windows either side of the outer door, so the office had very good light. The outer door opened onto a stoop five steps above the walk and was left open whenever the weather permitted, both to welcome Indian visitors and to air the room out, as well as to afford Boyd a better view of the bay. He was always interested in the comings and goings of ships and commented often on the commerce of the island. It was the time of the year when the Indians came to seek provisions, having sold their winter's peltries; very many of their big lake canoes could be seen beached along the bay. It was a busy time for the Agency, and a time of year I favored above all but sugaring, though I was many years by now done with that sort of thing.

It was my duty to lay a fire in the morning, and I was doing so when the steps clattered and Dr. James appeared in the window, then stuck his head in the open doorway. Boyd rose to greet him, first closing the sliding doors in the face of Thomas, who had just brought to his father a cup of coffee and might have stood there staring at the odd-looking, non-Indian guest, were his eyes not fixed on me. I showed him my teeth as the door slid shut. I lit the fire.

The Doctor was wearing a green plaid vest under a brown jacket, and wore a tall beaver which he removed as he came through the door and fiddled with as we spoke. He was telling Boyd of our meeting at Cape Girardoux many years before, when an old Indian came up behind him. The Doctor turned and the Indian spoke to him.

"Kitte-mau-giz-ze,"[3] the Indian said.

The Doctor nodded, turned to address Colonel Boyd. "He offers his greeting," he said, meaning the Indian.

"You say so," Boyd said.

I took my place by the side of the old Ottawa and Dr. James seated himself by the fireplace to observe. Boyd scooted his chair around and sat sideways to his table, looking out the window as the Indian spoke. The old man's family had been robbed of its traps and ironware, all its pots and kettles, early that spring. He had only his gun to provide them with food, and without the aid of a trader at Drummond they might have starved. The Saginaw had taken everything.

I related all this to Boyd.

"Did you go to the British agency on Drummond?" Boyd asked.

They would never do such a thing.

"Where did this theft occur?"

The Indian turned and pointed. They went every spring to make sugar on Manitoulin with their Ottawa kin, and this year several families of Saginaw arrived there as well. They were poor after their journey, and constantly bothered the Ottawa for food.

"We've had quite a few here," Boyd said.

I asked the old man had there been either Gish-kaw-ko or Benais-sa with them, and he stated he did not know of these two; for all their generosity toward them, they had not made a point of smoking with the Saginaw.

Hearing us converse thus in Ottawa, Boyd looked over. "Ask him about the princess," he said.

---

[3] *"I am in want."*

I asked the old Indian what he knew of rumors surrounding the death of a Saginaw woman on Manitoulin that year. The old Indian smiled at this question. "Hoh," he said.

She was a princess, or was said to have been the daughter of a chief—he didn't recall her name, nor that of the father—who had lost her nose. He had seen her. She was famously drunk, and very ugly. Yet she was said to have been possessed of rare beauty as a young woman, with a straight and narrow nose, but was caused by this gift—bestowed on a child of such a God-scorned race as the Saginaw—to be first vain and ambitious, then bitterly cruel. One winter night an un-manned lover took her pretty nose in his teeth and left her—with no more thought and in little more time than would be required to sever a thread—both hideous and—though not so quickly—hideously profane. The woman went mad over the ensuing years, and it was she who died in March on Manitoulin, wild-tongued and un-pitied, savagely denouncing her people, calling them *matchi annemoash*,[4] to the very end, her shrieks ringing in the snow-fog through wheeling, sky-clawing trees right up to the instant she threw up her arms in a final gesture of disgust and stumbled backwards into a great boiling cauldron of maple sap. Her last cry had, as it impressed others present, a questioning uplift. Yet the ruined sap—or whether it was in fact ruined—became, in the moments that followed, the dominant concern, even as her loosed hair spread speckled with ash over the surface and her feet curled and the heels lost their purchase and she slid out of sight. The tribal ring closed silently around the cauldron, and a worried fingertip was lowered into the broth. She was buried then without a proper funeral fire or, for that matter, a funeral. Her people had by this time decided to dump the sugar-sap; for sorrow it was sufficient.

---

[4] *Bad dogs*

As I interpreted this, embellishing with details provided by other witnesses (though in not quite the words I am equipped to employ now), Dr. James's eyes grew, and Colonel Boyd had to hold his mouth to keep from laughing.

The old Indian went on. The Saginaw now wished for the Ottawa to share their sugar, and being refused had painted their faces and made raids on the family encampments and crossed the island to harass the Ojibwa. Fights broke out. Being a peaceful people, and their group composed primarily of women, children, and old men like himself, the Ottawa packed up and left Manitoulin, though not before suffering great losses of trap and iron. The old man's family had lost everything. The Saginaw were animals.

"Just so," said Colonel Boyd, and he wrote out a requisition for the Indian to take to the La Framboise trading house.

After the old man left, Dr. James stood. "I didn't wish to intrude," he said to Boyd. "Do forgive me for staying." He reached over to stroke the fur of a white fox pelt that Mrs. Boyd had draped over the mantle. "But, my Lord, one might spend a year on a pirate ship without hearing such tales!"

"This one could tell you a few," Boyd said, jabbing a thumb in my direction.

"Indeed," the Doctor said. He looked at me, or my craven remains, steadily a minute. I was relieved when a pair of Indians pushed through the door. What they required I no longer recall.

Will you have tea?

Dr. James arranged to meet with me that evening. Boyd had interceded so I was given no choice in the matter. He brought a bag of books and followed me across the front veranda to my door. My room was a place only my children were allowed— Therezia lived then with the Catholic Sisters—and I had not been so aware, before the Doctor's visit, of its closeness; I noticed, whether for the first time or more potently than before, an odor remindful of bats in an attic, and for a terrible instant thought a dead man lying on my bed its source, though my eyes beheld merely the death-reach of unwashed linens. Clothing, dried leaves, rabbit bones, were everywhere underfoot. I was mortified. The Doctor's very presence had this civilizing effect.

"Sit," I told him, and when he sat and had reached into his bag I hurried behind his back to tidy up as best I could, pitching under-drawers and wash towels under the bed and tossing blued bits of bread, dried gristle, mole pelts I'd been collecting for God-knows-what purpose, into the fireplace, aligning a pair of moccasins—whatever I could manage behind his chaired back. He took no note of the flurry, but made a small pile of his books, then gazed out the open doorway and began telling me about himself.

I understood half of what he had to say, and dismissed half of that, until he spoke of the great western plains and the mountains; then I took a seat. In his explorations he had seen herds of buffalo so great that they covered the prairies to the horizon. Hills flowing with them. He described the Sioux hunters on horseback. I had followed such herds and killed many buffalo, I told him, with and without horse. He nodded. He spoke of the vast Sioux migrations and the nobility of their warriors. With this I became agitated. I attempted to impress upon my guest what I knew personally of the murders and brutalities inflicted upon the woodland Indians by the Sioux, throwing in the Eternal Crisis of Irresolvability, but as my blood rose my English faltered, as it was prone when tested, sliding into the fire-light conjunctives of the Ottawa. He waited me out, interrupting only to pick out a word or an oath for me to translate.

"But of course," he said, "there's the question of whose buffalo one hunts; where provocation ends and belligerence begins. No?"

I rose to my feet, not sure exactly what he'd said, or that I wouldn't grab his nose regardless.

"I quite understand. Did I mention I was the first white man to reach the summit of Pike's great peak?"[5]

This question, odd as it was, arrested me.

"It's true," he continued, speaking quickly; "Zebulon Pike's great unattainable peak. Unclimbable, by his claim. Locked in winter at the top the year 'round, not a living creature abiding, nor even birds but a raven or two. Naught but rock and ice. I was the first to make a practical proof of its accessibility. Can you imagine, I passed through the clouds and beheld them from above, like a god!"

I slowly sat again, feeling dizzy. Algonquin lore bore no such imagery, although it was legend among the Ojibwa that Ne-bah-quam[6] had climbed a ladder through the clouds into the white man's heaven, this many generations ago, and had come to a place of great abundance of game and beauty, where few white men resided and no Indian had ever set foot. In the case of Ne-bah-quam, such ascent was but a sacred dream; yet the Doctor's claim was upon the very earth I walked.

"I have gazed straight down into an abyss deeper than the distance from here to the mainland," he said.

"Which mainland?" I asked.

"That." And he pointed at the ribbon of green west of the humped back of Round Island and, beyond that, Bois Blanc.

---

[5] Edwin James, accompanied on his climb by two companions, is credited as the first of European decent to reach the summit of what is now known as Pikes Peak on the afternoon of July 13, 1820. Named "James Peak" by expedition leader Major Stephen Long in honor of this accomplishment, the mountain was even then more commonly referred to as "Pike's Peak," in recognition of its 1806 discoverer, General Zebulon Montgomery Pike. James himself, in his notes on the 1820 expedition, referred to the mountain as "Pike's highest peak." John C. Fremont made "Pike's Peak" part of the formal geological record in the 1840's, to Long's chagrin. Edwin James would, however, retain namesake rights for the Limber Pine (Pinus flexilis James), the narrow-leaved cottonwood (Populus angustifolia James), and the Cliffbush (Jamesia americana).

[6] A Catholicized Chippewa of Grand Traverse Bay (Traverse City), Michigan, said he had heard of the dream from another in his youth, and had considered it sacred.

"You lie," I said.

He shrugged. "I stood in a gale on the summit, the very grind of earth upon the limpid face of heaven, and shot with a bow into this terrible wind; I watched the arrow float, then plucked it from the air as one might a tamed sparrow."

"Hoh!" I said. "An arrow?"

"I borrowed a kit from an Indian guide," he said. "The bow made a first-class walking stick."

"Did you try a gun?"

He smiled. "Do you know, at the summit I peered upward into sky black as ink at mid-day, and counted stars."

"Is there no sun there?" I asked, thinking I'd caught him.

"Oh yes," he said, "the sun shines brighter there than below. The sky at such elevation becomes a veneer without body. It cannot shield the stars. Think, now, of water."

I saw that it was true. Hook, line, and sinker he had me. Yet I was compelled by my hardheaded nature, and a niggling sense that he was testing my intelligence, to ask if he had, in truth, climbed to this place of winter that touches heaven.

"I did, and without ropes."

"Did you have, then, ladders?"

"No."

"Well, you should have," I said. I fought to think. If he was telling the truth, I felt nonetheless at a loss, belittled. I realized at that moment I was leaning forward against the table with my hands conjoined against my chest like a child listening to a tale, or a squirrel feeding; I made a pair of fists and lowered them to the table-top. "I employed a ladder in my assault on Fort Douglas that had been taken by the North West Company from the Hudson Bay on the Assiniboine," I told him. "I made a ladder from the truck of a pine and took the fort alone, and alone captured Mr. Harshield and confined him to his bedroom." I felt uncomfortable boasting, but knew he would recognize this history and make the connection, and waited for his expression to change and for our equality to be restored.

"You don't say," he said, raising an eyebrow.

"I did."

"Why would you do that?" he asked.

"For Lord Selkirk!" I said. The question stupefied me.

"I'm sorry, Lord Who?"

I brought my fist down on the table and might have screamed had not the interior door, at that moment, been unlocked with a loud clack.

"Good Lord!" Dr. James said, staring at me thunderstruck.

"It's dinner," I explained. I got up. He muttered something as I went to the door.

The Doctor had no appetite, but rather than simply leave set out his inkwell and wrote notes, and as I ate I watched his pen trace the blood-glimmer of ink in looping patterns over the page. He assumed from time to time a pose I later came to know very well, resting his chin lightly on the knuckles of the hand holding his pen, the tip up and bleeding ink down through his fingers, eyes looking up or straight ahead, at nothing.

"To be," he said.

I looked up, and he met my eyes. My mouth was full of, I think, mutton.

He said, "If I might just run this by you: 'It's of general consensus among philologists that the northern tribes, specifically those of the Algonquin family, such as your Chippewa, have unique to them, *vis a vis* the general run of Indians, the use of the substantive verb declarative of existence. '*Iau*,' with the particle, for past tense, '*ke*,' prefixed, or '*bun*,' suffixed, is used in various forms, but only when attached to nouns or objects of animate vitality. That is, the inanimate object, for example a condition or emotion, will not follow the substantive '*Iau*.' The Indian does not say, 'I am happy,' or 'I am sad,' but, rather, 'I happy, I sad.' Yet, when a non-vital, or inanimate object is used, a corresponding substantive verb, *'Atta,'* may be used, provided the noun described is not, as uniquely exempted by a grammatical rule, an emotion.'"

The Doctor looked up at me without raising his head. "Is that, in your opinion, fairly sound?"

I continued to eat. He gave me a second glance, returned to his notebook.

"*'Iau,'* 'To be;' *'nin diau,'* 'I am;' *'ki diau,'* 'you are;' *'iau-bun,'* 'I was—'"

I set down my knife. "What is it you want of me?" I asked him.

"Your help with the conjugations, of course," he said. He gestured to indicate the scribbles in his notebook. "But would you say what I have here is fundamentally sound?"

I nodded, thinking it would provoke less discussion. I was still eating, and in any event had not understood very much of it aside from the Ojibwa. He stood the pen in its inkwell, looked at his fingers, then ran his hand back through his hair. He seemed pleased.

"Well," he said, "I'd like your ongoing assistance with my language studies, if you'd be willing. Not to take up too much of your time. A little light work. Translating the Gospels into Chippewa, ultimately. I can't pay you, I'm afraid, but I was thinking that should you require any medical attention, I could offer my services at something of a discount."

"I need much of the medical," I told him.

"Do you indeed," he said. "Or I could pay you a dollar a week, say. That I might manage."

I agreed to the arrangement, with the stipulation he not disturb me on Sundays, and he packed up his books and bade me good night.

Would you help me up? The tea—I fear I've waited too long. Miss Mesare, if you could put down your damned pen, please—

6

[He is wearing a clean shirt, but there is a sour smell as of intoxicating spirits upon his breath.]

He, Dr. James, took the language notes, then together we walked some evenings down to the town, and returning sat on a bench on the veranda of the Agency. The days lengthened into June. We sat until last light. The moon would rise over the Huron, and in its light could be seen the currents moving on the straits. The currents moved in gold braids at various rates of speed, and sometimes in different directions. You could see slowly turning eddies in the bay. I would watch this, and the figures moving up and down the docks, loading or unloading ships in the spare yellow glow of lanterns, and Dr. James would talk and pose questions. Soon we had worked together two months.

This, then; that, therefore; latter, former. Rules conditional and inviolate. Dissections, tracings to origins. While it is true my English was helped by our talks, my Indian tongue became patterned and strange to me; my mind tired of it; some nights I wished to speak it no more.

"Tell me about your mother," he one evening said. The question was abrupt, and I looked at him.

"My stepmother, her I recall well."

"Your mother is not a memory?"

"Not so much. But the event of her death I remember distinctly. We moved from our home on the Kentucky River soon thereafter."

"Then what of the other?"

"My stepmother was a good woman. She was the mother of my younger brothers and sisters."

"Of course. Was she pretty?"

This seemed a peculiar question. She was my father's wife. "She was a big woman," I told him. "I remember that she was very strong. She walked a certain way because a knee had been injured by a horse when she was very young. I remember this walk and her voice."

"How old were you when your mother died?"

"Two years."

"Do you remember her name?"

"No."

"I see."

"My brother Ned told me her name when I lived a time with him. He remembered being told, but we did not speak of her when we were children. There was my stepmother then. I did not commit the name of my mother to heart then or later. I wish that I had."

"Of course."

"It is a sadness."

"What was your stepmother's name?"

"Ruth."

"Your father's?"

"John Edward Tanner."

"I'm sorry— Edward?"

"Yes. My brother is Edward, or Ned, after him."

"Tell me about him."

"Ned?"

"No, your father."

"He had been, in Virginia, a minister, like Ferry. He died when I was living at Great Wood River among the Assiniboine."

"You were aware of his death?"

"No; word came to my lodge not of my father but from a prophet's messenger who urged me to kill my dogs. The Great Spirit had sent word that all were to kill their dogs. There was also the great earthquake."

"The New Madrid?"

"Yes. These events happened at the time of my father's death. This is how I mark that time. I did not know of my father's death until eight years hence. Maybe ten."

"Nineteen eleven, then. Interesting. Did you kill your dogs?"

"No, I alone did not. It was the beginning of my war with religion."

"Where did you live when you were taken?"

I told him.

"How did your family come to be there?"

I told him of Elk Horn, where my family first lived, and of the cavern there that I had explored with my brother, and of the hostile Indians that drove us out and the flatboat with bullet holes and blood on it that carried us down onto the Ohio, and the place where we settled near the mouth of the Miami. It was there that I was taken, beyond the protection of my home, filling my hat with walnuts.

"Let us go inside," Dr. James said.

This, more or less, was how the narrative began. It very quickly pushed aside the Doctor's language studies.

I would require a cup of water, please.

Thank you.

In the beginning we had our difficulties. It surprised me at the time, but for all his notes-scribbling and studies Dr. James was not practiced at transcribing, and this was made more difficult by my poor English and my Ottawa dialect, for which he was unprepared; so the work vexed both of us and became at times unpleasant. But time would correct his deficiencies, as it would improve my English, and with time the Doctor's confidence grew. It grew with time and in time his confidence became such that he would sometimes raise a hand to shush me and go on transcribing in silence for an hour. Of his art I knew next to nothing. But as his confidence manifested itself and my role became shadowy and the layout of our system uncertain, it disturbed me greatly, and I became, over time, more and more inclined to say fantastic things to get his attention back. This, I can say in all truthfulness, I came to regret. It was a central mistake.

I recall a sitting one particularly chill autumn afternoon, with the lake winds foretelling winter and the straits like iron and the Doctor sitting red-eyed and staunching a bloody nose, and me telling him of running thirty miles within the reach of a single day. I told him that I had run barefoot, exhausted of moccasins, over ice and snow and cold-blistered ground from a trading house on the Red River to the encampment of my family, a distance white traders there had determined to be thirty miles. For fear of freezing if I so much as slowed, I had run barefoot such a distance. So I claimed. The story was intended to increase my reporter's misery as much as it was to regain some foothold in the narrative process, but I'd have flown the distance on a jossakeed's drum, had it come into my head just then: I was certain he was deaf to me. Edwin, as he now had me call him, dipped his pen, looked up at the ceiling as if to catch echoes, transcribed. He paused, unfolded his hanky to study it sorrowfully, stuffed it back up his nose, transcribed.

Years later I discovered he'd not been deaf to me at all; no, he'd taken it all down, only he'd given me moccasins and an extra day and, thus equipped, had me to run seventy miles—not a mere thirty—and had me running not to escape freezing, but of all heresies back to my family's camp to marry Mis-kwa-bun-o-kwa. He then took it upon himself to add a fantasy that had me and an anonymous half-breed taking turns clinging to the tail of a trotting horse and thus covering this seventy miles in a single day—with no more apparent purpose than sport. A horse alone could barely cover such a distance. It would have baffled any Indian. Can you explain this? Could the popularity of Irving have had an influence?

[I ignore the question, though he waits.]

There were many such tales born of competing exaggerations, and you can be sure, Miss Mesare, that they did their work. It was pointed out by a reader who wrote me that my narrative contained four more years of hunting-gathering than my life had accomplished, that my five months as a trader with American Fur had been stretched to fifteen. We had stuffed them in, these months and years, my poor life inadequate to the Doctor's literary ambitions. I became, without a clue as to why, The Great Liar.

[Brings the cup to his mouth. He is quiet. His expression settles. His eyes narrow; he clears his throat.]

Anyway.

We worked on the narrative throughout the winter. In April the Doctor retired to his quarters to make it into longhand. He could not be bothered then. It took a very long time. Afterward, he wanted me to go to New York with it, but I refused. I had no desire to travel, and knew that Colonel Boyd would not relieve me for such a period from my duties at the Indian Agency.

It was at this time, with our work completed and its demands on my evenings relieved, that I sought to have my son John come to live with me. As my daughters roomed with Therese Schindler, so too my youngest son, John Jr., stayed with a family in town. (James, our eldest, boarded at Ferry's new mission school, and did not want to leave.) My visits were not welcome at this house where John Jr. lived, and my influence on the child not encouraged. This had become a source of enmity between that family and me, so when I went to collect my boy, having received Colonel Boyd's permission to make such an arrangement, I went carrying a rifle. A man and woman walking in a neighboring grove of apples saw me approach the house thus, and followed.

I knocked at the door with the end of my gun, stood back. The door opened, and the woman of the house stuck her head out. She quickly closed the door again, and I could hear shouts within, hers and then her husband's—McFarland was his name—and faces at the windows and much commotion of feet upon floorboards and doors slamming shut. After a moment it quieted, and McFarland opened the door and stood there facing me. He had armed himself with a gun carved from a plank, a child's toy. I smiled when he aimed it at me.

"Tanner," he said, "take thy leave of my house." He was a Quaker and spoke biblically; this, one would guess, also explained the gun.

"I will have my boy now," I told him. I had rested the butt of my rifle on the stones to show my peaceful intent, but my fists held it firm to speak also of my resolve.

"Is that thing loaded?" he asked.

I cocked an eye to peer down the barrel. "Looks like it."

"What is thy plan?" he asked. He looked very worried.

"To take my son home. I thank you and your wife for your past kindness, but I wish to have my family live with me now."

"Not your daughters—" His rifle, which had drooped a little, came back up.

"Of course not," I said with a wince. I refocused. "Deliver to me my son!" I said.

"No!" he piped. "Thou wilt not lay thy hand on the boy!"

"Now!" I roared, and brought the gun up. Inside the house, Mrs. McFarland screamed; I caught her face in a window to the right of the doorway and jerked the gun in her direction; I saw her drop exactly as if I'd shot her. Her husband ducked a bit, but stood his ground. His attention was arrested by something behind me, and I turned to see the two that had followed me now running in the direction of town. I noted that they were elderly, so would take a minute; nonetheless, I needed to complete my transaction.

"My son!" I said.

"Soldiers will be along soon," McFarland said. His face was white and he swallowed hard, so that his neck twisted a bit.

"I come on the authority of Colonel Boyd," I told him. The statement was not entirely untruthful.

"I— Colonel Boyd?" The toy gun wavered and he glanced over his shoulder into the house, then downward—seeing, I supposed, his wife.

"Colonel Boyd," I declared. "On his authority! Give to me my son!"

He looked at me, rubbed the back of his neck. "Shit," he said, in a quiet, Quaker voice. "Let me talk this over with Anne." He shut the door.

It took me fifteen minutes to realize I'd been duped. I stood there in the sun, squinting at the white clapboard wall of the house, waiting. I turned to see if any boats were out on the straits. I wiped my forehead with a sleeve. I watched the green door with its brass knocker. I looked back towards town.

I was charged with threatening a man's life and held in the new fort lockup—thank God not the hole—[7] for two days, until Colonel Boyd posted bail. Boyd and Dr. James made the climb together to collect me. I was relieved to see them. The Doctor chatted throughout the process, while Boyd largely spent his time pacing, only occasionally stopping to scream, *"On my authority?!"*

It was an uncomfortable walk home.

"He needs some time away," Dr. James said.

"He needs his head examined," Boyd said.

---

[7] The guardhouse at Fort Mackinac was rebuilt in 1828, with the addition of a large room to house prisoners replacing the infamous "Black Hole," which was little more than a pit below the guardhouse floor having no windows and accessible only by a trap door.

The Doctor told Boyd as we walked of his invitation to me that I travel at his expense to New York with our manuscript. I realized then that the idea bore some appeal.

"What manuscript?"

Dr. James explained.

"Not a chance," Boyd said; "he's needed here."

"I might substitute for him," Dr. James offered. I grunted at this, for I knew both the limits of his Ojibwa and the impatient nature of the clientele.

"You have a post," Boyd told him. "And in any case John's merely out on bail."

"Well, that's true."

Boyd laughed, a huff of breath. "The Indians would eat you alive."

"It was just a thought."

But Dr. James would not let the matter rest. He himself could not go to New York: the threat of cholera was increasing with the advancing season and that, he said, required his presence. So he was very anxious for me to go, and went so far as to write letters of introduction addressed to various New York publishers. He grew more insistent. He was feverish about it. He spoke to the McFarland's and prayed with them for the Lord's guidance, and in time they dropped the charges; but that came later, in June.

Boyd resisted until the first week of May.

"That's fine, John, you go," he said to me one day. I had made it a practice to place my request each morning ahead of the parade of Indians, hoping to catch him rested and of a favorable frame of mind. "You go to the big city. That's fine. Break bail. I'll be able to shut the fucking door for a change."

"I will not be gone so long," I said.

"Oh yes you will."

He wrote out a paper and had me make my mark upon it, then said, "Better get that damned hair cut first." Thinking the paper was a note to a barber, telling of my journey, I reached to take it.

He snatched it away. "Get out!" he shouted. He shouted three more times thus, and I understood I was dismissed.

Tomorrow I shall tell you of New York City. Have you been there? Have you ever been to the opera? Have you been anywhere?

[I ask has he been drinking.]

Of course not. I could not do this. Why do you ask?

[I thought I smelled it about you.]

I made for my eye a poultice. It was perhaps that.

[I apologize.]

Thank you for asking. I would not have you think that of me.

7

The manuscript of our narrative Dr. James wrapped in butcher stock and tied up with ribbon and put into a leather satchel that I was instructed to keep on my person at all times. I was given unneeded and unwelcome lessons in money counting, and told to stay clear of certain types that might be identified by a range of clothing choices, mustaches, and manners of speech. I was not allowed to take along a gun.

Colonel Boyd came down to the dock with the Doctor. He slid three silver pieces into my palm, patted my shoulder, and stepped aside so that Dr. James, who was dressed as for a Sunday, could provide more instruction.

"I had a belt sewn onto it," he said, putting said belt over my head. He turned me and, keeping a hand on my back, walked me onto the gangplank. "Now carry it like this whenever you can, and keep the flap-side against your body like so. If someone asks, simply tell them it's your life's story. They won't be interested in that. When you know you're going to need money, take a little out where no one can observe you and stick it in your pocket. The letters of introduction and queries are in envelopes with the publishers' names and addresses written on them—" (he paused, looking up and wincing as the ship's whistle blew four times) "—and do please stay out of public houses and establishments of the sort we talked about last night and avoid women like a chancre unless they speak to you first, and then just say, 'Yes, Ma'am,' and get away, and pray every morning and night and, good Lord, John, put a smile on that face and remember to bathe and God speed my good man; God speed!" He leapt back off the gangplank.

The boat did not move for five more minutes. When finally smoke started in great billowing bursts overhead and the gangplank was raised and the water began to churn behind the wheels, the Doctor and many others looked relieved and happy again and began waving their hats; I searched for Boyd, but he had apparently gone back up to the Agency. I was able to see Dr. James for a very long time. He had received word from the army that he was to be transferred to a post at St. Mary's, and I did not expect I would see him again soon. During our year working together I had come to admire his company, and felt regret at this parting.

We sailed southeast in a cloud of wood-smoke. The ship's sails were not raised—I guessed because they would catch fire—but in spite of this we made what I judged to be very good time. The cool air was pleasant and I felt the movement of the boat. The wheels made a sound like rapids, and when I dozed on the deck in my dreams there were many woodland Indians, and I was with Net-no-kwa as in my youth. I dreamed of seeing the thick and sparkling coat of frost on the inside of a puk-kwi lodge, and hearing my Indian mother say that she had kept a large fire in expectation of my arrival. I awoke, confused and unhappy, and the following day we docked to take on wood. I slept most of the way to Detroit. We arrived on the 23rd of May.

The boat waited there a day for unloading and loading before going into Lake Erie and on to Buffalo. I slept out on the deck and awoke early. The sky to the east was green, and the small birds were starting up. At mid-day of the 24th we entered Lake Erie. I had never been on this water, and took an interest in watching the shadow of the boat manifest from time to time over the bottom. The lake was shallow and deep green in color. A trailing wind came up and an aft sail was raised, bringing much smoke down upon the deck, so that I was forced to go below, where I became seasick. I slept as much as possible. This part of the voyage was the most unpleasant, and lasted two days.

There was a day spent at Buffalo, New York; there I purchased passage on a barge that would take me east on the new Erie Canal. The barge passengers were of the general class and, once they became familiar with my story, treated me with kindness and generosity, so that I never wanted for food, or for anything else. No one would take my money, and no one asked about the Doctor's satchel. It took us a week to reach the Hudson River. I was very happy during this time, and there were many heartfelt handshakes when we disembarked; I have never forgotten the kindness of those I met. Another ship took me down the Hudson between high wooded hills to the flat spread of land and the forest of masts and church steeples that was Manhattan Island, this near the ocean. When we landed, I watched from the deck above as passengers disembarked, waiting my turn to descend the steps—all the while the boat rocking as the weight of its passengers and wagons of cargo disbursed—and when I walked down the steps and off the boat onto firm ground I stumbled with my satchel and bag and turned in a circle, then thought it best to go in the direction others were headed, so directly found myself being helped into a carriage.

All along the wharf were warehouses and smoky coopers' shops and packing sheds smelling of meat and blood and men rolling barrels or standing alongside buildings smoking pipes with their hands tucked under aprons for warmth. I heard a saw cutting heavy wood. There were seagulls flying amidst the masts of ships, and many keeping from underfoot along the wharf.

Dr. James, when it was known I would be making this trip, and a week before I embarked, had written to a friend he'd known at university in Vermont to arrange that I should room with this man, whose name was Harrison, and put into the satchel another letter I was to deliver to him. The name and address of Harrison were written on the envelope containing this letter. This envelope I showed to the carriage driver when everyone else had gotten off. I was uneasy with the arrangement Dr. James had made, but, pressed by circumstances and the Doctor's enthusiasm, had little say in the matter. I attempted to convey this to the driver, as it was clear I was putting him to some trouble, but he delivered me to Harrison's house without a word of complaint.

Harrison's house was of red brick, and set narrowly along a row of many other such houses. There were young maples in full leaf to either side of the stone walk. A small, balding young man answered my knock. He had light-colored hair so arranged as to stand out on all sides like a jay's topnotch, and a large mustache. He had no chin to speak of. His eyes were big.

"I am John Tanner," I told him, and handed him the Doctor's letter.

He said nothing, but looked at his name on the envelope, then tore away the wax-sealed flap and opened it wide. There was paper money inside. "Yes, yes," he said, "Mr. Tanner. Very pleased." He gave me his hand. "I just received Edwin's letter the other day. You're most welcome in my home. Do come in. How are you liking New York? I will have to show you the town! Yes, of course!"

He led me from one room to another, explaining his house. "Edwin sent me this," he said, stroking the fur of a white fox, identical to the one on Colonel Boyd's mantle, that was here draped over the top of a chair. "He bought it from an Indian. Have you ever seen anything like it?" In the parlor room was a low and very long piano. Harrison sat down suddenly, threw his arms in the air, and began playing. He stopped as suddenly and laughed like a madman.

"I'll show you your room," he said. "You'll want to freshen up." I followed as he moved busily up the staircase.

He made a very good dinner of sea bass, beets, onions, asparagus, and pickled cucumbers. As he cooked, we talked about the narrative. He wanted to know all about it. He asked which publishers I would be visiting. I drew from the Doctor's satchel—which was still on my person, as I had felt a need to be equipped for any such questions—the envelopes the Doctor had prepared. Harrison held them one by one up to his eyes. "No," he said, reading. "No, no, and, *no.*" He ripped the envelopes in half. "I'll take care of it," he said.

I was very upset by this sudden destruction of Dr. James's letters. Harrison held a hand toward me, waving, and told me he worked for the *New York Courier* in advertizing and knew a thing or two about the publishing business. Edwin had been right to put him to the test. Absolutely. "*Carvill,*" he said, Carvill was our ticket. They advertized in the *Courier.* This was their kind of thing. He motioned for me to take a seat at the table, nodding his head. He sat, winked, shoved a biscuit in his mouth. "Carvill," he said.

After a minute eating he looked up and asked why Dr. James had not secured for us an agent.

I told him I did not know, thought of Puthuff and Boyd, and asked what purpose an agent, as I was not, as I thought he knew, an Indian, would serve.

"Well, good luck with that," he muttered. He ceased chewing, swallowed, then smiled and explained about agents.

I wondered would this put us at a great disadvantage.

"Some might say that's an invention; I would disagree. One *should* have an agent. The publishing business is changing, don't you know, John. It needs to change. The temple is under siege. The rabble is at the gates!"

I did not understand.

"Liken it, this literature of yours, supposing it's literature, to architecture. The architect designs a vision of order and beauty. All well and good. That's what architects *should* do. But it is at best a *personal* vision of order and beauty, invested with—*infected* with—the dreams and concupiscent deformities of the architect; it may be ugly to the average man, crawling with bric-a-brac; or it may have too few closets. But we, say we are the landholder, build it and hope for the best. Or the landholder holds out for a higher measure of commercial surety and spends his days not building, but reviewing a thousand plans from a thousand architects. Which is better? Do you see the problem? What is the solution? Of what use in the end is a design the average man cannot appreciate, or the landholder ill-afford to have constructed? Should not the architect first consult the real estate broker? To take it a step further, should not the broker consult the architect, i.e., as to questions of load-bearing and mortar specifications, etcetera, and simply correct the design himself, and should not all parties leave questions of beauty and the divine to accountants and priests—or, excuse me—medicine men?"

I did not respond. My mind was puzzling over many words.

"Brokers. Gatekeepers," he said, winked again.

I suggested, having learned much of the Bible from my sister and then from Dr. James, and having understood a few of his sentences, that the money changers might by this reasoning have been given dominion over the teachings within the temple.

Harrison looked at me; he shook his head, waved it away. "Bad example. But you see my point."

Yet we had not an agent. I felt suddenly very low.

"Edwin should have thought of this," he said, looking unhappy. Then his face brightened and he said, "Wait!" and struck his fists to the table, knife and fork erect as gateposts. "*I'll* be your agent! There!"

We celebrated with wine (I no longer suffered from the headaches), and after dinner Harrison had me sit beside him on the piano bench. At Mackinac I had made bullet wadding from the pages of hymnals, so knew something of sheet music; I told him this. He nodded and smiled, then began to play and sing, and singing hurriedly pointed to words on the page and nudged at my shoulder, encouraging me to sing with him. I was not inclined to do so. He stopped.

"Here's something I think you'll like better," he said, rearranging the books of music. "This is all the rage down at the Castle."

He sang something about an Indian princess. The song described her ankles and bosom. I began to feel as I had below decks on Lake Erie.

"I go to bed now," I told him.

He got up. He looked scolded. "Fine," he said.

Tea would be good, thank you. Are you tired? May we then go on?

In the morning I dressed in the new suit Dr. James had had fitted for me and combed my hair, which had been cut in the European style by Dr. James himself, and Harrison fixed a good breakfast of boiled eggs and ham and rolls. We ate, then set off walking for Carvill. I carried the satchel over my shoulder. I was very nervous, as at first light looking over a hilltop upon a sleeping Sioux encampment. Harrison spoke without stopping.

"Foreign rights," he said. "That's the thing. They'll make you feel lucky with a fat advance and move the shells so fast you don't know what's what, and before you know it they've taken the foreign rights and you've lost the game. Happens all the time. This book has appeal, John, *appeal!* My God, a white boy taken and tomahawked and raped and God know what and grows up in spite to become a naked chief! Foreign rights, John. We don't yield on foreign rights!" He went on like that. "Remember," he said, "Tell them I'm your agent." I agreed to do so, adding that I had never been raped. I thought it possible Harrison was nervous too.

Harrison led me to a tall yellow stripe of a building at number 108 Broadway Street. There was a gold-lettered sign affixed alongside the door: C. & G. & H. CARVILL. Inside, we were directed up a wide, turning staircase to a room where a woman seated at a desk looked up to greet us. She was an older woman, very handsome, with red hair bound up by several overlapping green ribbons; her eyes were blue and set in a pale, sharp-edged face.

Behind her on the wall was a full-length portrait of an Indian. She noticed my interest and, standing, extended a hand toward the painting. "Inman," she said. I corrected her, and she said, "*Inman.*" I let it go. I had no letter to give her, so left it to Harrison to explain our visit. He mentioned he was with the *Courier*.

"Publicity is on the third floor," the woman told him.

He explained further. She asked us to sit down. The chairs were of hide and very soft. I thanked her.

"Let me do the talking," Harrison said. The woman opened a door and disappeared.

After some time the woman came out and motioned to us. "Mr. Tanner," she said. She spoke my name like that: "Mr. Tanner."

Harrison stood with me and ran his hands under my coat lapels. "All right, John," he said, putting his face very close, "try not to say too much. In fact, what if you just speak Indian."

"Mr. Tanner," the woman said; "Mr. Horace Carvill will receive you now."

We proceeded toward the door. My head was light and my legs felt heavy. Harrison coughed.

She held out a hand to stop Harrison. "Just Mr. Tanner," she said.

"But I'm his agent," Harrison said. His bulging eyes reddened.

"Mr. Carvill does not see agents," the woman said. "Legal is on the fourth floor."

I was led in.

Horace Carvill stood. He was a young man very well-dressed in black, with a white collar and black tie. He had long dark hair worn straight down, a pointed ear that erupted into view as might a small dog's, an extraordinarily large nose, and a narrow overbite that gathered like a fistful of quills his protruding, crooked teeth; he was pale and clean-shaven. He asked me to take a seat. I did so; as he sat I reached into the satchel. I handed him the bundle and he held it, lifting it up and down once or twice to judge its weight, then untied the ribbon and removed the butcher stock and set the pile of papers, this pile that was the narrative of my life, on the desk before him. I was glad to be relieved of it.

"This being you?" he asked, pointing to the title.

I nodded.

"Dr. Edwin James," he said, and looked across the room at the door; "not the man outside, I take it."

"No," I said, and retrieved from the satchel the Doctor's book on Long's expedition and handed it to Carvill. He looked at it, nodded, set it aside. He took in hand the topmost page of my narrative.

"Captivity story, I see. We do rather a business in captivities here at Carvill. And this—quite a long one." He leaned back in his chair, smiled. "Would you care to synopsize for me?"

Thinking he too was asking me to sing or perform in some manner, I told him no, and like Harrison his face took on a scolded look and he said, "Fine."

I asked him about the foreign rights. He had me repeat the question, then smiled as might a buzzard and told me I was getting a little ahead of him, that he would have to look at the manuscript, and could I meet with him again in a couple of days, on Friday, say, to which I agreed. He picked up the stack of papers again and, muttering something about production costs, bade me good day.

Altogether I found him pleasant enough and took nothing from his words or actions to arouse alarm or cause me to suspect any trickery was afoot. I tried to tell Harrison this as we walked home, but the failure of his agency now weighed upon him and he would not be cheered.

"Then tell me this, John, why would they not allow you representation?"

There was nothing I could say to that. Harrison declined to walk with me to Carvill on Friday. In the day intervening I took it upon myself to walk alone through the city. The buildings were tall and crowded together and the streets shadowed, but otherwise I was reminded by the smoke and slow movement of numberless people of the gatherings of war parties, as at Turtle Mountain, or treaty councils, and wondered, having been approached by several people, if provisioning was as acute a problem here. I had supper at a house that had more tables than room for them, so dined outside under the limbs of a tree and observed the people passing and the variety of their hats, and afterward counted out money carefully. The serving girl waited as if I'd made an error, so I counted again. She lifted an eyebrow. I counted a third time, this time out loud, but the result was unchanged.

She looked at me stupidly.

"You count it!" I said, and a man came up to help. Others were looking.

"It's fine, sir," the man said.

"See!" I said to the girl, and left much distressed. Other than that, I had a strange and fine day.

[I ask has he never heard of gratuities, then explain the word for him. His face falls.]

That's enough for tonight. Tomorrow I will tell you about Inman. I'll tell you about art and beauty.

[Will you, now.]

Have you heard of Inman?

[I have, I tell him, which is the truth, and I think I know a thing or two about art and beauty.]

Good. Tomorrow you will know more.

Your hair looks very nice, drawn up that way in the back. They don't call it "clubbed up" any more, do they? You shouldn't cover your face. You have a widow's peak. You should show it. All right then, go.

8

I walked alone to Carvill's Friday morning. A haze hung in the still, cool air and shrouded the tall houses, and I sensed a violence veiled in the haloed sunlight, a voice telling me to be careful of stupid errors, stupid actions, for I knew that my trip had been—both with the bad news awaiting me and the destruction of the Doctor's letters—like everything—for nothing. For nothing I beheld the city that morning; it was for this the sun rose. I wanted by my actions to make nothing worse. I had on occasion done so.

The tall yellow building appeared around a corner and regarded me with the eyes of a great and ravenous fish, and I stopped. This, any trepidation, I thought, is as well of no importance; I crossed the street and entered. But misapprehension, the unexpected, the unexplainable, prevailed—for I was welcomed on the second floor by the same woman before the painting of an Indian, who now jumped to her feet and might have knocked over her desk in her fervor to greet me.

"Mr. Tanner!" she said. She grabbed both my hands. "I'll get the Carvill's!" Releasing one hand and dragging me with the other and taking two steps, she threw open the door to the other room. Two men bending over the desk looked up and straightened. They came around either side to meet me.

Mr. Carvill said, "John!"

I was introduced to Horace Carvill's father, whose name was Charles and who worked at the same firm; he grasped my hand and, though he was not so elderly, swayed a bit as he told me that he and the house of C. & G. & H. Carvill would be most honored to publish my narrative. This produced from me a stream of Ottawa which delighted these two men, and they sent the lady out after champagne and cakes. It was then, noticing that the two Carvills looked nothing alike, that I asked the younger, in words I do not recall but which must have drawn offence, if he favored his mother. The two looked at each other, then stood or paced as they waited for the champagne and said things, sometimes at once, about the wonderful book that was to be made of my life. When I asked, they declined yet to discuss the compensation Dr. James and I could expect to receive for this. The younger Carvill said they were mindful, however, of foreign rights, and we would talk about all of that tomorrow. Right now they simply wanted to celebrate. The woman came back. A bottle of golden champagne was opened, then another. There were cakes of ginger. We had a fine morning. They took me then to a matinee, an opera. I cannot describe the opera. Have you ever—no, you said not—but it seemed to me the most around-your-elbow-to-get-to-your-thumb exercise in history. After that I was taken to dinner and dropped at Harrison's house, where I had to pound on the door and shout to be let in. I told him of my day. He shook my hand and went back up to bed. I had had more champagne at the opera, and at dinner, and found myself now more apt to like Harrison. In my room I wrote a letter to Dr. James. I knocked over the inkwell on the desk and cleaned it up with the inside of my black coat. I could not read more than a few words of my letter the following morning, and knew no one else would be able to read those, so I threw it away.

The young Mr. Carvill told me in the morning that there was no time to lose, that they must get me to Inman. It was understood that I wanted to leave New York as soon as possible, yet it had been determined that the book must have a portrait of me, as

images were needed to jar the browser to purchase; so I was loaded into a carriage before I'd had a chance to say good morning or
take off my coat. They were taking me to Inman's studio, Carvill
told me. Henry Inman was the man of the hour. There would be
time later in the day to discuss finances.

During our ride he said one more thing I remember: "My
mother, you understand, is a saint." I presumed from this that she
was dead, so said no more.

Though I was not overly tall, the artist Inman struck me as unusually short, an impression perhaps strengthened by the empty
space between the top of his head and the ceiling of his studio,
which must have been thirty feet. The room was dark and raftered
above, so the light from the studio's great windows, looking out
on the river and stretches of marsh and hills beyond, made by this
contrast all distinctions of shape and line sharper, and colors
more vivid. He told me this himself. There were everywhere, on
scattered easels and leaning against the walls, paintings of landscapes and portraits—mostly, from what I could tell, unfinished—
and the room smelled pleasantly of turpentine. Inman was a
young man with bulging dark eyes, a protruding lower lip, and a
brush pile of dark hair that you'd have thought would have birds
and snakes popping out of it. He was wearing a red plaid vest and
a tie and a butcher's apron.

Carvill introduced us. "Mr. Tanner here holds, we think, the
record. Thirty years captivity."

The artist Inman looked impressed.

"Raised by an Iroquois chieftess, became himself a naked
chief—"

Here I stopped him. "Ottawa," I said.

"Carvill is doing his narrative. We need a frontispiece, Henry. A good quick likeness to take over to Cephas.[1] We need it today. What say you?"

"Good, fine," said Inman. "Whatever you say. Lady Astor can wait." He smiled. His eyes rolled.

"As I say," Carvill said, "today; God knows this one could take off tomorrow."

Inman tilted his head and said, as if addressing the bereaved, "How have you been, Horace?"

"Oh, Henry!" Carvill said, and they embraced. "Forgive me; I'm all at ends today. Good Lord—!"

Something had caught Carvill's eye over the other's shoulder. I looked. Reclining in a chair in the shadows to one side of the windows was a man stripped to the waist; where his face might have been one saw instead a mound of white I deduced—following an instant thinking how odd it was that Inman was as well a barber— to be plaster.

"It's all right," Inman said. "He's asleep."

"Jesus," Carvill said quietly.

"It's the new Governor," Inman said. "He can't make it up here all the time, you know."

Carvill left and Inman had me sit in a wooden chair on a little platform with my knees pointed at the sleeping man with plaster covering his face. Two straws stuck out of it, the plaster, and I was told these helped the Governor breath. I wanted to watch his chest to be sure he was alive, but was corrected each time I failed to look at Inman, so decided that whether the man lived or died or was already dead was none of my concern. He did not move the entire time I was there.

It took Inman less than an hour. He peeked at me from behind a small canvas on a giant easel and talked the whole time, now

[1] Cephus G. Childs, lithographer.

91

and then telling me to move my head. He talked about his clientele. Many were Indians. I asked if he always painted people. This question, or its answer, occupied him for some time.

"Not at all," he said. "Mostly now, yes, but I used to also paint landscapes and what they call *genre* scenes—children chasing carriages, lovers undressing, scenes from Irving, that sort of thing. The critics encouraged me to stick to portraits. Chin up. But there was a time I wanted to be a landscape painter. I went to England out of school and caught the bug for it. Half my class, too. It was an industry over there, and so it became here. Cathedrals of nature. The Romantic Movement. Later we all went west and that which had been green came back brown, but it was the same thing. The travelling beat me all to hell and all anyone could talk about in the end was Catlin, so I went back to doing portraits.

"Look here." He leaned over to get my attention and pointed to a spot between his eyes. "Here." He squinted, painted.

"Not all at once, mind you. I went through a transitional phase. A metamorphosis. It started with water. I was up in the Catskills for a summer, painting outdoors. Landscapes, of course, at first, but it's hard to avoid rushets and brooks and the like up there, and in my painting I became aware of the eccentricities of light on objects in rapidly moving water. I packed out to rivers and streams and painted landscapes with the water moving over cobbles in the foreground. I painted day after day, painting this scene, that stream, thinking I was on to something. But it didn't work, entirely; I was not capturing it; the results were lifeless, obscenely genteel; some key element was missing. But I painted like a pig; I used canvases over and over until they sagged and cracked, I jumped on them, threw them into trees.

"Don't close your eyes, please.

"In short, nothing worked. The results were, as I say, commonplace, on-all-fours. Then, on an impulse, I moved kit and kaboodle out into the stream, *e voila!* the universe opened up. In water up to my shins, the wind in my hair, the sun blinding, glorious. Light and color invaded my foregrounds; they took fire. Glimmers and movement and brilliant *actuality!* I was full of joy!"

He shook his head. Something, a pencil, flew out and landed on the floor. He didn't seem to notice.

"The change, the move into the water, naturally informed my work, and slowly over time I found my perspective shifting, the stream coming more and more to dominate; the meadows receded and became a fringe along the top or sides, mere framing. The water, the rocks, became clearly now the subject of my art. Now I *was* on to something, I said to myself. I pursued it, and as my pursuit advanced, the tree trunks and grasses disappeared utterly, and the perspective foreshortened and soon enough I was painting what I beheld of the ephemeral, flashing, shape-shifting creek bottom between my feet. It was an adjustment. I was dizzy a week. I fell over twice. But gad, man, was I happy!" He shook, rolled his eyes, grinning. All this time he was looking at me, or painting.

"But now a change began, or commenced, continued, what-have-you. It was late summer, and the stream bed came to the surface and the rocks dried and primaries went pastel. It fascinated me. Well, not so much, but sufficiently that my subject shifted again. I studied the contrast between the submerged and the unsubmerged. I noticed, more, the rocks themselves. This was a phase in and of itself, for the rocks did not move as they did underwater, and the still, dry, staring-dead stone demanded a certain level of objective respect. This was another adjustment. Don't underestimate it. But once I made that leap, it opened the universe anew. Objectivity was the future, the fissure. The rocks had become the subject.

"The water dried up and I looked for groups of dry creek-bed rocks with interesting variations in color, then interesting sameness. It occurred to me about this time that the subject matter could be moved and arranged back in the studio, so I packed up crates of rocks and sand and went home and worked, actually, here. I've been here that long. Five years.

"I set up by the windows there, and quickly realized I had a problem. You see that's mostly north-facing, so no sunlight could hit the stones. They sat there all round and subtle or flat, depending, and as I looked and puzzled over them I saw patterns emerge and take on gentle yet dreadful clarity, the complexity of each stone shatteringly beautiful. I rushed to paint this mapping, and fell into it; I spent a week on the first. Can you imagine? I mean the first rock, a week. But I was on to something, no question about it. The problem now was this: you had to be on top of the painting to appreciate its achievement. If you stood back, the subject, the detail, coalesced back into a whole, a plain rock. I knew I had to go bigger.

"Head up, John; you're drooping. We're almost there. Chin slightly to your right. Now, whatever you do, don't smile; remember you're now a writer, seer of voids, interstices; just hold still; please don't smile, John, no, don't smile, no! Hah! Gotcha!

"My canvases went huge, and the subject became the detail on the surface of a single, egg-smooth river rock. I painted with more and more economy as the canvases grew. I found I could dapple the canvas with more lurid colors tempered with space between, and the colors would blend in the eye at a distance into the pastel hues I sought. I followed this aesthetic to the extreme, on canvases twenty feet long and ten feet high, and the subject a single stone. But by now the subject was not the stone; no, it had shifted again, now to the brushstrokes, the process, the viewer.

"But there was still the objectivity, and as my brushstrokes dispersed and excited me more, the stone's reappearance upon standing back struck me as cloying, sentimental. Not aspects commonly ascribed to rocks not chiseled in the likeness of George Washington, but you get my drift. I abandoned the object. I dappled with random colors; I stood back. It pleased me. In my pleasure I dappled and streaked with warm colors. Then I stopped. My mood shifted, and I dappled and streaked with dark cools.

"To even me this soon seemed insipid, so I decided to go back to the rocks. I stretched a big canvas, and in the middle of it painted, as small as I could, the word 'ROCK.' It satisfied me. If the fucking viewer wanted involvement, there it was. It had economy. It did, however, have the singular drawback of being easily copied. My sales dropped off. I quit painting for a time. I moved back in with the parents.

"There. Come look."

I was not pleased. The picture had me old and worn and delirium-eyed, my jowls stuffed as with tobacco. The ear you could see looked like a drooping penis. My face was jaundiced, otherwise red, painted in garish colors highlighted by a green background. For this I'd paid half an hour's agony. This was how the world would see me. I was angry. I left without a word. It took me three hours to find Harrison's house.

[It doesn't sound to me as though Inman was a very good artist, I say.]

No. Some of us are born to hunt and others to tend corn. Inman understood this. He tended the corn but hated every stalk personally. My throat is dry, dear. Your rouge reminds me of a bird. Is it the Kinglet?

There isn't a great deal more to tell about New York. Harrison walked me back to Carvill's in a truculent mood and might have been invited in, our discussion now concerning money, but he could not produce agency credentials, so left in a huff. That was when the woman at the desk accidently pressed her bosom to my arm.

"How does it feel to be a literary man?" she said.

I could not quickly respond. "Yes, ma'am," I managed, and slid off my coat to drape over my arm.

The elder Carvill whose name was Charles and all his sons were there to help me agree to the financial arrangements and see me off. I was given an advance of fifty dollars, and an envelope to take to Dr. James. It struck me as a ceremonial occasion, so I rose to speak:

"I go now from the City of New York to the Michigan Territory," I said, "not knowing what fortune awaits or even if I should die on the journey, but knowing I have now the work done I was sent for, and the Great Father has given me here many good friends and I am bent low with tears flowing that I must leave, but with now fifty dollars to take. Thank you." I sat down.

The assembled Carvill's waited a respectable second, looked at one another, then applauded. The lady of the desk stopped applauding when she caught my eye; she lifted her chin. I was congratulated and toasted for half an hour, shown deference beyond that accorded a chief or child in my former world, and in truth was glad when the elder Mr. Carvill looked up and shouted at the clock. I was shown the door. The woman, Eliza, I think her name was, wrote her address on a card and pressed it into my hand. I regret I never took the time to write her.

It took them two years to publish my narrative. It was printed also in England, France, and Germany. The poet Pushkin wrote an essay on it. I became, beyond anywhere I resided, celebrated. Where I resided I became an object of ridicule. I saw no more than the fifty dollars. Dr. James and I never spoke of it. I did see the Carvill volume, however, and my picture. Have you seen it? Yes. You'll agree it doesn't look like me. There is a quality of injury in the eyes that is not mine.

[Perhaps not then, I say. He looks, makes a face.]

This is all I can tell you of New York. Everyone should go there once.

I was in a ruminative mood on the voyage back. In Detroit I would lay myself before Governor Cass, and it troubled me. I dressed in my buckskins and a calico shirt and wove the charms into my hair Dr. James had weeks ago removed. Although I was the subject of much attention, people left me alone. The trip across Erie was upwind, so there were no sails raised and I was able to rest comfortably on the deck. We reached Detroit on the 18th of June.

I shall excuse you early tonight. I fear my bowels are restless. Thank you for your kindnesses. You do look a sight. You should take a moment to describe yourself to the reader, Miss Mesare.

{Indecipherable}

You don't, I'm sure, do yourself justice. How do you find me? Write that too, if you care to. Henry Schoolcraft called me a liminal figure.

[He leans forward, head tilted—]

Do you find me liminal?

9

You didn't come last night. I worried about you. I made this for you today.

[It is a tiny horse fashioned from dried corn husks tied about with string.]

I will say things in simple words that are not meant to offend.

[I thank him and tell him I was not by any action or word offended; had I, he'd have been forgiven. He looks solemn.]

Shall we work? That [indicating the horse] I learned from Net-no-kwa. She would make them and put them in my hand as I slept. I still dream of this, and will be sad finding my hand empty in the morning. She taught me in the days we lived near L'Arbre Croche, where the corn was plentiful. The leaves were collected before the spring burning, and I amused myself making many animals like this. It is not hard.

[It is very nice, I tell him.

He smiles, shy.] I make all animals. Just tell me what you like.

[Can you make me a cat? I ask.

He compresses his lips, runs his fingers along the edge of the table-top, shakes his head.

I tell him let us just work, and he nods, takes a breath.]

Governor Cass was happy to see me. He embraced me and told me I looked well. He noted the charms in my hair and said something about you could take the boy out of the woods. I told him of my trip to the City of New York.

He interrupted me and clasped me by the shoulders. "John!" he said. "You speak so well—(he shook me)—I'm so pleased! I understand *every* word!"

I had last seen him two years before on Mackinac, when he was on his way to the Treaty of Fon du Lac, and it was true my English had improved much since then.

"No," he said, "it was Butte des Morts, last summer. No matter. You're doing very well."

Dr. James had helped me a great deal. I told him of our work together on the languages.

"Yes, yes, James. Highly esteemed botanist. You were indeed fortunate, John. And now tell me about this book."

I began telling of the narrative the Doctor and I had written, and as I was yet carrying Dr. James's satchel, it now proving useful, I took from it the cheque for fifty dollars and showed this to Cass. He took and examined it.

"Quite a sum," he said. "What of royalties?"

I nodded. He repeated the question, and I became uncomfortable. The Carvill's had seen to all that. That, as well as the foreign rights.

"I'm most confident they did," he said. "You'll want me to negotiate this for you, convert this to silver. This" (he waved the paper), "is of no use to you. May I do that for you?"

To this I readily agreed.

"Quite a sum, yes," he said. He called out and a soldier entered the room. Cass introduced us, gave him the paper, and told him what to do with it. The man obliged. "Now John," he said, "I think I know why you're here. I received a letter from our Colonel Boyd."

My insides fell away. "Father," I said, "there has been an injustice done me."

"Take your hands away from your mouth," Cass said. His eyes were stern. "He tells me you were arrested for threatening the lives of a man and woman. What say you to that?"

"The woman didn't count."

"I know that!" he exploded. "You violated your bail! Jesus Christ, John!"

My breath, suddenly, was gone, but I did not weep. I have never wept before any man, except from extreme gratitude. I struggled to control my expression, still my trembling lips, keep my hands away from my mouth. My eyes burned. I studied my legs (my buckskin trousers were mottled with wear and filth), tried to gather myself.

"It's all right," he said after a moment. "I appreciate that it was about your son. Boyd was kind enough to explain that. He is sympathetic."

I looked up at him. To do so was difficult.

"Dr. James has interceded on your behalf with the McFarland's; the charges have been dropped."

I watched his eyes, but they did not soften.

"Also," he said, looking down, "I forgive you."

I let out a whoop and sobbed uncontrollably.

He said, in a quiet voice, "Now John, you're a good man and I'm very proud of you. I have all faith that you will do better in the future. God is watching over you, and you have been in my prayers, and I know the divine Lord will guide and protect you. You have much good in you, John, and much good to offer the world. I believe there is a great purpose for your life. Your life has been more difficult, your road more lain with the stones of misfortune, than nearly any man alive, but I see your path straightening, John, the road leveling; I behold good things."

All this time I was recovering myself from weeping. His words enfolded me like briars. I felt very low.

"I have this news for you, my friend. It is good news. You are needed at Sault de Ste. Marie."

I look at him, wiped my eyes.

He leaned back in his chair. "It's true; I have for you a new post at Saint Mary's."

"With Schoolcraft?"

"That's right," he said; "with Henry."

"Thank you, Father," I said. I began to feel better.

"Schoolcraft has an Indian for an interpreter; even the Indians are complaining about him. They never know what provisions to expect. Anyway, he has been writing me whining about it, and I told him I had just the man."

"He offered me this post four years ago," I said, [Tanner, here, was changing his voice to denote the speaker; Cass had, by all indications, a higher voice.] "but I could not stay then. My property was taken at Mackinac to pay for the board of my children, and I had to go—"

"Yes, he remembers you," Cass said. He was looking over my head. The guard had come in to announce someone who'd just arrived to see the Governor.

"John," Cass said, "I'm going to write Henry and make things clear. I don't think he'll object. There's no better interpreter in the Michigan Territory than John Tanner, now; isn't that correct?"

I nodded.

"And he's available, right?"

I nodded.

"And willing?"

I jumped to my feet and clasped his hand in both of mine, and thanked him with a full heart. He stood, came around the table, and putting his arm over my shoulder said, *"John, John, John."* I was shown out. I was very emotional the remainder of that day, and remembered only in the evening about the money and the letter for Schoolcraft; I returned to collect them early the next morning before my boat sailed.

After so many days gone I was anxious to see my children, but enjoyed the three days voyage north. Tears filled my eyes when

Mackinac Island, with its tiny white town below the white fort, finally appeared. Though I had travelled much in my life and been without my family for many months at a time, I had never experienced more joy on returning home. I had a success and great deal to tell. The fact I had no place to live did not trouble me.

There were many at the dock, including Therese Schindler and Marianne and my girls. I was very surprised to see them. They had been coming down to meet every boat for two weeks, not knowing the length of the journey to and from New York; Therese had collected them and brought them down whenever a boat came into sight from the east. I was told that on one such day my wife Therezia had agreed to come down as well, but finding me not among the passengers had confirmed her thenceforth against such folly. Therese Schindler confided that Therezia had spoken harshly of me and of my treatment of her, and that her time living with the Catholic Sisters had, in this regard, been most instructive. On another day I might have been sorely vexed, but this day I thought the news very funny. Martha and Mary and Lucy were happy to see me. I was very happy too.

I roomed three months at Ferry's mission school, and was able to pass some time with my son James. I wrote Dr. James, who was now posted at St. Mary's, with my son's help, and enclosed the envelope from Carvill. The Doctor replied by letter to tell me he was very gratified to learn of my success and was satisfied with the financial arrangements I had made. He was further pleased to learn I was to be posted at the Ste. Mary's, and spoke again of the prospect of translating the Gospels. He wanted to know about Harrison. I replied, putting on it the best face I could. The children were less happy about Ste. Mary's. In the end only John Jr. and Martha came along. It was still more difficult persuading my wife, Therezia, who was only now learning a little English and was reluctant to leave the Sisters; but, without her, the children would have remained behind and I would have been alone.

We left Mackinac on the 18th of September, with two canoes and a company of eight voyageurs. We spent a night at Au Train, then arrived at the Sault on the 24th. This day too I can mark with some certainty: it was the day of John Johnston's funeral. I learned later from Indians I came to know at Ste. Mary's that the entire village attended the ceremony—all but for several men digging up a Menominee woman so that her cranium could be sent to a phrenologist friend of Mr. Schoolcraft. (If this lent the day a certain balance, as Schoolcraft later said, it was nonetheless a sad day for all.) The Agency did not have a room for us, so we went to board at the Mission.

I met then your Reverend Bingham.

This seems a good place to stop. Have you eaten? You should. You are too small. I procured a rabbit and some onions this morning, in case you would come and I might make us a dinner. If you can stay, we can work more after. I was very pleased to see you tonight, Miss Mesare. May I ask, what is your accent?

[Swiss, if I had an accent, I tell him, which I have not.]

What is the derivation of the name?

[I have no knowledge of this; only that I am of a Catholic family from Switzerland.]

Do you have relatives on the Canadian side? It is very Catholic there.

[I don't believe so; but my father told me there were many Mesare's in Canada that had emigrated from our country. My parents brought me to the Canadian Sault as a child. My father was a missionary to the Indians. They, my parents, both died in the rapids when I was six, God rest them, and I was taken as an orphan to be cared for by the Sisters at Saint Mary's. That's on the other side.]

I know.

[After going to university I came here.]

I am sorry for your parents.

[They hired an Indian to take them down the rapids in his canoe. He was intoxicated. The Indian survived.]

Was it Trinket?

[Anything is possible.]

We must inquire. Trinket is a drunken fool.

[Anyone who drinks is a fool.]

[Nods gravely.] Are you a student?

[I teach.]

Like Marianne Schindler. Then I selected well. [He sits quietly, looking at me.] You never had to come back here, you know. I would not have gone after you again.

[I did not think you would. I came of my own accord.]

Why?

[To help.]

Were you not afraid of me?

[Did you want me to be?]

I frightened you at the Mission.

[Your gun frightened me. In any event, it would take more than you, Mr. Tanner.

I had not Mr. Tanner's stomach for rabbit, nor have I ever been able to digest onions—and the dinner was almost certainly undercooked; nonetheless I thanked him for his thoughtful generosity, said a blessing over the offerings of that *soto*-savage grace—to which he did not object—and, without hesitation or subsequent complaint, partook of them. We talked about the ship's progress up Portage; it was now even with the school, which spectacle captivated and stimulated the children—especially the Indians and *Metifs*—with the effect that attempts to teach had become futile. Two workmen had died of accidents: one by a blow from a ruptured timber, another by fall from the rear deck caused when the ship's backward movement—the oxen having lost their footing in mud—was suddenly arrested, and which fall might not have proved fatal had not the man become gruesomely ensnared in the lines of a flag bollard. Several others had been injured, and many oxen had been lamed and taken to slaughter, the ship's progress frequently awaiting their replacement. No one knew the details of these disasters more thoroughly than the school children.]

The Sault—St. Mary's, we called it—was very different then. This was not twenty years ago, but it has changed very much, some say for the good. There was no hotel, only few houses. There was the fort, Fort Brady, as now, and the Mission buildings, and downriver the Indian Agency and, beyond that, this house. Travelers as we have now did not exist. The travelers were Indians. Ottawa and Ojibwa and Menomonee, Fox, Potawatomie, Saginaw. They camped on the open ground along the river belonging to the government. After my travels I found them depressing—squaws bending in scorched skirts over fires, men piping in high-toned conjunctives of glory or sprawling drunk out the doors of lodges, children yipping like coyotes or sitting coughing or staring silently as flies crawled over their eyes and nostrils—but I treated them with respect, and in my service at the Indian Agency made numerous friends among them. As at Mackinac, they came to lodge complaints or beg at the Agency. The American Fur Company also had a trading post then, and there was for many years the larger North West Company post on the Canadian side. It was a busy place in summer. But it was now autumn, and the very air was the color of ripened corn.

The St. Mary's River is wide above and below the rapids. The Sault occupies a low grassy peninsula overlooked and half-encircled by wooded hills on the Canadian side. Many elms and birch grew here, many more than today, and there were tall, weather-clawed pines with osprey and eagle nests big as lodges, and piney shrubs and growths of alder along the water. Cattle and sheep grazed among the Indians in the open places. The edges of the pastures were thick with trampled ferns, and the bracken grew tall back in the trees and nodded in patches of sunlight, and the woods were scented with them. The wind came down over the river, and in it could be heard the rapids. At night the lights of the Canadian Sault shone on the water and currents moved through them, and the sound of the falls was more distinct then. Although I missed James, Mary, and Lucy very much, I thought Ste. Mary's a good place to live, and was determined to succeed that I might remain here. I knew my children, though not Lucy, could be brought along soon. Martha and John Jr., who was but two years of age then, were a comfort.

We inquired at the Baptist Mission and were told Bingham was expected the following week. He would decide upon our situation. We had no place to stay so were lodged in the cellar of the Mission chapel. Therezia complained of the arrangement to the woman who saw to us; her ingratitude disgusted me, and I said nothing to translate her bitter words, which provoked her to employ some of the English she had learned from the Sisters, and possibly others.

"Fuck!" she said. "No sleep dirt floor!"

My wife was no longer a pretty woman, and very unattractive at that moment; I laid my hand on her shoulder and spoke to her sharply in her tongue. The woman from the Mission withdrew a step and looked back up the stairs. Therezia said, *"Een-gah-ke-way!"* indicating her wish to go home, and brushed my hand aside. The children were busy exploring the cellar and were not troubled by the exchange. The arrangement was agreed to and the Mission woman left us. Despite her complaints, Therezia slept well and snored very loudly that night, which fact I pointed out to her in the morning. This failed to reconcile her.

I also took the opportunity on the day of our arrival to inquire at Fort Brady, but was told that Dr. James had been called to an Indian village on Whitefish Bay to dispense vaccines, and would return in a week or so. I was shown the Fort commissary where we might be provided rations.

The next day I started off to see Schoolcraft, to give him the letter from Cass. As I was walking to the Indian Agency I heard a man screaming and much shouting and the crashing of timbers. I went running in the direction of this, which sounds came from the direction of the village, thinking I might lend aid, and fell in with many others apparently intent on the same. I came there upon a terrible scene. Behind the butcher shop was a confinement for animals, and on the ground therein a man was being helped who was bleeding profusely, so that blood burst from his mouth when he screamed. Blood sheathed his neck and shone on his shirt and ran to mingle with the mud. A bull nearby leaned forward on its knees with a man repeatedly driving a knife into its neck and others pulling its tail or straining upon its head. It fell over and kicked, then lay still. The bleeding man continued to scream. I learned later he worked for the butcher and had been preparing to shoot the bull when it pinned him to the wood of the confinement and gored him between the teeth of his lower jaw, through the tongue, and into the roof of his mouth. He was lying on the ground, eyes wide open, his head held by another man who was trying to speak to him. I could see blood pouring from the wound and from the man's mouth. He coughed and gagged and then was choking.

The man holding him shouted, "Ethan, can you hear me!" The wounded man looked at him wildly. "Ethan, can you hear me!" he shouted again. But there came from Ethan no reply.

"Dear Lord, he's deaf!" someone cried. Word came back through the crowd that the bull had rendered poor Ethan deaf.

"Ethan, can you see me!"

Ethan the butcher's man was carried off and given care and in time recovered. His wounds healed, but his face was not pleasant to behold and his speech, although not lost utterly, became such as to prevent his advancement in the butcher shop. He was treated kindly by his friends over the years, but cruelty found him often, and he is, even now, a favorite of the travelers.

Do you not feel well? I am suddenly very tired myself. May we strive on tomorrow?

10

Very early on the second day I went to see Schoolcraft at the Indian Agency. The office doorway was open, so I went in. It took my eyes a minute to see and my head another to take in what they beheld, for the room could not have been less bright or more dread had it been painted in black and decorated, walls and ceiling, with white palm-prints.[1] There came into the Agency office light from the doorway at my back, and a trickle of morning from the window at the opposite end, but beyond the glow of a brass spittoon at my feet and a pair of battered white chairs nearby, the floor stretched away into shadows thick as smoke, wherein the motes of glass eyes, the bone-dead gleam of countless age-varnished books, blackened pottery, blued urns, human skulls, birds stuffed and perched upon webbed, curling sprigs of cedar, and waterfowl hanging limp with wings crossed at their backs in dusty rows—confused and drew me no less than would images assuming form and color in an apowa.[2] Below, pressed against the walls, were cabinets of shallow, labeled drawers with brass handles, and a glass case glimmering full of dully burning stones, gems, metals, shells, green lumps of copper. Still more strange were the piles of ledgers and papers thrown upon the tables and cabinets and rugs, stacks of pamphlets spilling over the floor. In

---

[1] Tanner's allusion here may be to a jossakeed's, or seer's, lodge.
[2] *Sacred dream*, as preceding a medicine hunt.

the middle of this decay-smelling, half-lit treasure-hoard, before a huge stove with low smoldering flames wrapping candle-glows about his cheeks and temples, impassive as a boulder, sat Henry Rowe Schoolcraft. He was writing.

I advanced to his table, which faced the door, and in a low voice announced myself. I placed the letter from Cass on the table before him. He looked up slowly and exhaled. For no reason, or perhaps because the morning was dark and cool and the stove fire failing, I shuddered. Schoolcraft was a very large man. He had a thick neck, heavy face, a round forehead, and a large, broad nose that brought to mind a moose, if a moose wore spectacles, and struck me as looking ominously powerful, like a moose. His chest was broad and strong-looking, though he had not seemed so powerful when I met him four years past. In this place at the edge of the white world, this land of the providential crumb, he had eaten well.

"John Tanner," he said, as though speaking in his sleep.

He opened the envelope.

"I have received approbatory notices about you from my friend Colonel Boyd," he said, after reading the letter. "That, and other news. I'll see what we can do."

He resumed his writing. I waited. After a minute or two he looked up at me and sighed.

"Since you appear to be interested, Mr. Tanner," he said, his hands milling about the papers, "perhaps I should read you what I'm working on, here. It is called a *poem*."

"I wish to know of my situation," I said.

"As you wish," But he picked up the papers, blew on the topmost, cleared his throat, and read aloud,

> "'The falls were thy grave, as they leapt mad along,
> And the roar of their waters thy funeral song;
> So wildly, so madly, thy people for aye,
> Are rapidly, ceaselessly, passing away.

They are seen but a moment, then fade and are past,
Like a cloud in the sky, or a leaf in the blast;
The path thou hast trodden, thy nation shall tread,
Chief, warrior, and kin, to the Land of the Dead;
And soon on the lake, or the shore, or the green,
Not a war drum shall sound, not a smoke shall be seen.'"

He put the papers down, glancing at me, and commenced cleaning the tip of his pen with a rag.

"I'd like to finish this before setting down to work on a paper on the life of our late esteemed Mr. Johnston," he said. "I have another stanza but it's not finished. I won't bother you with it." He looked up, grumbled, "I require a little time and privacy." When I neither responded nor moved, he said, "What do you say?"

I told him I thought what he'd read was pretty, like a hymn.

"Not so pretty as regards your brethren," he said, and let his eyes run over me from my face to my buckskins.

"I am a white man."

"By most appearances," he said.

"I desire to know of my post here," I said.

He licked his lips, made a sucking sound between his tongue and teeth. "Right," he said.

I waited.

"Have you eaten?"

I told him I had not. Nor had my family.

"Then go out and get something," he said. "I'll meet with you at two o'clock. We'll discuss it then." He commenced looking through the papers and searching for the inkwell with the tip of his pen.

There was nothing to do but go out. I collected Therezia and the children and went among the Indians to find something to eat. I gave an old Ojibwa woman a coin and she provided my family a meal of boiled whitefish and fried corn. Therezia was not pleased, but very hungry, and afterward we sat in the ferns and grass and observed the Indians fishing with nets in the rapids. Martha and John threw stones and sticks into the water. They were joined by an Indian boy, and John and the boy found a tree-toad under a piece of wood and set him off down the river on an elm leaf. The Indian boy followed it down along the bank, shouting back to John, who was reluctant to follow. I went back to the Agency at what I judged to be the appointed time.

It was bright out and still quite darker in the Agency office, so that before I entered I did not see, nor expect to find, others with Schoolcraft, or would have waited. An Indian was there, and a white man. Schoolcraft stood behind his desk speaking to the Indian. The second man was interpreting. This too was unexpected.

"Back again," Schoolcraft said. He opened a watch and looked at it. The Indian turned to me. He was an old man, old as only an Indian can be old. He was wearing a loose red shirt and gray vest and canvas pants and was barefoot. Three eagle feathers hung from his braids to touch his right shoulder.

"Mr. Tanner, allow me the pleasure of presenting—" (he paused, looked at the interpreter, who said, "Ka-te-wa-be-da.") "—Ka-te-wa-be-da,[3] of Sandy Lake. Mr. John Tanner."

We nodded to each other.

"Our friend Ka-te-wa-da— Our friend Breshieu" (this was the old Indian's common French name) "is returning to his people today after a stay at the falls of a week, over which time we have received the honor of several visits."

The white man interpreted, making clear Schoolcraft's words had been addressed to me. The old man looked at me again, and I at the interpreter. The interpreter was not very good. He had placed the Indian in the falls and reversed the giving of honor. Ka-te-wa-be-da spoke then, and had me know that the Government Father had been very generous and was a *mit-chaw* friend of

---

[3] *Broken Tooth*

all Indians and could, if he were of a mind, break the bones of many bear and call water from above, from beneath, and all around—such was the Government Father's great distinction. He addressed this sentiment, with much gesturing, then to School-craft, who cut off the interpreter in order to respond.

"Now, Breshieu," Schoolcraft said, "remember this and take my words to thy people: that by this Agency a door is opened by which they can communicate their wishes to the President, and he is so enabled to hear them."

The interpreter got as far as the Indian's name, then stopped and looked at Schoolcraft, who repeated his words in two shorter phrases.

"Hoh," said Ka-te-wa-be-da approvingly.

"All who open their ears to the American father will be includ-ed among the recipients of his favors."

The man interpreting left out the American Father. The Indian glanced at him, but nodded.

"He feels kindly to all, but those who hearken to his council will be allowed, as you Breshieu have been, to share in the usual provisions which this Agency at this place has secured to them."

When the interpreter, who was by now sweating, finished, Schoolcraft extended his hand to Ka-te-wa-be-da, who accepted it and holding it spoke ceremoniously for a very long time. When he finally left, Schoolcraft dropped into his chair.

"Jesus," he said. Then, "Mr. Tanner, pull up a chair. Angus, leave us. If there are any outside, and I see there are, disperse them an hour."

We sat facing one another. His face was big and imposing, and he kept his head tilted back somewhat in order to better see me through his spectacles.

"What have you been up to, then? Travelling, I hear. Dr. James has been kind enough to fill me in. To New York, I'm told. You're having a book published?"

I asked him who was that man interpreting.

"Angus Woosley," he said. "Brother of Melanchthon, a friend of mine. Why?"

I asked if I was to take his place, to which Schoolcraft replied, "No."

"Governor Cass told me it is to be my post," I said.

"Still yourself," he said, cross. "I had no idea you were coming. How could I know you were coming? Something had to be done. I had an Indian. A rank trade interpreter, and hardly that. He didn't show up half the time."

I declared that the post was mine by authority of the Governor of the Michigan Territory.

Schoolcraft sat back and removed his spectacles, stroked his face. After a minute he spoke. "And I'm to understand you found a publisher on your own and negotiated a book deal," he said.

Though the question confused me, I made him know that I had done so, and this without an agent.

"An agent," he said.

I asked him if he had not an agent, for I knew from the Doctor that Schoolcraft had published as well.

"No," he responded. "We have both of us travelled a hard road." He made the sucking sound with his tongue and teeth.

To my knowledge Dr. James had not either an agent, I told him. Yet the Doctor's notes of the Long expedition had been published and was strong with sales. I asked Schoolcraft if the Doctor had told him of climbing Pike's highest peak to look down upon the clouds, and told him this mountain was to be named for the Doctor and for all days would be Dr. James's Peak. To this Schoolcraft did not respond, only brought his elbow slowly onto the table and clasped his chin, looking at me.

"Why don't we just stick to the subject at hand?" he said.

I agreed and, straightening my back, stated again that I had been given the post of interpreter here at St. Mary's by authority of the Governor of the Michigan Territory.

"Yes," he said, "were there a vacancy, which there is not. Not here."

I thought it best he repeat the words, as a powerful emotion was overcoming me. He did so. I stood.

"Wait," he said; "there is now—allow me to speak, please, Tanner—there is now a vacancy at La Pointe, at the sub-agency. I brought Angus in from the sub-agency. I had no choice. Now, the Sub-Agent is my brother-in-law, George Johnston. He will require your services. You will admire working with him."

I told him send this man Angus back to La Pointe. He was a bad interpreter.

"Well, I can't do that."

I asked him to explain how this could be so.

"Angus has moved his family here," he said, "and he is the brother of Melancthon, a friend of mine."

I was outraged. I expressed my disappointment most bitterly.

Schoolcraft's face had darkened. "I will *not* be addressed in such tones, Mr. Tanner," he said. "Nor will I tolerate belligerence. Not from any Indian, and not from you. Do bear in mind I offered you this post some years ago and you declined it."

"Read the letter," I said.

He said nothing, did not move. He put his glasses back on and tilted his head, watching me, let another minute pass. "Did I not just tell you," he said slowly and quietly, "that you shall have a post at the sub-agency? I might engage any man to fill that vacancy, but I have reserved such an important post for you. To serve with a member of my own family. Is this not an honorable offer?"

In spite of my unhappiness and anger, it became evident to me that I could not persuade Mr. Schoolcraft; nor was I certain even that Cass would help me if my complaint were merely over the location of a post. I recalled how the Governor's stern words had moved my heart, and was weary of the destitution that had plagued my life and wanted to secure a post as interpreter, even at the cost of taking my family far over Superior to La Pointe. I relented.

"When?" I asked him.

"In the spring," was his reply; "that is, if the War Department approves."

I was visited by a vision of my children again starving in the snow, and stomped my foot, screamed, "Now!" and Angus Woosley came quickly back into the room. Schoolcraft clambered heavily to his feet. I turned on Angus. "You!" I shouted, spitting in my rage, "You go! You go La Point!" And such as that. I called him *matchi annemoash*. It was regrettable.

Schoolcraft startled me; he exploded.

"Desist-now-you-insolent-*bastard!*" he boomed, "or I'll have you locked up!" And he called for the guards.

His thunderous words surprised and stilled me. As I beheld Angus's twitching, ember-red face, something round and luminous in the corner of my eye diverted my attention; I realized it was my fist.

I was led away by several men in uniform. They did not lock me up. One of them explained that Schoolcraft's son had died of fever the year before, and that he'd been hell to work with since. One had to take measure of one's words. This news weighed upon me, for his misfortune equaled, I felt, my own. I was overcome with shame.

It was a bitter day and Therezia did her best to worsen it, so I spent the night outside upon the grass with my daughter Martha, who at thirteen had begun her menstruations.

The next morning I returned to the Agency. I waited my turn with a variety of silent Indians. I was not disposed to listen to the interpreter within, and far from certain how I would be received by the Agent, so waited thus. When in time I entered, Schoolcraft rose to greet me and clasped my hand. I apologized for my outburst and explained my disappointment of the day past, which had been replaced by gratitude and a willingness to serve the government in whatever way I could, and wherever. Schoolcraft seemed pleased. Again he asked the interpreter Angus Woosley to leave us.

"I have been giving your case some thought," he said, once he was seated and the office door shut, "and I have a proposition that I think you will find generous and to your liking. Rather than wait on the La Point thing, I would assign you to this post immediately."

I asked if this meant I was to be interpreter.

"Not in so many words," he said. "You will *attend* at the Agency."

"Attend?"

"That is the word."

I asked him to explain the word.

"Back-up our Angus, here. Help him along. Fetch things."

There was much to consider, but I did not hesitate. I assented to attend. I was told I would begin my duties on the 10th day of October, for which I would receive daily rations at Fort Brady, one dollar per day, and nine dollars and fifty cents monthly for house rent. This news was very well-received by my Therezia, to whom I had entrusted thirty-five dollars and fifty cents from my narrative, and we celebrated by purchasing lines and hooks and sitting until dark on the riverbank fishing. Martha Ann and John Jr. had a fine day, and each caught many small whitefish.

Would you like to take a break?

Dr. James came to the Agency upon his return from Whitefish Bay. Word had been sent by a voyageur of the goring of the butcher's man, and he'd come back immediately. I was attending at the Agency, which I had come to learn meant interpreting full-time whilst Angus Woosley pursued other interests. The Doctor was happy to see me, and I him. Schoolcraft wanted to know what the Doctor thought about the butcher's man's condition. Dr. James told him that the wound was infected, his chances not good. The Doctor had cut apart what little healing there was and cleaned things out and stitched him up under the chin and cut out the necrotic vestiges of his tongue. The rest would have to wait.

"As will the man's appetite," Schoolcraft ventured.

"It's not good anyway," said the Doctor sadly.

"What he did to provoke the animal I don't know," Schoolcraft said, "but the old bull was tame as a lamb. This I know. He came to his name like a dog. It doesn't make sense. I say he must have been provoked. Did he say anything about it?"

"He did not," Dr. James said.

"Of course not."

I asked to be sure this bull had a name, as I had never heard of a chattel with a name except as what it was, such as, "Bull."

Schoolcraft looked at me, then at Dr. James.

"But this is the truth," he said, voice thick with emotion, "Jane raised that bull from a calf. It had the run of the Johnston place when she was a girl. She used to ride it. Did you know that?"

Dr. James expressed amazement at this.

"She once rode it across the river and back."

"Hoh," I said, and looked quickly at Schoolcraft. A young woman's legs astride the heaving black back of a bull, the foam of the falls, had invaded my mind.

"Full-grown, it was," Schoolcraft said. "Into the river and clear across and back. What a woman. She's heartbroken over it. I had a devil of a time convincing her to put it down. Fact is she never did agree to it. The beast was lamed and she would have had it devoured by wolves. Do you know how old it was?"

We did not.

"Besides which, do you know what's the value here of beef? I had Baines the butcher come get it the other morning. I think in fact he sent his man, the man—" Schoolcraft stopped, his tongue between his teeth.

The Doctor could not find words.

"Ethan," I said.

"Whatever," Schoolcraft said. "Good to see you back in one piece, Doctor."

There was little business now, as summer had given to fall and the Indians had gone to harvest corn and wild rice in their summer encampments and the young braves westward to hunt, so the Doctor and I went down to the river and sat upon the trunk of a fallen tree to converse. There was a breeze in from the northwest, and far out on the water a boat was making its way across from the Canadian side toward the government dock. The boat was turned up into the current, making very slow progress. It was an odd boat. It had side-wheels like a steamship but was no bigger than a rowboat, and above it a wide wheel fitted with small sails turned in time with the side wheels. There was a man at the rear holding a tiller and looking up at the turning sails. We both watched it.

"What in hell," the Doctor said.

I had seen nothing like it, but for a wind toy in a garden on Mackinac that had two carved beavers taking turns chopping at a tiny tree stump.

"Something breaks on that and he's in Au Train by nightfall," the Doctor said.

I did not think it would survive a heavy wind, nor fatherly swells.

"I should say not," the Doctor said. The boat was then crossing the channel below the chute and rocking badly. The rocking caused the upper wheel, hence the others, to cease spinning. The boat pivoted and headed downstream. "Well there you go," said the Doctor.

As we sat upon the tree Dr. James minded the progress of the boat and I told him of my position at the Indian Agency, and of its terms. For my first week I had received nine dollars and fifty cents for a month's rent and six dollars in specie, which could be used in James Schoolcraft's general store. James Schoolcraft was the Agent's younger brother.

"You don't say," said the Doctor.

"His prices are high," I told him.

"You don't say."

"He, the brother of Schoolcraft, told me he will make me a loan if I need," I said.

"You don't say. Most inventive. Sounds a laudably pusillani-mous enterprise."

I did not ask for an explanation of his words, as it had occurred to me to ask instead why we had not sought an agent for the nar-rative. The Doctor frowned.

"I might have a conversation with our Mr. Schoolcraft."

I told him he could if he chose, but that I would take care of my family on terms agreed upon with Schoolcraft. We had settled ourselves according to those terms. I had taken a house to rent on the street where the French and Indians lived. It was a very poor house, little more than a two-room shack with a small stove, but Therezia had set about cleaning it and sealing out the wind and locating a few furnishings with the money Carvill had given me. Each window had at least one pane of glass that had not been broken out, and I had nailed boards and pieces of the tanned hide of a young deer to cover the others. It was a little gloomy inside, but would serve our needs far better than any lodge might. Dr. James nodded, rubbed his nose. He was still minding the boat. It had corrected its course and was headed for shore far downriver. In a moment it would be out of sight around the river's bend. The wheels were turning again.

We sat for a long time talking about New York, Harrison, and of Carvill, until I was called by Angus Woosley to see to an Indian visitor. It was beginning to rain. Dr. James bade me a good day and ran in the direction of the Fort, looking more than ever like a gangly heron intent upon flight, and I walked to the Agency, which was a very large house on a rise overlooking the river that also housed Schoolcraft's family, which he had named Elmwood, where an Indian in a voyageur copec and Crane Ojibwa dress stood leaning against the office wall under the eaves. We entered together. Schoolcraft's spectacles shone as he looked up.

"Shut the door," he said.

The Indian, I-aw-ba wad-dik, said *bonjour* to Schoolcraft, whom he called *Nosa*,[4] and commenced the customary salutation by extending his hand and declaring his name, though a chief here at St. Mary's and very well-known to Schoolcraft. This took a minute, following which he stated his family was very large and, though not poor, had need of flour and corn and other provisions for the winter. He was speaking thus, pausing impatiently for my translations, when Schoolcraft interrupted him.

"Your name," he said, "interests me."

I translated this and the old Indian looked dismayed, then firm.

"The name denotes, does it not, a genus of deer?"

"A buck deer," I said.

"Reindeer," said I-aw-ba wad-dik romantically.

Schoolcraft made a pointing gesture in the direction of the Indian and hurried to find a clean sheet of paper and prepare his pen; the chief and I glanced at each other; Schoolcraft talked as he made notes. "This would afford an evidence of the manner in which a noun or adjective prefix is joined to a noun proper, or by the interposition of a consonant before the noun—" (he paused, writing) "—whenever the latter begins, and the former ends, with a vowel." He looked up. "Say your name again."

The chief did not understand, or pretended thus, so I repeated his name.

"Yes," Schoolcraft said. "You see, we cannot say, 'iawba addick,' or *male deer*; but euphony requires, does it not, that in these cas-

---

[4] *My father*

120

es, the letter *W* should precede, and soften the sound of the initial *A* of the proper noun. What say you, John?"

I sighed. Attending would be much the same as my time with Dr. James.

"This is why you're here, John."

In all practical respects he was correct, so I nodded.

"Good!" he said. "And of course 'ik' is a termination in the Ojibwa denoting some hard substance, such as addick, as in reindeer—as in its antlers, you see. Most instructive name."

He finished writing and looked up. "Now, what does our good friend require of the Territorial Father?"

But the chief remembered he had other business to attend to and excused himself.

For a time thereafter I assisted in tidying the Agent's office, and as we spoke came to the understanding that Schoolcraft was writing in many ledger books about the Indian languages, as had Dr. James. He wrote, it appeared, many times more. I would come to know from Schoolcraft that he was by far the more advanced in these studies, and I supposed for reasons of this stature did not for long condone mention of the Doctor's name. He noted my interest in the contents of the glass case, and named the flaking minerals and the skulls and small pelts of animals. There were ferrets, lapins, and a white fox.

"Did you get that one from Edwin?" I asked, referring to the fox and meaning the Doctor.

"What?"

It was on this day, in the afternoon, that your Reverend Bingham came to introduce himself, and this day too that I met Mrs. Schoolcraft. I would prefer to tell you of Jane Schoolcraft, but Bingham arrived first, so I must start with him.

He was then, even as much as now, a hideous man, with cheekbones like gibbets and the murderously solicitous, deepsocketed eyes of a mother eagle. His face was nested in reddish neck-whiskers and he had a dented scar on his forehead from a bullet that had grazed him in the war. Age has only sharpened his cruel features, as will death. One day, I expect, he'll look himself.

I am now tired, Miss Mesare. I do not wish to have nightmares. We will take this up tomorrow.

[I tell him that in my opinion he has embarked on an exceedingly unfair depiction of Reverend Bingham, who is not merely my employer but a devout and just man who has sacrificed for the Lord throughout his long life not merely his own comforts, but those of his wife and his children—one of whom, Angie, is a dear friend of mine.]

He is a cruel man.

[He is a man of God. You should in any case find it in yourself to forgive whatever injustice has, in your mind, been done you.]

You forgive him.

[I tell him he speaks spitefully.]

You chirp like a sparrow.

[Just the other day I was a Kinglet.]

You're making your way quickly to hen.

[You would do well to have such a friend as the Reverend.]

I have no doubt I would have.

[I tell him good night.]

11

Your Bingham arrived at Ste. Mary's on the 9th of October. There followed a most hap-hazard time in my life. It embarrasses me to speak of it. I became religious. I hope, Miss Mesare, that you won't hold this against me, but I am not by disposition a religious man.

Nor was I when living among the Indians. I don't know what I was. Like an Indian, I was keen on the workings of nature; I understood as much of the world as I could feel or smell or proved useful; but, unlike so many, I rarely drank to excess and was exceedingly pragmatic; so religion, which seemed not so abject as unimportant—beyond the simplest rites said over tinder and spark—had only the smallest place in my order of things. I knew, too, that men and beasts suffered for religion, and I was not a believer in useless suffering. It is true that I had been visited by and received words, even prophetic words, from the young man who sometimes appeared before me—descending through the fire-hole of my lodge—during my preparations for the medicine hunt; but no mortal man came at such times to present me such words, no man stood before me to interpret these dreams, and I was, in any case—in every case—deliriously hungry when the young man appeared, and have had vivid and prophetic dreams even without the hunger or the medicine hunt. Though, if truth be told, I never gave it much more thought than I had Glory, or, after meeting

Bingham, Hell, I despised religion. One could find God in every puddle of mud, if one set one's mind to it, and worship like pigs. It was imagination, I thought; that, or fear, hope, mindless conviction. I wanted no part of it.

I knew, or knew by word of others, many prophets when I was among the Indians. There was no greatest among them, but the most pitiful was Ais-kaw-ba-wis. He had flesh upon face and eyes to see you—and you knew this, for everyone knew this—only for his having eaten his wife rather than perish from hunger. This man as a widower made himself a prophet, and my doubt and irreverence against his claims inflamed prejudice against me—even within my family—so fierce that I was removed out of my Indian family and out of the woods and prairies and shot and very nearly murdered. Had I died, his history would be long forgotten.

But there were others before, and before him came the Shawnee prophet, whose followers travelled among the camps to tell of his revelations from the Great Spirit, which revelations would have us to act in foolish and impractical ways.

I had heard of such a man travelling in the area of the Great Wood River, and one afternoon, when I was hunting on the prairie near this river at a great distance from my lodge, I saw a stranger in Ojibwa dress approaching on foot. He had a wild and strange countenance and neither greeted or spoke to me or looked into my face, but told me, without giving any explanation, that I must accompany him back to my lodge. I did so, though I thought him probably crazy; and although I attempted to engage him in conversation, he said nothing at all to me, but walked at my side looking only forward, uttering nothing even when he tripped over a clump of grass and dove onto his face.

When we had smoked, he sat silent for a long time, then brushed at his nose and commenced to tell me that he had been sent with a message from the Shawnee prophet, and that all tribes must heed his words.

"Henceforth," he said, "the fire must never be suffered to go out in your lodge. Summer and winter, day and night, in the storm or when it is calm, you must remember that the life in your body and the fire in you lodge are the same, and of the same date. If you suffer your fire to be extinguished, at that moment your life will be at its end. You must not suffer a dog to live. You must never strike either a man, a woman, a child, or a dog. The prophet himself is coming to shake hands with you, but I have come before that you may know what is the will of the Great Spirit, communicated to us by him, and to inform you that the preservation of your life, for a single moment, depends on your entire obedience." He went on to say that we would henceforth be invisible to the eyes of our Sioux enemies, and that the obedient, in general, would be happy.

I asked him how it was we must not strike a dog, yet neither suffer a dog to live, but he was through talking. He ate the dinner I prepared, then slept the night in my lodge. In the morning I saw that the fire had gone out, and I called him to get up and asked him to count how many of us were living, and how many dead.

He pulled his blanket back to peek at the ashes. He covered himself again, farted. Slowly, for he was not a young man, he sat up and drew the blanket around his back and over his shoulders. He took in hand the butt of a burned stick and stirred the ashes. A little smoke went up.

"You have not yet shaken hands with the prophet," he said. He met my eyes for the first time and I saw one of the eyes was cast to the side, the iris milky. "By shaking the hand of the prophet your obligations and engagement with his words will be incurred. Heed thus and rebuild your fire."

"You are a fool," I said.

"Perhaps," he said. "Do you have coffee?"

There was much anxiety among my people after the visit of this man, nor did I rest entirely comfortable in my disbelief; many killed their dogs; children and women were abandoned to their will. The lack of dogs proved a severe disadvantage to many, and those who heeded the words of the prophet suffered and were resentful of my exception and scorned every success in my hunting afterward, and would only share in my success in their extreme hunger. I was a young man of about thirty years then.

Several years later came Manito-o-geezhik. This man was of no great importance, but well-known among the Ojibwas, for he had recently disappeared for one year and claimed to have visited the abode of the Great Spirit, though traders later told me he had merely travelled to St. Louis on the Mississippi River. At the trading house at Pembinah he had a great lodge erected, and all the men called together to hear the newly revealed will of the Great Spirit, whose messenger was this Manito-o-geezhik. He had a long, crooked neck and a nose very big for his small face, and spoke as would a goose.

"From this time forth," he said, "you are no more to go against thine enemies. You must no longer steal, defraud, or lie; you must no longer be drunk. You must no longer eat thy food or drink thy broth when it is hot."

We all looked at one another. Someone asked if the food was to be cooked at all.

"Of course," he said. "What kind of question is that?"

"Why then must it be eaten cold?" I asked.

He looked upon me with a trace of disdain. "Heat hath no nutritional value," he said.

Such revelations were of no great inconvenience and were well-received, especially as no injunctions against dogs or wife-beating were included, and the effect on the Indians for two or three years was notably positive.

But then there was Ais-kaw-ba-wis. His influence was very local, as he was a member of our own band then encamped at Rainy Lake. He was a very insignificant and indolent and quiet man, and was rumored to have persisted through an unsuccessful winter hunt by eating his wife—actually consuming her—rather than

126

perish, as she had, from hunger. Had he admitted to this he might have been killed by the Indians, who would never abide such an abject and worthless creature; instead he became, one day and for a long time, the most favored among us, and his ascendency over the superstitious and gullible minds of the Indians was frequently used to his advantage. By ingenious craft he had found a means of procuring food and rum, and to have wood brought to his lodge for his fire without the effort required of the ordinary man; only his desire for women was left unsatisfied. The gullibility of an Indian woman was not without limits.

Not long after the peculiar death of his wife, Ais-kaw-ba-wis called together the chiefs of our band and announced to them the revelation that had been given him by the Great Spirit. He showed us a ball of clay, rounded smooth but for some cracking and a chip or two, and painted red. "The Great Spirit," he said, "as I sat day to day crying and praying and singing in my lodge, at last called to me and said, 'Ais-kaw-ba-wis, I have heard your prayers and I have seen the mats in your lodge wet with tears, and have listened to your request. I give you this ball; as you see, it is clean and new; I give it to you as your business to make the whole earth like it, even as it was when Na-na-bush first made it. All old things must be destroyed and done away with; everything must be made anew; and to your hands, Ais-kaw-ba-wis, I commit this great work.'"

"Hoh!" said the others.

I asked him was in fact the world as round as this ball, but he ignored me.

Someone asked how this great work was to be accomplished.

"Fair question," he said. "But we haven't quite framed out the scope of work. It shall be revealed."

When he had dismissed us, I ridiculed him to the others, saying it is well that we may be made acquainted with the whole mind and will of the Great Spirit at so cheap a rate.

"We have now among us these divinely taught instructors, and, fortunately, such men as are worth nothing for any other purpose.

Here we have one too poor and indolent and spiritless to feed his own family, yet he is made the instrument, in the hand of the Great Spirit, as he would have us believe, to renovate the whole earth!" I lost few opportunities in the days that followed to express my indignation and contempt for this man's pretentions, and castigated and mocked him at every turn. But others were not so disposed against him, and my efforts in opposition were in vain. His influence grew. "Scope of work" became a phrase repeated in reverent voices, meaning almost anything.

One day Ais-kaw-ba-wis induced me to make a feast-sacrifice of a moose I had killed, then predicted the success of my hunting in the days that followed, which success would be due not to my unexcelled skills or the over-population of the herd then at Rainy Lake, but as a consequence of my sacrifice and his prayers. I was not happy to be manipulated to this man's ends, and tracked indifferently on the day following, cursing my luck when I came upon a fat cow up to her belly in a pond. I waded through dried, hissing cattails and made a sound to frighten her. She looked up at me. She laid her ears back, but otherwise merely blinked and continued chewing. I lifted my gun over my head to show her. She stuck her head back under the water. I waited. Geese flew over. A minute or so later her head came up and I shouted that I dishonored her and that God had abandoned her and all her kind, and I prayed that her meat would sicken Ais-kaw-ba-wis. Before she could do more than look over her shoulder, discounting options, I shot her. Her hump exploded water and fur and her flanks shook and her head went skyward; she staggered and sat down in the water. She turned to gaze at me with mirror eyes, went over sideways.

The godly hubris of Ais-kaw-ba-wis would become, I knew, unbearable, and it was this stupid cow's fault. I spat.

On another day I returned from hunting with an otter over my shoulder and found that all the lodges of our village had been taken apart and assembled into one very large one, this at Ais-kaw-ba-wis's instruction. No one of the village was allowed to enter, and the women and children and elders had suffered from the cold throughout the day and were shivering around a fire in the open air. I learned that it had been arranged by Ais-kaw-ba-wis that upon a signal, Ba-po-wash, followed by the others, were to enter and dance around the lodge four times, then sit each in his place. Hearing this, I entered the lodge immediately and, throwing down my otter, took a seat by the fire. Ais-kaw-ba-wis gave me a hateful look, then closed his eyes and continued with the prayer I had interrupted. After a moment he gave me another look, then commenced beating a drum and singing. There were three intervals of silence, the third being the signal to Ba-po-wash; the people entered, and with Ais-kaw-ba-wis singing and pounding his drum they danced around the lodge, and me, four times, then obediently sat down.

By drawing lines with a stick in a patch of smoothed earth before him, Ais-kaw-ba-wis illustrated what had been revealed to him by the Great Spirit regarding the lives of those present at this meeting. We were told that those who listened to and heeded the admonitions of the Great Spirit, as received by Ais-kaw-ba-wis, would live to the full age of man. This full life he represented by a long straight line drawn in the dirt. The wife of Ba-po-wash, on the other hand—who had apparently displeased our prophet by denying him—would live a life that, like her line on his dirt-chart, would suddenly divert from the long and straight to terminate abruptly. I too was singled out. My line was short and squiggly. Such had been earned by my insolence.

"For you, Shaw-shaw-wa ne-ba-se, who have turned aside from the right path and despised the admonitions you have received, this short and crooked line represents your life. You are to attain to only half of the full age of man."

I stood and looked at the lines he had drawn. "Yes," I said. "If the Great Spirit chooses, it will be so. And you, Ais-kaw-ba-wis, will starve. Draw that."

The meeting made a large impression on those attending, and word of it spread to other bands in the region. My life was never thereafter as peaceful or unmolested. Even some time later, when we espied him chasing the wife of Gish-kau-ko through the woods of a sugar camp and he desisted from the chase to sit with us—red breach-clothe standing disgustingly proud—Ais-kaw-ba-wis would remain above question. Yet, as I have said, it was this man's prejudice against me, as much as the bias against my race, that caused my children to be repeatedly kidnapped, my horses and goods to be stolen, and my life to be threatened by ambush or by my mother-in-law, mother of Therezia, who once wielded with some force a hoe upon my head as I slept. Religion had made most tenuous and crooked my path.

I detested religion. My sister Lucy in Jackson sought to teach me to pray even as she taught me English. I pretended not to understand a word she said. Ferry, at Mackinac, tried to convert me; I was able to avoid him. Dr. James, who was also very devout, gave up proselytizing lest the narrative cease.

I say this, and tonight have spent much time speaking of events already in my first narrative, to explain my indifference to Bingham and his religion when we first met; and as well the confusion and disasters that would come as I strayed from this indifference.

I found Bingham, first, a confident man. His hands hung still at his sides when he spoke. Though small and slight, he stood erect and looked one always in the eye. His eyes blazed. He had not a deep or powerful voice, but those about him listened attentively to his words. It was not too easy to dismiss him as a man, whatever one's predisposition toward his métier. One soon overlooked the ugliness as well. He was also very energetic. He did not waste a great deal of time visiting with Schoolcraft upon his arrival, but went to work that very day preparing the Treaty House to serve as a mission school. In only eleven days he commenced classes. He took possession of the chapel and began Sabbath services—in the morning for the white population, followed, a few months later, after Charlotte Johnston agreed to serve as his interpreter, by quite different afternoon meetings for the Indians.

He seemed kind. He paid me the respect of speaking to me and asking after my past and present welfare when we first met, sub-tracting from the attention paid Schoolcraft; he had heard of me and was anxious to become more familiar with my history; he shook my hand warmly. All this I came to suspect was, to some degree, craft—not false, exactly, mere cultivation of want—but later, when he would reprimand me harshly for beating Therezia, shaking his finger and shouting the fires of damnation up into my chest, I was startled at how little his words cut me, how little they tainted my behavior. You see, I was not inclined to fear your Bingham, yet laid myself open over time, by my respect and grow-ing sympathy for him, to be traduced. I see this is not clear. I will explain later.

That's a very sour look, Miss Mesare. I think tea would do you good.

During the weeks Bingham was preparing his work at the Ste Mary's, my Therezia was very busy. She had lived with the Sisters and become attached to their gewgaws and lace, but could not count money, nor comprehend its sources or limits. It became quickly a problem. She wanted another room added to the house, where she might sleep in peace and have a sewing table. That, or a new kitchen; she couldn't decide. If she thought a wall would be taken out in the winter, well, I had news for her. She would stare, call me stupid, and go out. She went through the Carvill money buying a bed and linens, then bought a drop-leaf table and chairs with rush seats, these and more against my account at the store of James Schoolcraft. She did all this while I was off attending at the Agency. Evenings, I would walk home fists, throat, and bowels clenched, and at my door take the fat leather latch-string in hand and with bile already rising in my throat draw it slow as a snake from a knot-hole to let the door swing open and slowly reveal, sitting square in the middle of the table, a painted iron dog. Or a brass surveyor's compass. Or a blue china leech-bowl. Therezia made a point to display, thus declare. Our fights were terrible.

"Pee-waw-beek ta-tah-koo-gaut-ta-was-sim,"[1] she said, glaze-eyed, as if addressing a stump. She had on her head a new beaver hat, was smoking a pipe, and smelled of rum. "English," she said. The children were nowhere in sight. I screamed and went after her.

This was not uncommon.

All of this came to a head in December. I was walking home as usual, but on this afternoon, though yet far down the street, I heard clearly the screech of nails being pulled and the clatter of boards; my heart seized and I began to run: the sounds came from behind my house. There, to my horror, I discovered a pile of boards and two men at work pulling apart the back wall of my house. When they saw the look on my face they dropped their tools and ran. Martha and John Jr. peeked out from the hole in the house; they ran as well. I pressed between the uprights and entered. It was brighter inside because of the hole, but not too bright—it was late afternoon and December—and upon ducking into the half-light saw Therezia lying on the floor with her head propped up against the wall. Her arms were straight out at her sides. Her eyes shone. *She's dead*, I thought, but a pink palm rose from the floor and the fingers waggled a greeting, and it became clear she was not dead but merely pie-eyed drunk. It occurred to me she was wearing a new dress.

I screamed.

"Fuck you," she said, rolling her head. Her English was difficult to understand under far better circumstances, but I thought I had understood her. I looked around the room. On the table was a clutter of combs and overturned bottles, and among these a rod of

---

[1] *Iron short-legged dog*

wood—I think, in hindsight, hickory—upon which at one end had been fastened a small hand, carved from bone or antler, with curled, claw-like fingers; I picked it up and studied it a second, for it was very novel, then approached Therezia with half a notion to strike her with it. Her eyes became big and she struggled as if to get up, fell onto her hands and knees, and cried out in Ojibwa; I quickly came around her, planted my feet, drew back the rod, and struck her hard on the backside with the hand-end of it.

"Ivory!" she cried. She made to rise again and fell into the wall, rolled over onto her hands and knees, and I struck her again as before, and she howled. The order of this process was repeated several times, until by accident she fell through the hole made by the workmen and crawled free. I did not follow but screamed after her that she would winter without.

Throughout the night I hammered the boards of my southwest wall back into place. I lit two lanterns and worked until the hole was gone. The Frenchman from the house next door came and saw the damage that had been done and worked with me. He sorted through the wood, held up the boards while I hammered, then returned to his house without having said a word other than, "Bon soir." In the morning, only a few slivers of light came through.

Your Reverend Bingham came that morning to Schoolcraft's office, taking up a position between She-gud and me. She-gud, who was not yet then an old man but very dignified, had come to make requests of the Agent.

"This man beat his wife," Bingham said.

Schoolcraft looked at She-gud in alarm.

"This man," Bingham said.

She-gud nudged me, but I did not translate.

"You don't say," Schoolcraft said. He tilted his head back.

"This man has against the covenant of God raised a weapon against his wife and beaten her most cruelly." He turned to me. "You will come and on thy knees confess all to God," he said.

133

"What manner of weapon, John?" Schoolcraft demanded.

I told him I did not know.

"You do not know!" he shouted. "Were you so drunk?"

"A back-scratcher," Bingham told him.

I looked at Bingham. Everything made sense now. Schoolcraft started to laugh. I took this as a positive sign and interpreted for She-gud, as closely as I could, "Beat wife with back-scratcher." He smiled and nodded. Schoolcraft steadied himself, pinched his heavy lips, and squinted.

"Why would you do such a thing, Tanner?"

I told Schoolcraft that Therezia had made me poor, and that I had come home last night to find men tearing apart my house for a new bedroom or kitchen.

"Bedroom *or* kitchen," he said.

"She couldn't decide," I told him. I had refused the addition, but nothing would waylay her.

"I think I understand," he said; "but could you lay your hands, Tanner, on nothing stouter than a back-scratcher?"

"Sir, you forget!" Bingham said.

Schoolcraft apologized and told Bingham of course he was right to check him and that this Therezia of Tanner's, even if an undisciplined squaw, was deserving as any of her gender to right and humane treatment, or the lack thereof; and he sent me away with the Reverend, who took me to the chapel and chastised me most severely. He had me to kneel. He spoke then biblically.

"Doest thou know how to pray?"

I told him I did not to his God, though my sister had tried to teach me, nor had I to any since long ago throwing away my medicine bag.

"When— Forget the stupid medicine bag," he said. He paced, rose on his toes to look out a window, paced. He said, "Say this after me." And he gave me a long prayer to ask God's forgiveness that described me, in real and frightening images, beset upon by naked red men with tails. I mouthed what he said and stared at the floorboards. Without intending, I made a laughing sound with my nose.

"What was that?" he said sharply, turning.

I apologized.

"Does it not feel better to have prayed?"

My knees ached. "No," I said.

He scuffed to a stop and spoke in a voice that seemed large in the empty, breath- and dust-pillared chapel, "Thou, my son, needst a revelation!"

I agreed that might be so, depending.

"Doest thou believe in the pagan spirits of the Indians?"

"No," I told him. He was standing there with his fists at his sides.

"Doest thou believe in the pagan Gitche Manito?"

"I do not."

"Doest thou drink spirits?"

"No."

"Good," he said. "That's a start. Get up." He pulled a pipe from an inside coat pocket and struck a match upon a brass button on his vest. "We'll talk more later," he said. He motioned me to go with three fingers of the hand holding the match to the pipe bowl.

I went back to the Agency. There Schoolcraft had told Angus Woosley of my crimes.

"Home improvements always test a marriage, John," Angus said to me; "take heart."

I told him mind himself. He cleared his throat, blinked, looked away.

Schoolcraft would tell everyone he met about it, the home improvements, in the days and weeks that followed—even after Therezia had packed up my son John and her blue china leech-bowl and left by dog train for Mackinac.

I managed to sell everything back to James Schoolcraft and the other merchants with whom my wife had transacted, but not for the prices paid. I missed my son John sorely; it was Therezia's cruelty to take him and leave me with a daughter. Life became very hard for a time.

There. That is that and now I am very tired. Tomorrow I will talk of Jane.

[Noting he is not one to tire of pedagogy, I thank him for the religious instruction, pack up my things, and, promising to mind puddles on my way home, lest I lunge wallowing in search of God, leave.]

12

Jane was young when I first met her. In the year before she had lost her first-born son, William Henry. She had given him the pet name Sweet Willie and always called him that, or just Willie, when she spoke of him. She wrote poetry. Her eyes were distant and her voice frangible and ghostly, silvery as dust, and her cheekbones were full and her hair drawn back in dark furrows from her pale forehead and held by combs. Curls hung and bounced from her temples. Sometimes I would find her eyes unexpectedly fastened on me, as a mother might look upon a child, or upon a mote of sunlight trapped in a cup, and meeting my eyes she would smile, lower her head, then look brightly up at someone else present speaking, usually Schoolcraft. She was very kind and I think very sad, and without question the handsomest woman I ever saw. Of course, you know she is gone now. But Schoolcraft had such a wife.

She came to the Agency office on the day I have described, the day Bingham presented himself. She was carrying Janie, who was then about a year and a half. Bingham had gone off to look after business; Schoolcraft had sent him to find John Hulbert, who was to show him the Treaty House and the Mission chapel. She looked in and Schoolcraft motioned to her as he was speaking to me about lake tides. He had been writing a letter about them, the lake tides. He was uncertain about them. She entered. Her breath was visible and then it was not.

"Mrs. Schoolcraft, John Tanner," he said, rising, the chair scooting.

She offered her hand, smiled. She had on buck-skin gloves, a long dark coat, and a red scarf. She smiled. "My husband has spoken of you," she said.

I looked at Schoolcraft.

She said, "Is your wife finding Saint Mary's to her liking?"

I shook my head.

"Do you have children, Mr. Tanner?"

I found myself somehow afraid of her, the more now that I had no recourse but to speak. "Three children in Red River country," I told her, "near Pembinah, I think. A son and two girls. Also a son and two daughters at Mackinac. Here a son and a daughter." My mouth had gone quickly dry.

She spoke to me then in Ojibwa. "You must miss those of yours that are so far away."

I told her it made me very low sometimes.

"Of course," she said, and touched my arm.

Schoolcraft cleared his throat. "Mr. Tanner and I were just discussing lake tides," he said. "General Dearborn believes he has discovered something." He tapped at the papers before him with the butt-end of his pen. "As if casual observation can beget, or casual conclusions claim, discovery." He grunted.

"Have you been to the ocean, Mr. Tanner?" she asked me.

I nodded and said I had been to the City of New York, which was, I thought, very near the ocean.

Schoolcraft said, "Methinks it requires more exactitude of observation than falls to the lot of these casual observers to upset the conclusions of known laws and phenomena. Don't you agree, Mrs. Schoolcraft?"

"Yes, Dear," she said. Then, to me, "We're having a dinner Sunday after next, in the afternoon. A true *Johnston* Sunday dinner.

Your Dr. James will be there, and the Hulbert's and the Cameron's from the other side, and I'm going to ask the Reverend and Mrs. Bingham—"

Schoolcraft said, "Dear—"

"We'd be honored if you and Mrs. Tanner could join us."

I felt Schoolcraft's breathing stop.

"The Audrain's can't make it, Henry."

I told Jane Schoolcraft that I would come, but without my wife. I sensed Schoolcraft slowly turning his face in my direction. Jane thanked me, said whatever it was she had come to say to her husband, lifted the child to be kissed, and left. Schoolcraft sat down. He made the sucking sound with his teeth.

"The lake winds blow the water to the east," I told him. "The water tries to move back. I have seen it on the Beavers where the lake is very shallow. It is there most easy to see in the bays, and the water moves in and out in two hours time and the change is half a man's shin-bone. Depending on the weather."

Schoolcraft looked at me.

I told him that when the water is low the smaller fish could be more easily netted.

"Seriously," he said, "Therezia can't make it?"

The Johnston house was long and low, the outside of stockaded and squared logs built as the French built log houses, and white-washed with many windows with black shutters. It was over-looked by tall elms and there was a row of small fruit trees between the house and the street. There was a gate and you walked over planks to reach the door, which was painted black and had in the middle a knocker of dull brass in the shape of a fox's head. You took the muzzle of the fox in hand to knock. On this day, the day of the Johnston dinner, a tall and handsome Indian woman some years older than me opened the door. She looked at my empty hands. She stepped back and without a word asked me in. I turned to her and announced my name, and she smiled and nodded and spoke to me in Ojibwa. She was Susan, mother of Jane who I had met; her husband, John Johnston, had gone on in the autumn, and she was happy to meet me as she had heard much of my life, and hoped I would find Saint Mary's a fitting and peaceful home. She smiled as she spoke thus, and put her hand under my arm and guided me into the room. She took the arm where the bone had been shot through, and it ached.

It was very warm inside, and noisy with voices and dishes, and smelled of cooking. The walls were plastered white with many dark paintings hung; over a fireplace was a portrait of a girl in a white dress I thought looked like Jane Schoolcraft. There were many women, some young and very pretty, bringing things to a long, lace-covered table patterned with plates of many sizes and colors, with rainbow-faceted goblets and ranks of forks and knives and spoons of polished silver. There were innumerable candles set on the table, with garlands of white pine woven between them. A young girl was lighting the candles from a long taper.

Through a doorway was another room layered in smoke and with many men talking. Between two men standing I saw there Reverend Bingham seated. He espied at me, reached to someone out of sight and spoke. A second later Schoolcraft came through the doorway.

"Mr. Tanner," he said, tilting his head. He looked like a man weighing upon a problem. "Still no Therezia, I see." Susan Johnston spoke to him. He bent toward her. Her voice was different in English; she did not speak it comfortably, I thought, and did so bashfully. Schoolcraft said, "We'll seat you at the place of greatest honor, Mr. Tanner, beside Mrs. Johnston."

Being not unaccustomed to ceremony, I faced Mrs. Johnston and bowed gravely. She laughed and put her hand on my shoulder. At that moment I found she reminded me of Therese Schindler, and I was pleased and relieved that I would sit by her.

Schoolcraft took me into the other room. There was a fire burning and the walls were lined with books. I had never imagined so many books existed. The men here, or some of the men, stood. A tall, fair-haired man approached me and gave his hand. "John Hulbert," he said.

Schoolcraft started to introduce us. "I'd like you to meet my attending interpreter," Schoolcraft said.

"Of course," Hulbert said, "Mr. Polyglotis. Most pleased."

Schoolcraft turned the red of an apple. "This is *Tanner*," he said. "John Tanner. I've told you about him."

Hulbert turned much the same color and apologized as he continued to shake my hand. I later came to know that Schoolcraft had taken to referring to me as Tanner Polyglotis, or T. Polyglotis, for the bird that can mimic any other, which bird is also called the Buffoon Bird. This did not please me, but I did not learn it until years later.

"Reverend Bingham you know," he said.

"Yes, we've talked," Bingham said.

Dr. James came up and put an arm over my shoulder. "My co-conspirator!" he said. "How are we, John? Settling in well?"

Schoolcraft reminded Hulbert that I had recently been to New York and had secured publication of Dr. James rendition, as he put it, of my autobiography, to which Hulbert responded by raising a glass of amber spirits in my direction and asking the Doctor when he might be able to read my narrative.

"Certainly quite soon," Dr. James said. "We're editing currently. Also I've made the decision to add a few sections."

I asked him what sections.

"Coming along, then," Schoolcraft said. "What do you think, a year?"

"I would guess," replied the Doctor.

(Well, it took another two years, and then six months beyond that for me to be informed. But that's another story.)

"Should prove an amusing read," Schoolcraft said, as he turned away. Hulbert and the Doctor then conversed on another subject while I waited for an opportunity to inquire of the Doctor about the new sections. After standing there a sufficient length of time to feel foolish, I went over to crouch by the fire. It was then, or after a quarter-hour or so, that Jane Schoolcraft came to the doorway and said she hated so to interrupt something or other exalted proceedings and that we were called to dinner.

Are you hungry, Miss Mesare? Then we'll go on.

By the time dinner was on the table the windows were dusky blue and the candles threw no shadows but shone on the faces of those seated, and the girls who were still supplying the table would bend into the candle-light and then withdraw into shadow and disappear into the kitchen or pantry, where Mrs. Johnston could be heard speaking in her Ojibwa. When she finally came into the room, Schoolcraft stood; everyone stood. I stood as well. Schoolcraft came around the table and pulled out the chair next to mine, and when Mrs. Johnston was seated he moved to stand at the head of the table; he motioned everyone sit, then took up a glass of wine and placed his hand upon the chair-back, cleared his throat.

Mrs. Johnston leaned toward him. I heard her say, very quietly, "I think it's fine."

He glanced at her twice. His large face was shiny and he looked worried. I surveyed the table and was satisfied there was enough food, so waited with the rest for whatever bad news he had.

"My dear friends—" he started, clearing his throat again. The table quieted. "We are gathered this day to offer a toast, 'neath beams raised high by our esteemed absent host. 'Neath beams with mirth and wassail rife, knew all joy in abundance, rare beset by strife. So raise thou a glass nigh up to the ceiling, for a sire of refinement and high social feeling!" At that moment there could be heard the scream of a pig being murdered several houses away, and Schoolcraft blinked. He swallowed, then spoke in a higher, somewhat louder voice: "'Neath beams stout and true as good lads and lasses—" Here he broke off with a gulp and looked suddenly down, swallowed again. The chair he held wobbled. He said then in a breaking, bleating voice, "The son of County Antrim to the hereafter passes!"

John Hulbert rose and excused himself, and making sputtering sounds hurried into the other room. I was a bit confused by the proceedings, in particular Mr. Hulbert's agitation, but recognized a poem when I heard one. I surmised it was an emotional occasion. Schoolcraft shook his head as if to clear it, set down his glass, then withdrew from his pocket a paper, which he commenced to unfold in trembling hands.

"I have here a letter from our Territorial Governor, which I should like to read; I find it a most succinct and eloquent expression of Mr. Johnston's high estimation." He picked up and shook loose a dinner cloth and ran it over his face, then continued. "Governor Cass writes, 'Mr. Johnston's death is an event I sincerely deplore, and one upon which I tender my condolements to the family. He was really no common man. To preserve the manners of a perfect gentleman, and the intelligence and information of a well-educated man, in the dreary wastes around him, and in his seclusion from all society but that of his own family, required a vigor and elasticity of mind rarely to be found.'"

Mrs. Johnston grunted. There was quiet chorus of, "Here, here," and some applause.

Schoolcraft picked up the glass again and said, "John Johnston!" and everyone drank. I did as well. Schoolcraft sat down.

"Very nice," Dr. James, seated at my left, said.

"I don't know," Schoolcraft said. He looked dazed. "I seem to be off my nerves."

"Rousseau wrote an interesting essay on introspective vertigo," the Doctor said. "Maybe it was in his *Confessions*. Do you know?"

"Dear," Mrs. Johnston said to Schoolcraft.

Schoolcraft glanced down at the plate in front of him and looked startled. He quickly rose and reseated himself next to Jane, across the table from us. Hulbert came back into the room wiping his eyes, then turned and exited again.

"Reverend, if you would do us the honor of blessing the food," Schoolcraft said.

Bingham, at the other end of the table, rose and said a long prayer. It was very different from the one he would later help me with. When he sat the food started around. I was very hungry.

It was generally more quiet while everyone ate. I had, with everyone, been given a glass of apple wine. It was good. One of Mrs. Johnston's daughters refilled my glass before it was empty. The younger girls filled glasses and took emptied plates and brought new dishes of baked fowl and pickled whitefish and jellied venison liver and rolls; I did not watch them as I spoke with Mrs. Johnston, but their hands floated in and out of my view without cease. I finished my glass of wine quickly to see if it would be filled again, and it was. I watched Mrs. Johnston carefully and used my fork and knife exactly as she did. Schoolcraft and Jane ate very differently. They held the fork in the left hand and pushed food onto it with the knife. I pointed this out to Mrs. Johnston, who told me it was the King George method; they all ate that way in Canada, she said. I asked did the Indians too, and she laughed and picked up a piece of meat with her fingers. Jane scolded her. Mrs. Johnston then asked me in Ojibwa about Therezia. I told her in her tongue about the house and Therezia's desire for more space and possessions. Jane Schoolcraft leaned forward over her plate to say she agreed it was difficult getting established in a new home. I told her it was hard on what I was paid. She did not ask me how much, but only looked at me in a way as to question, so I told her. She made a movement of her chin toward me signifying incredulity, and her mother asked Schoolcraft, who was talking to Dr. James at my left, how it was I was paid so little. Schoolcraft cupped his ear and shook his head, but a moment later, while the Doctor was speaking to him about the Indian languages, he looked at me sharply.

Down the table, hidden by the glow of candles, Bingham was talking with someone. Gradually others quieted to listen. He was

144

telling of his days among the Seneca's in western New York. There he had known a chief named Red Jacket. Red Jacket was the leader of the pagan majority opposing the Christian minority and, with them, Bingham. Bingham had wanted to establish a mission. He did so, and within two days was summoned before a pagan Indian council, where Red Jacket presided and told Bingham what the white people had done to the Indians, how they had driven them from their habitations into the setting sun, murdered them, stolen their land, and that he, Red Jacket, had been witness to the fact that ministers had taken the pay of poor people for nothing but preaching.

A few laughed at this last, but many had not heard, so Bingham repeated it.

"He asserted some had in fact made themselves rich by missionary work. This I too found hilarious, but thought it best to mind my tongue, and did not so much as smile. Red Jacket closed his speech by declaring I had to clear out, and I told him, 'If some of our fathers who were now dead had treated them badly, it was not our intention to do so, but so far as it was within in our power to do so, we would redress their wrongs, and we knew of no better way than by bringing them the Gospels,' etcetera, etcetera."

Mrs. Johnston leaning over said I hadn't eaten enough, and I thanked her and wondered could I take some food from my plate home, if I could not finish it, for my children. She called to a child standing in the kitchen doorway named Anna, and told her to wrap something for me to take. "But you're not leaving yet," she said to me. I told her no, and she patted my arm and leaned back. "Good," she said. She had spoken all of this in Ojibwa. I guessed she never spoke English if not forced by Schoolcraft. I wondered if Mr. Johnston had made her to speak English.

"He did not," she said. "He had me to partake of whichever I wanted, and sometimes we spoke French together. Do you force Therezia?"

I told her there was no forcing Therezia, and she laughed.

Bingham at the other end of the table was still talking. "Red Jacket sent word complimenting the mild and gentle manner with which I had addressed the subject, and said that when the Board of Missions heard about it, they would probably send for me. He left for Buffalo, but instructed the Tonawanda chiefs to see that I was sent off. They called a council themselves and demanded my presence; when I sent word I could not attend, as my Sophia was at that time ill with a fever, they came to my house. They reproved me sharply for not obeying them. If I didn't head for the rising sun immediately, they said, they could not be held responsible for the actions of young warriors. A chief by the name of Corn Planter then stood and gave a little speech on the vagaries of education, stating that while he had no doubt that education was good for white men, it was not good at all for Indians. No, it was apt to make bad men of them. Well, I thought on this and replied that if some men made a bad use of learning, it did not prove learning bad; no, it only proved that men were bad. A good man would make a good use of it, and a bad man would make bad use of it. Simple as that. It was so among the white people, and they would find it so among the Indians."

"Hah!" Hulbert said. "Aye," said someone else.

Bingham said, "This seemed to satisfy everyone but Corn Planter, and the interpreter rose and gave me his hand. 'That's good,' he told me; 'but I wouldn't push it.'"

Dr. James leaned forward to see Mrs. Johnston and, calling her "Neengay," told her in a simple Ojibwa phrase that the dinner had been very good. "And the liver, like nothing I've ever tasted," he added in English.

She smiled and nodded. She told him in Ojibwa it was the whortleberries as well as the dill that made it so. It required the liver be jarred three months, so it was only now ready, as the whortleberries and dill were not picked until late September. Dr. James pretended to understand her every word, but could not readily answer in her tongue, so I aided by saying, "The liver is a strong meat," and they both agreed.

"But this," the Doctor said, "this is most delicate in taste."

"Make strong," I explained.

Dr. James said, "Oh, quite."

"There was a chief of the Saginaws," I told them, "Og-i-maw kee-gi-do, who while hunting alone met with an accident by the discharge of his gun. The wound had caused his liver to be seen by him, and recognizing it he took his knife and with it cut off a small piece of the disgorged organ, which he ate that he might sustain himself."

The remark was heard by a only a few seated nearby, but one of these, a woman seated next to the man seated next to Jane Schoolcraft, responded into her dinner cloth and was excused from the table. The others, save Schoolcraft, thought it a funny story. I did not.

"Og-i-maw kee-gi-do was a man of strong passions," I said.

"I think you could do with more wine, John," Dr. James said.

Mrs. Johnston called to Anna.

"No," Schoolcraft said.

I looked at him. He was my employer, so I shook my head. "No wine for me," I said.

I looked down the table for Bingham, and found he had risen from his seat. He was saying, "So we stayed put. After a few weeks I was informed that Red Jacket was coming to remove us forcibly, and the day following my receipt of this news I was summoned before him in the Council House. The old chief addressed me sternly, and there was fire in his eyes—savage fire!—and he reproved me accordingly for not obeying the voice of his people." Here Bingham folded a dinner cloth and laid it upon his upturned head and gathered it behind to tie in the manner of an Indian; he screwed up his face and spoke as might an old Indian, were the old Indian ugly and sinister-eyed as Bingham: "'I will send two teams to your house tomorrow at twelve o'clock, and you may have the privilege of packing up, but go you must. But you must not speak!'"

He removed the cloth from his head. "I told him, 'No promises!'"

There was laughter.

Schoolcraft leaned forward and, as he could not get the Doctor's attention, said to me, "'The birds of heaven shall vindicate their grain.'" He made a circular motion with the end of his fork over his plate and looked in Bingham's direction. He shook his head. "Never mind," he grumbled.

I did not have a response for Schoolcraft, as he had made no sense. I have found, Miss Mesare, that the less a thing makes sense, the better I remember it. Is this normal, in your experience?

[I look at him.]

Mrs. Johnston then asked of me, "Does Mrs. Tanner provide you a good wife?"

This surprised me, and I found myself willing to discuss it, which also surprised me. "She is a good mother to our children," I said. "She is a terrible wife."

"It is made difficult in a new place," she said. "It is made difficult with children. You should set some time aside, maybe once a week, for just the two of you."

I told her in Ojibwa that I beat Therezia not so often as that, but could possibly find the time.

Mrs. Johnston looked at her daughter Jane, and they smiled.

"He jokes," Mrs. Johnston said in English.

"I think he's serious," Jane said.

"No he's not."

"He doesn't smile."

Schoolcraft turned and rose from his seat to talk to a pretty Indian-looking girl he addressed as Sophie; as he was doing so, a pair of hands refilled my wine glass.

Bingham said, "At noon a party of braves came to my house and, finding the key we kept hidden—not too effectually—on a hook outside, unlocked the door and went in. They packed up my belongings and carried them to a settlement five miles distant."

"Bloody magpie," Schoolcraft said to himself as he sat.

"He that would teach the children of Ham appears to be quite one himself," said Dr. James.

Schoolcraft smiled sadly.

"Speaking of Ham, what, if I may ask," the Doctor said, "is your feeling on the Mosaic history, in particular the deluvial, as it might bear on the origin of our Indians?"

Schoolcraft arranged himself comfortably and largely in his chair. He said, "One does well, in all inquiries of the kind, to keep the record of the Bible strictly in view."

"I agree, of course," Dr. James said, "but would you adhere to the view that the Indians of America spring from the ancient Cuthites, who are Hamitic?"

"That would be reckless," said Schoolcraft.

"Quite!" said the Doctor.

Schoolcraft said, "They have in their allegorical history, as have every race of man on earth, it would seem, the deluge—from which time, it must be presupposed, all languages were derived from a common surviving tongue, as all races were derived from Sham, Ham, and Japhet—but there cannot, not in any solid sense, be useful conclusions drawn from this."

Dr. James sat forward and tapped at the table with a finger. "None indeed! Were it so, would not the knowledge ship building, or other mechanical arts, say masonry—as in fact was not the Tower of Babel was built during Noah's lifetime—have survived the tribal wanderings of centuries and within any branch of the sons of Noah enabled a people to retain a common claim on the journey of improvement? And would not there be retained at least a traditional cosmogony and theogony?"

"I've said that myself a thousand times," Schoolcraft said.

They went on like this, so I turned my ear to Bingham, who again was wearing his dinner cloth.

"'The missionaries are like chipmunks! They fill their wallets, then clear out! The governor must remove them! He must make them go from our lands!'" (He removed the cloth.) "Whereupon Young King, a chief of the Christian minority, assured Governor Clinton that they did not want to be deprived of the benefits of the preaching of the Gospel, or of the teachings in school. The Governor said he had no laws to prevent men from teaching the Gospel or teaching school, where men were desirous to hear and be taught, but if any man moves onto your land to cultivate the soil, he can be moved off." Bingham broke off to catch Anna and have his glass refilled.

Schoolcraft said excuse me and got up from the table and went out of the room and when he came back interrupted Bingham, who was now with the cloth upon his head, and gave him a paper and talked to him. Bingham looked at the paper. Schoolcraft resumed his seat.

Bingham tapped at his wine glass with a fork. Everyone stopped talking and looked.

He said, "Ladies and gentlemen, it is my sincere privilege to offer the first public reading of a poem by our own gentle Mrs. Schoolcraft. I find it most apropos to the spirit of the evening. It is entitled, 'After a Shower.'"

"Oh dear," said Jane, and brought a dinner cloth up to cover her face.

Schoolcraft cleared his throat loudly and pointed to his head. Bingham looked toward the ceiling, removed the cloth, and grinned horribly. "Ahem!" he said, then read,

"'Come sisters, come! The shower's past,
The garden walks are drying fast,
The sun's bright beams are seen again,

And naught within, can now detain.
The rain drops tremble on the leaves,
Or drip expiring, from the eaves;
But soon the cool and balmy air,
Shall dry the gems that sparkle there,
With wisp'ring breath, shake ev'ry spray,
And scatter every cloud away.

'Thus sisters! shall the breeze of hope,
Through sorrow's clouds a vista ope;
Thus, shall affliction's surly blast,
By faith's bright calm be still'd at last;
Thus, pain and care, the tear and sigh,
Be chased from every dewy eye;
And life's mix'd scene itself, but cease,
To show us realms of light and peace.'"

There was much applause. Jane blushed and looked down. Her husband took her hand from her lap and kissed it. Bingham walked over and did the same with her other hand.

"My Jane writes poems," Mrs. Johnston explained to me.

"Good poem," I told her. Then I saw that Jane was very quietly crying.

"Just lovely," Dr. James said. There were many compliments from the others.

Something occurred to me I'd forgotten, and I asked Dr. James what sections he was adding to my book, and if there would be more money as a result. He told me a simple treatise on the Indian dialects in general, plus some material from our work together conjugating verbs and such. I asked him wouldn't that affect production costs and what did Carvill say about it, but he was talking to Schoolcraft again.

Mrs. Johnston asked me if Martha and John enjoyed Reverend Bingham's school; I told her my daughter did and had always been a good student; John was only two. I was very proud of my children, but missed those that had been taken from me by my former wife and by Therese Schindler, who it must be said I favored in my opinions, and by Reverend Ferry at Mackinac. Jane was listening and watching me as I spoke. Seeing tears in her eyes had made me feel sad, and this made me more so regarding the circumstances of my children, including those I would probably never see again.

"And the little ones, they grow up so quickly," Mrs. Johnston said in her faint English.

"Hoh," I said sadly; "Martha Ann menstruates now."

This brought several discussions to a halt, including mine with Mrs. Johnston; she was needed, she said, in the kitchen to help with the dessert. Dr. James and Schoolcraft had not heard, and were again talking about the languages of the Indians. The Doctor, in any event, was talking.

"I believe there will be found in the languages, manners, and traditions—not to mention the physical conformation and character of our Indians—proofs sufficient that they are derived from Asiatic stock. Have you come across *Asiatic Researches*?"

"I have," said Schoolcraft.

"Not necessarily, in my opinion, from that haughty, noble, and unconquerable branch of Asiatics that produced Ishmael; nor that race from which, according to the flesh, sprang the Savior of the World."

"Probably not," Schoolcraft said. He turned to ask Jane about dessert and asked for coffee.

Dr. James said, "As you no doubt know, there are countless among the pious and ingenious that see in our American Indians the long lost tribes of Israel. No basis in fact."

"None," Schoolcraft said. He sucked at his teeth, looked again at Jane, who was now talking to one of the daughters, her hand stroking the girl's back.

"There are certain similarities between the two cultures, the Hebrew and the Native American, no question about it. The Indians do not break the bones of animals sacrificed in war feasts, nor do the Hebrews. The Hebrews impose the rigid separation of females during menstruation, as do our Indians." (Here several people looked in my direction in dismay.) "Strong points of resemblance. On the other hand, and this would seem to be equally conclusive, Indians do not circumcise and Hebrews do not eat dogs."

"Point of fact," Schoolcraft said irascibly. He looked at me as if I should enter the discussion.

A parade of girls came in carrying plates of cakes. I ate mine then found everyone had waited to eat at once, so asked for another that I might eat with them. It was very good. After that I listened for a time to Dr. James and fell asleep in my chair.

You see, I remember this night very clearly, Miss Mesare. So now I'll say good-night.

13

My daughter was changing. It was not certain that Martha Ann missed her mother; she didn't speak of that or much of anything after Therezia left; I do not know what influence this abandonment had on her. But she became as one I had never known. Always she had been a good girl, and then she wasn't. Always there had been a child's chatter, a playful affection shown her father; now she behaved as a stranger. She was growing at this time. She would become tall for her age, and the first sign of this was a deliberate slouch. One could not believe it was not deliberate. She walked leading with her hips, as I have seen river otters do when trained to walk on two legs, and as she walked let her mouth hang open. She could not remember to close it. To me it—her mouth— looked like something mechanically broken, though in all other respects fine, and I chastised her vehemently for it, but to no effect. I tried to help her with the slouch, walking her back and forth in the yard and becoming very angry, but there was nothing to do about the mouth, so I learned not to look at her. I feared I was not a good father. It became more difficult. She stopped speaking in the Ojibwa, which was good, but started swearing in English. Within six months of Therezia's desertion, my daughter's language was scornfully profane, and made worse morning by morning by the fact her clothes would no longer fit. Had Therezia remained, she might have worn her mother's clothes and her mother's shoes, but now the clothes became short and tight and disappeared, and the shoes merely multiplied; and soon, worst of all, the pronouncement of breasts became an insoluble problem. All of this I watched with fingers splayed before my eyes in horror. She would change again, and became later a teacher at Mackinac and a very good and devout woman, but I could see no divine plan possible in any of this at the time I speak of.

She would not sleep in the same bed or same room with me, so had an Indian girl of the neighborhood help her sew together a mattress bag she stuffed with dried grasses and lugged home to throw in the middle of the room near the stove. I did not protest. Mice found the mattress a good place to live. On many nights I was awakened by the sounds of Martha struggling to get out of bed, and then by her beating upon the mattress and the floor with a broom; I did not mind being awakened thus. Even nights when I did not laugh out loud, she would shout insults at me. She blasphemed, Miss Mesare. She had my temper, and it was awful sometimes.

I did not know her friends. She did not bring them to our house. Instead, she took to spending her hours elsewhere. She continued to do well in school, but where she found time to study I had no clue. I would go looking for her evenings, knocking on doors to ask was she there, and created much alarm and disfavor doing so. But I was very concerned. I was fearfully aware that she was of a child-bearing age now, and what with her breasts and attitude, anything was possible. I had not enough money to support the two of us, much less grand-children. Not that the money mattered. I was mad with fear for her. But she always came home. Sometimes, after I'd gone to bed, I would hear her banging cupboard doors and fetching something to eat. I'd call to her goodnight and ask if she'd been overturned on the rapids or if wolves had treed her and she would decline to answer, but then I would sleep well, or would until the mice started moving.

One afternoon a boy came around asking for her. He was small and shy, a white boy with a very offended face. When I opened the door on his knock (his smile snaked around his pustules), there he stood; I asked what did he want.

"Is Martha home, please?" he said.

I repeated his question then told him I didn't know, I would have to check, and he followed me in. I called for my daughter in one room and then called for her in the other. We had only the two rooms. I lifted one end of the straw mattress, looked behind the stove. The boy backed up to the doorway. I called Martha's name again as I took down my shotgun. I was suddenly a little dizzy, my hands shaking. She didn't seem to be home, I said, looking down the gun's barrels, my back to the boy. Where did he live, I asked, maybe I could send her over later. As I said this I was slowly pulling back the hammers. The first locked with a loud *clack*. When I turned the boy was nowhere in sight. I went to the doorway and saw him diving into the woods a quarter mile away. You understand, of course, that I had no fixed plan to shoot him. Yet it is possible that, given half a chance, I might have been an over-protective father.

It was following this incident that Bingham took me to the Mission chapel a second time. He had me to kneel again, this time at the altar. He did not bother now to speak biblically. He sat down on the altar close to me.

"John," he said, then said, like Governor Cass, *"John, John, John."*

Here the light from the windows showed clearly the deep crease on his forehead, and as he did not seem at this moment so stern, I dared ask him what it was from. He told me of the British bullet that had stuck him down in the war, and saying he had thus learned to never spare powder in war or ministry, knocked with his fist upon his forehead and laughed. I parted my hair and leaned far over to show him where I had been tomahawked. He laid a hand on my head and studied it.

"And here," I said.

"My goodness," he said, "what a dent. Yes."

He patted my shoulder and said, "We have both of us been under the protection of Providence, have we not?" He smiled. "Here. If one is called to a purpose, then is not the other?" He looked me directly in the eye. "I am reminded of how the saints carried the hope and belief that life's afflictions, if rightly borne and properly improved, would work out for us such a weight of glory as should render our minds cheerful and happy. This feeling has carried me along, John; and so shall it you." He poked me with a finger. "You have, my son, a purpose."

I told him Governor Cass had told me the same thing.

"I am not at all surprised, not at all," he said. "You need only see your life's afflictions as a blessing, John, and know your wounds betoken an inspired cause not yet revealed to you."

I grunted thoughtfully. He took out his pipe and lit it. This took several minutes. I asked him may I get up. He shrugged and I sat next to him.

I asked him had he heard the phrase the birds of heaven shall something their grain. He smiled.

"The birds of heaven shall *vindicate* their grain, John," he said. "Shall claim. It means we are God's, and that our acts, be they for his glory, shall create our store in heaven as a field of ripened grain is to a flock of birds. Something like that."

"Schoolcraft said that," I said.

"Did he?" he said.

"He said it while you were talking about the Senecas at dinner."

He lifted an eyebrow, pleased. "Then I shall take that as an 'Amen.'"

I told him I did not think magpies ate grain, and how Schoolcraft had used that term as well. Bingham stopped smiling, ran a finger around his collar to free his beard, smoked his pipe diligently a minute. I looked around the chapel. It struck me as unusually empty.

"Was that not a wonderful dinner though?" he said.

I told him I liked the cakes very much. I liked talking to Mrs. Johnston.

"Great lady," he said. "And what talented children!"

I agreed. Jane appeared again in my mind, riding upon the bull, black, heaving; the image, knowing now her beauty, came as a concussion of thunder.

He asked did I want to talk about Martha and I told him no. It would work itself out. I understood what I had done wrong and would not do it again. I was happy Martha had friends, but to have a boy come around the house after her was unexpected. It was the first such time. It had put me on guard. But now I had been able to think it through.

"She's an intelligent girl, your Martha," he said. "Not a bad student. Of course daughters of any age can be difficult, but a girl of her age can be a father's perambulation through hell."

I told him when she was very little and hungry she would club me on the head with her fists as I carried her on my back. She was different that way. She did not club her mother. Her mother clubbed me but once.

"Do you beat her?" he asked.

"Martha?" I said, "No. I am not a fierce father. She is a fierce daughter, though."

He asked me if it were possible I had spared the rod thoughtlessly. I told him no, I had switched her until it no longer seemed fitting. Then I stopped. I never thought of it as beating, though.

"Good," he said; "then you've been on the right track." He unbuttoned his vest and straightened to scratch his belly. "Anything else you want to tell me?"

I told him no.

"Has anything happened since we last met you'd like to talk to me about?"

"No," I said, though it was a lie. I wanted to talk about Jane.

"How did you feel after our last talk?"

"Fine," I told him. Also a lie.

"Now John," he said, "you have omitted to discuss your wife's leaving you. Is this a very painful subject?"

I told him in the simplest terms possible—in fact with one word—"No."

"Would you like to tell me how you feel about her leaving?"

"Fine," I said.

"And she took with her your youngest son John?"

I told him I would get John back. I had already been giving it much thought.

He asked, "How were, if I may be so personal, *relations* between you and Mrs. Tanner?"

Relations had frequently come between us, I told him; her brothers hated me and had threatened to kill me, and even her mother had scored my head with a hoe as I slept; but it no longer mattered. I asked him what was the point of talking about this.

He looked at me, took a breath. "Do you have enough to do at the Agency?" he asked.

I told him no, there was little this time of year. It would change in the spring if I stayed there, but I was then to move to La Point to work as an interpreter for Schoolcraft's brother-in-law George, who was Sub-Agent at that post and the brother of Jane.

"I see," he said. He straightened again. "You mention Jane. Did you hear the poem Jane wrote? What a lovely sentiment; what was it called—'After the Shower,' yes—did you hear me read it?"

I told him I thought it very pretty, and that Mrs. Schoolcraft had herself asked me to come to the dinner. I sat across from her.

"I take dinner with them every evening," he said. "Jane and I have formed a most felicitous friendship."

I asked him what was felicitous.

"Happy, or fortunate."

"All right," I said.

"Lovely woman," he said, and puffed on his pipe, sitting looking across the empty chapel. It was late afternoon and sunlight was coming in from the south windows, making square shafts in the bright smoke that flattened yellow against the back wall. As we spoke, the shapes of light moved and dimmed. I felt the stale air change, cool, take on weight.

"Good talk," he said. I'm sure we'll talk again soon."

We left. I walked about the town, looked in windows. Many lights were lit. I sat for a time on a bench outside a store that sold, if the items in the windows were any indication, nothing but fudge and taffy. I fell asleep and awoke in the cold. I found I was holding something in my hand, wet and crumbling. Horse dung. I threw it down, got up stiffly, and walked back toward home, and beyond, to pass in front of Elmwood. No lights shone. I should have walked home directly. I wasn't satisfied. I felt restless. I felt something like rage, though at what I could not have said—rage at my lot, the horse dung, the treacherous sanctimony of Bingham, the grotesque fate of Jane Schoolcraft. I opened the gate of the Agency and crept over the bristly grass and swollen earth, around the moon-shadowed house, until I heard a voice. It was a deep, quiet voice at a window. The window sash was open an inch. I crept as would an Indian, feeling the wall, to crouch at the window. I held the underside of the sill in one hand and listened. I heard Jane laugh. I heard Schoolcraft. He was saying, in a low voice slightly more a growl than a whisper, "Ah... Let us pause and botanize this spot."

She giggled, then moaned.

I fled.

Do you blush, Miss Mesare? Your neck has these spots upon it. Are you warm? Is it time for tea?

When I arrived home, the house smelled of the woodstove, but was cold as a stone. I kicked at the straw mattress and felt it scoot weightlessly over the floor. My Martha was out. I lit a lamp, then went outside to gauge the time by the stars. It was midnight or so. No (I squinted); one o'clock. My mind reeled. Inside, on the wall dividing the two rooms, to the right of the doorway into my room, my guns were hung. My hands settled first on the rifle, then rose to take the shotgun down from its pegs. I went back out.

Over the steady whisper of the rapids a few coyotes were barking and, nearer, dogs; men's voices came intermittently on the breeze from town. The moon was down in the trees to the west, but it was not difficult to see. I stepped out into the frozen ruts of the street and walked across Portage and down the lane that ran along the west wall of Fort Brady down to the river. I stood on the bank and peered across at the lights on the Canadian side. I had no idea where to start, no idea what I would do if I came upon Martha and a lover, and the air was suddenly gray with my breath; but such was my fury that I bent over and, as if tracking a moving elk, walked, stumbled, raced—toward nothing, anything— deciding finally upon the warehouses near the government dock. They were locked. The docks were deserted. I made my way along the river bank below the Fort, watching for sentries (there were none), then up the east side past the garrisons to Portage Road, and on Portage leftward, eastward, away from town. A black dog came out from under the porch of a house and I pointed the shotgun at it. It stopped and sat up, took note, then decided to follow, wagging its tail.

I felt my way over the rocks and ruts. The dog went ahead, here and there exploring in the trees and weeds, now and then returning to my side. I patted him on the head. I became in his company less agitated, more in heart as one out hunting birds or rabbits. He stopped several times as if hearing something off in the trees to the right, but then would continue on. Then he stopped stock still and I heard it as well. A cart was approaching. It was far down a lane that terminated on Portage a short distance ahead. The line of trees to my right ended at the head of the lane and yielded there to open starlight, an orchard of naked, twisted apples, piles of pruning brush. The dog ran to this place, turned up the lane.

I became more excited, and in my excitement misjudged something; before I was prepared for it, a horse appeared out of the lane—dusty as the night and unearthly, ghostly, huge—and heaved a buckboard up onto Portage in my direction. I locked my legs foursquare in the road, sucked in breath, raised the gun. I pulled the butt against my shoulder, dimly aware of stars skittering over the barrel, and pulled back the hammers. I sought words to shout—calling for the whereabouts of my daughter, demanding an inspection of passengers, bulges under blankets—but found, suddenly, that I could not think in English. Panic seized me. I bolted off the road into the weeds and trees, old legs pumping, and tripped. Miraculously, the gun did not go off. I landed in snow amongst the roots of elms and lay still. The horse snorted as the cart passed. It did not stop. They had not seen me.

The dog came up and licked my face. I rose and picked my way through the brambles and snow-humped grasses and weeds back out onto the road. The cart moved away at a trot. A man was driving. A smaller figure sat next to him. I thought he had his arm around her. They bounced along together. Although there was no way to be sure, I could not for a second doubt that it was my Martha with him. Again I raised the gun. Shaking, I aimed down the barrel at the man's head, squeezed down on the trigger, hesitated. I shifted my aim to the passenger's side. Finally, knowing they were in any event going out of range, I closed my eyes, raised my aim, and, letting out an Indian whoop, pulled both triggers at once. The night exploded and I felt myself punched in the shoulder and flung through the air. The shotgun clattered on the road as my head came down onto the ice-hard mud. Ahead, the man was shouting at his horse and the horse was now galloping wildly. The cart lurched out of sight into darkness.

Before I'd made it halfway back to my house the horse and cart were back, now thundering maniacally and scattering sparks over the road. I clung to the fat behind of a cherry as they thundered by. The dog chased happily alongside.

I stayed out another hour. I sat on the riverbank and watched the reflected lights pass through currents as through clouds. When I went home, Martha was asleep on the mattress by the stove. I might have killed her, this feeder of ravens, strangers' delight, and for longer than an instant I'd intended to. But I hadn't. I watched her breathing.

She said not a word of it the next day, nor ever. She had no idea. Brady and Hulbert would send men out to talk to local Indians about it. Had it happened today, of course, they'd have come directly here. Yet I felt given such a gift of unexpected and undeserved relief that I sat up half the night watching her sleep, then in the morning walked down to the river, raised my hands to heaven, and said what may have been my first true prayer to Bingham's God.

I never asked Martha where she'd been.

[Good of you.]

14

[His gray hair is pulled back and tied with a frayed, dirty bit of ribbon that may have at one time been blue. I shall have to bring him a few of mine. He smells clean and his bruisings have receded; his eye, as he rubs it, wincing—though no long swollen—is still colored. He seems distracted, seemed confused when he came to the door. I brought with me cookies, and when I presented them he merely looked up and down the street over my shoulder. I went in. He told me he'd been drowsing and apologized for not having built a fire. I said the room felt quite warm enough to me. For tea, he said. You needn't bother on my account, I said.]

I was sleeping or it would be made.

[I offer to come back tomorrow.]

It's all right. I sleep like a dog, like a child. I dream.

[I do as well, I tell him. He is laying a fire.]

But they have now a tendency to linger.

[The dreams? I ask, and he straightens and nods.]

I have certain over-developed faculties, Schoolcraft said.

[I ask of what did he dream?]

Often I dream of a small dark woman playing at cards alone. But such dreams no longer frighten me. I do not mind to dream. In dreams I am warm enough, and never hungry. Often I run. I love to run in my dreams, though it makes me sad, as the memory of the dream fades, that I am now old and can no longer start off, on a whim and with every confidence in my abilities, for a ten-or-twenty-mile flight to find Net-no-kwa sitting by her fire, eyes not dried with age or vague, but bright and cunning—for the sole purpose of seeing her still alive. Sometimes I stop in my dreams and make out the landscape in utter perfect detail, down to the discrete movements of ten thousand blades of grass, and wonder at my creation—knowing, on some level, that the grass inhabits my dream and that over this realm I have been made a minor god by the gifts of a greater one. But I must awake and forget. I am left alone and old and poor again. I do not repudiate the pleasures for their price. They give a pale hope.

[I beg his pardon for having interrupted his dreaming. He sits.]

I am ready.

[As am I.]

It was in February of that winter, February 1829, that my war with Schoolcraft began. It started simply enough. He claimed the federal government had run out of money. Or it had misspent money. One day he guessed to me that there was not enough gold, that too little had been discovered, mined, or minted, and that in time his help might be required to find the vast stores of it he was sure existed alongside the copper in the west. He had seen the great copper boulder lying green in the sun alongside the rocky bed of the Ontonagon, and it had made an impression on him. He spoke of it from time to time with a certain wistfulness, as it had been too large and heavy—though it had been hacked at and burned as to be cut up—to be recovered; yet it seemed to prove to him that all material difficulties could be overcome if one just scratched deeply enough upon the face of nature, and that— had he not been denied the time—he might have been the one to perform such scratchings. But the money had run out and the War Department had no money. It owed the Indian Department a monumental sum. I came to know at a later time that he had been aware of this problem when he agreed to send me to La Point, but

165

in February I knew only that the sub-agency at La Point was to be closed. His brother-in-law was being recalled. I would have no job. It was a blow. I didn't think at the time that Schoolcraft cared. I was a face listening, a pair of eyes widening, a head shaking, a fist gathering. I was nature. He alone existed; in him alone was vested nature's ends.

"Please understand, John," he said, moose-face tilted back, fleshy knuckles gripping the arms of his desk chair, elbows out, "this is quite out of my hands. Eventually the Department will put this fiscal perplexity in order and opportunities will be restored; but for a time, say, two years, we will all have to make sacrifices. Retrenchments are necessary. I know it's disgusting. I am myself embarrassed. But, there you are." He sucked at his teeth.

I was very unhappy. My belly was already rumbling with hunger, and the sour ire of fiscal perplexity was more than my bowels could reconcile; I sensed destitution, vultures circling; I told him talk to Cass.

His directions came from the President, he said.

I would talk to the American Father myself, I told him.

"Do that," he said; "should make all the difference."

My head was suddenly spinning. Out of nowhere there appeared before me an abyss deep as the distance across the Saint Mary's, and at its crumbling edge my toes bulging in moccasins, ready to jump. I was dizzy.

He told me he had work to do.

I asked him how will I be paid.

"You will not be paid," he said. "You will need to find other work. If you like I can talk to the blacksmith, or to the people at American Fur."

"I beg you help me," I said.

"I'll see you get your March rent money," he said; "then you're on your own."

I struggled to my feet and in my confusion accidently thanked him.

"No problem," he said.

My son John I had hoped to recover from his mother at Mackinac. That would be hopeless now. She might take him to the Red River country and I might never see him again. I had so lost my first-born, Picheito, who I called "Little Pheasant," and I feared Picheito no longer thought of me. John Jr. was my youngest. He was a quick and lively boy and I felt very tenderly towards him. It seemed I had known him a very long time, though he was so young, and with the loss of my post I feared I had lost also my son. I told Schoolcraft all this in my embarrassment at having thanked him; otherwise—though in all practical and personal aspects my words were true—I would never have spoken so. I saw now he was looking at me as he had not before. He met my eyes. There was a crease above his chin not there a moment before, and, at finding his heart so opened, I suddenly felt sick.

"John," he said, "the word *time* is indeed a relative term, and ever means much or little, as much or as little as has been enjoyed or suffered. I am so truly sorry. What I could change I would." I nodded and turned to leave, suddenly fearful he might go on. He said, "I do not often speak of it, but I lost a son as well. I— Do you know, we called him 'Penaci.'"[1]

My back was to him.

"That is not so far from 'Little Pheasant,' I think," he said. His words were low and deep in his throat, as if not meant for me. He coughed.

There was nothing to do but leave. I could have turned and sat down, but it would have been unpleasant; there was no courage in me for humility. I had lowered myself into a dialogue that repelled me. I left without a word.

That, to correct what I said earlier, was the beginning of our war. We would not speak of our sons again. He would not again address me as "John" (not that he had so frequently before, except

---

[1] *Little bird*

out of casual disrespect); nothing was ever quite the same. My scorn for him increased as did my self-loathing; what I took away was a morbid temptation to take Schoolcraft's side in our war; yet I could not concede the ground his grief demanded of mine, if I had before—such was my pride. I retained the pride of one from the interior. It was a pride not fitting this new world. It contested merely one's death. If it died, like the prophet's fire it would draw out and destroy the soul. This was not vanity, Miss Mesare, but the denial of all vanities. I supplied my being by such pride.

All about the Agency spoke of the money trouble. It was real as the corpses of sheep in the morning after tame dogs have packed up in the night. It was hard on morale. Once serious men could be seen playing at cards during the day. They spoke mordantly of the new American Father[2] and made pictures of him with their streams in the snow. He was an odd-looking man with a long face, and his character was not hard to capture with even the most unpredictable of instruments. It was known he had killed many Creeks and Seminoles, and it was not long before the local Ojibwas took up the drawing. His image was everywhere, shifting, darkening, growing more monstrous, until the spring thaw came. I did not question the truth at the heart of it. I could not. My pay had stopped the month before.

I was given hope when word came through Dr. James that Angus Woosley had given up his post as government interpreter and was departing Ste. Mary's. He left before the ice melted. His wife was with child, yet with their daughters they hired a dog train to Mackinac and endured a prolonged portage through deep and ice-encrusted snow, harassed by wolves, in order to catch the first vessel of the year west to Chicago. But they found the straits still locked hard in ice, and stayed on at the Agency with Boyd until the break-up, writing a series of pious, melancholy letters that Schoolcraft read—in the order posted, though a month later—for

---

[2] Andrew Jackson, inaugurated March 4, 1829.

the amusement of friends. They sailed then to Chicago, and from there to St. Louis, over swollen and insect-infested rivers, and the letters became less frequent, but more amusing (to Schoolcraft), until one came, written in the back-slanted hand of Mrs. Woosley, informing the Agent that Angus, brother of Melanchthon, had contracted cholera and died. The news created a swell of ill will against Schoolcraft, but that is another story.

Woosley was not replaced by me. I accepted the news of his leaving with a feeling of great vindication and anticipation, but learned that Henry Sewakee, a French-Potawatomi sent up from St. Joseph, who had no wife or family or particular need of income but who was young and ambitious and therefore inexpensive, had been assigned my post. It was another blow to my hopes and produced, at least in theory, another enemy. When I visited Schoolcraft about it he leaned back in his creaky chair and looked upon me as if he had trouble focusing his eyes, or I were an object materializing in cold haze upon a snow-blighted landscape.

"Hello, Tanner," he said. "What is it?"

I told him my daughter writes to her mother and wishes to know how to properly spell the word "unemployed." It was a word I preferred she use. She would use otherwise another that described not my condition, but me.

"You're not unemployed, Tanner," he said. "You work for the Agency."

I reminded him I was no longer paid.

"You work now for rations, do you not?"

That was true.[3]

"If anything," he said, "you are under-employed. That's not the same."

Then please spell it, I said.

---

[3] As of March 1st, 1829, Tanner had, upon his own suggestion, begun working at the Indian Agency an hour a day in exchange for daily rations taken at Fort Brady.

He wrote it on a piece of paper torn from a larger piece of paper and handed it to me.

I said the words, he corrected me, and I nodded. "Good," I said. "My daughter and I thank you."

He nodded.

"Just in case," I said, "'Pusillanimous.'"

"What?" he said.

"It is a word."

"I know it's a word."

"Please spell."

"For Martha? Seriously?" He was grinning sourly.

I told him she writes my letters too, and that if he wanted no mistakes in the spelling of his name he could write that down as well.

"What is this?" Schoolcraft asked. He had not moved, and his breathing came as a series of short huffs.

There was a stomping of boots and the door opened. James Schoolcraft came in. He had a light mustache and was wearing a French capote of blue with a grouse feather pinned to sweep back from it. Behind him a red horse bowed to snort into the snow. The storm-house door swung shut on my view and on the sound of the rapids that had come in with him. He closed the inner door.

"Evil!" he said. He looked at me. "Mr. Tanner," he said formally. Then, to Schoolcraft, "Evil children. Evil, evil!"

Schoolcraft asked him what now. I took note, as I thought he might be speaking of my Martha Ann.

"She-gud," he said. "He wants open credit for his whole family."

"He's respectable," Schoolcraft told his brother.

"They're unattractive. They're evil. Evil children!" He made a face.

"Don't be an ass," Schoolcraft said.

"All right, you think?"

"He's all right."

"He's the one on the hook."

170

"I wouldn't have a problem with it," Schoolcraft said.

"Good enough," James Schoolcraft said. "How's our friend Mr. Tanner?"

I looked at him. He turned back toward his brother and walked around the desk to stand at the window and looked out; under the naked trees the river stretched green into silver and on it were moving rafts of ice with bright sunlight on the edges.

"Dinner?" he asked Schoolcraft.

"You're inviting me?"

"No, you fool, what time?"

"Six-thirty, I should say, as usual."

"Bells on!"

"Vagabond!"

He looked over his brother's shoulder. "Word from Washington?"

"None."

"Evil children!" he said, and left, shaking his head.

Schoolcraft smiled, watching him leave, then quit smiling and asked what more he could do for me. I left as well.

I watched James Schoolcraft wheel his horse and ride kicking up mud and grass upon the snow up to the road and toward town. Farther down he did not go left where the orchard began, but in the other direction, toward the river, where the Johnston houses were. I returned home.

Have you eaten, Miss Mesare? I have a fine turtle hanging in back. All right, if you're sure. Tea then. What are those?

My first winter at Saint Mary's was coming to an end. In the winter there was little to do at the Agency. Schoolcraft used this time to write his Indian studies, and he wrote all the time. He wrote papers for reviews. As he was on the Territorial Legislative Council, he had many letters to read and write. He worked on his biography of John Johnston. When the days lengthened and warmed, the Indians would come—hundreds and then thousands of them—and he would have no time for this work of his; he became anxious not to waste time, and sometimes took dinner in his office. He kept the door locked some mornings until after nine o'clock. A few times he pretended to be out and had me or Sewakee meet outside with Indian visitors. I understood this feeling his, of clawing against inevitability, so took it upon myself to bother him as often as possible.

If I need you I'll call for you, Tanner, he would say.

I thought you might have some need of me this morning, afternoon, evening, I would say.

Not at present.

Should I wait to be sure?

Get out.

Typically my visits did not occupy much time, but they threw him off, got his mind slightly unshackled. That was enough. Other times, he would be fatigued from his studies, and my visit, if it upset him at first, would provide him a needed rest.

"Do you know, Tanner," he might say, leaning far back in his chair with an arm draped over the top of his head, "that over the past ten years I have travelled not less than twenty thousand miles, and have written for publication not less than a half-million words, and over these years I have scarcely laid my head down one night without feeling that the next day's success or failure would depend on a fresh appeal to continued—nay endless— effort. Do you know? My path has not been laid over beds of gold, nor my pillows composed of down, and yet my success has served to arouse envy and malignity in many minds. True though it be these are small minds."

He straightened in his chair. "Nevertheless," he said, "good to receive word from a friend in Boston that I'm not altogether forgotten." He picked up a paper as if to read it to me, then laid it back down. "Only looking for crania anyway," he said to himself. He picked it up again and sorted through its pages, tilted his head back, and read in a funny voice, "'I require the best specimens of

Indian eloquence. It will be desirable to have as much as possible of the history of each head.'"

He seemed to think about it, a hint of contempt showing upon his lips, then to realize I was still there. He leaned back and let out a breath that was as well a grunt.

He said, "I remember an Indian that came here early on, a haggard-looking and forsaken Chippewa. He was dressed in tatters and wearing a silver medal of the type then given to the natives for meritorious loyalty to the American Father. It had Washington's image on it. Do you have one? No. Well, it was when Governor Cass and I were on our expedition of the west in 1820 that this Indian was given the medal. It was at the time we went up the Ontonagon and I first descried the copper boulder. The Governor had gone off alone to rejoin my forward party upriver and had cut across that mountainous county reckoning to shorten his journey rather than follow the bed of the stream. He had not reckoned the course of the river correctly, however, and managed to get himself hopelessly turned about and entangled in the sharp hills and ravines. This Indian found him and gave him aid, for which he was, at journey's end, given by Cass the medal in gratitude. I think he was called White Bird. Anyway. When he appeared here at the Agency he was forlorn and starving. When asked about the medal, this roused him from his melancholy and he reminded us of the events that won it for him. I realized who this man was, and was shocked at his changed appearance, for he was just two or three years before a young man. It became apparent that his service as a guide, evidenced by the medal, had made him unpopular with his band—that he had, in their minds, received an honor for which he should be condemned. He had aided those who would rob the Indians of their wealth. You see? He was an outcast.

"Such are my honors, Tanner, such is the weight of scientific and intellectual achievement. It hangs heavy about the neck, draws the ire of the slack and envious. Yet one must not be daunted."

I agreed and told him how my success at hunting had produced envy and prejudice even within my wife's family, and that I too had paid the price he spoke of and had known his life of a despised outcast.

He looked at me and compressed his brow. "I didn't say *I* was an outcast," he said.

Neither of us said anything a moment.

He frowned, then sighed and shook his head. "I have work," he said.

"Ah," I said, and asked was he paid for it. He looked at me sharply.

"Don't start sniveling to me about that again," he said.

"I have no money," I told him. "I have a growing daughter to support."

"That's not my fault," he said, in a slow voice. He made the disrespectful sucking sound with his tongue and teeth and this made me suddenly very angry.

"You rob me!" I said.

He got quickly to his feet. "Get out!" he shouted.

"You steal from me!" I screamed.

"Out, you Indianized *bastard!*" he boomed.

"*Matchi annemoash!*"

Our talks, my visits, were sometimes more restful than this. But I think Schoolcraft was not so busy as he was too proud, proud in a different way than me, and this led us often down the same path of antagonism. He would never apologize later; I did every time. His position did not require apologies, though it would have been nice. I still felt a tug of remorse, a feeling of pity for the man. This was misplaced.

Do you know, Miss Mesare, that during this time, this time which lasted nine months, when I was too deprived to provide for my daughter even by hunting—as it was a famously poor year— that my pay, the pay for the La Pointe interpreter—that pay which was said to have been cut off by the Department for lack of funds—that pay was not cut off, but was given to George John-ston—this in addition to his own pay, which was not cut off ei-ther; and this was all done by Schoolcraft himself, in spite of the fact the La Pointe post was closed, and George Johnston took this money and did nothing for it. Schoolcraft of course knew. I have no doubt James Schoolcraft knew. I fear, but cannot resolve my-self to it, that George Johnston must have known. They watched me work for rations and deprive my daughter and they knew. On-ly I did not know. I did not know and I am sure Jane did not know.

You look surprised.

[You slander the Schoolcrafts.]

It's my narrative. Thank you for the cookies.

15

In March I began working with Bingham as interpreter at his meetings with the Indians. He and Dr. James were translating the Gospels into Ojibwa and I was asked to help with this as well. It did not pay, but they were making a mess of it and appealed to me in the name of my Ottawa mother, who they said might by my efforts receive the Word, and by this be accepted into the abode of God upon her death. This I doubted, but I was left no way to refuse without in some wise repudiating Net-no-qua, so I agreed. It was very difficult work. The Gospel of John, in particular, made at first little sense to me in English (even the Doctor, after repeating its opening verses seven or eight times, could not explain it), and Ojibwa equivalencies could not be conceived of. I did my best. A room was prepared for us at the Treaty House, which now was the Mission House, and in it set two tables, one for Dr. James's books and supplies and the other for our work. There was a lantern on this table and we worked oft times into the night. The process was slow, and Dr. James wrote now in longhand, with much scratching out and correction; he questioned me constantly about my choice of Ojibwa words and phrases so as to understand their meaning, and made many decisions I did not agree with. Accuracy had for him suddenly a place at the table. I was not paid, but rewarded with added food provisions, clothing, and gifts for Martha, for whom both the Doctor and Reverend Bingham had formed an at- ⁄

tachment. Why, I didn't know. She was not improving, so far as I could tell, beyond the appalling, blouse-wasting enlargement of her bosom.

These endeavors occupied me through the remaining cold days of spring, and in May I plotted out and spaded a garden behind my house, where I would plant corn and beans and potatoes in early June. I thought the soil would be very good for potatoes. Seeds and starters were given to me by John Hulbert, who was suttler at the Fort. He was a good friend of Bingham's, and so became an ally after I became Bingham's religious conscript. I took satisfaction from my work in the garden. I also hunted daily, now that the days had lengthened, although this rarely added to our rations from the Fort. Still, we had little want, during this time, of sufficient food. We just had no money for anything else.

I stole once. I have never been in the habit of stealing, rather have sacrificed in order to share throughout my life; but on this occasion I stole. I will explain.

Early one Sunday morning, as I looked out over the frost-glazed earth of my garden, the idea came to me that I would need a scarecrow. I had not planted, but the garden occupied my mind throughout the long hours at the Agency and the Mission, and held my mind fast during chapel meetings; I came to fear the ravens and innumerable crows that would settle on every stalk, and to hate every rabbit and raccoon that might graze at will upon my beans. As I looked over the cold turned earth, a shiver ran through my bones, and I determined that I would on that very day, which was in any case a cold and misty Sunday, make a scarecrow. It would be a good scarecrow. It would not be a shirt hung upon crossed sticks, a mere roost. No, what I wanted was a shaggy, brimstone-eyed devil, something to scare off the neighbors along with the varmints. It would be, I decided, more or less *me*. Possibly worse.

Martha moaned and swore and the leather flap of her lodge stiffly rose. She was having her time, which required she sleep outside, and it made her very cross; she emerged, looked at me hatefully, then walked over the garden plot to the privy. When she came out I told her close her mouth, whereupon she fetched up a clod of dirt and threw it at me. Martha threw very well for a girl. The clod struck the house with a boom and did not break. She walked toward me, head down, hair like tattered rags in the breeze.

"Missed me," I said, smiling. She mumbled something and made to pick up another clod, and as she was very close at hand and a dangerous aim, I stepped forward and kicked her as she bent over—she went headlong—then hurried into the house before she could get up. I was laughing when she came in.

She had a ball of dirt. It was a big one. Her teeth showed.

"Don't!" I yelled, but she twisted back and shrieked a very bad name and the dirt clod, which was frozen solid as a rock, hit me in the face above my left eye with a blinding flash and a sound like a gun going off. I fell to the floor screaming in pain.

This has nothing to do with the scarecrow, except that it happened the same morning. Nor would I bother you about the scarecrow either, except that it became important later, and also had to do with my stealing.

[Go on.]

Martha dressed for church and left. I was no longer expected to go Sunday mornings, as I attended the afternoon meeting for Indians where, as I have said, I served as interpreter. I had thus the entire morning to work on the scarecrow without Martha about. It took about an hour of this time for my eyes to clear and for the bleeding to stop. I then set to work.

In a bag under my bed I kept the filth-stiffened rags I wore only for butchering. I took these out. I sewed the leggings and blouse of these together at the waist and stuffed the result all full of grasses and ferns, then buttoned up the blouse. A good pair of buckskin gloves I filled with sand, this to give them weight and form, and these I fixed to the sleeves of the blouse. Likewise a pair of worn and seam-bursting boots were fixed to the leggings. The scarecrow, once a coat was added, was startlingly big in our little house, and an oddly welcome addition; but it had no head and was, as you would expect, rigid as the neck of a day-dead goose. The body could be tied to a pole for support, but the head remained a problem. I set the thing on a chair in the corner to wait until I could think of something. I looked at it a long time. After giving it much unproductive thought I lugged it into my room and laid it carefully on the floor, slid it under the bed.

The morning next was Monday, and I went to the Agency and found atop Schoolcraft's glass cabinet a crate with four paper-wrapped bundles packed in wood shavings. The Agent had gone into the residence to get something for my wound. It was black where it had bled. He feared infection and said he would send for Dr. James. I felt the top of one of these bundles. It was round and hard and I thought it must be a bowl or skull. I moved aside the shavings and lifted one out, felt its shape, the rows of teeth. The lower jaw was there as well. Suddenly there were quick footsteps coming—Jane's—and I hurried to replace the skull in the crate.

"John," she said, and said my name, "John," again. She took my arms in her hands and held me firm and looked at me. I felt as a child. She touched my forehead. "Alcohol," she said in her silvery, ringingly alarmed voice, and turned and hurried out. Then I could hear her speaking to Schoolcraft somewhere in the house.

Something then came over me, Miss Mesare. I had heard her voice some nights before. I had heard hers and Schoolcraft's. Now I heard their voices as her hands could still be felt upon my arms and her fingers upon my face. I became angry as a child, murderously angry, and knew I must leave and never return, this to hurt her, and as I was thinking this I felt, as if still in my hand, the skull with its roundness and teeth, and a thought came to me of the scarecrow; I took again the skull from the crate and tucked it under my arm; I left running. Or not quite running. I did not put in my hour that day.

179

That was my stealing. I put the skull under the bed and did not finish the scarecrow for a long time. When the corn grew ears to attract crows I thought of it again. But I did not complete it. I worried continually over the skull. It must surely have been noted that morning missing; word of it grinning over my garden would inevitably get back to the Agent. I had not thought it through about the skull. I left it under the bed. The scarecrow's grasses warmed and moldered. In the late fall mice would burrow into its warmth and my winter nights would be disturbed by the shrill chirping of their brood, but I did not bring it out, except from time to time later in the year when I knew the mice would be gone, to look at it. I brought it out for use the following summer. But not until then.

[I apologize for daring ask but must: had he not at that time coveted Schoolcraft's wife?]

I know you're trying to follow me. But try not to judge me.

[I'm not judging, I'm asking.]

I did not covet; I denied myself this.

[I ask if he'd like me to read what he has just said.]

I did *not* covet. I flung my arms over my head against a storm of kindness and moaning and mercy and pity, but did not covet. She wrote terrible poetry sometimes and I did not covet. Once, sitting with her and Schoolcraft in the Agency office late in the year I served as interpreter, we were talking about the weather and she said, as if struck by a spell, "Autumn is a second spring, when every leaf is a flower—" then looked disconcertedly out the window. Schoolcraft said, "Quite," and left the room. In her embarrassment a man might have coveted her. She wrote beautiful verse and I did not covet then. In her happiness as well with Janie, and later John, I did not covet, nor in her weakness or her sorrow. Her sadness had divided her and this division might have drawn me except this repelled me as blood repels a deer. I think it is possible, Miss Mesare, that I had a pure heart. Maybe not. Let the reader judge. That is all I am going to say about Jane. I think we will leave it out.

[Fine.]

Is it now time for tea?

Bingham's meetings were a thing to get through. I preferred not to dress, but he had me to wear my New York suit and a high collar and tie and stand at his left. I was to stand very still. He discouraged any movement or gesture, lest it distract from the spoken Word of God, or his bantam strutting and fist waving—which stillness went against the basic mechanics of Indian communication, so was an insult to the congregation—but wished that I emulate by my voice his emotion, cadence, and volume, and, worst of all, to lead in Ojibwa the hymns. These, especially the hymns, combined to fill me with dread before every meeting, and discomfort to the point of dizziness as the realization stole over me that the countless pairs of eyes shifting from him to me were not so intent on the message carried within the Reverend's apocalyptic bombast, as on how I would, as a white man, bring it all off in the Ojibwa. Bingham himself, face fractured by hatred of inebriety into scarlet peaks and chasms, would turn his burning eyes on me as I translated, and the assembled Ojibwa and Ottawa and Menominee, with their silent children and rickety old men carried in on the backs of daughters, would murmur in anticipation of my words, and my bowels would smolder and my face burn from fear and humiliation. The chapel became as a sweat lodge. The air turned sour; I was sure it all emanated from me. I was almost always sick later. The first Sunday was so bad I sought a drink in the town afterward and was almost arrested, such was my fist-hurling fury at being refused because it was a Sunday.

It became easier with time. It helped that my ill-will toward Bingham subsided. He became something of a friend. Also, his sermons grew more predictable. As he reused religious anecdotes and metaphors I was able to fill in what he'd said before and left out this time, and using my head thus distracted and calmed me. From time to time I found a way to bring the message closer to the audience—by substituting whortleberries for figs, say, or talking jays for doves. He read the opening of the Gospel John and I substituted the opening of a medicine hunt song I thought very much like it: "Waw-ne-ge-ah-na gah-ne-gesh-na. Mainito-wahga gah-zhe-hah-gwaw gah-ne-ge-ah-na."[1] This drew a reverential response of "Hoh!" from the Indians that pleased Bingham.

He told the Indians they needed to prepare to meet the Great Father, and would then spend half an hour explaining the derivation of the word "prepare," or, "pre-pare," and explain how we needed to pare away, as the skin of an apple is pared away, the layers of sloth and indifference and concupiscence that smother our souls in order that we might receive God. This might have been all right, but he used this speech whenever he could think of nothing else to say, or had had no time to prepare for the meeting, so it came up very often. By the third occasion of this speech I found it desirable, thus, to substitute for the apple a deer, which by the end of the sermon was gutted, skinned, and quartered. I later used a snapping turtle to good effect, as this butchery was more difficult, thus more interesting; and, finally, a Sioux warrior, which process limited itself to a careful scalping, but which brought down the house. Bingham was surprised at the response and paced excitedly afterward, and spoke then of the apple even more frequently.

He took me away from the others after one such meeting and standing by the wall beside the chapel in the thin afternoon sun asked me how I was getting on with Martha, and wondered if I would like to meet with him to talk about her, or anything else. I told her she was fine, as was I, and thanked him to not worry over us.

---

[1] *"I wished to be born, I was born, and after I was born I made all spirits."*

"But John," he said, "I must by God press this. Do you think she might be, and you as well, happier if she stayed at the Mission? Is it not a hardship for a father alone to care for a girl?"

I disagreed. She cared for me. She cooked sometimes. I would need her as well for the garden. I made an effort to imagine her weeding and smiled.

"Be serious, John."

"I cannot," I said, meaning allow her to live at the Mission.

"I am to understand she is made to sleep outside," Bingham said, crossing his arms.

I told him she was of an age, and this did not concern him.

"Then you *do*. You make her stay outside, like a squaw. In the winter. That's barbaric, John; it's not done in civilized society. It's not even done in Saint Mary's."

I told him if he wanted to take her in for just that week each month I would agree.

This appeared to confuse him. I said good afternoon and walked home.

But I was not stupid; I knew talk was afoot to take Martha Ann away from me. Yet Bingham's notions of peace and faithfulness, of family and obligation, were apart from mine. Of more children than I could count she was the last with me, and the thought of her removal made me quake with grief and fury. She had changed in unexpected ways, but I still remembered the child and still felt tenderly toward her. She was my Martha Ann. No one would take her away. I would shoot a man off his cart that tried.

Bingham continued to press after that. He came to my cabin from time to time, I thought to observe my relationship with Martha, but Martha was of course never home. Come back at two o'clock tonight, I'd tell him, if you want to visit with my daughter.

"You must get her in hand," he'd say.

I'd tell him I don't dare, and point to the healing scar on my forehead, which you can see has a black cast about it to this day.

"Well," he'd say. "Well, well indeed." And he'd look thoughtful. "Yet she's such a good student. Hard to fathom."

"Well, fathom it," I told him.

"Then you must pray for her," he said.

I told him she was where she wanted to be. When she wanted to come home she would come home. She always came home.

"That's foolishness," he said. "It's leaving a child up a tree. Do not leave your child up a tree."

I asked what he meant up a tree. He pulled out a chair from the table and sat down to tell me.

"I say this because I once knew a Seneca woman whose son went up a tree in a fit of temper and would not come down. She let him stay up there all night. The next day I was told of it because the boy was still up the tree, so I went to see her. She was inside. I inquired of her had she asked the boy to come down, and she said she had not and would not. When he was good and ready to come down he would. He was, as you say, where he wanted to be. I went outside and called to the boy. He did not answer. He was sitting on a limb leaning against the trunk and was possibly asleep. I was afraid to startle him for fear he'd fall—or so I told myself—so I went home. I went again to her house the following day and found her nearby the tree; the boy had not come down. I was very concerned, but she merely pulled a blanket up around her head and said, 'He's where he wants to be,' or something to that effect, glancing upward, and wanted to be bothered no more. This continued another day. Near the end of the fourth day others in her village took matters in hand and it was found that the boy in the tree was dead. Of cold or thirst or grief he'd died; one doesn't know. But it's a true story. It was a terrible lesson. I was heart-broken. I thought it to myself I could have gotten him down the second day, but had been reluctant to interfere. How I prayed for forgiveness, and for the mother's! Now I interfere as much as I possibly can. Do you understand, John? And, by God, I will interfere with you, if this matter with Martha is not resolved."

"You will not," I told him.

"Oh yes. One way or another," he said.

"You will not, for I will take care of it."

"Be sure then that you do."

I thanked him again for his concern and opened the door. He smiled, lit his pipe, and said good night.

It was by butting heads in this manner that Bingham and I became friends. I forgave his awful appearance. He desisted from sending devils into my dreams. My sympathy for him grew. He missed his family in western New York State where he'd left them, and spoke often of his plans to go in April to retrieve them. Most of all, it helped soften my attitude that Schoolcraft had declared war against Bingham as well.

[The Reverend has spoken to me of that, of Schoolcraft, I say. He has not reconciled to it. I'm sorry, go on.]

To bind me to his service, Bingham had relieved Schoolcraft's sister-in-law Charlotte Johnston as interpreter at his meetings, and this had been taken as an affront to the Agency by the Agent. Charlotte was very young and pretty, and though she had all the qualities needed to help Bingham, she had more qualities than required, and had stirred talk and distracted the men of the congregation—even without undue gestures or movements—from the Word of God. Even Dr. James, who once or twice a month read in refined Ojibwa the Gospels we had so far translated, could not keep his eyes off Charlotte. Preparing for meetings must have also made Bingham, or possibly Mrs. Bingham, uncomfortable. I do not know. I was sought as a replacement without knowing any of this. Charlotte looked very much like Jane, but was taller and darker-skinned. She might even have been prettier. She was much younger than Jane and more talkative, and foolish in a strangely tolerable way. She came often to Elmwood to visit Jane, and would come into the office to tease Schoolcraft. She called him Uncle Fuddy. He liked it. She determined from time to time to make me smile, though I was immovable in that way as a boulder. I suppose

185

Jane was very protective of Charlotte, and this could have influenced Schoolcraft. I don't think so, though. Schoolcraft was out after wars then. He was a politician. He never spoke to me of it, so I can't be sure. Bingham was less careful. From Bingham I learned that Schoolcraft insisted Charlotte be made permanently Bingham's interpreter, and that he had written cruel letters to various authorities against the Reverend's character for dismissing her, though it was a turn she had agreed to. Schoolcraft's anger made no sense to me, and troubled Bingham greatly. The post did not pay, and permanence in such a position, or in such a young woman, was not to be expected. She had not wanted such permanence. Only Schoolcraft felt injured.

My sympathies for Bingham increased. He was new to Saint Mary's and finding his way as was I. He was, as I said, without his family. Now he could no longer take meals with the Johnstons. My empathy was a crack that widened into a ravine and stayed with me a long time. I put in extra time on the Gospels, tiring even Dr. James. I took to praying, though no man stood over me or gave me words. In little events and circumstances—changes in weather favorable to my garden, improvements in my bowel habits, a kind look from my daughter—I found, or invented, answers to my prayers, prayed with increased fervor, and, cunningly, came to believe.

You are looking at me that way again. If you would help me up I'll see you to the door.

16

The year I think I told you was 1829 went by in the way I have described. I skulked nights around the edges of town with fists huge in my coat pockets, chest pounding, looking for my daughter Martha; I interpreted, mumbled inchoately as I hoed the garden afternoons, paced the cabin nights, went out. Sometimes I brought out the scarecrow and set it in a chair to look at it. One night I drove a long stake down into it. Down through the collar. [He demonstrates with both hands clutching and thrusting downward an imaginary rod.] I impaled the grinning egg-brown skull upon the stake and with twine tied the jaw to the shirt through a button hole; with pitch I affixed a straw hat onto the skull, then put it, my construction, back under the bed. I was pleased and vaguely frightened by it, yet still dared not set it out.

I did not hear from Therezia, but learned she was still at Mackinac. I wrote letters to my children there with the Doctor's help. Jane Schoolcraft became large with child. It was, all in all, an unhappy year.

That summer the Indians came by the thousands, and it was very busy at the Agency. Schoolcraft had drawn me in to help with his language studies, and in the late spring, when only evenings could be used for this work, he would be vexed by my leaving to assist Dr. James with Bingham's Gospels. I think this possibly worsened his relations with Bingham, but I don't know.

There were other problems. Dr. James was frequently ill, and one evening when the Doctor was unable to work I went back to the Agency. The outer door was unlocked. This was unusual, as Indians were not accustomed to knocking. I opened it. The lamp on Schoolcraft's desk was lit. I heard a scuffling and saw two figures standing close together by the glass cabinet. One was Schoolcraft. He stood with his back turned. The other was a girl I recognized to be Sophia Cadotte, the Metif he called Sophie, a servant girl bound to the Schoolcraft's. She faced me and said hello. I said good evening and told Schoolcraft Dr. James was sick in bed and I could help him with his language studies if he wanted.

"Not tonight," he said, but did not turn to face me.

I left. That was in September. I did not enter his office without knocking after that.

Henry Sewakee was the posted interpreter then. He had been raised by a French-Miami father and Pottawattamie mother so was a good interpreter, though very young and inexperienced in the affairs of the fur trade both American and British; he also had some difficulties with dialects of the northern lakes tribes that I was able to help him with. He was polite and we got on well. He wore his hair short and was always well-dressed. I think Schoolcraft was fond of him; at least I never heard a harsh word.

One night when I was circling the Agency House with the intent of peeping in at the Schoolcraft's corner window, I saw them, Sewakee and Sophia Cadotte, lying in the grass. The moon was full and in its light I knew immediately who I'd caught coupling on what looked to be a tablecloth spread on the ground near the base of an old elm tree. Sewakee was on his back with his pants bunched down around boots; Sophia was sitting atop him. Her hair was down and she had on a white bed gown. The gown covered her and much of him. She was leaning forward with her hands pressed upon his chest and his hands were up under the bed gown. There was very much movement and the movement became more violent until Sewakee's back arched like a snake in a fire and Miss Cadotte sat bolt upright and flung her hair back and let out several shrill cries; I rose from my knees and fumbled for balance, got away from them.

Is that too much detail, Miss Mesare?

The sight of them made a strong impression on me; it bore into my thoughts and dried my tongue even as I stood with Bingham in the chapel meetings; and I took to going there, to the rear of Elmwood overlooking the river, whenever the nights were fair. A month or so later, on a warm night in October, I saw them again. I saw Sewakee first. He was standing under the elm. Some minutes later Sophia appeared carrying a blanket. She dropped the blanket to the grass and they embraced. He ran his hands over her hips and she unbuttoned his trousers, which dropped of their own weight, and he lifted her gown and standing they pressed together and kissed. He lowered himself to his knees and she laid the front of her gown over his head—

Thank you deciding to stay, Miss Mesare. May I call you Constance?

[In the present context I would prefer you did not.]

I will approach these events another way.

It seems that on one of these nights I saw them, or on some other night I somehow missed, Schoolcraft saw them as well. There must have been a terrible row after that, for Sophia ran away and Henry Sewakee was dismissed. I think he went back below to St. Joseph. Where Sophia went no one said. She came back, but not for several months. The next time I saw Schoolcraft, he had me to sit down. He was pale and his eyes were heavy and dark.

"Something unseemly has taken place under this roof," he told me, "here in my very home."

I thought not of Sewakee, but was certain he had discovered my theft and was going to dismiss me. For what might have been the first time in my life I would be unable to defend my actions. I sat silent, waiting. In my fear sweat bristled on my forehead and I began to tremble. He gazed up beyond me as if into the corners of the ceiling, then looked at me and carefully, slow as an old Indian assembling his words, said, "Our Mr. Sewakee has seen fit to carry on a heinous liaison with my servant girl, Miss Cadotte, who, as you know, is barely sixteen and hardly of a background to instinctively safeguard her virtue, such as it was, and for this, this imprudence and moral equivocation, this breach of ethics and professional fealty—not to mention debauchment, fornication, and buggery—" (he paused here to catch his breath, for his voice had at the last grown excited) "—I have seen fit to dismiss him."

He was very angry. To help calm him, and because I was suddenly a little giddy with relief, I asked him to please explain the word *buggery*, though I knew the word and its meaning and could even, at that instant, picture it and its object, Miss Cadotte, quite clearly. Schoolcraft glared at me a moment, then blinked; his face relaxed.

"Seriously?" he said.

I shrugged.

"To get to the point," he said, "I need an interpreter. I am offering you the post. You'll start immediately. Same terms as Sewakee."

I asked him what terms were these.

"Full time," he said.

I let it go at that. It was a mistake to do so.

It occurred to me then to ask about the interpreter's quarters. Though it was newer by half a century, Elmwood was arranged very like the Indian Agency at Mackinac, with a wing at either end for the Agency office and the interpreter's quarters, and I knew the one room would not be sufficient, because my daughter lived with me now and would not share a room.

"Good, yes," Schoolcraft said, squinting. "I have given that some thought too, in fact, and can put your mind at rest. We are in need of more guest rooms. The interpreter's quarters are to be rehabilitated and made suitable for visitors. The three rooms are a bit much for your purposes anyway. And now with the baby, you know, housing guests within the central residence is out of the question. The Perrault's are already lodged for the winter in the cellar, and that's quite enough. So Tanner—you will continue to receive a stipend for your rent, and you can live where you like. Only not here at the Agency."

"Three rooms?" I said.

"I don't think we can get four out of it," Schoolcraft said. He sucked at his teeth.

I was happy to have the position of interpreter and went home that evening to tell Martha of our good fortune. We could send for little John now. I would go to get him. If necessary, I would take him from Therezia as I had been taken from my parents when little more than John's age. I even resolved, as I walked quickly home that evening, to bring back Therezia as well, if it came to that. My resolve thus quickly subsided, and the business was forgotten altogether when I arrived home to find the cabin empty, dark, and cold as a cave, and Martha gone.

For an hour I sat at the table with my chair facing the door, at first merely waiting, grumbling like a horse, my mouth full of woody pemmican and my nose cold and running furiously; and with the futility of waiting came a counting and recounting of the year's takings and misfortunes; I thought of my John's shy enthusiasms and of the other children now removed, felt the sting of their absence; then of Sewakee and Cadotte coiling, sprawling, and felt the searing hatred in Schoolcraft's eyes; recalled with a chill Jane's childbirth screams and the knife-blade of sunlight on the stair rail that accompanied them; and Bingham lifting the dinner cloth from his head, grinning. My head ached. My thoughts circled back to Martha, and I rose and went out to look for her—though with cold indifference. On returning, I spent some time with the scarecrow to get the other pictures out of my head, then went to bed.

Sometime later Martha came in. I listened to her knock into things as she undressed, heard the mattress as she laid down on it.

"Father," she said. Her voice startled me, as would hearing a cat speaking. I saw in my mind her eyes open wide, staring into the rafters. I felt frightened; I can't say why. I said nothing.

"I want to go to Momma," she said.

I spoke and told her it could not be. I asked if she was sick.

She said no in a faint voice, then was quiet.

"I was today made interpreter at the Agency," I said. "I am full-time with pay."

The air sparked with silence. You could hear the falls. After a time she could be heard crying.

I'm sorry, Miss Mesare, my throat is dry.

At this time I had begun to distrust those around me that I had trusted, and to dislike those I had liked. My ways made people look upon me with disdain and enmity, or to look upon me not at all, or to seek advantages over me; and Martha's behavior made me wary of women that might want to take her away and hatefully suspicious of men, especially James Schoolcraft. James, the Agent's brother, was worse than the fawning, lip-wiping Ais-kaw-ba-wis about women, if less disgusting to behold.

I liked James Schoolcraft when first I met him at the Agency, and then at his store. I liked him because he made jokes. But then he joked that Ethan the butcher's man had learned Ojibwa from the bull, and I did not like him anymore. Schoolcraft the Agent excused his brother everything. James drank too much at a French ball on Mackinac and dirked a man and nearly killed him, and Schoolcraft, after it became known, said only, as if to explain, that his brother was high-spirited. I have heard this term applied to horses, but never to swine. He was a swine and a thief. He is still a swine. He is probably still a thief. Got forgive me, I hate the man. He is Henry's brother, but I would hate him if he were not. He mocked me.

192

"You have a bite here," he'd say if I went into his store, touching a spot above his eye.

I would not respond, but stood before the flour barrel waiting to be dealt with seriously.

"Jean Baptiste," he would say to another man there; "look at him. Is that not a bite?"

The little man who had taken up residency in Schoolcraft's cellar—and was the one who built the strange little boat with spinning sails because he had lost his life's savings through carelessness and hoped to gain it back through such whimsies as the boat and helped, for this kindness of Henry Schoolcraft, at the store—would tuck his face between me and the flour barrel and look.

"Oui, c'est un bite, I think," he'd say, pointing. "Spider."

"Very large one," James Schoolcraft said, looking.

I told them to mind their own business.

Schoolcraft's brother said to me, "Mind yourself tonight, for there is a very large spider in your house that could bite you again. It is an evil spider. But do not let it out to bite others."

The little Frenchman laughed as he walked away.

I told Schoolcraft's brother I needed flour and other provisions.

"For credit?" he asked.

I told him yes, for credit; I had not yet been paid for my services at the Indian Agency.

"Then credit for you and your spider," he said.

"Shut up about the spider," I told him.

"He is sensitive about the spider," he told the other.

But the other was looking out the window at the snow falling.

"It is understandable. A spider is a difficulty," he said.

"You are a fool," I told him.

"That may be," he said, "but I have not been bitten." He smiled and gave me what I requested without saying more. I made my mark for the goods and left.

Several days later I went back into the store. For what I do not remember. There were several other men there I did not know. He looked up.

"Is that a bite?" he asked me.

That is how he was. He trifled. That I did not respect him meant nothing to either of us; he treated me with the same distain he showed the Indians.

He liked to talk about the Indians. He had not his brother's need for diplomacy on the subject. He liked to talk about Indian women. He knew it made me angry when he did so. It could make his brother angry as well, but Schoolcraft allowed for anything that came from James.

"Tanner," he'd say, "tell me this: do Indian women lie down to have their babies? In the wild, that is. I have not seen a deer lie down to give birth. They'll drag a fawn by its cord a mile before they'll lie down. What of Indians?"

Schoolcraft would say "James" whenever his brother got started, and "James" several times before he was finished, and would scold him after, but Schoolcraft was amused by his brother and let him say anything. James had been seated next to Bingham at the Johnston dinner for a reason, I thought. It occurred to me as well that Bingham might not have stood and put the dinner cloth on his head had he been seated elsewhere.

Once James Schoolcraft said, "What say my natural scientists of the curious patch of fur to be found between the breasts of an old Indian woman? Is there a term for it? Henry? No? What, Tanner—speak up, man—seriously—her—" and he said a word that was a very bad Latin word as if I had supplied it. This joke did not make me angry at the time, as I failed to understand it; instead I committed to memory the Latin word so I could ask Martha had she yet been taught it at the Mission school. She had not, but asked her friends about the word, and told them her father wanted to know what it was. Her white friends knew this word, as did their parents, as did Bingham, and there was much alarm over this question. I might have killed James Schoolcraft for the damage done me by this joke, but avenged myself instead with a second theft from the Agency. I have now, if you'd like to see it, a book of Latin translation.

I became indebted to James Schoolcraft. My pay continued to be withheld me, though I was the posted interpreter, and was instead given—as I learned much later and have told you—to Henry Schoolcraft's brother-in-law, George Johnston. There must have been some lie told Johnston by Schoolcraft that prevented undoing whatever arrangement had been made; I can't think of another explanation. I did not think George Johnston a bad man. Schoolcraft told me it was the government's fault he could not pay me, and took to paying me a small sum in specie again. The specie was honored only by James Schoolcraft at his store. Schoolcraft gave it to some Indians, too. We were not to use it except at the store. His brother had one price for dollars and another for specie. It did not buy much. That is how I became indebted to James Schoolcraft. A few Indians were indebted as well, and some voyageurs, and half the soldiers at Fort Brady. James Schoolcraft was not well-admired in St. Mary's. "Mind you purse, mind your wife; mind your wife's purse too," was the saying. Stories were told on the streets.

One day I was collecting lard and cornmeal at his store and James Schoolcraft looked up from a book, said, "You are now into me for seventy-six dollars and eighty-seven cents." He said it and I thought he was joking. I looked at him and saw he was not.

"That cannot be," I told him.

"Not including interest," he said.

I asked him what interest.

"At ten percent," he said, as if that explained anything.

"What is interest," I asked him.

"What I am paid for extending you credit," he said.

"How much?"

He told me seven dollars and sixty-nine cents per annum at my current indebtedness.

I asked him what was per annum. He told me.

"It is too much," I said.

"I have debts myself," he said. "I must borrow to supply the store. I too must pay interest."

I asked him what interest per annum he paid.

"Two percent," he told me.

That was a great deal less than ten.

"Yes, but what I pay is none of your concern, Tanner," he said. "Fact is, rates are artificially low because the economy is in the state it's in. Things pick up and rates could go through the roof. As a creditor I must share this risk."

What risk, I asked him.

"Interest rate risk."

"My interest cannot go higher," I said; "it is ten percent now." I was growing both angry and afraid.

"I allay this risk in advance with the ten percent. I will not raise it," he said. "You have my word."

I thanked him.

"Only you must pay me sometime."

When your brother pays me, I told him.

He offered to have Schoolcraft pay him directly. This would reduce the interest.

Again I thanked him and left the store somewhat relieved. It took me a few days to figure it all out, whereupon I was angry again.

"You should be happy," he said, "I have long-term debt against the store itself and it is at a rate that did not come down when rates came down. I'm stuck at five and a half percent. Do I have long-term receivables to mitigate that? No. Now I am positively gapped in a falling rate market. It is not amusing, John. Do not laugh at me. It does not mean I am a bad businessman. Only that I am a victim of the markets. It happens to the best of us. What you owe the store is nothing, but if I allowed your rate, and everyone else's, to come down, I would lose any margin I ever had and would in effect be paying you for the privilege of extending credit."

This made sense to me.

"And if we project this situation into the future and regard my business through the lens of interest rate risk, my equity gets present-valued to zilch. I would be, in effect, a bankrupt. Would that amuse you, John?"

I apologized and left. It required a smile upon Dr. James's lips for me to see through it all. I resolved, in any case, not to discuss my debts further with anyone—although I did write Governor Cass a very bitter letter which went a long way toward inciting Schoolcraft against me, but in the end got me paid.

That's enough for tonight. I know you have to go soon. I wish you could stay longer and would put down that damned pen.

[I tell him that though I have listened biding my tongue, he should be aware that James Schoolcraft is a friend of mine, has been now for several years, and that he is both respectable and respected.]

Nonsense.

[You damn your daughter by damning Schoolcraft; do you not understand this?]

You're getting ahead of the story.

[It's clear enough where it's going, I say.]

Do I damn you as well?

[You know nothing about me.]

Maybe not.

[I leave.]

17

You'll please forgive me, but it came into my head—at first tentatively and then so firmly it would not leave my mind but choked it of all other thoughts day and night—that James Schoolcraft, to whom I was indebted and who demanded of me seven dollars and sixty-nine cents per annum and who was then thirty if he was a day, was seeing my Martha Ann nights—Martha, who was at this time fifteen, and, if she slouched like an otter, was nonetheless tall and bosomy. I tried more than once to trick him into admitting to it.

"Funny thing about daughters," I said to him one morning at his store, "they tell their fathers everything."

He paused from weighing and bagging seed as if to consider it. Drops of perspiration were beaded on his forehead. "As would a dog if he could talk, I suppose," he said, glancing at me. "Good for you and your daughter."

"Who they have been with, included."

"Jack," he said, meaning his dog, "is always with me, so it doesn't come up."

I told him Martha came in very late last night.

"What was last night?" he asked.

"You know."

"You mean you don't? It was Thursday, John. At least it was Thursday in Canada. Possibly here as well. You'll have to check. What time did you say she came in?"

I thought about one o'clock.

"Well," he said, "I didn't see her in Canada."

I asked why was he in Canada.

"I was invited to the Cameron's," he said; "along with Jack. Why do you ask? Did she have a school activity?"

I told him she had not been to any school activity so late.

"She told you that?"

"Yes," I lied.

"Does she skip many school activities?"

I said no she was good student and skipped nothing.

"Then that explains it."

I squinted at him. "Explains what?"

"Everything," he said, and smiled, tilting his head.

He retreated into nonsense like that, like a crawfish into mud, every time; I could never get a sensible word out of him. Yet I was certain he was seeing my daughter. Martha was crying nights, sobbing so that my hair stood on end and my chest tightened as in a vice. She may have been with child. There was no way to know. I could not ask her about it; I could demand nothing of her; being Martha, she'd have left me.

It was spring 1830 now and the nights were warming, though snow abounded in the trees and there was still ice on the river. One night I determined I would wait for her outside, to see what direction she would come from and perhaps in whose company, and hid first down on Portage where I had met the horse and buckboard half a year past. I crouched in wet snow against the base of a tree, the air cold and damp on my face, and fell asleep in a ball listening to the thin sound of the falls and the bells of the Episcopal mission across the river. I awoke and walked stiffly home and found her snoring on her mattress with her coat and clothes thrown this way and that over the floor. Another night I waited by the Fort in a thicket of river birch, but did not see Martha. I next sat on the bench outside the candy store and likewise fell asleep. I gave it up for a time.

I need to insert here, because I forgot to earlier, that Sophia Cadotte had returned to Ste. Mary's. She came back in March and Bingham admitted her to the Mission school the first of April. She was roomed with other half-caste girls. That she had left Henry Schoolcraft's service in violation of the law and was now allowed into the school threw Henry Schoolcraft into an apoplexy. I think he hated it she was in town at all. He brought it up daily. I don't know why he put himself through it; he was seized by a fit every time.

"By God!" he'd say, fists like boulders on his chair arms, face burning, "it was not the purpose of the 1820 treaty, nor the 1826, to benefit worthless vagabonds and runaways of the Indian race who turn a deaf ear on the instructions of the government and slander its agents! Damn it all! I'll have her arrested! Yes, by God, get Hulbert!" He shook, coughed to the point of sickness. I told him I'd go out to see what I could do.

John Hulbert was helping out at the time as sheriff. Everyone helped out one way or the other. Schoolcraft was helping out then as district judge.

"Get him!" Schoolcraft boomed.

But John Hulbert wanted no part of it. He was taking inventory at the Fort commissary.

"Bingham," Schoolcraft fumed, "is misapplying the federal annuity. By admitting and boarding as meretricious a specimen as Cadotte he's introduced into the Mission a corruption, a chancre! And in so doing has declared himself an enemy of the Department, and now stands openly opposed to its efforts—to *my* efforts—to improve the lot of the Indians. He's misapplying government funds, by God! That's what it is! I will write the superintendent about it! Where's my pen! Get me a pen!" He coughed, held up his quill. "Never mind!"

This is what I had to put up with. The Indians as well. One morning Nee-gau-be-un,[1] who was a minor chief of the Crane by descent, though a disreputable and intemperate man, visited to ask for provisions. He looked as ever haggard with his one eye missing and where it had been be-specked with dirt and gummy and his poor clothing smelling very bad. Schoolcraft, who was working intently on an angry letter to the Superintendent of the Office of Indian Affairs, swore vehemently when told Nee-gau-be-un was waiting. He slowly gathered himself as for a great exertion and rose, as I opened the door, to greet him. Though it was blowing outside and you could not see the river for the thin rain, Schoolcraft signaled me to leave the door open. I assumed a place to the left of Nee-gau-be-un. This was not my accustomed position, but was the side of the good eye, and I knew that if he opened the one wide the other wanted to crack as well, and this is what I wished not to see. The Indian spoke first and I translated.

"Father, I am poor; show me pity."

Schoolcraft waved his hand dismissively and had already seated himself again and was now leaning his face on his fist looking up at Nee-gau-be-un. "Why should I?" he said.

This surprised the old Indian, who understood this much English and looked at me as if I should explain. I was not so disposed, so said, "Tell him," in English, and tipped my head in the direction of Schoolcraft.

Before the Indian could speak, Schoolcraft said, "So how are my friends on Drummond?" and by this meant the British agency post on Drummond Island, which was a day's distance by canoe. It was known that Nee-gau-be-un visited there frequently. Schoolcraft, to correct any misapprehension, had no friends there.

The Indian answered that he did not know, as he no longer visited the British. His affections were with the American Father.

---

[1] *The west wind*

"Don't lie to me," Schoolcraft said in a soft and very dangerous voice. His massive face did not move, but for what the light of the lamp revealed of his heartbeat about the bevels of his spectacles.

Nee-gau-be-un again rolled his eye up to appeal to me and, without looking back at Schoolcraft, said again that he was poor, and added that he did not trouble the Agent often, and hoped that he would show him charity.

Schoolcraft told him look at him, and when he did asked when he was last on Drummond Island.

"Last month," the Indian said. He glanced sidelong at me.

"That would be March, this being whatever follows March. And what did you receive there?" Schoolcraft asked him.

Nee-gau-be-un told him freely that he had been given four traps and twelve rations. The British were not generous like the American Father, he said, shaking his head. They were not kind. He was done with them. His loyalties were now firm.

"Now, Nee-gau-be-un," Schoolcraft said, smiling and bringing his hand slowly down to grip the chair arm, "I have told you in the past not to misconstrue my charity into approbation of your conduct, especially as regards your visits to Drummond. Have I not?"

The old Indian, who was not steady on his feet, pointed a finger at Schoolcraft and said in his creaky Ojibwa, "I am poor and you have told my people that their needs would always be supplied, and if I have gone to the British you have forced me to do so."

I wanted to cover my head as I translated this.

"Don't you fucking start that!" Schoolcraft said, coming up out of his chair. The two men glared at each other as Schoolcraft collected himself. "You have misused this agency," he said. "You have dishonored the American Father. You land where you will with the politics of a fly. You have received charity the bounty of which you have employed merely to further your journeys to foreign agencies and you have persisted in taking these bounties, which are meant to supply the poor and suffering, while the fruits of your labor are spent on whiskey. You, my Nee-gau-be-un, discredit your race!"

The Indian's mouth tightened as I translated this. He turned to go.

"You stay right there!" Schoolcraft shouted in a breaking, you'd have thought panicked, voice. I made no attempt to translate what followed, as Schoolcraft spoke very quickly in a loud and passionate way, and I had not in any case either the language or heart for it:

"I have tolerated your bullshit remonstrances and heedless of your lies held the doors of this Agency open to you and your type even as my sympathies were squandered and generosity's stores looted and as dissolution and betrayal ran and ripened in staunched orthorhombic crusts down your leggings and I can tell you, my Nee-gau-be-un, that those doors are now finally and fastly *closed*—and if you find doors thrown open to you again you will find they lead not here but to the western territories where men of your example have prepared a destiny among the alumblinded locusts of the white desserts, because the Great Father, Nee-gau-be-un, will abide you no more! You, Nee-gau-be-un, are without faithfulness! You are without honor! You are *not*, Nee-gau-be-un, *a chief!*"

This last was understood. The Indian said in a weak voice that *Nos* was mistaken, he was a chief. His hands wrung the pitiful, wear-fringed blanket draped across his chest.

"You are chief of nothing!" Schoolcraft shouted. He sat forward and was shaking. *"You are chief of the dead!"*

Nee-gau-be-un made a final attempt to look resolute, then left, I think, in tears.

But if Nee-gau-be-un was in respects a special case, Schoolcraft's rage was greater and less specific than this forlorn old man could have guessed; for the Agent's dream of glory, his redemption of the Indian races, was in ashes; he had given up. Nee-gaube-un and his sons and their very forests were doomed. I knew this as well, and in a way it did not make me unhappy. I too, though in my own heart-split confused way, had loved the anguish of freedom that was in the end my, and their, hell.

Eventually Schoolcraft would turn his spitefulness against me as well. He minded that I had allied myself, that's how he put it, with Bingham and Dr. James. He couldn't even trust Hulbert anymore. Everyone was lining up against him. And for what, for whom? A mixed-blood, law-breaking, covenant-desecrating strumpet. (His words, Miss Mesare, not mine.) Yet it was not either about Cadotte. Schoolcraft was a shipwreck. I am told he was a just man once, that he had been greatly impressed by what he had discovered of the non-animal in the Indian, and had devoted himself to their betterment through his duties and his studies, but had been gravely disappointed. He spoke sometimes of Lake Pepin, as if he had himself been there murdered.[2] This, and possibly he had lost faith when his son William died of fever. I don't know. I never found him a just man. This is only what I have been told.

But that was in April, and really has nothing to do with my story. What I have to tell you happened in late March. Would you like tea before I tell you about it?

I wouldn't bother to guess how many nights I stayed out looking for Martha. It all seems a skiff of time now, those final weeks,

---

[2] On or about July 1, 1824, a war party of twenty-nine Ojibwa led by Kewaynkwut (Returning cloud) murdered, for no apparent cause, an American trader by the name of Finley, and three Canadians, at Lake Pepin on the Mississippi. The news of this atrocity, along with the scalp of one of the victims, was delivered to Schoolcraft on August 31 of that year by John Holiday, a trader. See Henry Rowe Schoolcraft, *Personal Memoirs of a Residence of Thirty Years with the Tribes on the American Frontiers: With Brief Notices of Passing Events, Facts, and Opinions, A.D. 1812 to A.D. 1842* (Philadelphia: Lippincott, Grambo and Co., 1851), 198. The events of Lake Pepin marked a turning point in the U.S. government's approach to Indian affairs, which course turned thereafter inexorably toward the removal of the Indians from the Northwest Territories. On June 22, 1825, the Ojibwa men guilty of shooting the whites at Lake Pepin were delivered by their tribe to Schoolcraft at Sault Ste. Marie. Schoolcraft himself conducted the inquiry and tribunal.

thin as the skin of leaves under winter's retreat; but it went on for a long time, or seemed to, and seemed then to have gone on forever. It went on into the warm, frog-shrill nights of spring. Then it stopped. It stopped in a heartbeat and with it ceased the face-clutching torment of a father. Fatherhood ceased, Miss Mesare. Not quite so immediately, but soon enough. Yet this change all began as a joke. A dead bear propped upon the seat of a trader's outhouse. Or like that.

One night I walked back off the road into the woods and came upon a deer path in the moonlight, and followed it that I might come upon their bedding place. The moon was up and full-red under the ashes of clearing fires. I liked to scare deer up from their bedding places; they would dance in their confusion and it was a thing to see in the moonlight. It excited me, too, possibly, that the moon was red. I did not see any deer, though. I saw, instead, at a distance interspersed with trees, a campfire.

The wind was up in the pines and in the wind the sounds of hardwoods rubbing and limbs rattling, and the air carried fingers of fog through the trees. It was cool and damp. The ground was soft and there were many sticks underfoot, but I walked forward toward the light of the fire without concern of being heard. It was sugar season, and Indians camping in the woods, even so close to town, would not have been thought out of place; nor did I worry lest my visit cause alarm. They would almost certainly be drunk. If not, friendly. Either way, this time of year they would be Crane Ojibwa from town.

A small clearing opened in the woods, and the trunks of pine and birch glowed red at its edges and shone dripping with sap. I stopped. Not far from the campfire was a woman lying naked upon a blanket with her legs apart and the darkness between visible and frosted with dampness in the firelight. When she sat up and turned her head I recognized her to be Sophia Cadotte. At that moment a man emerged from the trees. He also was naked, with a proudly wagging groin, and he carried a small earthen jug which he handed to her; it was James Schoolcraft. Remembering myself, I crouched down behind the base of a pine and watched as Cadotte sat up and with Schoolcraft's help raised the jug to her lips in both hands, then gave it back. Schoolcraft took a drink, brushed at his hairless chest to spread over it a sheen of moisture, then bent to set the jug on the ground. He lowered himself to stretch out beside the girl on the blanket. They were talking, but I could not hear what was said. When the girl, Sophia Cadotte, laughed, her belly jiggled and she sounded like a child.

[Mr. Tanner—]

James Schoolcraft took her hand and put it on himself. Very soon he was on top of her and her knees were up and her heels clutching his back and his dough-white buttocks were clenching and it was then that I sensed up in a tree to my right a movement, and looked. I blinked, looked. Without a second's hesitation I rose and fled, ran back through the shifting, darkened woods—eyes closing on webs, stung by feathers of hemlock, my arms flailing; I snorted, then bawled, wanted to scream: I had seen Martha. There filled my chest a dread fury of love and hate, shame and the horrible conceit that it would have been better, at least on this night, had my Martha been the one under Schoolcraft. Lights came into view, the eaves of the woods opened; I ran home.

I sat at my table. My neck ached from some stumble or other, possibly a look back over my shoulder, a crash into a tree; I could not remember. I could hardly lift my head for the pain, so let it hang, which tormented me equally. I groaned and waited for Martha. I would talk to her. This night I would let nothing pass. If I simply went to bed and awoke to her sobs, I was half-afraid I'd kill her. What I had feared about James Schoolcraft had been true.

[Or it might not have been true.]

Or it might not have been true. He'd exploited Martha Ann, mocked me.

[Or he'd merely mocked you.]

Or he'd merely mocked me. Now, either way, he had cast us down together unawares.

I got up, cracked the door. The moon was burrowing through the clouds to the west. I squinted into the pale blue haze south over the river bend, listened to the rapids to the north, frogs chirping below in the alder marsh, and it came to me:

Martha needed a revelation.

I heard myself cackle a little crazily as I got down on my hands and knees and dragged the scarecrow out from beneath my bed. I stood it up and held it against the bedroom wall to catch my breath. Light strayed in from the other room, and when the thing moved, settling a bit against the wall, I nearly came out of my skin. It was a good scarecrow. Suddenly afraid Martha would come home too soon, I gathered the figure in my arms, hauled it through the house, and lugged it out over the mole-bloated grass and around back by the spaded, sweet-smelling earth of the garden and to the black hump of sticks and hides and moldering puk-kwi that was Martha's lodge. There I laid it down and threw the hide door-covering back over the top of the roof of the wigwam. I ducked into its sour, pitch-black closeness and pulled the fat scarecrow by the collar in after me and, kicking pillows and dolls out of the way, horsed and pivoted it around so that its boots were at the far end; I arranged him so that his chest abutted the bedding and a searching arm and gloved hand—fat, cold—reached up over the threadbare blankets. I threw the covers back over all but his legs and boots, put the pillows and dolls more or less where they'd been, then withdrew, dropped the door-hide back in place. Once back in the house, I pulled in the drawstring, blew out the lamp, and went to bed.

My listening kept me awake for what seemed hours. I pulled the blankets around myself tightly and folded my arms. I rubbed the bones of my elbows with my fingers. I felt happy. I fell asleep.

Though it was the scream I would remember, I could not be exact, later—when it seemed important to Bingham and others to recall such things—what woke me. I did not hear Martha try to get into the cabin. She may or may not have knocked. I heard her scream with a sense of expecting a scream. What sounds woke me were more like the muffled violence of a bear fight. Yet she screamed, and I shook—jolted less by the sound than the terrible revelation of my own wickedness—and jumped out of bed. She was already pounding on the door. I lifted the latch and she stood there naked to the waist in the cold dew-glow of moonlight. The sight of her was a shock. It was not for any man's eyes. Certainly not a father's. She pushed by and got behind me, pulling at my arm and then holding me, crying. I turned on her.

"Stop it!" I shouted. She was trembling. I pushed her away by her hips and, because I was the more terrified of the two of us, began to laugh. She looked at me. I laughed and laughed, clapping my hands and bending over. She gathered her arms over her chest and looked at me, comprehension slowly stealing over her fish-eyed horror. She pushed by me to go out. I followed her back to the lodge. She threw up the flap and peered in.

I howled and held my knees. "Did he—" I made my eyes big, held my hands out like claws "—*Getcha?*" I laughed until I had to stop and hold myself, stark sober and suddenly afraid I was going to pee.

Martha ran back to the house. By the time I reached the door she had the shotgun down. She pulled the hammers back. She brought it up. Her breasts rocked under her arms. Her teeth showed.

"Ayee!" she screamed.

I ducked to the right as she fired. The cabin wall at my shoulder exploded in splinters, dust and smoke, shards of glass. I slipped and fell on the floor. She shot again and soot rained over my back and a section of stovepipe clattered around the room. I heard her grunting, going after the rifle.

"Fucker!" she screamed.

"Martha!" I shouted. "God damn you!" I was under the table then. I kicked chairs at her.

"Ouch," she said. There was a thumping commotion as if she'd tripped.

I crawled out from under the table and threw myself headlong over the threshold and rolled onto my back on the planking of the stoop. I looked up as she lowered the aim of the rifle toward me, her face contorted; I rolled away into the grass as the stoop exploded. I staggered to my feet in an acrid fog of fear and smoke and ran, head pumping up and down, sore neck all but forgotten, down the road and dove not a quarter mile on into the woods, making a mental note not to leave my guns loaded, much less primed, in the future.

Hoh.

[His mouth is round, expressive of surprise or exhaustion, or surprise at exhaustion. I tell him that is enough for tonight. That I must go. He nods.]

18

[Last night's account sent me back to his first narrative, wherein an Indian girl, a child, was sent off into the snow of night, presumably to die, as punishment for burning down Tanner's family's lodge. Which disaster clearly was an accident. So had he horribly renounced his daughter for an action that was for all purposes an accident, such is love? What say he to this?]

By allowing the lodge to burn this girl had endangered all our lives. This needed to be impressed upon her. Do you think me unjust?

[I should say so. Most cruel.

Looks me hard in the eye, presses a finger to the table-top.]

It is made clear in my narrative that she did not die that night. I would not, even in my anger, have permitted that.

[Permitted.]

Correct. She was allowed back into the band and provided food and shelter. And Martha—

[Should one so persecute a victim? I ask him. I guess this is my point. Or with Martha were *you*, again—as with the lodge-burning—the victim?]

Let me speak.

[Please do.

He sits glaring, his features stone-still and frighteningly dark in the lamplight.]

Your questions will be answered. I require water.

I watched from the woods as men and women popped out of houses onto the moonlit street; there was a general questioning one of the other, and shouts to Martha, asking if she was all right and had I tried to kill her; a few walked over to see whether anyone was dead. As Martha was half-naked, it did not take long for there to be a dozen or more gathered in front of my house. She was crying convulsively now, and led them around back to show them the problem with her lodge. A man had his arm over her naked shoulder and another took up a position on her other side and put his arm across the naked small of her back. Someone went in the wigwam and came out dragging my scarecrow. This, and the sympathy bestowed on my daughter in her state of undress, upset me very much, and I emerged from my cover and ran over screaming in Ottawa that they all go. The dialect and red moon combined to what must been considerable effect; they scattered; there followed a banging of doors, whereafter the street was completely deserted but for Martha Ann, who stood there shivering in the receding echoes like a trophy of war. I took her inside and made her to go to bed. I was tender to her and apologized fervently and humbly, though none of this counted for very much later.

The next morning I did not want Martha to go to school. She did not argue. She went on her own out to the lodge and did not come out all morning. Bingham came. He brought with him Susan Johnston. I said nothing to them in response to their questions, but only motioned to the lodge. They went over and stood outside for a time talking to Martha, who still would not come out. They came back to the house.

Bingham waited looking grim as a granite ledge while Mrs. Johnston spoke. She spoke in Ojibwa and asked if they might come inside. I told her no, I was sorry. I did not wish them to see the scarecrow, which just then was sitting at the table with a terrible grin upon its stolen face. Of course I did not tell her this.

"We think it would be best if Martha came along with us," she said, looking at Bingham, who nodded as if he understood. "The Reverend will prepare a very pleasant room for her at the Mission, and you will be able to see her whenever you wish. She can visit you. It is for the best."

I told her no, that this could not be allowed, and I would kill any man who tried to take from me my daughter. This threat I addressed to Bingham, for I could not say such words to Mrs. Johnston.

"Why isn't she in school?" Bingham said, lipless mouth compressed.

"Why aren't you?" I asked him.

"Enough!" he said. His weight went from one foot to the other and back in lurching movements. "Look what this has come to! Did I not tell you I should act? Had I acted sooner your daughter might not have been nearly orphaned last night!"

"She has a mother," I said.

He looked for an instant confused. "I said *nearly*."

"Please go," I told them.

Bingham shouted, "You put a scarecrow in her lodge! An effigy of the devil! How could you commit such an act of sacrilege against a child of God—a mere girl! Your own daughter! In the name of God, John!"

I would never tell them, nor—until last evening—anyone, why; I simply told them it was for a joke.

"Come to the chapel!" he snorted. His face was veined and red, about to explode. "Now!"

I told him no.

"By God, John," he said, "this shall not stand!"

They turned and walked to the street, Bingham stopping to shout, "If she's not in school tomorrow, I'll be back with the sheriff!" and turned back once more to say again it would not stand.

I felt very low afterward. I had lost the respect of Mrs. Johnston, who I had liked very much. But I never threatened anyone again, or not for a long time, and the words said against me, you must understand, were untrue. I simply scared hell out of them. I came running out under the red moon shrieking in Ottawa. The rest was remembered from their nightmares.

James Schoolcraft lit out for Mackinac the first of April. I do not know if he feared Martha or had the foresight to fear me, but he was gone within a day or two of that night. I was relieved when I learned of this. My course with respect to him was not worked out then, and I was tired.

The funny thing is, things improved after that. Martha stopped going out. She stayed home and studied under the lamp at the table, leaning on an elbow and holding back her hair with one hand; she cooked and sewed. She cleaned and would glance up at me as I watched. I said nothing to her about that night, said little about my days, did not invite scorn; but she became quieter of expression, and a kind of peace between us grew. Also, I burned the scarecrow. I think this helped. The birds and rabbits had their way. I didn't care. It was good to be a father again. We grew corn and potatoes that summer. The war was not between us, but between Schoolcraft and Bingham over Cadotte and the Baptist annuity, and I took no side. In May, Schoolcraft went to the Legislative Council in Detroit, and I was able to fish in the coolness of morning and hunt evenings, and days tended the garden with Martha. I did not go to the Agency. In August Schoolcraft returned. I did not know for several days that he was back; he did not send for me. It was then, in the first days of August, that they took Martha.[1] It was by then without a shred of cause. School was not even in session yet. It caused me great anguish.

---

[1] While in Detroit, Schoolcraft introduced legislation entitled, "An act authorizing the sheriff of Chippewa County to perform certain duties therein mentioned." The law, passed July 30, 1830 by the Legislative Council of the Territory of Michigan, empowered the sheriff of Chippewa County (then

They took my daughter in the morning. Not even by killing might I have prevented Martha's theft. Your Bingham and your Hulbert and their women packed her up at the very hour I sat over a log a mile south of here in the cold yellow dawn, nursing a sick stomach and squinting to clear my eyes and bowels and thinking through the day's requirements, worrying over my poor daughter's needs like a string of beads; so that by the time I'd begun hunting they'd already put her on a boat with all her belongings, along with whatever she cared for of mine, and took her below to Detroit. In the afternoon, when I walked home, the whole town must have known it; not a soul was out. It was cool and the houses were webbed with the smoke of chimneys and a haze hung on the river from clearing fires on the Canadian side, and as I walked beneath the elms and sycamores on the road near my gate I heard the scuffling of bark and without turning counted four men following me. Men from Major Wilcox's company, it turned out, but I'd already guessed as much. They threw open the gate and rushed me at my door and shoved their way in. One grabbed my gun and another, bigger, put a hand to the side of my face and pushed me to the floorboards. When I got onto a knee and grabbed a chair, the man's face reared back in the door-light and my eye caught the glimmer of the brass butt of his gun just before he clubbed me in the face with it. I fell onto my back and they rattled the muzzles of their guns down on my chest, swore and breathed sharply through their teeth. One of them, a small man with red hair, thrust a hand forward and proclaimed in a womanish voice the words written across a trembling white

---

Schoolcraft's brother-in-law, John Hulbert) to remove Martha Tanner from her father's custody and directed she be taken to a mission or place of safety, and further stipulated that "any threats of the said John Tanner to injure the said Martha Tanner, or any person or persons with whom she may be placed "would be "punishable by fine and imprisonment, at the discretion of the court." It remains uncertain, outside the question of Tanner's loyalties and the infamous discord within the Tanner household, what motivated Schoolcraft's extraordinary action.

broadsheet. When he finished, he let the paper fall by my side. Their feet squirmed.

"Fie!" the small one with the nervous hand yelled; the others ducked a bit and looked confused, as if not sure whether they'd been ordered to shoot (it was a bad moment for me as well, I can tell you), and as I got my elbows under me they bumped their way backward out through the doorway. The small one shuffled about like a spaniel until he was safely out, then stuck his head back in to spit on my floor. "Fie!" he screamed again.

"Mind you!" I told him. It was all I could manage. I was, I will admit, at a loss. Their feet pounded up the street.

I got up from the floor and later studied, by the light of the lamp on the kitchen table—my eyes dimmed more by disbelief than the blow from the soldier's rifle-butt—the patterns on paper made by words yet ringing in my ears, crawling scribbles ordering my Martha's removal, and saw that the paper was indeed signed— perhaps, as asserted later by Schoolcraft—by Lewis Cass. I would-n't have thought it of him, for he was a just man and had never done anything but reached out his hand to help me; Henry Schoolcraft, him I instantly suspected. Only he was not in Ste. Mary's then; at least I thought he was still in Detroit; yet the words had borne his prejudices as they bore his way of piling sen-tences like wobbly steps up the face of a thunderhead, and there could be no question he'd had a hand in it.

Just raise your hand when you'd like tea, Miss Mesare. Ah. Well I'll have some anyway.

I complained to General Brady about the soldiers. Of course it did no good. What was done was done, he said stupidly. They were, up to a point, acting on orders. The two soldiers either side of me watched warily. "You have created much ill will and fear hereabouts," he said. "What goes around—"

"I want my daughter," I told him.

"She is not here," he replied. He was a calm and confident man some years older than me, with an eye that winked from a tic of some sort and drew my attention away from my central concern. I minded to be sure he was not thus communicating with the soldiers.

He looked at one then the other of the two. "Do I speak the truth? Is she in fact not here?"

They both said yes sir, and he winked at them.

I told him see my face what they did, and described the man that had hit me with his gun and the other that had spit on my floor.

"What would you have me do about it?" he said.

I thought a moment, then told him my arm is not strong, so have this man club you in the face with his gun. I will myself do the spitting.

One of the soldiers, the one I had indicated with my thumb, laughed, but the General shot him a glance and he turned solemn.

"Get out of here before I have you locked up," Brady said to me.

They saw me out.

I went to the Agency to ask after Schoolcraft, and was surprised to find him there in his antlered office. He was at his desk writing. He looked up slowly when the door opened, then started as might a cat on finding at its raised tail a dog sniffing; he scooted back his chair violently, but did not rise. He gave me a miserable little wave, called out for Jane. She entered the room and upon seeing me took on a look as one suddenly smelling blood.

"Dear, go and call on General Brady," he told her. "Ask if he and Mrs. Brady might join us for dinner tonight. Take the children."

"Of course. Good day, Mr. Tanner," Jane said quietly. She was pale as only an Irish-Indian can be pale, and I did not think her very pretty at that moment. I was half-tempted to say as much, such was my anger. I looked at her. She left the room, her shoulder bumping against the door casing.

216

Schoolcraft watched her go. "Are you ready to get back to work, Tanner?" he said. He looked fat and was tanned. He had whiskers now, I thought to make his face seem less fat. Outside it had begun to rain. The trees through the window behind him and the river beyond were blurred with rain. There were canoes overturned along the shore.

I asked him where was my daughter Martha Ann.

"I wouldn't know," he said. There was a babble of children complaining from within the residence; a door opened and closed. "Why do you ask me this now? Has she not been unaccountable?"

"She was taken," I told him.

"Not by me," he said.

"You lie," I said. I felt a tail-twitch at the base of my spine.

"Never speak to me thus," he said. He tried to appear firm, but his features would not resolve to it; he looked afraid. It occurred to me he had sent Jane after soldiers. Jane, who was now with his children out in the rain.

I told him in a strong voice that he was weak and cowardly and had used the legislative council to bring grief upon me because he was not such a man as could take my daughter himself, and now sent his wife and children out into the rain to bring him help against a crippled old man, and that in the Indian world he would have been killed for such despicable and dishonorable behavior. I shouted show me my daughter now. I stepped forward toward his desk as I spoke this.

Schoolcraft turned in his chair toward the window as if seeking a way of escape.

"Yes," he said in a trembling voice, "I see it's raining." He looked back over his shoulder at me, then rose and touched the window sash. I believe he did intend for a passing instant to open it and jump out. He then leaned against the wall next to the window and faced me.

I picked up from his desk the blade he used to open letters. My hand shook. "You *injure* me!" I screamed.

His mouth opened and he let out a moan as one about to die by murder; he grabbed the seat of his pants. I knew then that for all his bluff and boasting he was, in truth, a coward.

"Cass!" he said. "Is it not his signature upon the document? Would I not undo what injuries he has done you? Have I not been—" and at that moment the door at my back opened and several wet Indian faces appeared there looking quite alarmed. Schoolcraft shouted their names, as they were locals known to him, appearing very happy to see them. I took it upon myself at that point to leave, knowing that in any event I had said my due and also that soldiers would be along any time. I had one more thing to say, and delivered this message from beyond the doorway: "I'll have the wages due me!"

I went to the Mission House. I found the door locked and pounded upon it repeatedly and called for Bingham, but he would not come out or show his face in the window, so I stated my grievances for him and his family from where I stood in the street in the pouring rain. People about stopped and observed me from a distance. I told Bingham that if he would come out I would go with him to the chapel, where we would examine what his actions, now that he had acted, had worked upon me. I then recited his "Prepare" speech, and advised him mind its message that he might be received into the Kingdom of God. This was cited later as a clear threat against the Reverend's life, although I was careful to frame my words in the most general and disarming manner. I did not swear; I did not throw stones through every window of his house; I did not in direct language call his children into danger. Yet all these things I would later be accused of. It did not matter.

I went to the Fort to see Dr. James. I was quickly surrounded by soldiers and led away. I went thence to that area of the stockade on the west side closest his office and stated in a voice sufficient to be heard within that his part in the taking of my daughter was not unknown to me, and that he would not be under the protection of soldiers outside the Fort. The first was not entirely true, but he had made me look so ridiculous in the narrative, I was then learning, that I suspected him of everything. That and the money issue (did you think me such a fool?) had festered. This seemed as good a time as any to be heard out. The second statement about protection outside the Fort, that was a simple statement of fact. Not, technically, a threat.

I ran around to the east side of the stockade and similarly addressed John Hulbert, who as I think I've said was suttler of the commissary. Where I positioned myself did not matter, I realized. The entire garrison could hear me. Men were crowding the towers, filling the slits between the pilings; ladders were thrown up so that eyes could peer over the pointed teeth of the stockade. People from town gathered near both corners of the wall in growing numbers. Canoes held against the river's current; Canadians amassed upon the opposing shore.

It came upon me then, having assembled such an audience and having been schooled by Bingham in the art of divine terror, that I should make an impression on these townsfolk. Who, after all, be it actively or sympathetically, had not taken part in the abduction of my Martha Ann? And how much time might be saved, versus a tedious door-to-door approach later, if I acted here and now? I resolved to give them all a revelation.

"Know this, all of you!" I shouted, throwing up my arms, or the one I could (my voice boomed back from the stockade like thunder—in fact it thundered at that instant; I ducked a bit), "I am as the water that rises from the ground and the rain that falls!"

They waited, motionless, struck fast by my words. I was struck by the discomfiting feeling that I didn't know, in English, what to say next. I had strayed, in my exuberance, and perhaps because of the storm, into something like a medicine song. I had no time to think, so went with it: "I walk about in the night time! I am such! I am such, my friends! I hear your mouth! Now I come up out of the ground! Your own tongue kills you!"

They were motionless. Silent. Thunder rumbled.

"You have too much tongue!"

A small boy at the far end of the stockade by Portage came alone a distance from the group there and now put his tongue out and danced in a circle. A few people laughed. His mother ran out to retrieve him. She shouted at me in red, hysterical anger. This produced more laughter. I suddenly realized I could lose them. My mind raced. I cast about through what I could remember of the medicine songs, translated feverishly.

"Throw off, woman, thy garments! Throw off!" I bawled at the top of my voice, and instantly regretted my choice.

The woman stopped and turned on me, pointed indignantly. Then many soldiers shouted at once to the woman, using my words, and the laughter in the rain became as the falls. It grew into a roar that echoed off the stockade wall, and when I turned to walk away in disgust the children started running after me. I turned on them. They screamed. A man ran up.

"Look in Detroit!" he said. He tilted his head. "For God's sake, man, get hold of yourself! What's one child more or less?"

That night I paced my tiny house clutching at my clothing, my face. My chest burned, my brain was exploding. I pounded the table with my fist. *The injustice!* I stood outside and howled that I might not weep. I cried out in Ottawa at my fate, swore oaths against the Gitche Manito as well as Bingham's God. The town was otherwise silent, as if under a spell. After a time I went in and sat down, exhausted, and composed a very strong letter to Governor Cass. I wrote it upon the back of the document that bore his signature. It was, I knew, a pitiful letter, knotty mess of misspelled grunts and scattered kekeewun, but in the morning I handed it to the first man I met on the street that was not a Frenchman or Indian and demanded he mail it to the Governor. The man, Ethan the butcher's man, as it turned out, agreed to this without a word.

I did not venture back to the Agency. Schoolcraft, who was never again to be seen unaccompanied by guards, sent word in a few days that I was dismissed, and sent along as well enough of my pay that I was able to purchase passage on a schooner that would take me below to Detroit. I hoped I would find Martha there, and that I might arrive ahead of my letter. It, the letter, would require some explanation. If I did not find her there, I would go on to Washington to lay the matter before the Great American Father. I made my preparations.

Tomorrow we go to Detroit again. Do you know, Miss Mesare, something wonderful happened to me there.

[I tell him something wonderful needed to happen to him. Wouldn't hurt him now, either. I might suggest salvation versus revelation.]

I do hate it when you leave.

19

It was very warm south of the Saginaw Bay. A haze rose in yellow streaks into gray cloudless skies, and the winds were so poor that the sails hung limp or filled as half-empty sacks. I suffered in my buckskins, and would have preferred to have been in a canoe that I might have reached into the water; in Detroit it was but much worse. There had been rain only days before and the air was like steam. Dogs laid about wracked with panting. I looked once at the window of a shop as I walked on my way to the Governor's house, and saw how it was I looked. But there was nothing I could do.

Cass suffered from the heat as well, so was not seeing visitors in his office. It was as well a Saturday. The sentry reminded me of this, but I begged he carry word of me inside; when he did, Cass sent word out that he would receive me in his residence. I found him undressed to the waist and seated at a table wearing the same hat of yellow straw such as you see farmers or scarecrows wearing. The room had several windows open. I looked for animals outside about the farm but saw none, and guessed then that the Governor's bowels were discomposed. I asked him was this the case. He laughed and was very forthcoming and called his condition mutinous. And with such heat, he said. He told me how it was first thing in the morning. Not every morning, he said, but the Poop Fairy set her own schedule. He explained his condition thus. I was distressed to hear the Governor talk to me in so personal a fashion, and to speak seriously of woodland spirits (not that such a fairy in Algonquin lore was known to me), so asked him abruptly why had he made a law to take my Martha away. He denied any knowledge of it; when told of my treatment by the soldiers and how Schoolcraft had said ask Cass about it, he seemed quite upset, and said in any case he signed bills willy-nilly all the time.

"I will write Schoolcraft and set things aright," he said. He looked doubtful. "Why do you think they took her?"

I told him I did not know, but thought it best he be told by me about the scarecrow. As I was doing this he raised a hand to stop me and called for Mrs. Cass.

I was happy to see her again. I apologize that I have failed to mention Mrs. Cass, as I met her on my previous visits and she was always very kind to me. She sat next to me now, and when I then started again about the scarecrow she made a face as though to cry.

"Mind you," the Governor said to her, "I'll remember that one when next you criticize my company."

She laughed loudly then, and I saw they both understood that the scarecrow, beyond a terrible mistake, had been meant as a joke as well as a lesson. She put her arm over my shoulder and brought my head to press against her own. I resisted—not to be impolite, but from concern over being unbathed—and after a brief struggle had then a good visit. Mrs. Cass made us lemonade and showed me many card tricks. I protested that I did not believe in magic, and had her show me a particular trick several times, then how she did it. She seemed quite jolly, although when she told the Governor about the Scots Ball, it made them both unhappy.

There had been many French balls on Mackinac and at Ste. Mary's, but no Scots balls. Here in Detroit they had both. The ball was the following night. Cass did not want to go. Mrs. Cass did not want to go. He did not feel he could refuse. She said, "Of course not, Dear," and they looked at the floor. I asked why they did not want to go. I told them of the French ball at Mackinac that I had gone to and taken Therezia. Therezia did not dance, but drank very much and was happy to get away from the children. Afterward she had thanked me. I was not thanked very often, so would have taken her to more French balls, only she became Catholic.

"But the French are all Catholic," Mrs. Cass said.

I told her the Sisters did not approve of our Indian marriage.

"What has that to do with it?" she asked.

I told her they did not countenance the thanking. She looked at me as you do now.

Cass brightened and said to Mrs. Cass, "I know what!" and asked her to find the invitation. She did this and he went to a cabinet that dropped open to make a desk, wherein he found an inkwell and pen, and he took a seat and wrote upon the invitation. I was relieved to see him happy again, though Mrs. Cass looked uncertain. Then the Governor went out of the room to put on a shirt and jacket and, coming out, put on his straw hat again and sent a man to prepare his carriage.

He rode with me to the Woodworth Hotel. The hotel was a long white frame building very much like Ferris's mission school at Mackinac, but with a veranda across the front, and was located not far from the Governor's mansion; on the way he talked about Indian affairs and of the Indian Agency at Ste. Mary's. I told him I thought the Agent Schoolcraft might be of a better temperament if he worked less and got out more, to which Cass nodded agreement. He had plans to get him out in a real and meaningful way next year.[1] He told me then that Schoolcraft had volunteered to name all of the townships in the Michigan Territory; Cass thought

---

[1] Schoolcraft's expedition to the northern Minnesota Territory for the purpose of gauging Indian hostilities, encouraging fealty to the federal government, and vaccinating the Indian population against Cholera would embark in only ten months, in June 1831.

it wonderful Schoolcraft had decided that half were to be named after notable Indians, and the other half after General Wayne's officers that had killed them. He mentioned also the Indian Removal Bill, which he said made him sick but was the only course left open given the speed of western migration; then he went with me inside the hotel.

In the lobby Cass led me to the counter where Mrs. Woodworth, who knew him, threw out her hands and shouted that her husband and those employed by the Woodworth's might come and greet the Governor. Cass introduced me and told them I was a personal friend who had led a most interesting life, of which was told in a book just published in New York and London.[2] Cass slapped me on the back. "Treat him well or I'll have the Secretary examining your license," he said, and they smiled. He handed a paper to Mr. Woodworth and spoke to him, then said goodbye and asked me to come outside with him.

"John," he said. *"John, John, John."* He stood close and, squinting into the sunlight, said, "Listen to me, John. You are to go the Scots ball tomorrow evening as the Governor's representative. The assignment is imperative. I am counting on you, John. One thing is important. Tell them you are a Whig. Can you remember that? A Whig. Otherwise you are permitted to enjoy yourself. Woodworth will see to everything. He is a good man. I will see you Monday morning. Come and report to me Monday, John." He seemed very serious.

He climbed into the carriage.

I was left alone.

Inside, I was examined closely by all until Mr. Woodworth clapped his hands twice, upon which signal I was taken upstairs and shown my room by a small dark woman not Mrs. Woodworth. It was a small room but bright and comfortable. The wom-

---

[2] The narrative was subsequently published in Paris in 1835, and in Leipzig in 1840 without the sections on Algonquin vocabularies.

an, who told me her name was Wildereen Duncan, made me a bath in another room, and I bathed until the water was very nearly cold. Afterward I was hungry, but too tired to dress, so laid down upon the bed while it was still light and listened to the gulls. It made me think of Ste. Mary's and all that had happened there, and I felt after a while very sad. It grew dark and I fell asleep.

[I think the water is ready, I say.]

Yes, thank you, Miss Mesare.

In the morning I went outside quite before the sun was up, and found the woman sitting there on a bench wrapped in a blanket and smoking a small clay pipe and staring across the street that had shown me my room and prepared for me the bath. She looked up and said hello, and I thanked her for her kindness of the night before.

"Is that an accent, or a pallet deformity?" she said. She made a smile as though she'd forgotten to be polite and it had just occurred to her. She had a small mouth, and it was a taut and sudden smile.

I was accustomed to questions about my speech early in a conversation, so—if I did not understand her perfectly—told her I had been raised by the Ottawa and had only recently, as a man, learned English. Many had helped me, but my English was still very poor. I hoped it would improve.

"My grandmother always said the truest sentiments are not spoken," she said, still with the small smile.

I told her it was good her grandmother had made that one exception. She frowned and looked across the street. There was nothing of interest in the direction she looked. A few small houses; behind them, trees. Pigeons walking back and forth along the rooftops, occasionally flapping their wings and jumping upon one another; the sun was rising and would soon be in our eyes; there were a few streaked clouds. It was not an interesting view. I asked what did she look at.

"What is it you want of me?" she said.

I told her I sought nothing of her.

"Then we'll get along," she said. She smoked her pipe, looking across the street. "Sit down if you like, it's a free country." She moved her blanket.

She was silent a minute, then told me she started every day collecting her thoughts and planning. She had a great deal to attend to and she needed this time to think. It was her one time of day. She would tolerate me this morning, but don't look for any special treatment tomorrow.

I understood and thanked her. She was very small and dark, had a nose like a cupboard drawer knob, and wore spectacles. Her hair lay upon her shoulders in disorderly waves as if just unbraided. I thought her pretty in an odd way. I wondered if she was Indian or part Indian. Her given name sounded Indian, but I could not make it out as meaning anything. The nose was decidedly not Indian. Indians could be very small, though. Therezia was not small. I had this preference for small women. I had no prejudice against Indian women or big women, but I liked that this one did not look at all like Therezia. I spoke none of this.

"I suppose you want me to make up your bed and get you breakfast," she said.

She did not need to do anything for me, I told her. She could think and plan first. I was happy to keep quiet in order she might do this.

"So you're a friend of the Governor?" she said.

I told her yes, Cass was a very kind man and done much to help me. I was here that he might help me once more. I told her about Martha and asked if she'd seen or heard of her. She said no. I told her I was going to the ball tonight as the Governor's representative. She said she knew that, but could not be impressed. She was a Whig. I asked her please explain, and she explained a long time about Democrats. When she finished, I told her I would attend tonight as a Whig. She offered me a pipe. We smoked together. She wanted to know about my narrative, so I told her about the City of New York and the Carvill's and Inman. After that she became more friendly, and in time made a good breakfast of eggs and ham and sat with me and talked about her own writing, and then about city and territorial politics. She talked a long time. She was a woman of passion and possessed good knowledge on every subject, and I was very pleased to listen to her talk. After this we went upstairs. As she made up my bed she talked about how a hotel should be properly run; if the Woodworth's put her in charge for just one day, she said, she could straighten this one out. She thought one could make a business telling proprietors how to do things. She was, I decided, the most intelligent woman I had ever met.

She told me her husband Wallace had died four years before. They had gone west to make a new life on Portage Prairie near St. Joseph, where the soil was black as coal and the Pottawatomi's docile as cats, and what did Mr. Duncan do but felled a tree right on top of himself. It was just like him, she said. So she went home to Dexter, then on to Detroit, where she took a position in a fish market that fronted a busy street and offered its backside to the steaming, reeking chaos of the wharf; there she watched in horror as the fishmongers, crafty and dexterous as magicians, rolled, blink-quick, lumps of copper or lead between their fingers and cheated customers at the scales. She complained and lost her position. To one bureaucrat after another she went, seeking justice and a crumb of retribution, and in no time was assisting blank-eyed, stupid—though in some cases, in some measure, earnest—territorial officials in the development of regulations for the fish trade. She advanced, but only to encounter sneering misogyny, intractable corruption, and predictable incompetence, and soon determined to be rid of the frustration and abuse and retired. But she had misjudged her wealth and appetites and was soon exhausted of money. Now *this* was her lot. *Not*, she said, making a gesture, *for long*.

She had other rooms to make up, and as I listened to her talk to one or two other men on various subjects, I felt strangely displeased. I thought she must talk to dozens of men every day. She was telling a man several rooms away about Mayor Williams's dog. The Mayor's Pug had been taught by His Honor to sing and to throw back its head and howl, "Mayor, I love you!" But having strayed out alone into the Mayor's city, the dog was now learning many other phrases and songs as could be read as cartoon captions in the *Gazette* or provided, in this case, by Wildereen. The man laughed and said something that made Wildereen laugh in return. At this I clenched my teeth and went downstairs and out for a long walk.

When I got back she pretended to be pleased to see me; she cocked a shoulder and called me "Howdy." She looked a bit odd doing this, with her spectacles and lump of a nose, but I decided then and there that any displeasure I had felt was false or unimportant, and determined that this small dark one would be favored in my imaginings that night—or, if I fell asleep too quickly, in the morning— But it was not necessary, Miss Mesare. You see, something wonderful happened to me.

[Lord help us.]

What happened first was that Wildereen, that was her name, accompanied me to the Scots Ball. I was a little fearful about going; she said she had a solution, that I did not have to go alone. She thought it would be very good, the ball, for my contacts and exposure, and that I might surprise everyone and enjoy myself as well, and she would see to everything. I told her Mr. Woodworth was to see to everything, and she made with her hand an upward fluttering gesture that I came to learn meant she did not suffer fools gladly.

"Then go on and check your arrangements with Woodworth," she said. "I'm going out for a smoke." And she went out. I did as she suggested, then found her and apologized.

Later in the afternoon, Mr. Woodworth, who asked me to call him Ben, knocked on the door of my room and carried in a bundle of clothes and leather strapping that he dropped upon the bed. The Governor wished I be properly attired for the ball, he told me.

"This is your purse," he said, picking up a silver box. "It will not match your shoes, but tonight that shouldn't matter." He smiled. Woodworth was tall and bald and boldly friendly. He stood too close and had foul breath. He insisted on helping me dress. I sat on the bed a long time after, wondering about this friend of the Governor's, and if I could go out dressed so.

I had come to know Scots during my employ hunting buffalo with the Hudson Bay Company. Lord Selkirk had moved one hundred Scots onto the Red River settlement at the Assiniboine, and Mr. Hanie engaged me to secure meat to provision them. I there killed over two hundred bulls and fat cows, and, as the herd was at a great distance from the settlement, Hanie sent out twenty Scots laborers, and four clerks to beat them, to retrieve the meat. I thought them, the Scots, the most brutal and disgusting men I had ever met,[3] and my estimation would not have been improved had they dressed in the fashion Woodworth proposed. Nor did I want to be mistaken for one of them.

I was thinking these thoughts when Wildereen knocked on the door. She was dressed in a skirt like mine, though slightly longer, and a hat with a partridge feather pinned to it, and looked very

---

[3] Tanner was employed hunting for four months in the summer of 1817 on the prairies west of present-day Winnipeg. "Even when they had plenty, [the Scots] …ate like starved dogs, and never failed to quarrel over their meat. The clerks frequently beat and punished them, but they would still quarrel." See John Tanner, *A Narrative of the Captivity and Adventures of John Tanner (U. S, Interpreter at the Saut de Ste. Marie) During Thirty Years Residence Among the Indians in the Interior of North America* (Minneapolis: Ross & Haines, Inc., 1956), 193.

pleasing. She did not fail to tease me, and such was my consternation at this that I determined to take off the Scots clothes. She desisted and became her serious self and we went downstairs, where Mrs. Woodworth called me her highlander. I felt considerable trepidation as we waited for our carriage. I would rather the Governor had sent me out alone to kill an army of Scots.

But do you know, Miss Mesare, I had a fine time that night. Or I did for a while. There was a platform raised upon a gathering of crates in the middle of a warehouse or armory or some such, and troops of dancers or bagpipers or drummers or assortments of these would ascend to the platform and dance or play or drum or both; and Wildereen, who sat close at my side and saw that I was supplied with whiskey—which on this night against my better judgment I did not refuse—would instruct me on what was happening or being played, and tell me the merit of each performance. She leaned against me and moved a great deal with the music, and kept time to one song with her hand patting not her own knee but mine. This familiarity increased, but I did not object. At one point during the music I looked at Wildereen and—as she had moved her spectacles up onto her head, so pushing her hair back from her forehead, and the heat and excitement had reddened her cheeks—noticed she looked very pretty. I told her close to her ear that she was glowing like a tree afire, and she smiled and blinked her eyes and looked a little drunk.

The Scots music was very loud in my good ear, but I found it satisfactory and very much like Indian singing. We ate Scots food and it was very good. Then everyone stood and sang "Auld Lang Syne." It was up to this point that I had a good time. Then the dancings commenced.

I cannot tell you, reader, the humiliation and trouble I then endured. There was a table near the dancing space where whiskey was being poured and I spent as much time at that table as possible; but Wildereen was a dancer, and if I was to remain near her I was compelled to dance. I had never, not in my childhood or youth or adulthood, neither with the Indians or whites, enjoyed dancing. I took pains to avoid it. I was never one for show or exhibitions. I thought of dancing as a bodily expression of the mind's passions, and always wondered if men dancing knew what they were telling of themselves. I preferred to keep my passions in check or to beat the party provoking them; dancing had never a place in my order of conduct. But reader, on this night I danced. There was my duty to the Governor as his representative, and there was Wildereen as well, so I danced. This dancing consisted of rapid shuffling and occasional leaps into the air. After each dance all would clap hands to show approval of each other's dancing, and Wildereen would laugh, and I would hold my aching right side and lick at my teeth with a dry tongue and try to steer Wildereen back to the whiskey table. But then the music would start up, and we'd be back at it.

Wildereen danced very earnestly. She looked sometimes at me, but mostly her eyes were cast downward or off to one side. By this I could see she was serious about her dancing and danced very well, or was of this opinion. She moved her hips more than most of the women her age (she was a number of years older than me, which is to say not young), and did things with her hands in the air. Even with spectacles glittering upon her nose, the effect was creditable. At one point she brought our bodies into contact and moved herself against me. I smelled her hair and for some reason, perhaps to slow her dancing, I pressed my hands tenderly to the small of her back, or slightly below.

Soon after this I realized I had become very drunk, and upon stumbling into a woman decided to sit at a table. It was not our table. It did not matter. Wildereen disappeared the instant I sat down. She was dancing with other men. I got up and went to the whiskey table, balefully surveyed the room, sat down again. Time passed. In all that time Wildereen was not to be seen, but was nonetheless visible to me out on the floor waggling her hands and feet in the air and looking down or off to one side, pressing up against chosen strangers, dancing. I became at first morose over my neglect, then very angry. I determined to leave. I would leave and walk back to the hotel and never speak to this woman with the small sudden smile again. I went first to the whiskey table to thank the woman there. She told me that from what she could tell I'd had enough. I did not thank her then, but did my duty to the Governor and told her I was a Whig and that she could go hang herself. Then I left by a back door with the help of several men.

Outside it was black night. I took two steps, whereupon I slipped in something and fell headlong upon the cobbles. I got onto my feet with some difficulty, and after satisfying myself that I had not broken my bad arm started walking in the direction I judged from the lights to be that of the City of Detroit. A man stopped me and asked was I all right. I told him yes thank you and he said no you're not and took me by the arm and led me around the warehouse or armory and back in through the front door. In the light I saw there was blood all down my shirt and Scots jacket. The man asked who I was with and I told him. Someone found Wildereen and brought her to me. She was very alarmed at my appearance and called for a wet towel and with this cleaned a considerable quantity of blood from the left side of my face. She asked what I'd been up to. I told her just getting some air. She called me a silly fool and was very tender towards me. My anger thus subsided.

We were taken back to the hotel in the buckboard of the man that had found me bleeding; Wildereen sat next to and spoke to this man throughout the drive about farming, as the man let it be known he was a farmer, and told him the names of prominent farmers she was acquainted with and of the relative merits of various farming programs the man might want to look into, and was just getting onto the subject of dairy subsidies when we arrived at the hotel; the man asked once more to be sure that I was all right, then said goodnight.

At the door of the hotel Wildereen turned to me.

"So what do you want to do?" she asked me.

I told her what I wanted to do. This with six or seven words, none of which were unspecific or polite. She was looking with keys clutched in the fingers of one hand, her chest still and small, head tilted back. I looked to judge her reaction, but could not see her eyes behind the spectacles. Then I saw her move up. Then again moving up. She continued moving up.

"I see you're feeling better," she said.

"That could change," I told her.

"Can you make it up the stairs?" she said.

I had determined by our conversation earlier that her room was on the first floor, so told her no.

"All right then," she said, in a tone as one presented an unpleasant task, and we went in.

Wildereen's room was in the back of the hotel off the kitchen. There was one window and the light of the moon fell upon the bed. The bed was pushed against the wall. It was not a single bed, but a stacked pair. There looked to be someone in the bottom bunk. I stepped closer, reached to steady myself with a hand on the upper bed, and looking down at the sleeping figure perceived that it was very big. Wildereen did not light a candle.

"Upstairs or downstairs?" she said.

Thinking she was again giving me the choice of going up to my room, I thought a moment, discounted the strangeness of the arrangement, and said, "Downstairs," whereupon she drew back the bedding of the lower bunk to expose a large field of striped nightshirt to a shaft of moonlight, and slapped at it. The figure, Mrs. Woodworth's figure, rolled toward the wall.

"I'll be right back," Wildereen said. Her hand whispered upon the door, found the knob, and she went out. I heard an outer door and understood he'd gone out to the privy. I undressed and got into the bed. It was warm between the sheets and smelled clean. Though I was dismayed to find myself in bed with Mrs. Woodworth, I was of a practical nature and at that moment very sick, so

I stayed put, only propping myself up on an elbow so the room did not move so violently. I listened for Wildereen. Mrs. Woodworth rolled over, threw a leg upon me (I pushed it away), and recommenced to snore.

When Wildereen came back in, I laid back and closed my eyes and pretended to be sleeping. It made me ill to lie back and close my eyes. She approached the side of the bed. I heard her undressing and laying her clothes upon a chair. Then, Miss Mesare, I felt the bed move and opened my eyes. I beheld in the moonlight Wildereen Duncan crawling naked, innocent as a child, up the far end of the bed, her ankles disappearing as she drew onto the top bunk. I heard, felt, her burrow beneath the covers. The room was still rolling.

It was then—or, rather, in the morning, after Mrs. Woodworth awoke and with a flushed, saw-toothed smile said good morning and went to see to Mr. Woodworth, and in spite of losing my breath some moments later on finding the image of a coiled blue snake and the words DON'T TREAD ON ME tattooed over Wildereen's heart—that something wonderful happened to me.

Do you dance, Miss Mesare?

[Is it your object to shock me?]

Do you go to the balls? There still are, are there not, the French balls.

[Not all French, I tell him.]

Do you go?

[I do not answer.]

With James Schoolcraft?

[My personal life, I tell him, is none of his concern.]

I thought we were friends.

[Then behave as one. Respect my privacy.]

Is he not old for you?

[At this I stood and, feeling attacked on the basis of my associations and pressed on an indefinably yet vaguely frightening personal level, chastised my host with some vehemence on his poor manners and cruel inclinations. He declaimed back, slandering James Schoolcraft and asking what kind of woman, setting herself up as an example to children, would have anything to do with such a man. My temper rose, as did his, and I left hastily, lest he lay a hand on me. I did not go back the two succeeding nights. I shared my experience with my friend James. This, I fear, was a bad error, as he has now assigned someone from the Fort, one of the outliers with whom he meets to play cards, to look after me. Should I never have been pressed to tell him of my project at all!]

{Last bracketed entry is in Mesare's longhand.}

20

[All is prepared: a fire is burning again on this very warm evening; the kettle hangs above, steaming; yet there is not a lamp lit. Mr. Tanner says not a word as I prepare. He seems satisfied I am here, as he evidently expected, or as if incognizant of the fact I was not here the night preceding or the night before that. He designs, I suppose, to injure my feelings.

I ask if he is ready, and he nods, his face cast downward, watching me with eyes half-hidden by his heavy brows.

He begins to speak. Every quiet word, as though I should transcribe thunder, is spoken in an Indian dialect.

I pack up and leave as he goes on. He neither stops nor moves.]

{Last two paragraphs entered in Mesare's longhand, subsequent to event.}

21

I spent the next several days in Detroit. I slept secretly with Wildereen in the swaying, crashing top bunk, and staggered out into the light Monday morning and the next morning and morning after morning after that, but did not find Martha. I did not gain word of her. I sailed back to Mackinac aboard the Totosh[1] on the 23rd of August. Wildereen refused to see me off. She had dined with another guest of the Woodworth Hotel two nights before, which second act of neglect I failed to condone as I should have, and this put her against me. I had asked questions that would have seemed sensible anywhere but there in Detroit. Detroit was a modern city, and one led a modern life there; to ask questions attacked the honor of the party questioned. I would learn one did not question Wildereen wherever. You did not question anything. If you did, you where left to devices cast off since meeting her. That and you otherwise did not know. Rules were as she made them, and she made them readily, as she was a very intelligent woman. Much of what I came to understand came later, but even that week in Detroit I was never entirely sure of myself in her company, yet was very unhappy to leave her.

Governor Cass sent out assurances he would write Schoolcraft, but would not receive me. I fingered and picked at the wounds

---

[1] *Female breast* in Ojibwa; possibly a mistake on Tanner's, or Mesare's, part. No ship of that name is found in registries of the period.

tightening down the left side of my face, winced at the sun (clouds covered it), as the sentry resumed his pacing. I felt as one rebuked. I was not allowed to explain about the ball, or my bloody Scots uniform, nor my nights with the Woodworth's housekeeper. I felt as a son disowned. Nor was it possible to go on to Washington. I had assumed anything possible after my journey to the City of New York, but now I had no money, and no letter, nor help of any kind from Governor Cass. And not even Wildereen came out to see me off.

I was alone then, alone as I had not felt since being taken from my family by the Saginaw. I was tormented. I chased down old men and women and young children on the streets of Ste. Mary's and huffed into their fear-twisted faces in grief-broken English where is my Martha Ann, what have you done with her—but it was false; my rage was against Wildereen, or my violent need of her. My heart clenched at the thought of another guest lying awake listening for her return from the privy. I was visited by visions of her formless nose and flashing spectacles; they ate at my heart. Yet that too, all of it, was false. It was not, or not entirely, Wildereen at all. It took me years to understand: I feared aloneness. I understood only that I was confounded and denied and in great suffering. Nothing, nor God, could have comforted me. Though, of course, Bingham, who was not home when I pounded on his door that day, and who had, in any case, forgiven me, tried.

"How are we sleeping, John?" he'd ask.

I told him I did not sleep, or slept fitfully. If I slept it was only to wake needing to relieve myself, whereupon I would sleep no more that night. I awoke sick with woe. My appetite had withered; my belly howled, yet I could not eat.

"Are you drinking?"

I looked at him. "I do not drink," I said; "drink has done its worst in my life." I told him nothing about the occurrences in Detroit. I never told anyone. Cass may have; I don't know.

239

"With my blessing you might have a drink before you go to bed," he said. He was looking across the empty chapel. "It might help." His face flinched as he said this. I nodded, thought about Wildereen dancing, the air filled with fierce music, wild laughter.

He asked was I praying, and I told him not at present.

"I mean generally," he said. "Do you seek the Lord's comfort?"

I did. It didn't seem to help.

"His grace will be revealed to you," he said. "Keep praying."

"I will drink and pray," I told him.

He looked at me as if to scold, then took out his pipe. "Good," he said.

I had frightened a good many people, he said, and needed to rein in the demons that caused me to act so; if Martha had been taken away, it was out of love and concern for her as well as her father, and that which had occurred had occurred by the will of God, and no man should question it. If I had allowed her to board at the Mission none of it would have been necessary, and my life would have been spared loneliness now. We all miss Martha, he said, and he himself wished I had complied to his requests, that she might still be here in Ste. Mary's to delight him daily with her presence at the school. She had a natural aptitude, and he thought she might have soon helped with the teaching. It was a shame. He shook his head, blew a ring of smoke into a shaft of window-light. "Now some other school will have her," he said sadly.

All the time he spoke, I was thinking of Wildereen. I too knew Martha was better off. I had not been an altogether wicked father, but life had been wicked for Martha in my home. But my concern was for Wildereen now. Or for myself. I had taken to praying that Wildereen's heart might be softened towards me. I prayed this in the morning, standing outside the doorway looking out over the Ste. Mary's, watching the gulls and eagles and ospreys, and I was praying it now, for that which might change by my prayers and pull the pins that afflicted my mind and heart and end my pain and aloneness and otherwise there was, would be, nothing. My thoughts strayed to the Ste. Mary's and thence to the Mother of Our Lord, and it came to me as a lightning bolt that I might have impregnated Wildereen; the idea gripped me like a fever. *If only*, I thought, *if only I have impregnated her.* By such grace—slathering grunt, spurt of life—might my prayers have been already answered. I became agitated and asked Bingham could I be excused.

"You have to go somewhere?"

I told him I must write a letter.

"I could help you with that," he offered.

I thought he might at least help me with the word "impregnate," but instead told him perhaps not, and bid him good day. I hurried to the Mission House. A pair of women there caught sight of my approach and hitched up their skirts to flee like deer in opposite directions.

Dr. James and I had been working all through the year on the Ojibwa Gospels in the room I have described with the two tables and stacks of books. A great many sheets of paper were laid in store there, and inks and quills and pens. I sat down at the table and pulled the cork from a squat green glass bottle of ink and dipped into it the tip of a pen. I bit my tongue, brought my nose to the page, sought to draw words. But it was no good, I had not the skill. I muttered, tried to concentrate. Finally, my fist holding the pen death-white, I resorted to a kekeewun image of a woman with a circle-belly, within which sat cross-legged a tiny stick-man that brought to mind Ais-kaw-ba-wis pouting in his lodge; I followed this with a question mark. I took it home and started my stove-fire with it.

That afternoon I sought out Dr. James. It was early for our day's work, but he had no obligations, so came out of the Fort, hair rumpled and eyes dark, to walk silently with me to the Mission House. He sat at the table and scratched at his forehead, took before him a half-filled page, opened the Bible to leaf through it a minute, then asked was I ready. I nodded.

He read to me a verse from the Gospel of St. Luke. I thought a moment, said the Ojibwa for it. He wrote. He read, I spoke, and he transcribed again. This was how we worked, and we had worked thus now a year. When the page was full, he laid it upon the stack of transcript and drew from the other table a fresh sheet. I did not listen to him after that, other than to note when he stopped to await my translations. My mind was very busy. My heart pounded.

I thought poetry would be effective, so said in the Ojibwa, in the style of the feast-song:

"I reach out to you, I reach; my heart is filled with sadness. I am lonely and dream of the great feast under the moon; your breasts and stomach I feast. I lay upon you. Under the moon I lay upon you and enter you and see your mouth open and your tongue up-on your lips. Hear the wildcat; you are the wildcat."

Dr. James looked up at me suspiciously once or twice, but kept transcribing. (Of course this was not said all at once, but meas-ured out according to the Doctor's readings from Luke.)

"I pray God to touch you. I pray my seed grows in you; my child grows. Feel my child, wildcat. Bring out of you my child; bite free its cord; bring my child to the feast of names. Live in my abode, my abode; be my wife."

In this way I turned the tables on Dr. James. I went on, de-scribed how life would be abundant with provisions of deer and bear, and of our nights of love-making forever under the moon. I thought it a very good letter. When the page was filled and anoth-er begun, I reverted to a truer translation of Luke.

We finished, but then the Doctor did something unusual: he picked up the stack of pages and put them in his satchel. He left with my letter. I should not have to tell you, reader, of the anguish this caused me. My plan had been to take the page to an inter-preter at some other post and pay him to translate, on some pre-text, the letter back into English. Now I would have to steal, possibly, the satchel and all its contents. Possibly I would have the opportunity when next we worked to find the page. But I worried over this dreadfully. I needn't have. The page came back to me the next day. This was a Sunday. Dr. James read from the Ojibwa Gospel at the afternoon meeting for the Indians.

I will not blaspheme to tell you who from the Gospel of St. Luke spoke the words of my letter, but when he did it awoke the slumbering congregation like a canon-shot. I was seated in front by Bingham at this time, sweating profusely—like Schoolcraft wondering would the window nearby open that I might escape the consequences of my treachery—and when the first words of my letter were read I saw a hundred heads snap to attention in unison. Bingham noted it as well. He noted the fervent, hungry looks upon faces, the women rubbing their legs; and when he rose to conclude the service and asked was there anyone would come down to the alter to be saved by the grace of Our Lord Jesus Christ, half the men and all the women stood and approached. He later wanted to know what verses the Doctor had read, and this is how I got the letter back. Dr. James handed it to me to translate for Bingham, and I ran into the woods with it.

Would you be good enough to make tea?

It was about this time, this time I have just told you, that Schoolcraft engaged an interpreter to replace me. I approached this man, a very dark Ottawa named by his father Mow-wy-un,[2] but now called David, to seek his help. He shrank in terror that I approached him thus, as he had been told many lies about me, but came to see I was not to be feared and agreed to help me. He was very educated and had a good writing hand. He came to my house. Upon reading my letter he smiled and put his hand upon my shoulder. He sat down at once and wrote out the translation into English upon a sheet of clean paper I had taken from the Mis-

---

[2] *Doth he cry*

sion. "I think we might leave this out," he said, meaning the part about the cord, to which I agreed. He was very kind and took the translated letter with him to mail. He would not take any money, saying that in the cause of love he was my servant. I thanked him with much emotion.

In a month a letter arrived from Wildereen. Mow-wy-un read it for me. She had been very moved by my letter and wanted me to know that she thought often about me and our nights together as well. She did not think she was with child. In fact she was sure of it. Oh by the way, she said, the City Council was considering a measure she had herself put before them that would order the collection and disposal of all cats living wild in the City of Detroit, that certain diseases might be prevented. It was her hope this would give the Council something useful to do. She wanted to know did I have a house, and if so was it large and comfortable. The rest of what I'd said in my letter she would have to think about. She was very busy keeping the Woodworth's out of the poor house, but would think about my proposal. She signed her letter with just a "W."

We wrote a letter back. I started by stating my concern about the mice and rats, should all the cats be removed, but Mow-wy-un shook his head. Then I told her my house was very large and had a room for sewing and a kitchen both. Mow-wy-un looked at me. I pointed at my room and said "sewing" and indicated the room we occupied and said "kitchen." He scowled, but wrote it down.

"I think a sentiment would be appropriate," he said.

I told him then put it in, and he did.

He left to mail it.

Another month passed and a letter arrived from Wildereen. She said she would agree to marry me, but there needed to be certain conditions met. We were to be married in the parlor of my house and the entire population of Ste. Mary's was to be invited, that they might witness for themselves our joy and love and see how well we lived; she said what the date was to be, which was the

15th day of June, her birthday, and told me I needed to go fetch from Mackinac any possessions Therezia had taken with her, as they were mine by rights. Also, she wrote, if you have not been baptized in the Christian faith, go get it done now. She signed the letter, "W."

Mow-wy-un cocked an eyebrow. "She is a forceful woman," he said.

"She expects much," I said.

"Better marry her in Detroit," he said.

I concurred.

In late autumn winter occurred, and in late winter, spring. It was now 1831. I don't remember a great deal more about it. My mind was fastened on Wildereen. There were many letters. I worked with Dr. James and Bingham on the Gospels. The Ste. Mary's was frozen until April, and thereafter remained very cold, so there were not too many converts until summer. But then it was time to get to Detroit, and my baptism would have to wait until July or August. The water was quite cold then as well. The Ste. Mary's poured out of Superior without distance to warm, and, without a canoe, getting into the river was for Frenchmen and fools.

Bingham was such a fool.

"John," he said, holding out an arm and beaming, "come, my son."

I stood in the grass wrapped in a sheet, though otherwise na- ked. To one side a woman was squeezing the river water out of her hair, and beside her a man was sitting on the grass shivering like a dog. I looked at Wildereen. She waited, watching Bingham. Her face showed no interest; it showed nothing. She had been very disappointed about the house. A pair of men from the Fort stood by her. They had become friends shortly after her arrival and these two men had taken to accompanying Wildereen about the town. I did not like these men. Wildereen had gone to Fort Brady immediately upon her arrival and gained permission from

Brady to give a talk she called "Operational Readiness: It's Not Just About Indians!" and these two had fastened onto her. I thought one of them might have been the runt spitter, but I wasn't sure. I think he was. The two talked frequently to my wife about salvation, and Wildereen talked to them about records organization and federal accounting standards; but the religion took precedence on this day, and the three were there to be sure I did not slip the baptismal noose.

I walked up to my thighs into the water. The current tugged at the sheets and the stones hurt my feet. I worried about fishhooks.

"Come on, John," Bingham said. He was ten feet away, in up to his ribs.

The cold stung at my scrotum. The pain was blinding. "Shit," I said.

"*French*, John, if you must," Bingham said. He shot a smile up to Wildereen and the others and gestured for me to come.

I went to him, and Bingham put one hand on my forehead and the other upon my back and pressed in hard with both. "We're just going to dunk you a little," he said secretly, and I nodded, preparing to go forward into the icy green water.

"In the name of the Father, the Son, and the *Holy Ghost!*" he shouted, and threw me over backward. My nostrils and throat filled with water astringent as vomit and I flailed and screamed great bubbles into the current. I punched the Reverend in the side, though not hard—as to do so would have been impossible underwater—and kicked at nothing, eternity, certain I was about to drown. Within several seconds, though, he plucked me back upright and shouted, "Alleluia!"

I coughed up river water a minute as Wildereen and the others looked on, then wiped my eyes and grinned at her. She looked off. The others piped their alleluias and turned to go. They took Wildereen. They were at my house when I arrived; Wildereen was at the table, drawing flowcharts. We were then married two months.

Schoolcraft was gone much of the summer on his expedition to the Mississippi headwaters. There was much unrest among the Indians west of Superior in 1831, and he was to look into it.[3] Cass wrote me to say he had enjoined Schoolcraft to take me back on as an interpreter, but of course this did not happen. My income was but little from my Mission duties, and Wildereen did not have employment, and was too busy with civic projects to look for a position, so we were very poor. She was not kind to me about it. If I protested it became an attack on her honor, so I desisted from saying too much.

Many parties were coming from the east now to visit Ste. Mary's, and I was able to secure a few brief engagements as a guide. I took a party of men and women to the Apostle Islands to look at birds. While we were on the government dock preparing to embark, another group arrived aboard a lake steamer. Among them were two young Frenchman from France who were the subjects of much attention. One in particular was slight and handsome, with fine European manners. He paused from talking to a delegation from the Fort to look me over curiously. We did not speak, but he asked an interpreter about me. I later came to know that this man was Alexis de Tocqueville, and mention him only because he became quite famous later, and one imagines that the reader has an interest in such encounters with celebrated personages.[4] He would have himself been very interested to know I was

---

[3] Hostility arising from the westward white migration and the practical implications of the Indian Removal Bill culminated in the Blackhawk War the following year.

[4] Tocqueville and his compatriot Gustave de Beaumont arrived in Sault Ste. Marie aboard the steamer *Superior* on August 5, 1831. They remained less than a full day, leaving by canoe for Mackinac early the following morning. Tocqueville and Beaumont, during their journey studying American social and political systems, travelled as far south as New Orleans and as far north as the Sault, although the majority of their time was devoted to interviewing political figures in New England and Washington. De Tocqueville's diary contains mention of "a taciturn Englishman" noted on the dock at Sault Ste. Marie, which would seem to confirm Tanner's version of events. In fact, De Tocqueville took

John Tanner, as he would read the Paris edition of my narrative when it was published there four years later.

Schoolcraft was in the west still on this day, so it is for the record that I mention he missed the visit of these Frenchmen.

Have you heard of—

[Of course I have.]

back to France a copy of Tanner's *Narrative*, where he had it translated into French. It's publication in Paris followed in 1835.

22

Therezia became homesick during the summer of 1831 and left John Jr. with me on her way to the Red River country. She looked as though she had eaten a great deal in preparation for her journey. I told her about Martha Ann. This she knew already, as Martha was now on Mackinac boarding with Therese Schindler, as was Mary and, of course, my youngest daughter Lucy.

"Do not trouble her," she said in Ojibwa. "She is happy now and does not wish to see you."

I told her I would not, but might visit her sometime later. She said sit still and give it some time, and then do not be harsh with her. "I have listened to your voice and trust you are not, or possibly are no longer, a bad man," she said.

Then I mentioned about marrying Wildereen, who was not then at home, but out discussing the Trinity and the best route around the town for a shipping canal with her two friends.

Therezia's face darkened and became the shape of a wedge. This face I knew well. "You are a whore," she said. "You are the dog that shits as he eats in order to make room."

"You wrong me," I told her. "The very thought of you stops my bowels to this day."

She shook her head and left.

I was very happy to see John Jr., and very happy his mother had not carried him off to the Red River country as I had feared. He seemed at first shy, but soon, when we went down to look at the river and throw stones, he laughed and was very affectionate. He was then five years of age.

Wildereen came home and was surprised to find a dark, Indian-looking boy in her house. She stared at him and then at me, and on being told this was my son crouched down, smoothed his hair, and spoke to him as if he were a grown man. He did his best to respond in English that he would come to an understanding that mates came before children in the ordering of a man's affections. Wildereen was good to John and, though somewhat strict, I think came to love him very much. She had been like a mother to her brothers and sisters, she often said, and had always loved children; and now John was here and would remain. This calmed Wildereen down a bit, and she became less guarded and more inclined to be impregnated. By October this was accomplished in a singularly loud and powerful way.

In the center of town, at the crossing of the plank road and that road laid out by John Johnston from the Fort west along the shore of the river, that which is now called Water Street, a thick post made from the trunk of a storm-broken elm had been shaped round and smooth and sunk deep into the earth very many years ago. This had been erected as a gathering-post, where men came to joke and boast of their season's hunting whilst urinating upon something that would not die as a result, and, as it offered the second benefit of discouraging the nearby presence of wives, it became known as a good place to gather, and so was called thus. This post also came to serve as a place for visiting Indians to paint or carve their totems, after which the urinating was more or less permissible, depending which tribe was minding the place and upon which side was done the urinating. It later bore the carved names of soldiers and traders and missionaries and boys, and many parts of the post were effaced of the grayed and weather-ribbed totems to allow for these fresh carvings. The post had narrowed in this manner, but it was still a very big post. When paper came into abundance, the post was used by tradesmen and attorneys and the sheriff to nail up public notices, and the urinating became prohibited. You always saw one or two people standing about reading these notices, and they were watched carefully by the women of the town out sweeping their boardwalks; but the urinating did not entirely stop until the building of public privies nearby and the planting of roses around the post. It was just down the hill west of the Crane Indian cemetery. It is not there anymore.

In my time at Ste. Mary's, the post also came into common use among the citizens to post papers regarding personal items for sale, or to communicate personal opinions. Wildereen took note of these, the opinions, and took to posting her own. She spoke sometimes that she was going down to the kiosk. I was ignorant of many words still, and did ask about the kiosk; nor did I seek English instruction from my wife, as it was provided freely without the asking; but I was surprised to learn later that she had been going to the pee-pole. She would go there often, sometimes many times in a day. She would be overcome by the stupid or horrible things she had read upon the pee-pole, and burst into our home agitated and sit down at the table and, without saying a word—without noting me standing by the window pouring steaming water into the dish-pail or turning fish upon the stove, and after making the gesture with her hand that signified she did not suffer fools—would commence writing. Then she would leave again. She would come back laughing derisively and write more. This would go on for several days or a week and then would subside and her time would be devoted back to her two friends from the Fort. But in a month, maybe two, it would start up again. She brought the postings of others home and sometimes talked to herself as she wrote her responses.

"I laugh at you!" she'd say. "I laugh aloud!"

"What is it about?" I'd ask.

Wildereen would say it was about nothing, or tell me, where-upon it was made clear it was about nothing. One time it was about cats locked up in a warehouse on the government dock. A few citizens, primarily old women, wanted to be given access that they might feed the cats. Wildereen pointed out that the cats had found their way in and could probably find their way out. If they couldn't get out, in fact, they'd have been dead by now. This provoked a number of hostile remarks from others, none of whom would use their real names on their opinion posts. They admitted that a window had been broken out by one of their group, which was now a group, in order to feed the cats. Wildereen said you would not do so if you had a lick of sense, as that will let in weather and only teach the cats to stay put and starve should you get bored of your charity. They posted that the cats were fed through the broken window because they had feelings, which clearly she, Wildereen, did not. It was wondered if Wildereen was a mother or barren or what. To this Wildereen responded that she laughed aloud and if they wanted the building unlocked to feed the cats they should ask General Brady, who would no doubt see to the cats in the proper way. Wildereen had a special feeling for cats. She told in her posts about disease and waste and the odor a cat-owner carried unknowingly about on her person, and was surprised at the lack of reason shown by her antagonists, but only a little, as intelligence and hygiene versus cat-ownership had been shown in studies to be anti-correlative. She was from a real city, the City of Detroit, and there they had learned how to deal with the problem proactively. She herself had seen to it.

It would go on like this, as I have said, for several days. One afternoon I told her I thought the pee-pole arguments a bad idea, and that I had seen her posts and did not like it that her opinions carried upon them my surname. There was enough against me in Ste. Mary's, I said mildly, without her cat-fury. At this she flew, as they say, like a hoot-owl into my face, and did not speak to me thereafter a week. This also upset my son, who was fond of cats.

But then she took it upon herself to tell Ste. Mary's, or the pee-pole, about her canal idea, and it became more serious. There was, she said, a malaise regarding transportation hereabouts, and the town as well as the Territory needed to be shaken out of its lethargy. She called St. Mary's a backwater—where everyone knew it to be a virtual headwater—and opinion against her canal idea was quick to form. It got ugly. What chance, I asked her, do you give a federal grant petition with such an approach? But her mind was always firmly set, and without an awl one could not through her ears reach her brain. Her unnamed detractors raised a silent howl. The canal idea died. It left her quite bitter, and, like me, suspicious of nearly everyone.

She decided then to get baptized.

I asked her why.

"It's something I always wanted to do," she replied.

"You are not baptized?" I asked her.

"Of course not," she said, standing small and dark and reproving before me. "You knew that."

"What!" I cried. "Why were you not baptized with me?"

"Is there a law I have to get baptized with my husband? Can a woman not get baptized alone?" Then she told me she was sick of my always and forever attacking her decisions and she reminded me I had not been supportive of her with the cats or the canal.

I protested that this was not true.

She mimicked me, which was in its way quite funny, saying I did not like my name on her posts, because it brought shame on the high and mighty name of Tanner, and oh, how do you think you'll ever win a federal grant with that ignorant attitude, and she made the hand gesture.

I told her I never said those things, or quite those things.

"You're always attacking my honor!" she shouted, and her face was very dark and firm, yet not far from tears.

I told her fine get baptized. This made her still more angry.

"I don't need your permission to get fucking baptized!" she said.

"Fine!" I shouted.

"I have already arranged it," she said. "It will be December 4th and you don't have to come. I wouldn't want you there."

I thought how the river would be on such a date, and told her I would not miss it. I asked why wait for December. The river could lock up.

"It's the only date that works for both Arvil and Benjamin."

I asked what they had to do with it.

"We're the three of us getting baptized together," she said.

I did not react well to this, reader. I spent the next week sleeping in Martha's lodge.

Life was not improved when in November Bingham had us to move into the Mission. I would not have agreed to this, as it cost me not only my house and privacy but also my garden, but Bingham would not relent, and I was afraid my new wife would be taken from me if I did not comply. Wildereen had been extremely reluctant to stay in the lodge during her time, and this might have contributed. I am not at all inclined to believe moving into the Mission House was entirely Bingham's idea.

We lived among children. I slept on the floor. I ate at table with children when told to, or went without food. The children tested their limits with me. I was called surly by the adults. I was compelled for my sanity to spend all hours but those sleeping out of doors, or working with Dr. James. As it was cold out and I not young, this was very hard on me. I was exhausted all the time. I had nothing in life to look forward to, save perhaps Wildereen's baptism. The longing for the old life with the Indians, utterly free—if such thoughts were romantic heresy—tempted me now with every harangue and platitude, every over-warm room in audience with the rampant pride of untested soldiers and virginal old women; it was a constant struggle to remain sane. Then it got very cold and the river locked up, and I took a hope.

Tea?

I loved Wildereen very much, but she seemed never to have loved me. She might have loved the house with both sewing room and kitchen, but what I had to offer was not that. I was very poor, and this made her very poor, and for this she came to hate me. When we argued, she hated me afterward with such vehemence that I wished not to live, and could not work well on the Gospels, could not sit still in a chair, could not eat, nor could I sleep. My mind was vexed by the constant anticipation of disaster—of accused wrongs, omissions, abandonment—and I took to walking down evenings to the river to sit in the grass far from Wildereen's sullen silence, her cruel indifference to my fears. The breeze would come across from Canada. Downriver the lanterns of boats and boathouses hunkered at the water's edge, and now and then, higher up, deeper, the lights of houses blinked in and out of view amidst the hills. Straight across was the Hudson Bay Company post. There were campfires along the shore, and voices floated over on the breeze. A part of me wanted to join them. Another part wanted to shoot over the river at them, rein them to silence. Some of this was Wildereen; some of this had been always with me.

These two men that I had come to hate, these two that rarely spoke to me when they came by for my wife—with whom she laughed and with whom she was as I had known her at the Scots Ball but never since—were to be baptized with her. There was this, and her choice to be baptized with them and not with me; it confounded me; she had needed them present even at my baptism. I wondered now only how it could be a woman could love two men at once, and how either of these two could tolerate the presence of the other. It was simply incomprehensible. I thought it sick. I hated these men. I did not hate Wildereen, though. With Wildereen I had mated. That, whether a man was white or Indian, was that. A man mated. There might have been exceptions, but a

255

good woman was in this way like a man. Wildereen was very like a man, but not in this way. She had not mated. She did not love me. She ripped from my chest my heart and pressed it by her heel through the bedrock into Bingham's hell. She caused me great anguish.

She spent a great deal of time with her hair and rouged her cheeks in order to be dunked in the river. I asked about this, and was told I would be wise not to attack her honor again on this day. I asked if the three of them would go into the river together, naked but for sheets, and what impression would this make on God, and she made the signal with her hand and did not speak to me. I wondered would her friends want to dunk her one after the other when Bingham was done with her, and maybe they'd dunked her plenty already, and she started speaking in a very bad temper, and told me she would not be home this night or ever again, and that she was done with me.

I felt at that moment quite ready to kill her, and told her what it was she was—but in Ottawa, lest she understand and in fact never speak to me again—and went up to the town. I went into the Shamrock, that sold only whiskey and ice cream and taffy and fudge, and—though it was Sunday—no one refused me a thing due to my fierce countenance; after having my glass refilled twice, I went down to the baptismal place to sit on the frozen grass and wait. I waited a very long time, and it was very cold. The sky clouded and it became still colder, and I thought it would be a very satisfactory baptismal day.

They all came together walking from the Mission chapel, the whole lot of them, which was about twenty persons. Bingham walked in front carrying his Bible and looking happy. Behind him came the three condemned, wrapped in sheets under their coats. Wildereen ignored me. She looked very pretty. I stood.

"Good afternoon, John," Bingham said. "Praise the Lord!"

"River's froze," I told him.

"So it is, so it is," he said. He looked around. "Praise the Lord!" he said. "Trinket!"

Trinket was very young then, and Bingham had been working hard to correct his penchant for thievery and bring him salvation; he was among the congregates present and was the one chosen by Bingham to go break up the ice. He walked down and stepped out onto it. He stood looking down. Everyone watched. Wildereen and her two friends spoke in low voices and Wildereen laughed, said something or other, and one of them put his hand on her back and gave a slight push. I felt on the verge of attacking this man, but Wildereen at that moment walked down to join Trinket out on the ice. She stood next to him, and the two of them stood looking down. She put a hand on Trinket's arm and stomped at the ice with the heel of her right foot. She was wearing shoes, but the stomping made hardly a sound. The ice did. It did like a musket-ball ricocheting off a rock, and a white crack shot across the surface. Wildereen became more excited and turned to motion her compatriots they come help. She did not motion to me. "You're going to get wet anyway!" she shouted, so they went down to her. One, the one named Arvil, who was the runt and who had a very wide mouth and big teeth when he smiled and tended to smile when he was not spitting, walked out much farther than Wildereen and Trinket on the crack as to make a show, then turned and—grinning brightly and widely at us and holding his sheet to his side with a fist and waving his other arm— commenced jumping up and down.

I saw what was going to happen. "Praise the Lord," I said to Bingham. Bingham looked at me and was smiling heavenward when the ice opened. It opened and then closed with a gulping sound and Arvil was by full immersion gone. Wildereen made a sound like a goose shot in flight and dropped flat on the ice; a number of others behind me screamed. I alone remained calm. I was interested in the outcome of Arvil's baptism, so watched and could more or less follow his progress downstream, as it was a dark and sunless day and he was, white-cold naked under the ice with his flowing sheet, quite bright. It was Trinket ran downriver following him, and where the river opened up it was Trinket ran in and saved him. Everyone walked down along shore watching and being horrified and exclaiming, then clapped and shouted praises as Trinket hauled Arvil up and laid him out on the grass coughing and puking; Bingham threw up his arms and shouted praise the Lord and Wildereen threw herself over the naked runt and later claimed to have saved him.

That is why, Miss Mesare, Trinket is not allowed on my property.

Wildereen would call me a coward afterward, as I had not moved a finger to help, apparently afraid of the cold water—whereas she had gone out to do what no man but Trinket and Arvil had been willing. I was nothing. Trinket, at least, was a man honest enough to acknowledge his weaknesses and seek redemption, and had in some slight way helped save Arvil and the baptism. She received, she reminded me, only abuse from me. There was nothing left of her husband to be admired but what happened long ago and might have been mere tales told Dr. James and her. None of this was spoken quietly or kindly, reader. The face I loved changed; the eyes slanted and glinted like flints; my toes curled, my ears buzzed, my sperm turned to dust.

Worst of all, they finally held the baptism that day. In the spot Arvil had been spared death all three, one at a time, were baptized. I stayed, but could not watch; I looked over them at the open water far out. I looked upon Wildereen once or twice, as one presses at a painful tooth, but otherwise did not watch. There was much hugging and laughter and righteous pride afterward. I left unacknowledged, despairing, disgusted. I turned to look back down from the prominence by the Agency, saw their bright faces, the lights starting along the Canadian shore, and ran as on all fours for home. I remembered then that I had no home. They would, if they chose, press in on me where I lived at the Mission. I lifted my head and screamed. A doe in my path froze, then leapt and danced into the woods.

[He leans back, turns to look at the fire.] I thank you for coming tonight, Miss Mesare.

[You may call me Constance, I tell him, if you think it will help.]

23

It was immediately after the baptism Sunday that Wildereen declared she would no longer live with me. She demanded to be given another room at the Mission. Bingham responded by asking we meet with him jointly, by which he meant the two of us at the same time. This we did. It was in his office, which was on the second floor of the Mission House. The room was painted white like all the others. There was a picture of our Savior on the wall behind Bingham's head, and a cross above that, then the ceiling. The ceiling was white with no cobwebs. The room was cluttered with papers and books but was very clean, and a stove-pipe ran up through the room at one corner and warmed the right side of my face. There was a window to my left and on the grass below many large and small sticks that had blown out of the elms in a storm. Beyond the trees the long east wall of Fort Brady ran down from Portage to the river. The river, where it was not frozen, looked green and very cold. It was starting to snow.

"How does this make you feel, John?" he said, after Wildereen had stated jointly her intentions.

I told him it was crazy. She was with my child. I would not allow it. I would kill any man that tried to take her from me, and had given such action much thought already, as she seemed to be attached by affection to these two men from the Fort.

At this Wildereen laughed and asked Bingham could she go now, as this was obviously pointless.

"What two men?" he asked me.

I said the two she was baptized with.

He looked at her and asked was this true she was with child, and what did she have to say about the two men. Wildereen made the fluttering upward gesture with her hand and stood to leave.

"Sit down, Mrs. Tanner," Bingham said sternly, and she sat and looked very angry. "Would you like to respond to your husband's assertions?" he asked.

She told him no, but that the two were her friends and together they discussed such things as John could not possibly process or have any interest in, such as ethics and decency and respect for the Word of God.

I mentioned I was translating the New Testament, what about that, and she shook her head as if I'd spoke gibberish.

"And how to behave in a relationship and show consideration for your partner, and not always attack the honor of the other and bring politics into the home and belittle and chide me and say vicious things," she said, facing me. Her face looked as if carved from hickory.

"John?" Bingham said, turning to me.

"I don't do that," I said.

"Am I a liar?" Wildereen said. "You see he's calling me a liar. This is typical. I do not easily tolerate such abuse. I have tried to be tolerant, but he says these things and I have to stop and just look at him and ask myself did that just come out of his mouth and what did I do to deserve it? My first husband did not treat me like this. He could never have heaped upon me such abuse. No woman I have ever known has suffered under such an abusive relationship."

I said for Bingham's benefit that her first husband had killed himself, or he might have gotten around to it.

"Case in point," she said. Her eyes had gone the strange shape. "How *dare* you."

To calm her, Bingham asked if she would share some specific incidents of my abuse, and she launched into the cat postings and my vicious attack on her for using her married name publically, as if she were something I was ashamed of and wanted to keep hidden under a rock.

Bingham nodded and, leaning back in his chair, glanced at me.

Then she mentioned a time I suggested she close the door of the privy when she used it, as it faced the street. "He all but called me an exhibitionist and said in no time there would be tour carriages for the Indians to come watch me using the privy. Said he'd sell them taffy and we wouldn't have to worry about the money anymore."

"Well, indeed," Bingham said. His face had turned red.

"It's behind the house," she said to me. She was very upset.

"I have seen you from the street," I said.

"You *would*," she said.

"I have *not*," Bingham said. We both looked at him.

Wildereen said, "Oh, and did I mention he would have me placed nights in a lodge, a *wigwam*, behind the house during my time?"

"Not again— *John*," Bingham said. He shook his head sadly.

I protested that I had forced nothing, and indeed she had not spent a single night out there, whereas I had spent plenty.

"He asked me to," she said. "I'm a dog to him, something to abuse."

"It was only a request. Furthermore," I said, raising a finger, feeling *my* honor attacked, "I do not abuse dogs."

"You do understand, don't you, Wildereen, that John here was raised by Indians. This, actually is some progress that he—did you say he asked?—that he asked."

She waved it off. "He doesn't approve of what I read. He tells me all the time how ignorant I am, how what I read is of no value and beneath him."

"Really?" Bingham said, and looked at me with his eyebrows raised.

I told him she misunderstood about the reading and persisted in this misunderstanding. What she didn't like she misunderstood. The misunderstandings seemed intentional. She could read what she wanted, but she read in bed and used much lamp oil.

Bingham said to her, "Lamp oil is expensive, you understand, and John here is not a wealthy man."

"Tell me about it," she said.

I added what she read made her laugh and I had difficulty getting to sleep, as did John Jr.

Bingham wanted to know what she was reading.

"Marquis de Sade," she said.

"Haven't read him," Bingham said quickly. "And what's this about bringing politics into the home?"

Wildereen told Bingham that I had become a Democrat, and was in the habit of bringing political pamphlets home supporting insufferable political positions.

I protested, saying this had happened but once, and that I could not in any case read. I had asked her to explain this thing that had been handed me in the street. There had been an argument over it, as she had insulted my friend Lewis Cass, and much bitterness afterward, and I had brought this event up a few times to demonstrate how she was given to claiming insult where none was intended. The same argument ensued each time. I added that she had a tattoo I thought very like a political cartoon, and started to describe it.

She cut me off. "It's from a *flag*, Newton." Then, to Bingham: "And I'm sick and tired of having to share my life with his ex-wife. He refuses her nothing. It's as if she runs our lives!"

263

"This surprises me," Bingham said, cupping his chin in his hand.

I told him I had not seen or spoken to Therezia in a very long time. I did not know where Wildereen got this.

"He refused to go get his things from her after agreeing he would. She has everything she wants, whereas I have nothing. I think sometimes he still loves her, that he intends to go back to her."

Bingham, who had met Therezia, was buying none of this. He asked if she really thought this.

She did. Absolutely. She just wanted to feel, was it so much to ask, that she had some importance, that she counted too. Yet I had not even consented to divorce Therezia.

"To be fair, they were never technically married," Bingham said.

"What the fuck does that have to do with it?" she snapped.

I felt I needed to step in, so told Bingham there was nothing Therezia had taken that I wanted, and that she was then at Mackinac, which was a long distance to go for a blue china leech-bowl.

"Then why did you agree to it?" Wildereen asked.

"To be married," I said.

"There you are," she said to Bingham, who leaned forward as if wanting to speak. "Just like you lied about the house," she said to me, and turned back to tell Bingham how I had described it. "I expected a little more honesty from a mate," she said, and glared at me. I noticed her spectacles sat crooked upon her nose. This I had noticed many times before when she was angry, and it had moved me to feel sorry and protective and loving. But not now.

"She wanted only the house," I told Bingham. "Not me. She tells me I never smile or laugh."

"Well?" she said.

"She never loved me. She loves those two."

Wildereen laughed, and I told her straighten her stupid spectacles, and she made the hand motion.

264

Bingham must have seen this was going nowhere, for he raised his hands and commenced to explain about the Triangle of Vituperation, and how it was a triangle. He traced this imaginary triangle with his hand in the empty air above his desk, and showed by pointing where Wildereen and I were on the triangle. I think we were at the bottom. He talked about the Hymeneal Phase that was here on the ascending side, and how it peaked briefly then went into the Phlegmatic Phase, which occupied the descending side, and then showed how the Vituperation Phase, with all its attendant ugliness, was there flat on the bottom of the triangle, and that's in fact where we were. It repeated like that, he said, and each time it repeated like a dinner chime being rung, love was by degrees withdrawn by the object of such vituperation until there was none left, and only by turning to God could the terrible cycle be stopped. He made suggestions for how to stop fights before they happened. They, the suggestions, had to do with praying and managing one's temper by having the other restate insults in more digestible form. They, the suggestions, struck me as insipid. I also thought the triangle too simplistic a form, given our circumstances, but could not think of the names of six- or eight-sided shapes, and wondered why this triangle seemed to apply only to me, and if it was time to eat.

"Try these things," he said, "then we'll get together in a week, see how it went, and talk further. That sound all right?"

Wildereen asked about getting a separate room.

"Don't be impractical," he said; "you're pregnant. You'll require your husband's attentions."

"I've done just fine without them," she said.

"Tell me about it," I said.

Bingham held up a hand. "But I do have some good news," he said. "I am going to write Bolles in Boston and ask again that the Board provide funding for a full-time interpreter. Your work here has been exemplary, John; I don't know what I'd do without you. Can't lose you to the Presbyterians, now can I? He he! No, it's time you were properly remunerated. That would make life a little easier, wouldn't it? I think it would help relieve some of the pressures the two of you are experiencing."

Wildereen asked if he needed any help with the letter to the Baptist Board. She knew a thing or two about funding requests. That, or she could merely evaluate his request before he sent it off. Bingham thanked her and said he would consider it, but that he hoped to get the letter out on the next morning's mail train,[1] so needed to finish it today.

[There is a sound, a scuffling outside, and he rises and goes to the window facing the river. He opens the door. I ask him what it is, and he raises a hand, then, after a minute's listening, returns to the table.]

Is it time for tea?

We met with Bingham sometimes weekly. Sometimes Wildereen met with him alone. Very often she did this. I don't think it helped her. Her attitude hardened where it should have softened, and I thought Bingham must be spending the hour looking at her blouse-front, then telling her she was right about everything. I took to telling them what they wanted to hear when we met jointly, whatever I thought might restore to me relations with Wildereen; but any hopes I had dried like dung. Her pregnant belly and swelling breasts drew and mocked me; she looked upon me as one would an old dog that has bitten and spoke to me only, in painful and incomprehensible detail, of the progress of various projects she had been drawn into. She was rarely happy in my company. If she was home she sat sullenly and played with a deck

---

[1] Dog "trains" were employed to transport mail overland to St. Ignace and Mackinac following the close of the shipping season.

of cards, aligning the cards in rows upon the table that she would add to or shift about until suddenly gathering them all up and starting over. She would wrap up in a blanket and go outside in the dark and cold to smoke. In our home—our room—I was miserable. With her I grieved the silence, my inarticulate stupidity, or stood until I could stand no more, looking interested as she went on angrily about territorial governance or mineral rights. Without her I paced and was needlessly cruel to my son. With her two friends she went out as often as possible, and they laughed and talked; but if they provided her respites of happiness, I was not thankful for them in my prayers. They had stolen my wife's affections; I had thus far spared their lives. It seemed enough. "Thus far," I said aloud to God, kneeling at the bed with the knuckles of my thumbs pressing into my head like the buttons of horns into a calf's skull.

But, Constance, I loved my wife dearly. I thought always of her as sweet and good and charitable, even if she was not; that is what my heart will not relinquish even now. I loved her smallness and her dark, forbidding strength; I loved her voice that was that of a farmer's daughter, and how her *R*'s hung on the air, and how with that voice she spoke very many words I did not know; I loved the odd shape of her nose and the shape of her face when she pulled her hair back, and her little smile. But she did not love me. If she looked at me, it was with the indifferent, burning eyes of a cat.

"What is it?" she would say.

"My arm is in pain," I'd answer.

"Not my fault."

Prayers and funding requests were not answered. I wrote Bolles myself, with Wildereen's help, in May, that was May 1832, but still no word came from the Baptists about my position and salary. Bingham said they were clerics, not businessmen, and poor clerics at that. Dr. James told me that the American Bible Society was interested in publishing our translation of the New Testament when it was finished, and he went himself to Boston to meet with the

Baptist Board on my behalf also in May. But nothing came of anything until it was too late.

In the meantime we borrowed from James Schoolcraft, who had returned from Mackinac more or less permanently. This doubly terrified me, as there was no way to keep Wildereen out of his store, and he was—is—a very dangerous man. I owed him hundreds of dollars. But if the notion that I thus owed him Wildereen had crept into his febrile brain, neither would anything come of that until it was too late.

My son Luke was born on July the twentieth in our room at the Mission. Dr. James delivered him of Wildereen on a hot and hazy afternoon, with many women attending within our room and the hallway crowded with girls. Arvil and Benjamin stood on the yellow lawn below our window. It, the childbirth, was a terrible thing to witness. Some of the hair matted upon Wildereen's temples was gone gray with age, and, as she was also very small, the birth caused her considerable agony; the Doctor was for a long time very worried. She complained in low throaty screams; when I touched her she told me to go away, get away, that she wished to die. I was very afraid for her. I became faint and started to go out of the room once, but a woman there in the hallway said see what you've done to her and the girls backed down along the walls; I went back into the room and stood in a corner until it was over.

There was great celebration afterward.

Wildereen recovered and cared for the baby and soon became very bored and irritable. She announced one day that she was going to take up her writing again, and would I go get her what she needed in order to write, then take the baby so she could do so. I did as she asked and she wrote—occasionally suckling Luke when he bawled, as the bawling was worse than the suckling for her concentration—then slept half the following day. She was happy when I woke her for the baby. She had written an opinion, and this, for some reason, made her happy. I asked her should I go put it on the kiosk, and she looked as though she would become angry, so I said tell me your opinion.

"It's nothing," she said. "Just something I needed to get out of my system."

"Hoh," I said. For this I had stayed up all night.

"Maybe," she said, "if it's good, I'll let Henry put it in his *Muzzegenin*."

She told me that the Asiatic Cholera outbreak, which had taken so many lives that past summer, was said to have broken out on ships carrying soldiers to fight Black Hawk. She had been told by Henry Schoolcraft that the ravages of the Cholera were tenfold worse than the Black Hawk War itself. This, she said, her eyes sharpening, was the fault of the federal government. This is what she had written about. She had explained this blame, she said, and to do so more effectively had adopted a voice. She thought it a good voice.

I asked why was she talking to Schoolcraft. He was my enemy that had laid me low and stolen away my daughter and cheated me of my pay. She held me in contempt for our poverty, yet would talk to Schoolcraft. I did not understand this.

"Our poverty is not his fault, John Tanner," she said. "You make it everyone's fault but your own. Your precious daughter is gone and it's everyone else's fault. Well, let me tell you something about Henry. He at least takes responsibility for his actions. He at least has integrity. He at least respects mine."

"Do not call him *Henry*," I said.

"I will call him *Henry*. I will call him whatever I please. And he calls me *Wildereen*."

I became exceedingly angry, and her voice had grown sharp, so I saluted her with the hand motion she had invented and turned to leave the room.

"I try to share something with you and you accuse and belittle me!" she shouted. "You always belittle me! You're always attacking my honor!"

269

I turned and grabbed her papers from the table.

"Give me that!" she screamed. Luke jerked awake and started bawling.

Thinking it possible that she had written an opinion not about the Blackhawk cholera but about her husband, and with my mind twisting around such thoughts as that it might be a note to Henry Schoolcraft, I took Wildereen's opinion to Mow-wy-un down at the Agency. He was sitting in a chair out on the boardwalk in the sun, smoking a pipe. There were many Indians seated or walking about in the grass waiting on Schoolcraft to reconvene for the afternoon. I told Mow-wy-un that Wildereen admired his education and wished sound advice on her writing. He squinted at me curiously, but took the papers held out to him and read Wildereen's opinion.

"She's British?" he asked. "I didn't realize."

"No, she is from Dexter."

"Certainly sounds British here."

"Is it good?"

He glanced up at me, then reread the opinion. "What I can understand might be a little over-mannered and affected," he said. "Like I said, British. Except where it's French. Wait. 'If sacrifice be demanded, so be it; it is always by way of pain one arrives at pleasure.' Strange. That sound to you like de Sade? Anyway. You can't see the point she's trying to make through it." He handed back the papers. "Just my opinion."

"Could you write those words on a paper?"

"What words?"

I told him "over-mannered" and the other. He shrugged, got to his feet, and led me into the Agency office.

"Long as we're at it," he said, writing, *"Fa-tu-ous."*

I took back to Wildereen the opinion she had written and lied that I had read it carefully, and shared with her, in Mow-wy-un's words, my assessment. I believe this was the only abuse I ever heaped upon my wife. I felt very bad about it later; and Wildereen

270

did prove herself commited as a writer, for she did not speak to me for six weeks and would not share her bed or anything with me ever again, and we never had relations thereafter.

She spoke openly and bitterly about this abuse, though without such specifics as would prevent the citizens of St. Mary's from presuming I was beating her savagely. Women visiting—and they visited continually—looked her over as they would a tomato, but there were never any scars or bruisings, and you could see their eyes relax and the disappointment. Life became more vexing. Women who months ago would have fled at the sight of me stood now foursquare in my path (if they were at least two) and glared.

Things descended from there.

[You make her sound horrid, I say, then apologize, asking if he is finished. He shakes his head.]

She was difficult. Very like me, in ways.

But I remember a day. It must have been mid-June, as the light was unusually clear and the cottonwoods releasing. I had taken Dr. James to Vermillion Point for the purpose of vaccinating the Indians there, and as John Jr. wanted to go and Wildereen's friends were required on government duty, she, though then very large with Luke, went as well, and we waited for a time under a broad and tall pine. Wildereen spread out our dinner upon the weathered-clean trunk of a fallen cedar. We had corn bread and pickled whitefish from a green glass jar, and had also apples. The sand was covered with fallen needles and was cool in the shadow of the pine. We were very comfortable looking out at the lake and watching the seagulls. I rested my elbow upon the smoothed gray cedar log. To the west a stand of cottonwood stood high against the lake and released their cotton into the breeze. The cotton glowed in the sun before the trees and the darkness of the lake, and the cotton glowing floated toward us, and John was fussing to keep it out of his food. It was Wildereen first commented on how pretty the cotton looked in the sun. She said, "Look how it rises out of the trees, John." She did not say it looked like snow. That is what one would have expected.

"See how it rises first from the trees," she said. "They go *up*. Look."

Or the front of the canoe rising and falling and Wildereen in the evening with the sky at sunset spreading and running upon the water sitting next to John in the center and her arm around him.

It was not all bad, Constance. It was sometimes very good. It was the goodness made me go mad when it was robbed of me.

[We bid each other good night and I leave.

Lt. Tilden is waiting outside. He follows me about continually. I think he has taken leave of his post for the purpose of minding me. He is outside the school; he is at my door in the morning; he stands below my window now. The man is a fawning, dog-grinning idiot.

I shall speak to James about it tomorrow. I will not stand for this.]

{Bracketed entry is in Mesare's longhand.}

24

There was no use of anything. Nothing was going to help me. All creation withdrew, clenched like the roots of trees; God turned away. Bingham's arms moved mechanically as he took out his pipe and lit it, staring at me. Dr. James staunched his nose and let his gaze slowly waft over me on its way to the ceiling. My wife wrote notes to her friends, this as she suckled my child, or looked up at me and stopped speaking, face gone blank, remembering herself. I was already alone. I lived with Wildereen while in terror of her leaving me. I was not this, yet not that, neither here nor there. At the mere sound of Wildereen chatting and laughing with others, I became sick with jealousy and fear. It took no more than that. This most intelligent woman that had once loved me now merely judged me, and judged me stupid and bad and cast me looks as she beheaded chickens and wanted to spend no more time with me. She no longer made the first pretence of affection. It became so and was so for many months, and I lost a terrible amount of weight. It became that I did not care if she loved me. My needs, as one starving, became simple. I wanted only not to be deprived of her. I felt my mind being eaten. I could not think, much less reconcile myself. Still, a part of me refused to believe it could not be corrected.

I implored of Bingham that he try to intercede with Wildereen, but she would make the hand gesture and have nothing to do with it, recounting only my sins so as to make them sound many, when I knew them to be few, and Bingham would puff on his pipe, shrug. "I'm sorry, John," he'd say, then ask how the New Testament was coming.

I was sick all the time. It was generally a burning in my chest and belly, straying like flames up my neck, but if I saw Wildereen with her friends there was suddenly a fire deep and hot in my face and my mind would be upset as to make me dizzy, and I would dream of murder. I was careful not to drink at all.

To be alone I went out hunting, and alone I was able to worry aloud over Wildereen. I spoke thus to my dog. He began to stray off. I became at this time a fierce father. John would ask to go with me hunting, and I would refuse him. I wanted to be alone. He would insist and whine and I would strike him. I said cruel things, told him he would never be a hunter, that he would one day starve, or that he might first hang himself. It broke my heart, so I would do or say worse to increase my remorse, my pain. Finally, in September, he ran away. He could not be found. He was then but six.

[Oh John, I say, overcome. I apologize for interrupting.]

It is your function to interrupt.

From this it became known how I had been treating my son. Bingham was very fond of children, and this touched his heart and stirred anger in him; he came to believe—from this act of John's (kidnap, then, was not an element of concern)—that whatever Wildereen had said against me must be true. So he too thought me a bad man. I came at this time to understand the Indian suicides as I had never, despite my grim life, been able before, and said this to Bingham one day in the street. It was to gain his sympathy I spoke of being so low; but it startled him and made him react so that I realized he seemed not to care so much about me as to fear losing a certain investment. He said come up to his office immediately. I told him I would do so, but must first go to the

Shamrock. It had befallen me in my low state that I had grown addicted to the taffy sold at the Shamrock.

It was late afternoon in early autumn. The setting sun was bright and showed the white and yellow houses in the trees on the Canadian side, and reflected like stars in far-off windows. As I walked back to the Mission I pushed what taffy I had left into my mouth and bit down and felt it squeeze and tasted it. It was good.

"You must never talk like that," Bingham said. His eyes were urgent, dark.

"I cannot thtand it," I said.

"You mustn't talk so. But I do understand, John. I have counseled many desperate souls."

"You have never yourthelf been dethperate."

"You are wrong."

"You have never loved thuch a woman ath my wife."

"I am quick to agree."

"Ekthcuthe me."

"That's fine, John, take a moment."

I worked at my teeth and the roof of my mouth with a fingernail and in a minute could talk, but wanted now more taffy. It took a minute to center myself.

Bingham spoke as he lit his pipe. "God put man on earth that he might glorify Him and find joy in His creation," he lisped. "Life is to be *enjoyed*, John. Man's true end is *joy*, not suffering."

I told him I had known joy but a few moments in my life.

"That makes me very sad to hear," he said. "But I am not surprised. It tells me you have not truly been saved. You could not behave as you do had you truly been saved. One could not be so low. You have lived your life in a state of nature—in more ways than one—and have served many lusts and pleasures."

"It is true," I said, and hung my head, craving taffy.

He looked at me sharply, but with a hint of compassion, or sorrow. He opened a book he drew from a shelf at his side, found a page, read: "'Because there is not one man who does good and commits no sin, and because the best of men may fall into great sins and provocations through the power and deceitfulness of their own indwelling corruption and the prevalency of temptation, God has mercifully provided in the covenant of grace that when believers sin and fall they shall be renewed through repentance to salvation.'"

He looked up at me. "Do you follow?"

I nodded, still picking at my teeth.

"'Saving repentance is an evangelical grace by which a man who is made to feel, by the Holy Spirit, the manifold evils of his sin, and being given faith in Christ, humbles himself over his sin with godly sorrow, detestation of his sin and self-abhorrency. In such repentance the man also prays for pardon and strength of grace, and has a purpose and endeavor, by supplies of the Spirit's power, to walk before God and to totally please Him in all things.

"'As repentance is to be continued through the whole course of our lives, on account of the body of death, and the motions of it, it is therefore every man's duty to repent of his particular known sins particularly.' And so on." He closed the book.

[Amen, I say. He scowls.]

"John," Bingham said, "you have fallen from grace. Behold: In the eyes of your children, in the eyes of your wife, in the eyes of your community, in the eyes of the Church—I daresay in the eyes of God Almighty—thou hast fallen. Passions of the flesh hath cast thee down."

I told him I was a despised outcast.

"Not to put too fine a point on it, but yes, quite."

We sat a moment in silence, reflecting.

"It is time you repent," he said. "Before God and the Community of Faith."

I nodded gravely.

"Before your wife. And your wife's friends."

At this my bowels moved down in fear and disgust. I told him no.

"You must. It is the only way, John. Yet this is but the first step. Without it there can be no redemption, nor salvation; no marriage. Without it, at worst, what you spoke of before."

I asked did he think it would soften Wildereen's heart toward me.

"Couldn't hurt," he said, relighting his pipe.

Bingham arranged that I would stand before the Sunday morning Baptist congregation and confess my sins and pray for the community's and God's pardon. I was very afraid at the thought of this, and the fear prevented me from thinking clearly, and this prevented me from preparing very well. It made me sick to think of Wildereen's two friends sitting either side of her looking at me. My English was very far from perfect and I had a fearful accent, so it would be, I knew, some kind of experience for the congregation, and—if it went badly—a humiliation not merely for me but for Wildereen. Yet I was willing to do this, to risk anything, to regain her love; and such a sacrifice of dignity in the cause of her honor and love I hoped would touch her heart and make her feel tenderness toward me again. It, her heart, required correction, and I was such a fool—though I had no choice and little sense—as to undertake to correct it.

It was one thing to agree to do what amounted to flaying from bone and muscle one's own skin for the amusement of one's enemies—full of hope and the scornful, depraved bravery of a war party gathering to feast and dab with fingers at face paints—and quite another to do it. To do it brought to the nostrils the acrid smell of death. To the mind it brought the keen desire for death's ease. Though I moved deliberately from one side of the room to the other and took down my clothes and laid them out on the bed without a howl of pain or a storming run for the river, my world seemed enclosed in fire. My brain screamed. It was all I could do to haul the coat of my New York suit onto my shoulders. My hands shook; my face felt numb, yet burned. I mumbled, babbled. The spit left my mouth. I was as a deer encircled by wolves.

Wildereen opened the door and I spun, nearly fell down. She'd been downstairs at breakfast.

"Christ, look at you," she said. "You can't even dress yourself." She took up her hair brush and dabbed at the front of my coat. "These look like fucking cat hairs," she said. "Who the hell have you been with?"

I smiled and felt suddenly childishly happy. She hadn't spoken so much as a word to me in more than a month.

"All right," she said, "There is something I have to say; let me say this. Don't talk or get angry, just hear me out."

I looked at her. She was not very pretty just then, with her hair falling about her face and straying out like searching vines, but this is how she looked mornings, and I loved her very much.

"I admire what you're doing, and I think I understand why you're doing it. I honestly don't know if it will help us. I may simply have been put through too much for it to make any difference. I've been numb, just numb, since our last fight. You say such things to cut and belittle— I don't know, John. I will have to hear what you have to say, and then weigh that together with everything, and I'll need some time to think through it. I can't promise anything. I have to tell you I am not optimistic. But I will consider it. Is that fair?"

She waited for me to respond, looking up into my eyes. I did not think it fair but nodded.

"Just one thing," she said, looking at my chest and laying her palm flat upon it; "there is one thing I ask."

I grunted.

"There will be nothing about the hotel." She looked up at me and made her sudden little smile. "The night of the Scots ball is just something special between you and me. All right?"

This was the morning of my confession.

Tea?

It, the morning of my confession, was a bright cool dry morning. I think it was the first of October. Many kitchen fires were dying, and the sky held a thin haze and the air smelled of smoke and hay and of dried corn stalks. It was going to be warm. I walked alone to the chapel. Wildereen had left saying she would see me there, and went toward the Fort to collect her friends. This, under the circumstances, seemed a cruel and selfish act. Yet such neglect provided me something to seize upon outside my fear, and anger was far superior at that moment to fear, so by Wildereen's heedless grace I was able to walk erect and with quick and resolute steps, fists at my sides, jaw set and eyes like ice, through the gathering, unsettlingly large crowd outside the morning-dappled, white-frame Baptist chapel. Silence ran before me like a wave.

I sat myself in the front pew on the left side. The room filled in behind me. I did not look back or around. The hubbub rose and I waited to see Bingham, but he was so long in coming I began to fear having to fill the hours with my confession. When he came in through the rear door behind the pulpit I felt an instant's relief; then he stepped down off the altar and walked straight to me and bent over.

"Dammit, I was waiting for you in my office," he said. He put his hand on my shoulder and leaned his weight upon it. His face was angular and severe and smelled of bacon and coffee. "You were going to meet with me before. I sent word. Did you not—"

I looked at him stupidly.

He straightened to say good morning to several behind me.

"No matter. Have you eaten? Have your bowels moved? Good, good, you'll do fine. We'll do you after the readings; I'll introduce you; remember to go to the lectern, not the pulpit." He looked over my head back into the congregation. "Then just sit down again. Do not leave. All right?" He looked me in the eye again. "I might refer to you here and there in the sermon. Just don't take any offense. Understand?"

I blinked, which he took as a reply.

"All right," he said, then squeezed my shoulder and turned, walked up to the altar, and sat down. He leaned over his clasped hands and closed his eyes. I breathed in and out and looked at the dust and dried bits of moths gathered in corners of the window-sill at my left side. A woman who'd seemed to be dozing startled me by suddenly banging on a piano and Bingham, everyone, stood. I jerked to my feet.

Whatever I had done in my life that threatened my life I had done knowing the moment of trial must one way or another pass; yet I felt now held by the thorny tendrils of eternity itself, and felt myself not one but of many, and the threat not against my life but all lives and existence, and I did not believe, standing there on quaking legs before Wildereen and her friends and Hulbert and James and the Johnstons and the new Presbyterian minister Porter and General Brady and the cocked heads of half the Fort, that re-lease from this moment, even by death, was possible. The room swayed. I clutched at the sides of the lectern. I took a great breath.

"I am John Tanner," I said. I glanced over at Bingham sitting against the wall with his hands locked together and his hooded eyes fastened on me, mouth set, cheeks drawn taut; he nodded just perceptibly. I tried to calm myself. I needed water. Someone, an old woman, coughed and I looked back as to find her and locked my eyes instead on the rear doors of the chapel. Into my mind then came, quite clearly, crafty old Net-no-kwa, sitting stir-ring sparks up out of a night-fire, and I found myself addressing my words, as the congregation became as a landscape of winter-dead shrubs and stones, to her:

"The Reverend has asked me to reach my words to you and lay before you my sins, and call upon your hearts that you will find it to pardon me and accept me as a son come home and forgiven."

"Good," Bingham whispered. I glanced at him.

"I speak to you and tell you my sins. I am fallen low to many lusts and pleasures—" (I glanced again at Bingham, but he was now cleaning the thumbnail of one hand with a fingernail of the other) "—and have been cruel and unjust to those I love. I have scared by threats of violence my friends and visited death upon mine enemies." Here the congregation stirred, averted faces turned forward, and having gotten their attention, if at the slight expense of the truth, I could not resist peering into the eyes of one, then the other, of Wildereen's two friends. They blanched. I felt myself relax a bit. "I have lied and allowed others to lie about me and to steal from me. I have caused my children to be stole from me and taken far away where I cannot see them or know even if they are alive or dead. For years my tears run for my children; they are taken from me by their mother who would not see them live with their white father, and by you because I have acted and lived as a man not of you but of the Indians who raised me. For this by you I was stripped alone and thrown down to the dust, for which I ask your forgiveness."

Bingham cleared his throat.

"These things I have brought upon myself," I said. I let go the sides of the lectern and placed my hands and forearms atop it and leaned over them as I had seen Bingham do countless times. There was a familiar, hollow ache in my right arm. I felt suddenly strangely at home.

"Last year I took a wife. She gave me a son. Yet I have not provided for them except pitifully from the Mission by your offerings. We thank you your merciful kindness. Governor Cass gave me the post of interpreter for the government but Mr. Schoolcraft took it and gave it to his friend; then, when I was made interpreter, I received no pay. I was dismissed for my grief over my daughter, her taking, and had become very poor and in great debt to the Agent's brother." I wanted to tell them at what interest per annum, but let it go.

"I have worked faithfully at my duties for the Mission translating the Gospels and interpreting at the Indian meetings, but for this have been paid but very little."

Bingham moved in his chair, cleared his throat again, coughed weakly.

"All the time I have tried to be a good husband, but my ways have troubled my wife and she desires to leave me. She thinks me stupid and cruel. She tells others I abuse her. I would not willingly do this; I love my wife; but I pray to God every day for her forgiveness and that he softens her heart toward me; but I fear I must lose her, for I am very poor."

Wildereen, now, was glaring at me, her face gone very dark. Her breathing worked up and down a fold in her blouse. She looked away. I saw that none of this was going to help. I found I did not care.

"I lived with the Indians until I could no longer. Their ways were my ways but their gods were not my gods. I did not learn of the God of Abraham until a grown man. If I was taught as a child, I had forgotten. This, with my home and parents, had been taken from me. As a child I was taken by the Saginaw or I might have no sins. I would be as you. I had then an Ottawa mother. She, whose name was Net-no-kwa, was very kind to me. She bought me from the Saginaws for a keg of rum, or maybe two; I would have died at their hands otherwise. She raised me herself as her son. You would think her nothing but a poor dirty squaw, but she was wise and in the eyes of her people a noble woman, and led a large family with no help of a husband, who had died, but with only me and an indolent son to help her. I have not seen this woman in many years. I do not know if she lives. I never saw her again after I came to seek my family in Kentucky. I did not look for her when I went back to the Red River country to find my children; I never bade her good-bye." At this my throat tightened and a heat akin to rage filled my face and chest, a welling of unpardoned grief; tears started in my eyes, and at this moment I believed everyone in the chapel could see clearly as me old Net-no-kwa raising her eyes from the fire and tightening one side of her mouth, shaking her head at such foolishness.

282

Bingham coughed again.

"For this I ask God's forgiveness," I said. "I do not ask yours."

There was silence. The congregation remained still; I could feel Bingham's eyes, feel the great hollows of his face deepen.

I decided to sit down.

I walked down to the pew but felt a great force of their eyes upon me and did not wish to be there longer. I could not look at Wildereen. I felt their judgment as one feels the sun on one's cheeks, and not wanting to be there longer strode down the aisle to the doors and out and walked far back into the woods where it was morning and in the woods the trees full of the calls of crows.

Did you hear that?

[I did.]

Has someone followed you here?

25

You ask if I loved Jane. I do not think so. It was something else. Jane was no longer the woman Schoolcraft had married. I wondered how she had been then; I had only the girl on the bull to imagine from; but she was something else now. It had nothing to do with me. But I will tell you it ached at my side and was such a torment that I pressed my hands over my eyes and yet there was nothing but repeating her name to help it. She could be insufferable, calling the dew dropping into puddles from the eaves morning's pizzicato prelude, yet this did not help me. Nothing stopped it. But I didn't know her to love her. I knew instead her son had died. This had divided her. The division called me like a wolf to blood. I cannot explain it beyond that. It was like a scent.

[I tell him I had not asked about Jane, that we had discussed her many nights ago. He is looking at me. He had said something quite different before. He said her sorrow had repelled him.]

Well I do not think so.

[He had been talking about his wife, Wildereen, I tell him.

He looks at me. I ask if he is all right.

He looks.]

You're very late.

[I had a dinner, I tell him. I failed to mention it last night. I'm very sorry.]

There won't be tea now.

[That's all right; I can't stay long.

He looks.

She was a wicked woman, I say, his wife.]

She did not love me, but she was not wicked. I could not understand her. We had in common only a dislike for cats.

[She was very bad for you.]

She was a very strong woman. I admired this strength. It drew me. It caused me to have faith. Then she used it, this strength, this faith, against me. This caused me great pain.

[What happened, I ask.]

She was taken from me. She asked to be taken from me. She asked that it be made as it had been for Martha. This happened as she asked. She knew what Schoolcraft had done with Martha, and sought to have it done for herself. She had no money. There was no other way. She had her friends come to the Mission. They were to help her. I did not want her to go to Schoolcraft; I hated the man; and I would follow her sometimes to see where she went and always asked where she had been to see if she lied, so she had her friends come now to the Mission that they could carry her message to Schoolcraft to make her a law. They were snuck in and were in a room and she said I need to go out and I said where and she said to the sutler's commissary and I said fine I'll go with you. There is no need, she said, and picked up Luke and went out. She went down the hall and knocked on a door. I watched her. She did not see me watch her. The door opened and she went in. Well, Constance, I went to this door, which had closed behind her, and listened.

"I can stand it no more," I heard her say in a low and angry voice, not pitiful, and then listened and heard one then the other of her two friends speak. "You should not have to," one said, the runt spitter, head tilted (I imagined), groin swelling with sincerity; "Something must be done," said the other. She told them they must go to see the Agent Schoolcraft for her and what they must demand of him. She began to weep and I imagined them embracing her, or one of them embracing and the other waiting his turn; and standing there in the hallway I felt at a greater remove from anything that I had tolerated or understood than at any time in my life; and preferring anything, crime and apprehension, to this smothering dream-confusion, I knocked gently on the door, as might a woman. It was opened to me.

The look on the face of this one named Arvil was very funny. He did not expect to see me. He looked to meet the eyes of a woman, then up to find mine, and made a face as if about to sneeze. I put my hand to the door and Wildereen cried out my name. The other friend named Benjamin let out a hoot and shied away from her and climbed into a wardrobe. Arvil followed his example. Luke started to bawl. I wanted to laugh. It was not difficult to frighten these men. It was much more difficult not to kill them.

"You dishonor me!" I said to Wildereen. She attempted a defiant face, then screamed and fled with our child.

The wardrobe was tall and with two men shaking in it very heavy, but I was able to pivot it around and shove it doors-first against the wall.

"You come out I kill you!" I shouted. "You want take my wife! I avenge! I *tomahawk!*" This last word I shrieked for my own amusement, and though it did not help my case in future days or years, I think it must have been very effective, for no one heard from these two a full two days. When they did come out, it was with a thunderous crash that shook the Mission half off its foundation. They, with Bingham, then ran to find John Hulbert—who I have told you about and was then sheriff—and now too a judge—and he collected soldiers to bring.

Wildereen did not come back to our room those two nights her friends stayed in the wardrobe. I do not know where she went. But with Luke in tow I knew she would have to come back sooner or later, so I waited outside the Mission for her. I saw her then in the late afternoon when she was far down Portage, where it crosses the plank road, and went to meet her. She stopped upon seeing me, but having Luke in her arms could not run. She scooted into the shop she'd stopped in front of. She was pretending to look at a bolt of cloth under a hanging lantern, holding Luke in one arm, when I went in.

"Get away from me," she said quietly.

I asked where she'd been.

"Stay the hell away from me," she hissed. She looked at me with her hard, slanted eyes.

I told her I loved her and I was very sorry and would she please take me back and not take from me my son, and she started right then and there to cry. I put my arm around her and led her out of the shop; all the time she was shaking crying and Luke looking at her. The shop-woman locked the door behind us, and I saw far down the street a boy running hard toward the Fort, but did not think anything about it. It was late in the afternoon. As it was October, it was almost dark and very cool.

Near the Mission a group of Indian boys passed by, and with them I saw my son, John Jr. When he saw me he began to run, but could not take three steps before I had him in hand and had commenced punishing him very severely for running away. I did not fail to strike him many times very hard, but he covered his head so I could not hurt him badly, and it was at this time that the soldiers came, but I did not see them coming because of working John and when I did they were taking Wildereen and Luke away. They grabbed and held me and took John Jr. away as well, and carried Wildereen into the Mission House, where she was locked away in an upper room by your Reverend Bingham, who would not release her to me but said your wife is in my hands now and you will not see her again as long as you live; and the next day she was walked down to the dock by the entire Baptist missionary family and set on a boat that took her below and there was nothing I could do. They had collected money and sent her to Detroit and then made us a law, this Schoolcraft's second law, and by this law divorced us.

[Leans back, fists on the table, takes a breath.] They jailed me two days at the Fort. They collected money and put her on a boat. They jailed me to do this. They could not have otherwise without killing me.

I was moved out of the Mission and lived in a small house abandoned on government property. Not a week had passed but the soldiers came, this time six with bayonets fixed upon their rifles. The soldiers did not force their way in, but stood back from my door with guns ready and hands on the hammers and said nothing but an officer whose hat was pulled down and whose eyes I could not see stepped forward and said you are divorced by Wildereen Duncan Tanner, and then no more but handed me a paper and turned away. Never one day or night had my tears stopped running, I said, and I told him I have nothing to say but you have robbed me of my wife and baby and what did I ever do in this world to be brought to this, and I watched him and he looked to the others but not one had a word more to say. When they had gone, I looked at the paper and saw that it was signed by a judge but not John Hulbert, who was brother-in-law of Henry Schoolcraft and a judge as well as sheriff, but I knew whatever man signed it Schoolcraft had a hand in it and more than that, for he was on the boat that took Wildereen off, or led her onto the boat, I wasn't sure but that he was behind it.

With no money and winter locking in I could not follow Wildereen; but in June, with twenty-four dollars in hand, I went to Detroit to look for my family, and it was in the village of Dexter, fifty miles from Detroit, where I found her, and she told me she was made to leave by Schoolcraft and Bingham and the others and she could not come back, though she held nothing against me. It's just what people made me do, she said. But she would not show me my child, that was just three months old when I last saw him, so I gave her ten dollars, which left me but five for {my} return trip—which was not enough and caused me to suffer terrible hunger and seek help from Cass in Detroit—and she kissed me and wished me well but would never show me my child or tell me where he was. I asked in town was there anyone could tell me where was my child, he is one year old and very dear to me, but no one would help me except some men sitting outside a house said stop bothering about it, we heard you were coming so we killed it yesterday and buried it last night. I asked them show me the grave, but they would not but said if you want your child so much we will dig it out of the ground and give it to you and you can take it home with you and raise it. Two days I spent begging to be shown the grave of my child, but no one would help me; no one would tell me the truth, not a man, nor would any woman do more than look at me; so I went home suffering in grief, not knowing to this day if my child is living or dead.

[There is the concussion of an explosion. He looks toward a window, then another. I remind him it is July the fourth, the anniversary of our nation's independence.]

Lock your doors tonight.

[I do always, I tell him. He nods, looks again at the window, refocuses.]

I became as one gone mad. I renounced man and God and made myself a great trouble in the town. I demanded of everyone had they given money to send my wife and son away. I knew everyone had had some part in it, including Bingham, and one night, not long after I'd been relieved of my position and room at the Mission, I stole into the Reverend's office and, as he was occupied with his books, was able to creep to within a foot of his back and reach over his shoulder and grab his nose before he was aware of me. He flung his arms and legs about and squealed like a pig. I twisted his nose, he told Hulbert, *most spitefully*. This I did. John Hulbert's wife was sitting downstairs with Mrs. Bingham and other women and all of them in fear of me and as I left said to Mrs. Hulbert in my rage, "Mind the flowers of your garden!" meaning her children, and for this, as well as Bingham's nose, I was jailed again. My home was broken into, my things stolen. John Jr. was taken away to Mackinac.

And that is everything about Wildereen. I did not hear of her again. I let my hair grow long and became smelly. I did not care. I withdrew, became legend.

Schoolcraft, he moved to Mackinac.

My daughter Lucy drowned in Lake Michigan. Later Mary {died} of fever.

Years passed.

I saw Schoolcraft but once more. He had been made an officer of the new State government and was assessing the value of Indian lands, counting shacks and apple trees that annuities might be paid for them and the Indians removed to reservations. He passed on his way west through Ste. Mary's. My heart jumped at seeing him—it had been four or five years—and something not unlike affection overcame me. I was confused by this, wondering if such an emotion sometimes preceded murder, and followed him silently to a canoe shed he'd gone alone to inspect.

He was fat now and carried a cane. He saw my shadow, turned, and lifted the cane to hold it in two hands. "Ah, John Tanner, hello!" he said.

I said nothing. I might have told him he looked fat, but it felt strange seeing him and as I beheld him could not speak. He had also grown a large beard.

"Good seeing you; trust you have fared well, my friend. You look well. Yes," he said. He looked around. There was no other door. Neither were there windows. My shadow fell over him.

He tipped back his head; his spectacles flashed. "Good news—! I received recently notice of my election as one of the vice presidents of the American Society for the Diffusion of Useful Knowledge, at New York!"

I said nothing.

"I did. Quite unexpected. And at its annual meeting in March, which happened to be held at my offices, I had the honor of being selected president of the Historical Society of Michigan. They—we—have a deep interest in the history of the aboriginal tribes, you know. Gave me something of a foot up. Yes!"

I took a step toward him.

"And the American Lyceum requested me to prepare a paper for the sixth anniversary. That's in Washington," he said, backing into the shed a step and speaking now more quickly, even as his voice trailed off. "Something, I suppose, of an honor.

"Oh, this will amuse you—" (he swallowed) "—the agent of the dead-letter office at Washington transmitted me a diploma of membership of the Royal Geographical Society of London, which appears to have been originally misdirected and gone astray to St. Mary's, Georgia." His face glistened. "Ha!" he said.

I thought I smelled bowel.

"And I was named president of the newly formed Algic Society, in Detroit, and the American Philosophical Society at Philadelphia informed me of my election as a member!"

His throat caught and he swallowed again, you'd have thought painfully; we were silent together. He slowly raised the cane in both hands like a weapon.

"I am named a regent of the University of Michigan. Not that one needs be impressed," he said, a whimper. He broke wind, blinked. The cane came slowly down.

"John Tanner," he said, letting go with the cane with one hand long enough to push at his spectacles, "stand back. Listen. You won't be troubled by me further. My work with the State is near an end and I will be going back east, to my childhood home, very soon. You won't see me again." He drew a breath. "As from your crimes I would pardon you, let your indulgence—"

"You," I said, "have only helped me."

I can't say where this thought came from. Certainly I was emotional at seeing the man again, remembered something of him that had stirred in me long ago an awareness of, or an awe at, a terrible power beyond nature, yet to say he'd helped me was to say

I'd helped ten thousand beavers, two hundred buffalo; but I found myself moved by my words, convinced from my head to my scrotum they were true. It wa a strange moment—as if the birthshriek of bone-white sun upon the door casing had split apart to set bands of vivid colors dancing in my eyes, sending through me a shiver not unlike joy; I pushed back against this sensation, this illusion, with the most spiteful, untrue thing I could think of: "Even as you have helped the Indian tribes in their improvement."

He squinted, studying me as if to confirm such words were issuing from my mouth.

"Your honors will be known through all ages," I said.

"Of course; thank you," Schoolcraft said quietly, and took another step backward.

I turned and walked from the canoe shed. I never saw him again.

[Sound of another explosion. He does not this time bat an eye.]

Leaves sprouted, fell; stars spun over the uplifted, spirit-haunted eyes of starved Indians; I married again; she left me; foxes snatched eggs and bears burrowed, death-smelling, into the snow.

[Two explosions, in succession.]

I grew old.

[He sits quietly a while as the rockets burst out over the river, staring at me.]

So then, enough about me.

[He continued to stare, as if there were something he was waiting for me to say. I thanked him. For what, he wanted to know, then lifted the fingers of one hand from the table top and nodded. I told him I would prepare a draft and we could go over it together. He nodded again. His shoulders settled and he seemed somewhat sad. I told him as I gathered my things that I would miss our nights working. He said he would miss them as well, but that it had tired him very much. You will come to visit, he said, and I told him I would not make him have to come after me again.

292

As I rose to leave and was thinking of my first visit seeming such a long time ago, I thought of something he'd said then and asked, do you remember when on our first night you spoke of going up to Bingham's room to request something of him?

He grunted.

I said tell me.

Said he, I asked could I be allowed to live again at the Mission, to have a small room. I told Bingham I could endure my loneliness no longer. There must be a change. I told him I would help him as interpreter again and bring upon his home no trouble. If I could only eat at table I would keep to my room and disturb no one. That was my request. This is what he refused. I did not think he would refuse me. I had worried only over my pride. Is that not a good joke?

Then you came for me.

For anyone.

I told him I thought it had worked out according to God's will.

God's will, he said. Yes. As you wish.

We said good night. As I moved toward the door he asked me to sit back down. I asked him why.

We have more to discuss, he said.

I said I don't think there is the time right now, and added we would be seeing each other again soon enough, and could discuss whatever it was then.

Sit down, Constance, he said.

I said excuse me, Mr. Tanner, and reached for the door latch, whereupon he rose out of his chair and taking two steps grabbed me by both my arms above the elbows and, pivoting me, backed me to my chair and saying sit down and giving a violent push, forced me down upon it. He stood over me. He demanded I tell him to what degree I planned to twist and barbarize his narrative, and said, his face marbled red and twitching, that I should not think he had any more respect for me or my abilities than I had for him, then demanded I tell him who I'd dined with.

I became very angry, more angry than afraid, but his turn stung so deeply that my response was at first neither angry in tone nor timid; I told him I thought him a treasure, that I treasured him, and I would never hurt him as he was now hurting me. I think I then began to cry. I told him look what you're doing. I told him do what you will to me, but I'm leaving, and I stood.

My words drew a confused look, and he did not for an instant react as I walked around him to the door. But then he howled, and as he put a hand to the back of my neck I turned and grabbed him and turned him as he had turned me and taking his right arm—as I knew it to be his bad arm—drew it up behind his back and threw him into the wall. I pressed him into the wall with all my strength and forced his arm up and heard him cry in pain.

I release you! he screamed. Go to Schoolcraft!

There came a pounding at the door.

You were born bad, I said; you have a bad heart; you wish to blame the world for what was in you; you blame everyone but yourself for your very birth.

Then I should blame God, he said.

At that moment the door burst nearly off its hinges and Tilden entered.

I release you, I whispered in Tanner's ear.

Tilden took Tanner in hand and tore me away. He flung Tanner to the floor so that the house shook.

Get out! Tilden shouted to me. Tanner was screaming.

I picked up my things. I heard a blow, a sickening crunch; I shouted at the lieutenant don't hurt him, even as I heard another blow, and another. There was a sound as of chimes as I fled the doorway and a body flew by me, dark—I thought for an instant a winged creature—and in the sudden light of an exploding rocket imagined the figure of an Indian crossing before the shifting red brilliance of the house behind me. I ran.]

{Bracketed entry is in Mesare's longhand.}

26

{The ensuing, final two entries are written in Mesare's longhand. The second concludes about midway through the last of seven ledgers containing her transcription of John Tanner's second narrative.}

July 5, 1846   John Tanner's house burned to the ground last night. Today his body was not found in the ashes, nor any part of him. He is not seen today. There was no effort to put out the blaze, as quantities of gunpowder were exploding within and no one could get near the place. I have spent the day in earnest prayer.

July 7, 1846   There is but time and duty, and loss. Duty is a pig, takes all it can. Time swallows up the rest. What is done against duty is, I think, or should be, forgivable. Against the midnight black of loss should be held bright torches, be duty denied. I write this, now, for no one, myself.

Where the wretched bend on knees or lie, is there bird-song in that place? What vindicates faith where faith is gone, forgives bitter scorn and waste?

I will give this morning to Reverend Bingham a letter, detaching myself from the school. I did not attend to the matter much thought. I cannot remain here. Here resides a murderer. I was, unwitting, his accomplice.

Word came yesterday, which was Monday the 6th of July, that James Schoolcraft was felled by a murderer's bullet. I conceived that he was surprised and struck down unawares by a coward hidden in the brush at the edge of his garden, which lies south of Portage and east of the Mission; he was dressed in nothing more than his dressing sack and slippers, and was determined to have flown from his slippers six feet when struck by the bullet; he died, by all indications, instantly, shot through the heart.

My children were at their mid-day recess when word came, carried by a boy newly arrived in Ste. Mary's and not enrolled in the school, Peter White; he had followed the shouting and ran with the adults to the place of the killing. The boy himself had viewed James Schoolcraft's mortal remains and was sent back to town, as were several others, to spread the word that all were to take up their guns and hunt for John Tanner. This boy spoke to several of the children, who were attracted by the growing excitement about the town, including Flavia Poissen, who brought to me the terrible report. She stuck her head in my classroom and cried, "Miss Mesare, James Schoolcraft has been murdered by John Tanner!" and left me alone in a state of disbelief and horror. I fell as in a swoon.

Class, so far as I know, was not resumed.

My mind seized on the violence done Tanner by Schoolcraft's Tilden and the words spoken against James Schoolcraft by Tanner, and I became anxious—as anxious for him as I was anxious to confront him—for it did not seem at all out of boundaries to imagine Tanner had committed the crime. If another had been arrested, I was equally anxious to clear such horrific misapprehensions from my mind. I did know he was a hunted man. He must have known it himself. I was not to linger long on the question, but went directly to Tanner's house, as if to find him waiting amid its smoldering ruins, then walked through town and in an aimless way west up Portage until the countless filth-smelling miners—turning as if slapped or rolling over upon their stomachs to see a woman passing—compelled me to quicken my gait to near a run; then over darkening clods of manure I stepped until past the great stupefying hulk of the *Julia Palmer,* foundered in sand and gravel on the riverbank above the rapids, at which point I came up behind, though at a distance, a small contingent of soldiers from Fort Brady; without being seen I veered south-ward, stumbling into the woods.

I thought he would be this way, west. There was no reason for supposing it, other than it was west. He would not have gone east. In this way I was thinking as I walked, hoping, foolish as it was, to find him. Only desire moved me. I had not hope of success, nor the first reason to expect it. I had in some way to act, and in this way, tugged one way then another by brambles and vines, I found in acting an overwhelming sense of anarchic satisfaction. I fell many times, inhaled the dank aroma of moss and fungi, clawed the cool damp earth, and, falling finally into a shaded clearing of ferns and grasses with a small stream running down from a hillside and feeling hidden and protected and utterly spent, I lay still a time lying on my back and breathing sharply, thinking—then whispering aloud with the sibilant, syllabic rhythm of the brook—without fully comprehending the emotions behind my words— "God forgive us, God forgive us, God forgive us."

At length I dozed, and think I must have then slept soundly, for when I awoke my eyes beheld, as though a curtain had been raised on a strange and unexpected stage, a man sitting cross-legged upon a mat before an elegant tent of black duck, arranging the elements of a silver tea service. He was dressed with shabby formality in a suit and beaver hat, beneath which his hair was gathered behind the ears into braids that hung forward over the front of his medal-ornamented vest. He wore pairs of silver rings in his ears and his movements, as when he turned his head toward a sound in the trees—a chipmunk—were accompanied by a jingling of medals and jewelry. He seemed very odd, even for an Indian.

Between this man and me a small fire was burning, over which a black pot steamed suspended from a trio of sticks. Several twigs were bent toward the fire wrapped in colored threads. Rings and medals turned on threads suspended from the twigs. Jays and Towhees were calling and there was a slight cool breeze to be heard in the boughs of pines; a cottonwood rattled overhead. The sun was aslant upon the trees and yellowed the edges of clouds within a cobalt sky.

My senses vibrated with sleep and confusion; I rose upon an elbow and asked of him, "Are you Trinket?"

He smiled a moment without answering or looking in my direction. When he'd finished moving things about on the mat he faced me, lifted his head, made an O with his lips, and said, in a dark, soft voice, "Wil'am, Miss. You may address me as Wil'am." He spoke with a grotesque English accent, such as might be imagined of a London cab horse turning to address its driver. "I trust, Miss, I find you well-rested," he added.

He was deteriorated, yet not elderly, with the repentant, alluvial eyes of an inebriate. I met those eyes with a look I intended to be indignant as I sat up, arranged my skirt. Several tall ferns touching my feet and legs waggled stiffly between us. I told him I had no wish at this terminus of my stay in Ste. Mary's to make further acquaintances, or offer to strangers explanations; I felt my privacy, under the circumstances, quite compromised enough. It was not a Christian or charitable thing to say, but I was in fact quite resolved not to exhibit the slightest fear.

He nodded in response and motioned me toward the mat. "Come," he said, with a very large O and very long M. Without hesitating I did as he bade.

The silver service, tarnished to deathly colors, and the chipped blue china cups and saucers were marshaled in rows upon the center of the grass mat, large to small, with scrupulous attention to order, yet none to function. He had not a single tray that might have helped. It was as a child or a raven might have arranged. He spent the next five minutes making tea.

"I am told you quite enjoy your tea," he said at length. He placed a strainer over a cup and poured, then carefully put down the silver pot, moved the strainer to the other cup, and poured. As he did so his hands shook. "Sugar?"

I nodded, and with his long black fingers he pinched a quantity of course brown granules from a silver caddy and dropped them into my cup. He met my eyes. I saw then that his nose was swollen, his nostrils black. His blouse and vest were stained dark brown.

"Fine, thank you," I said, and shivered.

He nodded. "I regret there is no cream."

I told him I did not take cream.

"E'en so," he said.

"James Schoolcraft has been murdered," I said.

He looked at me. "So I have heard. Pi-ty." He ran his tongue over his teeth inside his closed, pleated lips. There was a slight turn of his ravaged face as he asked, "Are you on the run?"

I told him it was a ridiculous question. One side of his mouth pinched; he shrugged.

"Did Mr. Tanner kill him?" I asked.

He shook his head to signify he had not. I watched his hollowed, draped eyes as he gathered sugar to transfer in an open palm to his tea, and for some reason believed he told the truth, and believed by his quiet confidence he had reason to know whereof he spoke. I asked him why then did Tanner burn his house.

He carefully picked up his saucer and teacup, gathered the cup's handle in his fingers, and when he'd found the cup steady enough, rolled his eyes up to meet mine. "He did not burn his house, Miss, nor will we find that he killed Mr. Schoolcraft. It would seem that one points to the other. But I would say something different." His eyes blinked thickly.

I demanded he tell me what he meant, and in my agitation swore once and called him Mr. Trinket; yet there was suddenly a most urgent fear arising within me.

"We should both of us be most circumspect in our words as regards this incident, Miss. For my part, I'm leaving town."

"I have nothing to fear from Mr. Tanner," I told him.

"Rather not," he said.

I waited.

"I should only wish to share with you an old Indian fable, Miss. For this purpose I have waited here for you."

I did not comprehend what he meant and asked him to explain. He did not.

"Mr. Tanner told it me several times; to console me in some measure, I think, for I lived at times a difficult life—though it was a very sad story to be offered as consolation. I remember it most clearly. I do indeed. He was quite fond of it himself. He did not speak of his family with me. He did not tell of his troubles, or the wife and children who were taken. With me he told only Indian stories. Traditional fancies. To help me, I came to understand. To provide me what I had not been given by my family. My family had rather disowned me, you see."

I said it was my understanding he was not even allowed on Tanner's property.

He smiled, shook his head. "Mr. Tanner could be rather jealous of his time. No one's perfect." He blinked and his back slumped a bit; he took several more minutes to drink his tea and I waited, confused and sick with trepidation. His hands shook badly; each time the cup and saucer rattled against one another his eyes glanced up at mine.

"It comes to me now, this fable, as though he were speaking it." His gaze drifted and his mouth fell slack.

I waited. I sensed that something, beyond the horrors already inflicted upon Ste. Mary's, was terribly wrong.

"I give this you as he gave it me."

He set the teacup down then, and with no further explanation or preamble, commenced to tell a beautiful and melancholy and altogether strange story of a boy turned wolf, in gentle language distinctly Indian in cadence and framing. He dispensed with the English pretense. I had not pen or paper but will here set down what I can recall of it.

At the conclusion of the story he fell silent. Eyes that had looked inward during the telling of the tale met mine and it was as if, in that still moment, no words, not even a fable, could speak so clearly or convey with such depth of conviction, love, and genuine sorrow the truth of my fears. I stood and thanked Trinket for the tea and for the story. He stood and bowed. I wished him Godspeed, bade him good-bye, and walked, my heart laden with grief and my sight dimmed by tears, through John Tanner's forest, back to town.

{Mesare did not include the story in her transcription, perhaps interrupted by the work of arranging her departure from Sault Ste. Marie; or the story might have been written in a separate, lost, folio. The tale referred to is almost certainly the same included under the title "The Forsaken Brother" in Schoolcraft's *Algic Researches*, I, pp. 191-199; *Historical and Statistical Information Regarding the History, Conditions and Prospects of the Indian Tribes of the United States* (Philadelphia, 1852), II, pp. 202-204; *Myth of Hiawatha*, pp. 52-70; and *The Indian Fairy Book*, pp. 98-101. The story was prepared for inclusion in Schoolcraft's *Muzzegenin, or The Literary Voyageur* in 1827 by Jane Schoolcraft, who almost certainly would have learned it from her mother, Susan (Mrs. John) Johnston:

"It was a fine summer evening; the sun was scarcely an hour high; its departing rays beamed through the foliage of the tall, stately elms that skirted the little green knoll on which a solitary Indian lodge stood. The deep silence that reigned in this sequested and romantic spot seemed to most of the inmates of that lonely hut like the long sleep of death that was now evidently fast sealing the eyes of the head of this poor family. His low breathing was answered by the sighs of his disconsolate wife and their children. Two of the latter were almost grown up, one was yet a mere child. These were the only human beings near the dying man. The door of the lodge was thrown open to admit the freshing breeze of the lake, on the banks of which it stood; and as the cool air fanned the head of the poor man, he felt a momentary return of strength, and raising himself a little, he thus addressed his weeping family. 'I leave you—thou, who hast been my partner in life, but you will not stay long to suffer in this world. But oh! my children, my poor children! You have just commenced life, and mark me, unkindness, and ingratitude, and every wickedness is in the scene before you. I left my kindred and my tribe, because I found what I have just warned you of. I have contented myself with the company of your mother and yourselves, for many years, and you will find my motives for separating from the haunts of men, were solitude and anxiety to preserve you from the bad examples you would inevitably have followed. But I shall die content if you, my children, promise me to cherish each other, and on no account to forsake your youngest brother, of him I give you both particular charge.' The man became exhausted, and taking a hand of each of his eldest children, he continued— 'My daughter! Never forsake your little brother. My son, never forsake your little brother.'

"'Never, never!' they both exclaimed. 'Never—never!' repeated the father, and expired.

"The poor man died happy, because he thought his commands would be obeyed. The sun sank below the trees, and left a golden sky behind, which the family were wont to admire, but no one heeded it now. The lodge that was so still an hour before was now filled with low and unavailing lamentations. Time wore heavily away—five long moons had passed and the sixth was nearly full, when the mother also died. In her last moments she pressed the fulfillment of their promise to their departed father. They readily renewed their promise, because they were yet free from any selfish motive. The winter passed away, and the beauties of spring cheered the drooping spirits of the bereft little family. The girl, being the eldest, dictated to her brothers, and seemed to feel a tender and sisterly affection for the youngest, who was rather sickly and delicate. The other boy soon showed symptoms of restlessness, and addressed his sister as follows. 'My sister, are we always to live as if there were no other human beings in the world? Must I deprive myself the pleasure of associating with my own kind? I shall seek the villages of men; I have determined, and you cannot prevent me.' The girl replied, 'My brother, I do not say no to what you desire. We were not prohibited the society of our fellow mortals, but we were told to cherish each other, and that we should do nothing independent of each other—that neither pleasure nor pain ought ever to separate us, particularly from our helpless brother. If we follow our separate gratifications, it will surely make us forget him whom we are alike bound to support.' The young man made no answer, but taking his bow and arrows left the lodge, and never returned.

"Many moons had come and gone after the young man's departure, and still the girl administered to the wants of her youngest brother. At length, however, she began to be weary of her solitude, and of her charge. Years, which added to her strength and capability of directing the affairs of the household, also brought with them the desire of society, and made her solitude irksome. But in meditating a change of life, she thought only for herself, and cruelly sought to abandon her little brother, as her elder brother had done before.

303

"One day after she had collected all the provisions she had set apart for emergencies, and brought a quantity of wood to the door, she said to her brother, 'My brother, you must not stray far from the lodge. I am going to seek our brother; I shall soon be back.' Then taking her bundle she set off in search of habitations. She soon found them, and was so much taken up with the pleasures and amusements of society, that all affection for her brother was obliterated. She accepted a proposal of marriage, and after that never more thought of the helpless relative she had abandoned.

"In the meantime the elder brother had also married, and settled on the shores of the same lake, which contained the bones of his parents, and the abode of his forsaken brother.

"As soon as the little boy had eaten all the food left by his sister, he was obliged to pick berries and dig up roots. Winter came on, and the poor child was exposed to all its rigors. He was obliged to quit the lodge in search of food, without a shelter. Sometimes he passed the night in the clefts of old trees, and ate the refuge meat of the wolves. The latter soon became his only resource, and he became so fearless of these animals that he would sit close to them whilst they devoured their prey, and the animals themselves seemed to pity his condition, and would always leave something. Thus he lived, as it were, on the bounty of fierce wolves until spring. As soon as the lake was free from ice, he followed his new found friends and companions to the shore. It happened his brother was fishing in his canoe in the lake a considerable distance out, when he thought he heard the cry of a child, and wondered how any could exist on so bleak a part of the shore. He listened again more attentively, and distinctly heard the cry repeated. He made for shore as quick as possible, and as he approached land discovered and recognized his little brother, and heard him singing in a plaintive voice—

Neesya, neesya, shyegwuh gushuh!
Ween ne myeengunish!
    Ne myeengunish!
My brother, my brother,
I am now turning into a wolf!
    I am turning into a wolf.

"At the termination of his song, he howled like a wolf, and the young man was still more astonished when, on getting nearer the shore, he perceived his poor brother half turned into that animal. He however leapt on shore and strove to catch him in his arms, and soothingly said, 'My brother, my brother, come to me.' But the boy eluded his grasp and fled, still singing as he fled, 'I am turning into a wolf—I am turning into a wolf,' and howling in the intervals.

"The elder brother, conscience struck, and feeling his brotherly affection returning with redoubled force, exclaimed in great anguish, 'My brother, my brother, come to me.' But the nearer he approached the child, the more rapidly his transformation went on, until he changed into a perfect wolf—still singing and howling, and naming his brother and sister alternately in his song as he fled into the woods, until his change was complete. At last he said, 'I am a wolf,' and bounded out of sight.

"The young man felt the bitterness of remorse all his days, and the sister, when she heard of the fate of the little boy whom she had so cruelly left, and whom she and her brother had solemnly promised to foster and protect, wept bitterly, and never ceased to mourn until she died."}

AFTERWORD

The case against John Tanner in the matter of James Schoolcraft's murder was never proved conclusively, though there never arose a reason to question the evidence pointing in his direction; that is, until many years later, when Lieutenant Bryant Tilden, an officer posted to Fort Brady at the time of the incident, confessed to the murder on his deathbed. There had been, he said, a quarrel between Schoolcraft and himself over a woman. Tilden was also known from military records to have taken three solders out with him on a hunt for Tanner the afternoon of the day of Schoolcraft's murder.

In 1847, the skeletal remains of a man dressed in clothing similar to Tanner's, and lying alongside a rifle believed to be of the same make as Tanner's, was discovered in a wooded swamp near Sault Ste. Marie. Word of this conflicted with other reports that placed Tanner in the Red River country of southern Manitoba. Such was the uncertainty surrounding the case, and so damning the circumstances, that historians to this day have been reluctant, even in the face of Tilden's confession, to relieve Tanner of all suspicion.

The burning of Tanner's house the night of July 4, 1846, two days prior to the murder, was from the start regarded as proof he had killed Schoolcraft. Yet, this editor wonders, why—save pure and simple madness—would he burn his house two days before a planned murder? And if he were planning an escape to, say, the

Red River country, why would Tanner bother destroying his home? It was reported by Constance Mesare and others, including Angie Bingham, daughter of Reverend Abel Bingham, that quantities of gunpowder, as though used as an accelerant, were exploding within the house as it burned. One wonders, first, if Tanner would, in his poverty, have possessed such stores; and, if not, who would have access to such quantities, or motive to employ them?

Mesare's comments and observations are in the end vague; readers are left to draw their own conclusions. There is, however, found within the final entry of Mesare's notebook this passage: "I cannot remain here. Here resides a murderer. I was, unwitting, his accomplice."

T. F. T.

EDITOR'S ACKNOWLEDGMENTS

I have not frequently found myself in a position to publicly share credit or broadcast gratitude; rather, having spent my adulthood clambering the lower rungs of academia, my experience has been to have intellectual ownership, like a succulent breast cheated from the smacking lips of a drowsing infant, evaporate. Yet it occurs to me that the imperative to share credit itself now evaporates: I am retired. Moreover, I am, here, the editor. Moreover again, I required no agent. Nonetheless, I will acknowledge certain debts.

My father was a layman historian. His passion carried him in the mid-nineteen-seventies to the presidency of the Michigan Historical Society. It should not surprise any of you to know that my upbringing, the shouts and whispers of childhood and beyond, sparked and resonated within walls lined with somber-faced books concerned with, for the most part, the history of the State of Michigan. It was inevitable, then, that I became familiar at a young age with the life of John Tanner. My father had, in his collection, the 1956 Haines & Ross edition of Tanner's 1830 narrative, this with the wonderful introduction by Noel M. Loomis and the captivating frontispiece image of John Tanner himself—Tanner of the wary, beleaguered eyes—and it was this book that made me an apostle of Tanner's strange gospel at the Michigan College of Mines, and made it all but inevitable that the folios of the *Second Narrative*, once delivered there, would find their way to my desk. So I thank my father.

Of course this book would not have come into being without the astute and unselfish actions undertaken by Stuart Bartkowsky and George Zech, who are recognized in my introduction so require no further mention here.

Nor would this book have been possible without the dedication and indefatigable labors of the staff and volunteer graduate students, under the direction of Helena Pratt, of the School of Administrative Assistance at the Business College of Eastern Michigan University, who undertook the difficult—one would suppose stultifying—task of translating Constance Mesare's antique Pitman shorthand into pages of editable manuscript.

I would like to thank the administration of the Michigan College of Mines for its ongoing moral support, for the University's generous sponsorship of this project, and for the press offices made available to me since my retirement (which roughly coincided with my acceptance of this project) in the foggy heights above the ice rink in Ross Field House.

Finally, to the men of the collegiate hockey team, whose quiet Finnish manners have made it possible for me to conduct work throughout practices, and whose record has kept those sports enthusiasts sprinkled over the escarpments of Ross's bleachers reserved as relatives of the accused at a trial for murder, I offer this salute: Go Miners!

T. F. T.
August, 2025

AUTHOR'S ACKNOWLEDGMENTS

A significant aid in organizing the frame of life-history within this fiction was John T. Fierst's excellent article, "Return to 'Civilization': John Tanner's Troubled Years at Sault Ste. Marie," *Minnesota History* 50/1 (Spring 1986). Other touchstone sources inevitably included Tanner's *A Narrative of the Captivity and Adventures of John Tanner (U. S, Interpreter at the Saut de Ste. Marie) During Thirty Years Residence Among the Indians in the Interior of North America,* ed. *Edwin James* (Minneapolis: Ross & Haines, Inc., 1956), and Henry Rowe Schoolcraft's *Personal Memoirs of a Residence of Thirty Years with the Tribes on the American Frontiers: With Brief Notices of Passing Events, Facts, and Opinions, A.D. 1812 to A.D. 1842* (Philadelphia: Lippincott, Grambo and Co., 1851). Reverend Abel Bingham's daughters, Ann Hulbert, Angie Gilbert, and Sophia Buchanan, published or presented to historical associations a number of papers drawn upon here, including: Ann and Sophia, "Sketches of the Life of Rev. Abel Bingham," *Michigan Pioneer Collections,* Vol. 2 (1880), Angie, "A Tale of Two Cities," *Michigan Pioneer and Historical Collections,* (1899), Angie, "The Story of John Tanner," *Michigan Pioneer and Historical Collections,* Vol 38 (1912), and Angie, "Memories of the 'Soo,'" *Michigan Pioneer and Historical Collections,* Vol 30 (1906). Other print sources, in no particular order, included Joseph H. Steele, "Sketch of John Tanner, Known as the 'White Indian,'" *Michigan Pioneer and Historical Collections* (1893); John E. McDowell, "Therese

Schindler of Mackinac: Upward Mobility in the Great Lakes Fur Trade," *Wisconsin Magazine of History* 6/12 (Winter 1977-78); Henry Rowe Schoolcraft, "Sketch of John Johnston," *Michigan Pioneer and Historical Collections*, Vol 36 (1908); Henry Rowe Schoolcraft, "The Literary Voyager or *Muzzeniegun*," ed. Phillip P. Mason, *University of Michigan Press* (1962); Jeremiah Porter (Lewis Beeson, ed.), "A Missionary in Early Sault Ste. Marie," *Michigan History* 38/4 (December 1954); Maxine Benson, "Schoolcraft, James, and the 'White Indian,'" *Michigan History* 54/4 (Winter 1970); Charles H. Chapman, "The Historic Johnston Family of the 'Soo,'" *Michigan Pioneer and Historical Collections*, Vol 32 (1903); Donald A. Ringe, "William Cullen Bryant's Account of Michigan in 1846," *Michigan History* 40/3 (September 1956); Thomas L. McKenney, "Detroit Half a Century Ago," *Michigan Pioneer Collections*, Vol 4 (1883); Detroit Evening News, "The Old Cass House," *Michigan Pioneer Collections*, Vol 4 (1883); Dr. Peter Lorenz Neufeld, "John 'Falcon' Tanner's Death," *Manitoba Pageant* 20/3 (Spring 1975); and George S. May, "John C. Pemberton: A Pennsylvania Confederate at Fort Mackinac," *Mackinac History*, Vol 1, Leaflet 11 (1968). In addition, online resources too numerous to mention were consulted over the course of this project.

Where possible and deemed appropriate, the writings of Tanner, Tanner/James, Bingham, and Schoolcraft, from sources cited above, have been incorporated into the text—sometimes paraphrased, sometimes taken several words or a phrase at a time, and occasionally used freely, with slight alterations, by the paragraph, as in a quoted monologue.

The College of Mines Press, though a publisher for my purposes, is, for the purposes of this novel, a fictional entity.

J. Todd Gillette

A Note on the Type

This book was set on the linotype in Lutefisk No. 2. Linotype Lutefisk is a contemporary cutting from the type matrices designed by Venslaw Lutefisk (1521 – 1569).

Lutefisk was a pupil of Geoffrey Troy, and, like Troy's better known student, Claude Garamond, was believed to have based his letters on other models—in Lutefisk's case, those of Garamond. Lutefisk began his apprenticeship as Troy's gardener, and, while credited with several advances in zoological topiary, and known as the father of the combined exclamation point and question mark within a single block of type, he was destined to spend his most productive years defending himself against a charge of artistic plagiary brought by Garamond. Lutefisk eventually won the case on a claim of insanity.

Lost to history is Lutefisk No. 3, which was rumored to have challenged the very foundations of type design, as well as the alphabet itself. The prototypes were said to have been buried by Lutefisk between the gate-posts of his father's farm near Oslo, Norway.

Composed, printed, and bound by College of Mines Printers, Houghton, MI.
Typography and binding design by T. Forrest Treadle.